Silhouettes
South of 27

Silhouettes South of 27

Wil Glavin

Copyright © 2021 Wil Glavin

First paperback edition July 2021
Book design by BuzBooks

ISBN: 978-0-578-90754-3 (paperback)
ISBN: 978-0-578-90755-0 (ebook)
Published by IngramSpark

To the people I love most—my parents and brothers.

To my friends, old and new, thank you for always being there for me. And as you know, I will always be there for you.

And lastly, to the strangers—I love every single person who purchased my debut novel, *The Venerable Vincent Beattie*, and proceeded to email/DM/Zoom/text me expressing their adoration for the characters, setting, plotline, style, etc. I never would've had the courage or confidence to write a second novel had it not been for my many wonderful fans constantly cheering me on and wishing to have lengthy discourses about specific sections and themes. I hope all of you enjoy *Silhouettes South of 27*!

Table of Contents

Cash Moreau

MAY 28, 2017

AT SOME POINT IN THE lives of all parents and children, there's a role reversal.

And when I first thought about that, I pondered what it'd be like to change my parents' Depends, to stick my face near a soiled behind, or to get exhausted following miles of slaloming around New York City with an occupied wheelchair in front of me.

This idea continued to dart around my mind as I sat across from my mother and watched her down her third gimlet on the rocks. Prior to glass number one, her behavior was tolerable as always, and the conversation topics flowed from her ever-racing mind. Then the waiter brought the second, which led to an unattractive haughtiness joining the meal. And by the time the third had been guzzled, my mother became a near-silent and dreary version of herself. I've watched this series take place a few hundred times in my life and always remember seeing the happiness gradually vanish from her face.

"Cash," she said as her dehydrated tongue slipped out of her mouth. "Take pictures of me."

"No, Mom. I can't."

"Why not? You never take pictures of me."

"It frustrates me when we can't go out for a nice dinner without you taking your phone out and bothering me, the waitress, and the maître d' for pictures."

"I'm paying," she said. "What do you care?"

"It's classless."

"I don't care what these people think of me."

"Lower your voice, please. And you taking pictures of every person and dish makes it very clear that we're Crow's Nest interlopers."

1

"Here's my credit card. I'll be outside."

My mother left the indoor portion of the restaurant and stood outside, taking pictures of the opalescent horizon while I paid the bill. It was the first second of relaxation I'd had that night, and I was only able to cherish it for 30 seconds before I saw my nearly immobile 60-year-old mother attempting to walk down a 20-degree decline toward the beach.

"Mom, stop. What are you doing?"

"It's so beautiful here."

That was something on which we agreed. That night, The Crow's Nest became my favorite restaurant in the Hamptons. It was nestled next to the shores of Lake Montauk, and whoever the owner was, they definitely knew how to maximize space.

The indoor restaurant contained an understated elegance. The walls and floors were what I believed to be acacia wood, while balls of light cascaded toward the cushioned chairs.

Upon exiting the bucolic, timber-filled restaurant, one then became transfixed by sprawling green countryside to the right and a diminutive beach on the left. If there were ever a time and place to take out one's iPhone, it was standing atop the hill at The Crow's Nest that led to the idyllic scenery of both perfectly maintained sand and grass. My mother would certainly be able to create many Instagram-worthy images, even in her drunken stupor.

"Honey, there's a bar at the bottom of the hill. Look, by the beach."

The last thing my mother needed was a fourth drink, which would inevitably lead to a domineering version of herself intruding on the waitstaff and bartenders. However, I knew how to walk on eggshells around this eruptive version of her, and if my mother wanted me to hold her arm as she limped to the bar area, that's exactly what I'd do.

We walked past five-foot-tall wooden pergolas that each had adjustable chaise lounge chairs beneath them. And then there were the twinkling, overhead string lights shining above the pathway toward a salient fireplace and the lake itself.

"Honey, I'm gonna order a drink. I'd ask if you want one, but you're my driver."

As my mother stepped away and began talking to anyone who would or wouldn't listen, making sure to show each random person shaky iPhone photos of the scenery that all could see in person, I found a cozy stool next to the fire. Anyone who's been to Montauk even once can tell you how chilly Memorial Day weekend is.

After less than five minutes, my white linen shirt proved to be powerless against the harsh winds whipping across the lake. This, along with several other reasons, made me desperately want to go back to the hotel room, despite it being only 7:15 p.m. over a holiday weekend.

"Mom," I said as I rose from my uncomfortable stool. I was the word "whine" personified.

"What?" She turned around as I approached.

"Let's go home. I don't want to drive when it's pitch-black."

"Oh, stop. You're fine. We're all fine."

"Look, Mom, I can only provide you with filial affection for so long."

I took the tumbler from her hand, placed it on the bar, and gently looped my arm through hers. My mother and I walked side by side at a glacial pace until we reached the top of the hill.

"Here are the car keys. One sec though. I need to give the maître d' my card."

I took another glance at the Edenic scenery and then guided her to the leering hostess.

"'Scuse me."

A different voice was approaching my mother and me. It was of a younger woman, but her voice was raspy and of a lower octave. My mother and I turned left and saw a sultry, black-haired twenty-something gliding over to us.

"Yes?" my mother said as she frantically waved her business card.

"Didn't I see you two at Sunset Beach last night?" She turned to me and said, "your mom had us take pictures of her. I think that was you?"

My mother and I looked at each other, ostensibly drawing the same conclusion. She didn't remember last night, and I must've been sitting alone somewhere, pondering my future.

The black-haired lady realized she was going to have to be the next to speak.

"Yes. It was definitely you two. You guys are so cool. You're, like, a dynamic mother-son duo taking on the Hamptons. I love that."

My mother and I nodded warily. We were both raised to adhere to an inveterate creed that made us assume all strangers were either dangerous or needed something. This is not an uncommon mindset for Manhattanites who are approached by a wide array of seedy characters on a daily basis.

However, at that precise moment, my mother was intoxicated, and I was becoming more enamored with every passing second, so our typical vigilance was impeded.

"Oh, yes," my mother said gleefully. "Now I remember you. I love your Star of David."

"Thank you. You know what, you should come sit with us. My friends and I are over there waiting for our table. We don't bite."

"Sounds great. I'm Andrea Moreau. Nice to meet you."

"I'm Kinsley Avital. And you are?"

"Cash," I said as we shook hands and walked toward yet another fireplace.

Kinsley led my mother and me to an outdoor area at the top of the hill where 11 extremely well-varnished chairs surrounded a raging fire. Nine well-dressed, well-kempt mid-twenties women occupied most of the seats. They didn't dress like Hamptons' veterans but were by no means unrefined.

My mother took one of the empty seats, and I stood waiting for Kinsley to sit next to her.

"Andrea, can I get you a drink? My treat. I was gonna get one for myself anyway."

"Sure," my mother said. "Surprise me."

"And you, Cash?"

"No, I'm her designated driver."

"Aw, really? That's so sweet of you. You raised a kind son, Andrea."

Much like the ancient Greeks hearing the lilts of Mediterranean women on their journeys home, I was enchanted by this lovely Israeli-American walking away from us. I remember the following series of events as well as any from my brief time on this earth.

Kinsley was wearing a white t-shirt and matching skinny jeans that juxtaposed well with her complexion. While her prominent black eyebrows and copious strands of intentionally messy hair were her defining features, I also managed to notice a birthmark on her left cheek, little ears that jutted outward, and a petite, pointy nose. However, as inimitable as her look was, I found her naturally convivial, affectionate, and energetic personality to be even more praiseworthy.

I stood and offered my seat to Kinsley but was met with a quizzical look.

"That's sweet to offer, but you don't have to get up for me. Andrea, your superb mothering skills are on full display."

"Well, I can go grab another chair," I said.

"Don't be silly. Scooch over. We'll share."

Kinsley handed my mother her drink, and 18 curious eyes stared at me like I was a doltish antelope that had mistakenly wandered past Pride Rock.

"Kins, who are your friends?" one of them asked.

"This is Cash and Andrea. Remember I was taking pics of a stunning, blonde woman last night? That's Andrea."

My mother gleamed as if she'd never heard the word "sycophant" before.

"Welcome, you two," another friend said. "We're always happy to take in any strays Kins finds."

The friends then returned to their separate conversations as my mother and Kinsley sipped their drinks. I grappled with whether I wanted to drive back and sit in our hotel room or stay and see if Kinsley had any interest in me.

"So, where are you guys from?" I attempted the latter.

"Oh gosh, we're a weird group. We all grew up in Cincinnati and went to high school together, but then we split up for college. Some went to OSU, some to Ohio, some went to Miami, and I went to Duke."

"Wow, so what are you all doing at The Crow's Nest?"

"I tried to organize this mini-reunion. Five of us live back in Ohio, and the other half live in NYC, so I felt we should all reconnect. It's been years since we've hung out together."

At that point, the wind had picked up, and the under-clothed Kinsley began to shiver.

"Are you cold? Mom, do you have a jacket in the car? I'll be right back."

Kinsley seemed to be attracted to this loving, mother-doting son dynamic, so I leaned into it. I returned with my mother's oversized white jean jacket and wrapped it around Kinsley's shoulders.

"Wow, you're the sweetest," she said. "Also, do you have a solution for this fire? I tried putting my sunglasses on, but the embers keep blowing into my eyes."

"Kinsley," my mother interrupted. "You know I have my own agency. Andrea Moreau PR. I'm trying to get clients now."

"Andrea, that's awesome. You're such a good role model. You raised a great son. You're working. You're your own boss. Can afford to go out to the Hamptons. I'm super impressed."

"You know," my mother said, "Cash is a rising senior at Penn. And he went to Hollandsworth, you know, the all-boys school, before that. He has a *very* bright future."

Kinsley simply laughed at her blatant attempts to pawn her son off to a potential suitor willing to fill the massive void that would exist in my life after no longer living at home.

"Why don't I take a picture of the two of you," the tipsiest person in our circle said. "You'd make an adorable couple."

My fashionable, bubbly seatmate agreed, placed one arm around my shoulder and her other hand on my lap, and smiled. I couldn't help but be elated at this chance encounter that wound up shaping my entire future.

Following our photography session, Kinsley and I hung out for what could've been anywhere from five minutes to three hours. I learned she was 23 and worked as a social media manager at a beauty start-up called Guépard. Kinsley also did freelance graphic design on the side and could work remotely whenever she chose. The raven-haired woman lived in Manhattan on 40th between Second and Third, and this was her first time in the Hamptons.

She continued to ask me all sorts of questions about my background, and I learned the following about her:

-Started a charity at 15
-Could play the harp
-Loved to ski
-Played shortstop on Duke's club softball team
-Rode horses
-Majored in sociology
-Enjoyed pop culture
-Pilates thrice a week
-Ran along the East River twice a week
-Her photography and Instagram were crucial in her personal and work lives
-Loved to travel internationally

I was so preoccupied with Kinsley I had no idea what my mother or the other nine women were doing. The next moment I remember is a random man of about 30 sauntering over to our group, armed with a Rolex watch and a Sigma Chi smile. He parked himself on the arm of one of the chairs and proceeded to flirt with the other young women.

Kinsley and I were rubbernecking at the train wreck occurring to our right while my mother stood up.

"So, I had a pretty good year at the firm," the man was explaining to deaf ears. "I'm in IB, and just two good years bought me a boat that's sitting in Montauk Harbor as we speak. You should come out with me," he said to one of the ladies.

The friend was deathly silent and still hoping Animal Planet's theory of remaining speechless and calm will cause predators to walk away. Unfortunately, the situation only worsened as a red-faced woman sped-walked to our circle and whispered something in the man's ear.

"Relax," he said as the group looked on with increased curiosity. "I'm just having fun until the table's ready."

"Who are you?" Kinsley's friend asked the woman.

"I'm his girlfriend. He does this stuff all the time."

"What do I do? Can't I have a friendly chat with some friendly people? You're so overly protective."

Then my mother, like an overzealous camp counselor, moved to the middle of the area and spoke.

"Everyone, let's all calm down. Girls, let's take a picture together. Who wants to remember their first night at The Crow's Nest?"

The group looked at one another, smiled, and began filing in next to the fire with the beach and sunset in the background.

"Excuse me, sir," my mother said to the misplaced man. "May you please take a photo of us?"

"Shhh-ore," he replied with a long sigh at the end of the word.

"Just the girls," my mother added. "Cash, you have to position us."

I told my mother where to look and how to angle her hips, and then she announced to our generous photographer:

"Take it high up so I don't have a double-chin."

The man, with his girlfriend attached to his hip, began taking both horizontal and vertical photos of the 11 women, praying his nightmare would end.

"Wow, we all look like sisters," my mother shouted.

That could've been the final line of that night's story, but the investment banker had one more snarky comment left in him.

"Well, not sisters, obviously. Maybe...maybe half-sisters, 'cause, you know."

His light-hearted but ill-advised response caused five-drinks-in Andrea to explode.

"What do you mean? Of course, we could be sisters. Are you calling me old? How ageist can you be? Didn't your parents teach you to respect your elders?"

My mother was frothing at the mouth as Kinsley and her friends returned to their chairs with metaphorical popcorn in hand.

"Well, I mean, you're like a senior citizen, and these girls are in their 20s. You're not sisters."

"Please," his girlfriend begged. "Let's just walk away and check on our table."

Then tears started to form in my eyes. Not because I was so proud of my mother for standing up for herself and the baby boomer generation, but because the embers of the fire had blown straight into my corneas.

Kinsley looked over, handed me her sunglasses without a word, and continued to watch my mother attempt to emasculate this supposed ageist.

"Haven't you ever heard of class?"

"That coming from the woman drunkenly shouting at The Crow's Nest?"

My eyes itched through the sunglasses as the moon was rising in the background. Poor Kinsley was now wiping tears from her eyes as we were sitting in the exact spot the fire's artillery could hit us.

I handed Kinsley her sunglasses, took her hand, and walked her away from the fireplace and that pointless argument.

"Sorry if my mom's ruining your guys' night," I said as we walked down the angled hill toward the water.

"Are you kidding? She's made my night. Your mom's my hero. She's so courageous and stands up for what she believes in. That guy was a jerk."

I laughed and then wiped the tears from my irritated eyes once again.

"Sorry, I usually don't cry this often."

"Yeah, you're such a baby." She laughed. "The fire and wind were rough. I must look like such a wreck. I can feel my makeup running."

"No, not at all."

Kinsley smiled and stared at the sunset.

"Kins," a voice called from up the hill. "Our table's ready."

My mother had also stopped berating our unsuspecting guest, and the outdoor area was serene once again.

"It was so nice meeting you and your friends," I said. "What's your number? We should hang out when we're both back in the city."

"I'd like that."

Kinsley typed her number into my phone before I guided her back toward the restaurant and the active fireplace. We both wiped our eyes one final time.

"I hate fire," she said.

"Oh God, I love it. I've always found it to be life's greatest amalgamation of beauty and danger."

"Hmm...I think I'm definitely going to see you again, Cash."

Kinsley then left me alone, hugged my mother, and rejoined her friends. They were all staring, waving, and giggling as they disappeared into the restaurant.

I then looped my arm inside my mother's and walked her to the parking lot. We both climbed inside the car, and I spent the entire ride home thinking about where to take Kinsley on our first date.

MAY 25, 2018

Just About One Year Later

I met Kinsley on 40th and Second with a green and black-striped duffle bag in one hand and two peanut butter smoothies from Juice Generation in the other. It was approximately 3:30 p.m. on the Friday of Memorial Day weekend, and I wasn't looking forward to what promised to be an extremely congested drive out to Montauk. Luckily, I had the best travel companion the world had to offer.

My girlfriend of over 11 and a half months double-parked her white 2016 Toyota Prius C-One on the northwest corner of the street, and I quickly jumped in to join her as horns blared behind us.

"Ready for the greatest summer of your life?" she said.

"Of course I am." I then kissed her and followed that with an "I love you, Kinsley."

"Love you too." She placed one hand on my face at the next red light and added, "Have I ever told you how handsome you are?"

"Maybe."

She then drove out on the Long Island Expressway and managed to let out a few shrieks and groans when we were held at a standstill.

"Easy Kins," she said to herself. "Oh, my playlist. Grab my iPhone. Plug in the Aux. Play the 'Million Dollar Music' playlist.'"

"Clever."

"I thought so. 'Cause you're Cash."

"Oh, I got it. Never gets old."

did as I was told, and we listened to Kinsley's eclectic playlist that
had the following:

"Closer" — The Chainsmokers
"Motorsport" — Cardi B, Migos and Nicki Minaj
"Closer" — The Chainsmokers
"Cecilia and the Satellite" — Andrew McMahon
"I Miss You" — Blink 182
"Call Me Maybe" — Carly Rae Jepsen
"Dog Days Are Over" — Florence and the Machine
"Crazy on You" — Heart
"Layla" — Eric Clapton
"Closer" — The Chainsmokers
"Sexual Healing" — Marvin Gaye (Kygo Remix)
"Free Fallin'" — Tom Petty
"Over the Love" — Florence and the Machine

Even today, I have all the lyrics to the male part of "Closer" memorized. It's a fantastic duet song. Kinsley had wonderful taste in music, and singing was just one of her countless expertises. She could hit the high notes on '70s ballads but was also keen on mimicking the famed Migos rapper Offset by screaming "Offset" every time his verse appeared on a song. So, while the 116-mile drive took three hours and 28 minutes, I enjoyed every second of it.

The initial plan was to stop at Campbell's house to put our bags down and unpack, but we had to make the 7:00 p.m. reservation, so we drove straight to Navy Beach and arrived at 6:58 p.m. Kinsley and I may have been a tad sweaty and slightly underdressed, but it wound up not being an issue.

The maître d' led Kinsley and me to the outdoor area where Campbell and Skye were sitting, unsurprisingly at the best table at Navy Beach. The four of us were placed at a spot on the sand with nothing obstructing our view of the bay. And the chivalrous Campbell proved he hadn't forgotten our etiquette lessons at Hollandsworth as he elected to sit with his back to the water.

"Hi, I'm Kins—"

"Ms. Avital. Pleasure." Campbell kissed her hand. "Moreau here has told me so much about you."

"He puts me on a pedestal, so hopefully you'll temper expectations."

The group chuckled, and then Skye stepped forward and hugged us.

"Kins, I love your hair. What do you use?"

At that point, Campbell pulled me aside and said:

"Moreau. Great to have you. Been a bit, hasn't it?"

"Last time would've been our junior years. I came to visit you up in New Haven for the Yale-Penn game."

"That's right. You guys spanked us." He ran his hand through the middle of his blond locks. "Gotta love Navy, right? Best table in the house. Two beauties on our arms. This is heaven, eh Moreau?"

The waitress came by and delicately placed menus in each of our hands.

Kinsley was given the seat overlooking the water while I was on her left, and Campbell was on my left.

"So," Kinsley spoke first. "What do I call you? Jeff? Jefferson? Campbell?"

"Call me whatever your heart desires."

Campbell was wearing tight, white jeans, a navy short-sleeve button-down with pink flamingos, an expensive pair of tortoiseshell shades, and navy Rivieras. It was sleek.

I glanced over the menu, and even though I'm not a heavy drinker, I felt I might as well join my friends.

"I'll have a Moscow Mule."

"Moreau, you haven't changed. You know, Skye and I typically grab the prix fixe, but I told her about your famed pickiness, so that's a no-go."

"Not gonna lie, but the fact you barely eat fish is gonna be a huge problem," Skye said.

Campbell's girlfriend was part Puerto Rican and objectively quite attractive. But she was only 20, and given my love for Kinsley, I didn't have interest in anything other than Skye's personality. But for the sake of painting a picture, I'll say Skye Pellegrini wasn't the type of girl you'd take to a black-tie function or one who could be buried beside you in a Jewish cemetery.

Immediately on that first night, I noticed the following tattoos (although I assumed there were more):

-A sea lion on her left wrist
-A meticulously carved tiara next to the sea lion
-The word "Consciousness" on her right wrist
-Audrey Hepburn's face on her upper left arm
-Some numbers on her upper right arm
-An ankle tattoo I couldn't make out

In addition, she had a horizontal earring-line piercing the top of each ear and three small, round diamonds dotting her outer cartilage.

At the genesis of the evening, Skye's dirty blonde hair was tied in a bun, but she let it down later. I would've guessed she was a natural brunette with dyed streaks. Beneath her locks was an outfit consisting of white short shorts and a navy and white billowy, checked long-sleeve button-down. Skye went with her sleeves rolled past her elbows and only two buttons fastened, so her navy bra was visible from several angles.

Lastly, her face's defining feature was the distinctive eyebrows— thick above the nose, tailing off to a thin strip.

"My lady friend and I will have the Bérénice rosé, please," Campbell said to the waitress.

"I'll have a piña colada, but can you please go heavy on the coconut and light on the pineapple? Thank you very much," Kinsley said.

The waitress then disappeared into the restaurant situated 30 feet from the bay's edge.

"Moreau, your girl orders like you."

"Well, Jeff, there's a distinct difference. I'm particular. He's picky."

There was a brief silence as we all seemed to stare out at the water simultaneously. It was a crisp May evening, but the deep orange sun was still visible on the horizon, and the sounds of waves crashing and seagulls squawking permeated the rock-filled beach. Skye interrupted the tranquility and asked:

"Kins, whaddya do for work?"

Like Kinsley, Skye spoke with a deeper, more raspy voice than the average young woman.

"I'm a social media manager at this beauty start-up. You may know it, Guépard?"

"No, I don't, but sounds lit."

"Yeah, it is. I'm building our company's engagement on Twitter, Facebook, Instagram, LinkedIn, YouTube, everything. Just trying to get the word out about our products."

Even though Campbell and I went to Ivies, it was blatantly obvious that Kinsley was the smartest among our group. And the kindest. And the most likable.

"You have, like, any Insta models reppin' your stuff?"

"I mean, a few micro-influencers, but we have a limited budget."

"You know, if you're nice to me, I'll hook you up. I've got 75K followers. I'm, like, famous a-f these days, right, Jeff?"

"Yeah, Skye's a really talented musician."

The waitress then arrived with our drinks and took our food orders.

"For apps, I'll have the hamachi ceviche, and my girl will get the shrimp ceviche. Then soy-glazed tilefish for me and swordfish for her."

"Very good, Mr. Campbell," the waitress said.

"May I please have the Atlantic salmon. And may I please have a side salad in place of the soba noodles and a side of capers if you have them?"

"Miss, our menu specifically states 'no additions or subtractions.'"

"Moreau, are we gonna be able to take your girlfriend to any nice places this summer?"

"Easy, Campbell. Miss, I'll have the New York strip, medium rare, but with the roasted garlic butter on the side, please. And fries, but with no truffle oil."

"Moreau, didn't you hear the waitress? Come on, lady and gentleman." He then turned to the waitress and said, "Sorry about them. They had a long drive. They're exhausted. Tell Jacques he'll be doing a special favor to Jefferson Campbell. Here's a 20."

"Thank you, Mr. Campbell."

After the smiley waitress left, Skye piped up once again.

"Cash, how'd you and Jeff meet?"

"Oh, you didn't tell her? Campbell and I went to Hollandsworth together. You know, the all-boys K through nine school? Met him when we were five. We were best friends back in the day, but you know how life goes. Went to different schools, lost touch for a bit. Reconnected at the Hollandsworth five-year reunion. Campbell told me about this National League-only fantasy baseball league he needed an extra guy for, so I said yes."

"Damn Moreau, that's right. Tough league, huh? Always has been. 10-team league, nine pitchers, 14 hitters, four bench spots, one DL."

"That first year, I was baffled at how deep the league was. Two catchers are absurd. I still remember rostering guys like Jordany Valdespin, Kyle Kendrick, Ryan Vogelsong, Chris Stewart. Those types."

"Cash, darling, maybe you want to stay on topic here? You're losing half the table."

"Right," I laughed. "Sorry. Anyway, the fantasy league kept us together. We'd call each other to check-in on our players and lives. Talked about sports and our futures. Campbell came to Philly for the Penn-Yale game our sophomore year, and I returned the favor in New Haven the next. Or maybe I got the years mixed up?"

The music then turned on in the background, and Campbell interrupted me.

"Skye, who's this?"

"Sleepless by Flume. Duh."

"Skye knows every EDM song ever made. You like this one, kid?"

"Not at all. It's dull and repetitive," she said before taking out her phone.

"Tell Moreau and Kinsley who you like."

"I'm high-key obsessed with Kygo, old Avicii, Marshmello, CamelPhat, Gesaffelstein, Robin Schulz, Yellow Claw, Alison Wonderland, Layla B."

"Moreau, ever hear one of Skye's songs? Kinsley, you have a SoundCloud? Check her out. She's super talented."

"J, stop." Skye was now scrolling through Instagram.

"I'm serious. She taught herself saxophone and violin as, like, a toddler. Right, kid?"

"Yes, okay. Can we move on, please? Stop being embarrassing."

"God, you guys should hear her stuff. It's perfect Hamptons music. Like tropical beach house. It's got hard, unexpected drops and then snaps, claps, real sax and violin. It's incredible dance music."

The waitress then came to our table with the Navy Beach manager in tow.

"Here are the ceviches, Mr. Campbell."

"Mr. Campbell," the manager said. "How are we this evening? I see you've brought some fresh faces."

"Not sure how fresh they are after four hours in the car."

The manager and waitress laughed way too hard.

"Mr. Campbell, you let me know if you need absolutely anything."

"Thank you both."

After the pair exited, it was finally time to ask the pressing question I'm sure was on Kinsley's mind too.

"So, Campbell, thanks again for the invite. Super generous, man. But now do you want to enlighten Kins and me about what to expect this summer?"

"Ah, the grand plan. So, first off, you and Kinsley are more than welcome to stay in the big house with us, but if I know you like I think I do, you'll prefer to be in the pool house 'cause of privacy."

"Correct. Thank you," I said.

"Anyway, it's not some shack. It's a two-story guest house with a kitchen, bathroom, TV, couch, and bed. Whole thing's fully furnished and stocked. Eighty percent of American families would consider my pool house a step up from their current domicile."

Kinsley rolled her eyes but maintained her pearly white smile in front of our hosts.

"As for the rest of the property, we're right on the Atlantic with a boardwalk that leads past the backyard onto the dunes. Then, there's the pool and Jacuzzi, of course, and I turned the garage into a half-gym for me and half-studio for Skye. The maid and gardener come by on Wednesdays. Moreau, let me tell you, the place is super sleek. I'm leaving out some of the good parts, trust me."

"Yeah, Kinsley and I are so thankful for the invite. So generous of you."

"Of course, man. I always hook my boys up. And if it gets to be too much of the me and Skye show, drive off in Kins' adorable car and explore the rest of the South Fork."

"Thanks again, Jeff."

We were then interrupted by the manager: "Mr. Campbell, are the beverages to your liking?"

"Yes, thank you, my good man."

"I've taken the liberty of ordering another round for the table. My treat, of course," the manager said.

"Where was I?" Campbell continued. "Oh, this summer. I'm thinking sailing, jet-skiing, horseback riding, polo matches, drinking rosé by the pool..."

"The food J, tell them about the food and the ice cream."

"Oh, well yeah. Navy Beach is awesome, as you see. I'll take you to Sant Ambroeus, DOPO, Tutto, 75, Crow's Nest, Sunset Beach, Lunch, Cittanuova, Coche, Il Mulino, Solé—"

"Don't forget La Fondita and Gosman's," Skye said. "And Kins, we have the best ice cream in the U.S. Literally every town out here. Scoop du Jour is the GOAT, of course, but Sag and East have dope places too. There's, like, this new ice cream place in Sag where you can get turnt and eat ice cream. They got their liquor license. J thinks it's extra, but not gonna lie, I'm all for it."

"Okay," I said. "I remember a lot of those places from when my family used to have the house out here."

"I wasn't *quite* finished, Moreau. We're gonna go on a vineyard trip, and we'll sleep under the stars in the state park. Wiffle ball, golf, football. Moreau, we've gotta go to Maidstone for 18. Best course you'll ever play at. And that's strictly a no-girls'-allowed trip."

The waitress and manager then brought out our smorgasbord, and let me tell you, it looked positively delectable.

"Kins, you and I will have to have a girls' day. We'll go to spin classes and, like, Pilates. And you know Gwen Paltrow's store, Goop, is in Sag. I've met Gwen before, you know. That's a girl whose look is always on fleek. Goddamn. Perfect skin, 'specially in person. I mean, talk about someone with just insane drip. It's unreal."

"Okay, sounds fun."

After the food was situated, Kinsley and I began sharing fries and steak like we always do. It felt innocuous and cute. The splitting of fries or ice cream was yet another activity that made us feel closer.

Skye then reached over to try Campbell's tilefish, and he glared.

"Come on, kid. You know the rules."

Skye then took out her iPhone and started scrolling at the dinner table. She barely touched her swordfish.

After our dinners were finished and the plates were cleared, the petulant Skye, using her baby voice for the first time that summer, said:

"J, can I have just a widdle dessert pwease?"

Campbell stood up, kissed her on the head, and said:

"We don't need dessert, kid. Not tonight...I'm gonna go to the restroom. Be right back."

There was an awkward silence, which Kinsley's gravelly voice halted.

"Skye, do you ever play cornhole here? I saw the tables with the holes back by the parking lot."

"I'm alright. J is the best, though. He's one of those dudes that's really good at everything. Makes it all look so easy."

"Well, let's start a game. And Jeff and Cash can join us in a bit."

The two jovial young women walked across the sand and rocks to the cornhole playing area. I was left to reflect on an ambivalent beginning to our three-month stay in the Hamptons.

Campbell came back outside, stopped in front of our table, and said:

"Moreau, my man, you joining our girls? We'll all play. Great idea."

"No problem, just waiting for the check."

"Come on, man, you know I got it. Paid for it inside."

I stood up, shook his hand, and smiled at his munificent gesture. That was the kind of person Jefferson Campbell III was.

The game began with the couples on the same teams. Kinsley and Skye stood at the other end, throwing their bags into our tables' hole, and Campbell and I were doing the same on our side of the beach. It's a relatively enjoyable party or tailgate game, and Campbell was predictably adroit.

"So, what was with the Skye dessert thing?" I asked Campbell as we were out of earshot from the ladies.

"What ever do you mean, Moreau?"

"Does she always listen to you?"

"Skye and I have a good system in place. She'll thank me tomorrow. Trust me. No one knows Skye like I do. You know her father ran away, and her mother died when she was seven? Lived with her grandma until she met me."

"Jesus."

"She's loyal, man—a good girl. But don't get me wrong, I wouldn't marry her. Been together, what, eight months. I love how agreeable she is. Everything I say, she listens with no argument. It's like I'm a 1950s husband. You ever get yourself a girl that worships you?"

"I don't want that. With me, Kins is the smarter one. And the breadwinner. She's a role model for me."

Skye threw her bag inside our hole, started jumping, and gave Kinsley a high-five.

"Way to go, Skye!" Campbell shouted. "Keep crushing it, kid."

We then tossed our bags to the other end.

"You see that movie *Baby Driver*?" he said. "Ansel Elgort. His girl in that is so agreeable. He robs banks, makes dirty money—doesn't matter. She'll go with him anywhere. Loyalty is very important to me, as you know. Well, and looks too. That Lily James actress from that movie? Hundred percent smoke. So is Skye. But anyway, my point is, my father always tells me to find someone laidback and not argumentative. That's the key."

"I'm happy with Kinsley. I want someone who challenges me."

Aside from a few shouts at impressive shots, we played the rest of the game in silence. Campbell and I enjoyed the light zephyrs blowing at our backs while watching our lovely companions chatting and smiling from afar.

After Kinsley and I lost the game, Skye came running to Campbell.

"Great game, J!" She planted a long, slobbering kiss on him. "I missed you."

"Folks," Campbell said. "Let's procure one of those lounge areas there and get another round of drinks."

Shortly after, our waitress led our group to a long couch-like piece of furniture with a white base and navy cushions. It sat no less than 10 feet from the shoreline. Campbell ordered some rum-based drinks, which I stopped nursing after a few sips, but Kinsley quickly knocked back two. We had agreed before the trip I'd be the designated driver most nights, which wasn't a problem.

Kinsley turned down a third drink, but Campbell insisted: "We're on vacation, after all."

This was a comical sentiment, considering he and I were unemployed post-grads, and Skye and Kinsley could work remotely. None of us were on vacation from anything.

Skye, though, in full-on vacation mode, must've had four or five drinks, and she couldn't have weighed more than 105 pounds. She stopped before number six and retired to smoking her Juul and snap-chatting her friends.

Meanwhile, Campbell offered me a cigar, which I declined. However, it had felt like I accepted because the malodorous scent from beside me was forcing its way into my nostrils and lungs. I was surprised one could smoke that close to the restaurant, but I suppose Campbell always did whatever he wanted without consequences.

"You ever think about heaven, Moreau?"

"It's not really something I believe in."

I noticed Kinsley was falling asleep, and Skye was in her own ethereal world.

"I think about heaven every day," Campbell continued. "You know what really bothers me? This whole idea that anyone can get in. If you're honest and you repent, and you live a life without sin, you can get into this magical, Elysian place."

"What's wrong with that?"

"Exclusivity."

"What do you mean?"

"A place isn't worth going to if everyone can go. Look at Fifth Avenue apartments or resorts in the Mediterranean or even nightclubs with bottle service. All these high-priced things are meant to keep the detritus out, you know."

"I don't think I agree with your point."

"Lemme finish. If everyone can get into heaven, then I want there to be a more exclusive spot in heaven that only, say, five percent can get in. Or better yet, 0.5 percent. A Luxe Heaven. The only places in life and the afterlife worth going to are the truly restrictive ones. That's my two cents, anyway."

I closed my eyes, thought about how unlikely it was that Campbell could get into this fantasy heaven, and then tried to fall asleep, but Skye's shrieks interrupted my three-second slumber.

"J, can we leave? I'm so bored. Let's go dancing."

"You wanna go dancing, kid? Then that's exactly what we'll do. Come here."

Skye jumped on top of him, and they passionately kissed.

"Kinsley and I are exhausted. We'll just call it a night and head back to the pool house."

"You sure, Moreau? Key is under the flamingo float to the left of the pool house door."

"Yeah, we've got all summer to stay out till two."

I woke Kinsley and walked her toward the parking lot. We said our goodbyes and I watched Campbell tip the valet $20 to drive his black Audi R8 convertible 10 feet. Meanwhile, I handed the man three dollars and felt like a scumbag.

I'd only had one drink, so the drive to Sagaponack was simple enough. Kinsley slept the whole way. I was moderately nervous about Campbell driving with three or four drinks in his system, but nothing bad ever happened to him, so that thought left my mind.

By the time we arrived at the pool house, Kinsley was wide awake, and I was ready to doze off. Campbell was right, though. It was a quaint little guest house with a fully furnished downstairs area and then a lonely king-sized mattress lying on the ground of the second floor, without a box-spring or headboard.

The pool house walls were all white, and the place had the distinct smell of hot sand, which was likely caused by the beach towels and umbrellas stuffed in the closet.

"Sorry, I fell asleep." Kinsley's succulent lips pressed against mine. "You wanna watch something on Netflix? *Stranger Things?*"

I heard her but was entranced by the only decorations in the diminutive house. Campbell had four different blown-up black-and-white images of nude women posing in nature. They weren't grotesque but rather tastefully done, and each of the women had a word painted on her body. There was "Serenity," "Sedation," "Strength," and "Tranquility."

"What? Yeah, sorry. Yeah, sounds good."

"It's a nice little place. I can't wait to see the inside of the big house tomorrow. Cash, I'm really glad I'm out here with you."

"Same here. I love you so much."

We cuddled next to each other on the couch and started to play the show. Kinsley paused during the theme song because she loved drinking a sugar-free Red Bull after having alcohol earlier in an evening. It was a habit she picked up at Duke.

I fell asleep in Kinsley's lap after one or two episodes but woke up to several cackles and the jingling of keys outside the pool house door.

"Kinsley and Moreau? My favorite couple?"

We both screeched as Jeff, Skye, and a female companion burst through the pool house door.

"Jesus Christ, Campbell. What the hell's a matter with you?"

"Girls, be quiet. Shush. Moreau, come back to the big house with us. Let's drink and dance and swim till morning."

"No friggin' way. It's 1:30. Get the hell out of here. Don't do this again."

"Sheesh," Skye said. "You're gonna have a major case of FOMO, Cashie."

"Jeff, please," Kinsley said. "Cash was sleeping. We'll see you in the morning."

Campbell nodded and then turned around as Skye and the other young lady began removing their tops and sprinting toward the pool. After the door was closed, locked, and dead-bolted, Skye began blasting music on her Bluetooth speaker from outside.

"Kins, I can't deal with this right now. I'm half-asleep."

"No worries. One sec," She said before opening the door. "Jeff, turn the music down, please."

"Can't, sweetheart. House rules."

Kinsley closed the door again. Falling back asleep, I muttered:

"I'll talk to him tomorrow. I've known him for a long time. He needs a little discipline."

"What have you gotten us into?" Kinsley's wry smile and dimples were on full display.

"Let's go upstairs and check out this mattress."

We made the bed with the sheets and blankets provided, and then she sat up by the pillows while I went downstairs to shower.

"I trust you, Cash," she shouted from upstairs. "We can handle anything."

MAY 26, 2018

THE VERY NEXT DAY

I WOKE UP EARLY TO the sound of Kinsley clacking away on her iPad.

"Oh, I'm so sorry. Did I wake you?"

"Don't worry 'bout me. I couldn't be happier. Come here."

Kinsley's kiss tasted like our shared minty toothpaste. Her wavy, black hair was draped over my blue Hollandsworth wrestling shirt in which she frequently slept.

"Sorry about last night," I said.

"You don't have anything to be sorry about."

"They got too rowdy and sorta broke into our house."

"It's summer. We're on vacation. I'm sure there will be a few bumps, but there's so much to look forward to."

Her cheery tone led me to believe her.

"Do you know what's on the agenda?" Kinsley said as she walked to her suitcase.

"Yeah, uh, Campbell texted me. He told me to meet him in his garage and told you to come along. Said wear workout clothes."

Kinsley and I followed our orders. We exited the pool house 10 minutes later and walked toward the garage. She was wearing black leggings and a white, long-sleeved lululemon top.

"Aren't you gonna be broiling?"

"No, it'll be good. I'll sweat out all the toxins."

"Who knows what we'll be doing."

Kinsley rarely wore revealing outfits. Shin-length summer dresses and loose, flowing white outfits were her seasonal specialty. She chose to stand out using her color palate as opposed to her skin and various assets.

I knocked on the garage door and found Campbell shirtless with a protein shake in hand.

"Do you want us to come back?"

"Nonsense, Moreau. Join me. I thought you and I could work out in the gym here, and the ladies could go into town and take a spin class."

"Kinsley, go knock on the front door. My girlfriend's waiting for you. Take your car."

"Sure, I'm always down for spin."

"Kins, are you sure?"

"'Course I am. Let's all loosen up, right?"

"That's right. Moreau, your girl's got the mindset...now come spot me."

Kinsley left the garage gym and presumably drove off with Skye to East Hampton, while I was handed some chocolate Muscle Milk and began plotting out my next 40 minutes.

At that point, I still hadn't seen the inside of the house, but I imagined this garage gym was the house's least grandiose room. Everything was grey aside from a black-and-white photograph that clearly belonged to the set in the pool house.

This one was of a nude twenty-something woman standing alone in a Pacific Northwestern pine forest. She had a sullen look on her face. The black-painted words above her chest read "Ferocious." I thought about asking Campbell about her, his collection, and how many were displayed throughout the big house, but I didn't.

"Last night was a good time," he said between sets.

"Yeah, Navy Beach is immeasurably beautiful."

"I don't want you to think this house is all I can afford."

"What are you talking about? This place is paradise, man."

Campbell was four or five inches taller than me but had a gaunt frame. He must've been around 6'2" 170 pounds. His torso was flat, his arms were vascular, and his ample blond hair remained coiffed even as he sweated.

"I don't know, man. It's alright. But remember my father used to have that nine-bedroom place on Meadow Lane? Right on the beach. That's what I want."

"As far as I'm concerned, any house out here is nice."

I laid on the adjusted bench and was doing dumbbell presses.

"When I turned 18, my father gave me a hundred K as a birthday gift," he said.

"Goddamn. Lucky you."

"And then my last two grandparents died when I was in college. One gave me this place in the will, and the other gave me another hundred K. None of it was taxed because you know the Campbells, we've got some whiz kid Jew accountant on retainer. But anyway—"

"Yeah, why are you telling me all this?"

"I just want you to know I've made some money on my own too. I've followed my father's stock tips, and you know how well I do with fantasy sports. And I'm a real card shark. You should see me at the poker tables."

"Oh yeah?"

"I don't want you to get the wrong idea about me."

"Campbell, I've known you for almost 20 years. We're friends no matter what. Now take Kinsley's advice and loosen up. Let's not talk about money."

"Whatever, man. Let's go for a dip when we're done here."

After our brief chat, Campbell put a Rick Ross album on the garage speakers, and we spent the rest of our gym time in silence. I specifically remember having a realization while "Stay Schemin'" was playing. I'd known Campbell for 20 years and Kinsley for basically one, and I felt much more comfortable around her.

"Let's hop in the pool now," Campbell said as he toweled the sweat from his face.

My old Hollandsworth pal burst through the garage's side door and headed toward the pool. His soccer player physique allowed strangers to ignore his potential emotional frailty, but it was good to see my old friend wasn't as infallible as he led others to believe.

Campbell and I swam in the pool for a while before our girlfriends eventually returned and found us lounging in the water on Skye's two pink flamingo pool floats. Campbell had sunglasses on and somehow managed to sneak a flask onto his flamingo.

"You girls up for a morning skinny-dip?"

"Stop it, Campbell."

"Be right there, bae," Skye shouted, luckily keeping her sweaty clothes on her body.

Her style was vastly more revealing than Kinsley's. The 20-year-old wore white bike shorts and a royal blue sports bra over her sun-kissed figure. Her buxom torso and chipper personality must've made her very popular throughout high school.

"I'll be right back. I'm gonna change into my suit," Kinsley said.

Moments later, Kinsley stepped out in a lively, striped one-piece, which caused a few squawks from the peanut gallery.

"Give us a twirl, sweetheart," Campbell shouted.

"Work it, girlfriend," Skye added.

"Campbell, seriously? Ease up."

"Relax, man. Kins knows I'm messin' around."

Kinsley, never one to back down from a fight, dove into the water and shoved Campbell off his flamingo float.

"Okay, Kins. Okay. You wanna play that way? Let's have a little fun. Skye, come here. Get on my shoulders. You know what to do."

We proceeded to have two chicken fights, with me holding Kinsley on my shoulders and Campbell and Skye doing the same. Our girlfriends grabbed and shoved until Skye fell off her mount and into the heated water. After a second loss, Campbell decided to switch games.

"Here, follow me to the deep end. Let's do some races. Crawl in race one, then breast, back, and butterfly. We'll see who the champs are."

"Sounds fun," Kinsley said and swam toward him.

"Skye, baby, you should win the breast contest with ease."

Skye playfully yanked on her boyfriend's wavy hair and shoved her tongue down his throat.

The races then commenced, and despite it being his home field, Campbell was the least deft swimmer. He was correct that Skye won the breaststroke lap, but she also beat everyone at the crawl and back-stroke. I suppose coming-of-age in East Hampton gave her a leg up on the three of us. I won the butterfly, though.

Every time I drove to the Hamptons, I was slapped with this blissful feeling that I was free from the endless concrete and grime of eight-million peoples' voluntary prison.

"Skye, go make some mimosas and pour them into two big Nalgene bottles, please. Let's head into town. Moreau, you and your girl should go get changed. We can take my car."

"Jeff, may Cash and I please have a tour of the house?" Kinsley said as she squeezed the water from the tips of her jet-black hair.

"'Course. Follow me. But dry off first. Skye, bring out two extra towels before the mimosas, please."

"Kk, brb."

Kinsley and I dried off, changed into more comfortable clothes, packed an extra bathing suit for a potential beach trip, and joined Campbell in the main house.

There was a man-made rock walkway from the pool to the patio area, which had a glass dining table and six surrounding chairs. Then, Kinsley and I entered through a wide doorway that would evidently allow a lot of light into the home. The outside of the five-bed-room house was complete with the classic Hamptons shaker siding. Truthfully, it was a gorgeous place.

"Okay, Moreau and Kins, we've got the living room, dining room, den, and kitchen in this main area here. Then if you follow me down this hallway, these are the two guest bedrooms. We got the one with the two twin beds and the other with the queen and the bathroom. Then, follow me upstairs. California-king room with small bathroom on your left, locked door on your right, and then at the end of the hallway is mine and Skye's place. California-king, 72-inch flatscreen, bathroom with removable shower head there and bathtub with jets on your right. Plenty of windows in this place."

"Campbell, man, this is all super cool. I envy you big time."

"You haven't seen the basement, my man."

The three of us walked down two flights of stairs, while Skye texted on one of the white couches in the living room.

"So, lady and gentleman, three sections in the basement. There's the video game area with another 72-inch flatscreen, an Xbox One, PS4, and Nintendo Switch all hooked up. Then, there's the casino area in this section. We have four poker tables, and I have a roulette wheel and blackjack table buried in Skye's garage studio."

"Jesus, Campbell. This place is the dream. I don't ever want to hear you complaining. My God."

"Awfully big for two people though, isn't it?" Kinsley added.

"Skye and I are rarely here alone. Always have various hedonists and interlopers coming over—and look here, got this other station."

"Come on," Kinsley said. "You have a stripper pole in the middle of your basement? When does that get used?"

"Never does really. I had it installed to impress guys that come over. Just for show."

"Yeah, okay, Jeff."

"Let's go to EH now. Skye," he shouted upstairs. "Hop in the car. You'll ride shotgun next to me. And don't drag any sand in this time."

Campbell sped up Townline Road and made a right on 27. The traffic was as bad as expected, but he kept ducking off onto back roads to avoid the brunt of it.

After parking the car, Campbell led the three of us into the Hamptons staple, The Golden Pear Cafe.

"Moreau, I'll see if they have a kids' menu for you. Girls, what do you want? All on me, of course."

"If you're buying," Kinsley said, "I'll take the, uh, challah French Toast with a Core Coconut Water."

"Moreau?"

"I can order for myself, thank you."

I asked the cashier for a grilled chicken sandwich with bacon, and Kinsley recited back her order. Then Campbell requested his egg whites before it was Skye's turn to chime in.

"J, what should I get?"

"Just get a smoothie, kid. Strawberry banana. I'll take care of it."

Skye then groped him, while I found a four-person table in the back of the narrow cafe.

We ate our breakfast while watching homogenous groups of people enter the establishment every few minutes. The Golden Pear's clientele consisted of primarily impossibly fit mothers in yoga pants with their too-formally-dressed sons and daughters, or businessmen trying their best to pull off tennis whites or golf polos. We were the only group of millennials in the quaint Hamptons chain.

After finishing our meals, we put on our bathing suits in the bathroom and proceeded to Atlantic Ave. Beach in Amagansett. It happened to be one of my favorite sandy spots in the entire United States—a picturesque view of the Atlantic Ocean along with soft, Caribbean-like sand and dunes in the background to separate beachgoers from the parking lot.

We laid out four towels and an umbrella in a quiet area and listened to the soothing sounds of breaking waves and distant seagulls.

Kinsley was the first to take out a book. Hers was *Improving Social Media Engagement One Like at a Time.* I, on the other hand, was reading Fitzgerald's *The Last Tycoon* at the beginning of that summer, and Campbell had McInerney's *Bright Lights, Big City.* Skye passed around the two Nalgene bottles filled with mimosas while no one said a word for an hour. Everyone always discusses the Hamptons as this rich person's paradise with golf, tennis, large houses, and boating, but to me, it was times like these that made the area so wonderful. Laying out on a stunning, tranquil beach with your close friends and not worrying about the soul-sucking job you were planning on taking that September.

Eventually, we went in the water, splashed around, and bodysurfed before returning home. Campbell had everyone change into something chic, and he drove us into East Hampton for some Italian food at Cittanuova.

The four of us, drained from a busy and rewarding day, had little to say over dinner. Campbell, Kinsley, and Skye drank several cocktails, and I responsibly drove the Audi home.

Kinsley and I then snuggled together on the pool house couch and watched *Before Sunrise*. The '90s classic romance intentionally acted as foreplay because right when the closing credits cascaded, Kinsley was guiding me to our upstairs "bedroom."

MAY 28, 2018

Our One-Year Anniversary

"We're not going to Vineyard Vines."

"Why, what's the problem?" I asked Kinsley.

"If I'm out in East Hampton, the goal should be to buy stuff you either can't get anywhere else, or it's at least difficult to find back home."

"Fine, fine. You're the expert. And you look really pretty."

Kinsley and I walked hand in hand up Main Street toward Newtown Lane.

"So, where are we going?"

"I want to check out Zimmermann for rompers, also Clic and then Henry Lehr. Is that okay, Cash? I don't want to bore you."

"I'm never bored for a single second around you."

We walked into the stores of her choosing, and then eventually stopped for ice cream at the place Skye continually referred to as the GOAT (greatest of all-time) of ice cream stores, Scoop du Jour.

"Excuse me, sir. May I please try the pistachio?"

The vendor handed Kinsley a tasting cup of ice cream, which she licked instantly.

"How about the cookie dough?" This achieved the same result. "Oh, now may I please try the cookies and cream?"

"Kinsley, c'mon."

"Oh, stop." She shoved me playfully. "And the rocky road, please."

"Kins, you know—"

"I know. I know." She then imitated my nasally voice and said, "'Allow yourself to be surprised. Haven't you ever heard of spontaneity? Blah blah. You're 24. You know what pistachio tastes like."

"Wow, well played."

"You're one to talk. You have the weirdest pet peeves."

"Well, at least I don't always feel the need to speak up whenever someone pushes an already-lit elevator button."

"Come on. That bothers you too. What are they hoping is gonna happen? Pushing it three times makes it come faster?"

Kinsley proceeded to get two ice cream flavors she never even tried, possibly to spite me, but I loved her anyway.

"Sir, we only accept cash."

"Ugh, I only have cards."

"Cash, I've got it. Relax."

"Are you sure? It's our anniversary, and I wanted to pay for everything."

"It's no big deal. Now, if I had to pay for dinner at Sunset Beach, well...I dunno."

"It's your anniversary?" the ice cream vendor said. "It's on the house."

"Seriously? You don't have to do that," I said.

"Thank you so much," Kinsley added and then whispered. "Cash, this is my money we're talking about now. Don't talk the guy out of being generous."

We left the store smiling and laughing as usual. She brushed a few wisps of black hair from her eyes, and I felt her s'mores-flavored breath on my lips.

We finished our shopping and ice cream date, placed our bags in the car, walked about a mile and a half to East Hampton Main Beach, and then laid out two towels.

"I haven't done any swimming yet," I said. "So, I'm gonna go in right away."

I took my white t-shirt off, and Kinsley lowered her sunglasses on her nose and then made that construction worker whistle sound.

"Now give us a twirl, hon," she said to me.

I rolled my eyes and sprinted into the freezing water. Unfortunately, after about five minutes of diving under waves, I realized the late-May Atlantic was still too brisk for my liking.

"Too cold? Lay next to me. Keep me warm, please."

Moments later, Kinsley fell asleep on my chest. I then stroked her long and wavy black hair that had some unwelcome grains of sand nestled inside.

After a few hours and several sun-tan lotion applications on my pallid skin, we returned to the pool house. I'd made a 6:30 p.m. reservation at Sunset Beach weeks ago, and it wasn't a quick trip, so we essentially had to get changed and leave immediately.

I put on my white pants and pale-pink linen shirt and exited the bathroom to find Tranquility staring at me. She was sprawled out on an Arabian desert with the lower half of her spine dug into the peak of a dune and the middle third arched in the air. The painted word was displayed down her left side as her profile faced the camera. However, her left eye was looking out toward the viewer of the photograph. She did seem tranquil.

"Almost ready, Cash?"

"Oh, um, yeah, just grabbing my Rivieras. Who's driving?"

"I'll do the way there," she shouted from upstairs, "And you take the ride home."

"Anything for you."

Kinsley took her time walking down the steps, intentionally ensorcelling me with her orange-and-blue paisley print summer dress.

"Kinsley, you look—I mean, wow."

I loved the tiny black birthmark on her cheek. It was as if God saw this flawless face and said, "'I want to give her one more additional, inimitable detail. No one shall replicate this woman's internal or external beauty.'"

Kinsley was a fast, aggressive driver who was obsessed with the horn. She'd never been in an accident in seven years of driving in Cincinnati. Although, and she'd hate that I'm repeating this, she'd received seven tickets. Kinsley had a propensity for illegal U-turns and rolling stops.

"If we get there fast enough, we should have time to go into that little jewelry shop right next to the restaurant."

"Well, can we get there in one piece? You almost hit that car when you were merging on 27."

"It takes two to make an accident." A toothy grin accompanied this.

I played along and said, "Suppose you met somebody just as clever as yourself?"

"I hope I never will," she added in a 1920s mid-Atlantic accent. "I hate careless people. That's why I like you."

"Wow! That was great. You remembered that Jordan quote out of nowhere."

"Glad I can still impress you after a year."

"Every. Single. Day."

Kinsley drove her car onto the ferry that led to Shelter Island. And without a word, I knew she'd want a few pictures of herself overlooking the water, so I left the car with her. Taking photos of her wasn't my favorite activity, but I was always willing to do whatever it took to make her happy.

We arrived about 20 minutes before our reservation, which gave Kinsley ample time to shop at the adjacent boutique. I purchased a pair of earrings she seemed to like, and then we took our seats at the upstairs portion of the restaurant.

I'd always loved Sunset Beach. It was a transformative experience whether you were a multi-millionaire celebrity or a five-year-old child like I once was. I remember playing on their outdoor ping-pong tables after my parents placed their orders. However, on this particular occasion, Kinsley and I were seated at a table overlooking the Shelter Island Sound, and there was no ping-pong to be played. That summer, the restaurant had these Parisian bistro chairs and yellow checked table cloths that created an aesthetically pleasing atmosphere. And listen, I know a lot of outsiders complain about the turgidity of the Hamptons, but Sunset Beach was a nice compromise given its kid-friendly ambience.

After the waitress delivered our menus and waters, Kinsley said:
"So...one year together. It's a crazy feeling."

The waitress took our drink orders and then left us alone underneath the roofless restaurant and overhead string lights.

"What's your favorite moment so far?" Kinsley asked.

"Oh, good one. The first two that immediately come to mind are meeting you at The Crow's Nest with my mom there—"

"Who could forget?"

"And that time you were in Philly on business, and we stayed at your hotel together. Your company had you at the Aloft, and we'd been together maybe three months?"

"Right. Right. You were finishing up Penn and uh—"

"It was the first time we were ever, you know."

"Of course."

"What about yours?"

The waitress brought our bottle, filled our glasses, and left.

"Wait. Cheers. To Kinsley Avital. May there be many stupendous years to come."

"And cheers to you, Cash Moreau." She gave me a quick peck on the lips.

At that moment, a child had thrown their bread on the floor, which caused two lurking seagulls to pounce and feed. A manager then sprinted over and quickly shooed away the birds.

"Okay then, um, where were—right, well, my favorite was when we went to Six Flags together that first summer." She closed her eyes and continued. "It was like a 95-degree day, and the crowd was sweaty and miserable, but I couldn't keep my hands off you. We didn't have Fast Pass money, so we waited in hourlong lines just kissing and touching and laughing to pass the time before the Superman or Green Lantern rides."

"Oh, jeez. That's right. I was scared to ride Kingda Ka, but you convinced me. That was the first time you said you loved me. Although you may have had an ulterior motive."

She laughed and said, "Well, how else could I have gotten you to go with me?"

"I think the quote was 'would you rather die today going 128 miles an hour on a rollercoaster with a girl that loves you or die when you're 75 and alone?'"

We then looked over the menu, ordered food, and reminisced about the mock graduation I had at Penn back in December. I'd finished school a semester early, and Kinsley and my whole family came down, and we went to the Franklin Institute and the Philadelphia Mint Museum. She'd been a true part of the family ever since.

"So, what does the future hold?" she asked, brushing her hair behind her pointy ears.

"With us? Couldn't be brighter. With my job, who knows?"

"Look, if you don't want to work for your dad, you don't have to."

"I made him a promise."

"People break promises to their parents all the time. You've gone three months without eating a vegetable."

"Good one."

"He gave you six months to find a job in Manhattan after graduating. You didn't. What's another six months? It's better than doing something you're not passionate about."

"It wasn't like I didn't have a job. I helped kids improve their SAT and ACT scores. That counts."

"You know what I mean, Cash. A career."

"I know. But look, my dad was generous enough to allow me to vacation out here with you for three months. I owe it to him to start work in September. Besides, I'll make a lot of money."

"As a real estate apprentice."

"Let's change the subject. What about you? How's working remotely going? Your boss is still cool?"

"Yeah, she's the best. I love the freedom a start-up gives you. I work when I want, where I want, and as long as the work gets done, no one cares. It's exactly how jobs should be."

"I'm so delighted for you. Really. You're the smartest, most driven person I know."

A toddler from another table then came running over.

"Uppie?"

"Aw, you're so cute," Kinsley said.

"Sorry about her," the mother said after jogging over. "Diana, back to the table. You want fries?"

The mother and daughter walked away, almost crashing into our waitress, who was bringing our dinners.

"So," Kinsley said, "would you rather tutor high schoolers or baby-sit toddlers?"

"Either. I love being around kids. I always wanted siblings. I've always dreamt of having a house with a bunch of rambunctious kids."

Kinsley hesitated and then said:

"Don't grow up too fast. It wasn't long ago you were a kid who probably loved running around and breaking things and catching frogs or whatever Manhattan boys do."

"You know me so well," I laughed. "I used to love hanging out by the creek on 88th and Park nabbing frogs and eating crickets."

We ate our phenomenally prepared meals. Kinsley then had three more glasses of champagne, and we eventually made our way downstairs and across the street to the beach.

She skipped toward the water, held her paisley print dress, and waded up to her knees.

"Cash, my darling, c'mere."

I walked over; my face stuck in a permanent, goofy smile.

"Hold my hand," she said. "And look at the moon."

I ran my hand through her hair.

"Cash Moreau, I'll love you till the day I die."

Kinsley's bubbly lips grazed mine as the water ran across our ankles, and our shoes watched from the sand.

After an hour or so of frolicking by the beach, I guided a sleepy Kinsley back to the front seat of her white Prius. She dozed off immediately as I pulled out of the parking lot. I played one of my playlists:

"Hot Stuff" – Donna Summer
"In Your Eyes" – Peter Gabriel
"It Was a Very Good Year" – Frank Sinatra
"Can You Feel the Love Tonight" – Elton John
"Feels Like the First Time" – Foreigner
"Layla" – Eric Clapton
"Your Song" – Elton John
"To Love Somebody" – The Bee Gees
"Vienna" – Billy Joel
"Wish You Were Here" – Pink Floyd

We arrived back at the pool house around 10:45 p.m. I carried Kinsley's svelte figure up to our bed and hoped she'd be able to sleep through the night. But I knew Kinsley and therefore knew she'd be up at 3:00 a.m., working on her iPad, killing her chances of falling back to sleep with nonstop blue light.

JUNE 16, 2018

BOYS' DAY

CAMPBELL AND I WERE STANDING at the tee box on the first hole at Poxabogue. It was a basic, 304-yard par four, and my old Hollandsworth pal drove the green with his brand-new Callaway.

"Nice shot," I said.

"How 'bout us? Ditching the girls for a day. A little peace and quiet. What's better than this?"

I sliced my drive into the rough on the right, about 80 yards from the green.

"And *that* is why I said we should've gone to the range first," he said.

"Relax. It's one shot. Walk with me to my ball."

"Such a tragedy this place doesn't have golf carts or caddies."

"How long's it been since you played here?"

"I was probably three at the time and still shot an even 30."

"It's a par 30, right? Nine holes?"

"Yeah, Moreau. Remind me why we're playing here again?"

"Look, you wanted to play Maidstone, and I haven't golfed in probably nine months. I needed an easy course to warm up and lose a few balls."

"It's so degrading. If anyone I know sees me here, my reputation as a five handicap will be shot."

We arrived at my ball, and I hit my pitching wedge long, 15 yards past the green.

"Either you need to start playing better, or I need to find someone to carry my clubs. This is gonna be a bad day for my shoulders. What's your handicap? 36?"

"17, probably."

"You couldn't shoot sub-100 at Maidstone if I gave you $1,000."

"Do they allow Jews there?" I said. "How many of these Hamptons' courses still don't?"

"Are you Jewish?"

"Are you serious?"

"Oh, well, you're like a mutt, right? Half-Jew?"

"Not sure Kinsley would like to hear you call Jewish people mutts."

"Relax. Today's a no-girls'-allowed day. I may let a few heinous things slip out. I keep these crazy thoughts cooped up in my head all the time for the sake of decorum."

"Maybe that's a good thing."

"You're my friend of 20 years. If I say something offensive, I know you'll still be there for me. I told you how important loyalty is."

I chipped my third shot past the hole and then two-putted from there to finish with a five. Meanwhile, after watching Campbell's short game, I knew my day was about to get a lot worse.

He missed his 12-footer right by four feet and then his birdie putt by two inches. Several curse words were uttered, and by the second tee, Campbell's trusty flask was seducing his silver tongue.

"Put me down for a three, Moreau."

"In what world?"

"You know where I got this flask?"

"The Poxabogue gift shop?"

"Good one. No, my father bought it in Cairo. It's genuine silver, and the nozzle is made out of an elephant's tusk. Hundred percent real ivory. Thing cost him one or two K."

"Cool. You're away, Mr. Birdie."

Campbell's pitching wedge flew over the 124-yard hole and may have landed in the woods.

"This course is so goddamn idiotic. This is where people bring their four-year-olds to learn golf. The holes aren't long enough. It's messing with my swing."

My wedge fell short of the green and left me with a chip and putt for par.

"It's a beautiful day, Campbell. What's this? 84? I love how it's sunny out here but never too humid like Manhattan.

"You know they're playing the U.S. Open out here? It's this weekend."

"Where? Shinnecock?"

"Yeah. They're playing the third round as we speak. 30-minute drive from here."

"What happened to the Maidstone plan later?"

"What? Yeah, that's still on. Oh, you thought—no, I'd never go watch pro golf live. You'd have to be a huge loser to do that. I was just saying it's funny we're playing so close to, like, Johnson and Reed, Koepka and Rose."

We finished the second hole, and I elected not to comment when I may or may not have seen Campbell kick his ball out of the woods to improve his lie. I've known him for a long time and used to play golf with him before high school. If there's one thing I learned, it's when Campbell is having a bad day, one needs to keep their mouth shut. Comments and suggestions go in one ear and out the other, and shouting, screaming, cursing, and overall vituperative behavior wasn't simply a possibility but a guarantee.

That morning, I actually begged Kinsley to create an excuse for me, but she wanted time to go to the vineyard alone with Skye, so there I was, on the third tee of Poxabogue, already regretting not faking a fever.

Campbell's third tee shot went into the woods on the left, but apparently my shadow was in his swing path so he deserved a free mulligan. Oh, and then I accidentally walked in his line on the fourth green, so he took a mulligan. And later in the round, he may or may not have used his proverbial "hand wedge" to assist him from a difficult lie.

By the time we were standing on the seventh tee, the scorecard I had in my pocket said I had a 27 and Campbell a 21. However, the scorecard in my head said I had a 27 and Campbell a 33. But there was no need to bring any of this up or to fight with him. I'd seen the guy three times in the previous eight years, and he still allowed us to stay with him rent-free in one of the nicest areas of the Hamptons. I was prepared to let anything slide. And I think Kinsley was too.

"I've made three hole-in-ones on this hole in my life. 72-yards out." He began to take his club back and talked during his own backswing. "Flagstick in primo position." His wedge was fully cocked. "Wind's blowing a few ticks east, and—"

Then a rather noisy crow cawed as Campbell's club descended toward his ball. It caused him to jerk upward and hit the ball directly into the woods on the left. This unfortunate event cost him about $120 because needless to say, Campbell launched his club into the woods out of spite or anger or idiocy or, I'm not sure why he did it. But immediately after the club throw and the profanity-laced speech about how God is out to get him, Campbell was pacified by what amounted to a silver and ivory sippy cup for a 22-year-old.

After we finished nine holes, Campbell suggested we eat at the Poxabogue restaurant, Fairway.

"So, what'd you shoot," Campbell asked as we sat at the casual, outdoor eatery.

"41. So, 11-over."

"Ouch, bro. You have me at 32 on the card, right? I would've shot even-par if not for that crow on seven."

"Right."

The waiter came with a coffee for Campbell and an orange juice for me.

"You order this?" I asked.

"Yeah, do I know you or what?"

"You certainly have a memory."

"Excuse me, sirs. Are you ready to order?"

"Sagaponack omelet for me," Campbell said. "And chocolate chip pancakes with sausage links for my buddy here."

"Excellent, sir."

"How'd I do?" he said to me.

"Nailed it, but what if someone wants to order for themselves?"

"Why would they want to do that?"

"Spontaneity? Freedom? I don't know."

"Every person in the world likes when things are taken care of for them, and they don't have to lift a finger."

"Does Skye?"

"Kid loves it. Adores me." Campbell paused and said, "You bet on any baseball these days?"

"No, only year-long fantasy sports."

"I got a bookie I text my daily picks to. It's addictive, Moreau. Let me tell you."

"Who ya got today?"

"Castillo against Nova and the Pirates. Scherzer's Nats against the Blue Jays. And my boy Junior Guerra at home against the Fightins."

"I'm afraid to ask. How much a game?"

"Usually a grand, but if I have a razor-sharp bet, a mortal lock, I'll bet five."

"Jesus Christ. Some life you've got."

"You got that right. I'm 22. Got a Hamptons house with my name on the deed. Got 400K in the bank and have a smokin' hot girl. Tell me someone else from Hollandsworth with a better life?"

I missed Kinsley.

"You got a job lined up for the fall?" I asked.

"Mulling some things. Weighing my options. Don't stress me out."

Campbell took his flask from under his chair and poured what amounted to three or four shots into his coffee.

"You want a little morning jolt?" he asked.

"Nope."

"Pussy as always. I'll be in the bathroom. Be right back."

After another half-hour, we finished eating, and Campbell paid. He started to make a beeline for the driver's side of his Audi, but I cautioned him against it and took the wheel.

I followed Google Maps to Maidstone Club in East Hampton, where we were planning on playing 18 more holes of even more laborious golf. And this extremely arduous course was made all the more difficult when one had, let's say eight shots of scotch, or whatever he had, and however many lines of coke Campbell snorted. I should've driven us home. But I didn't. Maybe Campbell was able to furtively bring out masochistic tendencies in people. Who knows?

I parked his car; we checked in at the clubhouse and shortly thereafter made our way to the first tee.

"I got this game I play with Mathewson and O'Reilly sometimes."

"Oh, they're out here?"

"You kidding? Mathewson has the nicest boat of anyone in our class."

"So, what's the game?

"I'll tell you, but please, please don't be a pussy."

"Okay."

"Here's how it works. Every time you miss a fairway in regulation or green in regulation, you have to take one of the pills I have in my golf bag. Gotta take a shot for any double bogey or worse, and you have to shotgun a beer for every bogey. Although I only brought six cans. I call the game Gamblin' and Scramblin' with Campblin'."

"I gotta drive the Audi home. Sorry."

"We'll take an Uber."

"No, man. You've been so generous. Like seriously, thank you so much for all you've done for Kinsley and me. I don't feel right about taking an Uber when we have a car I can drive."

"Whatever, man. Just wanted you to have fun with me—and I'm also doing a line every third hole."

And so that wound up being one of my least favorite days of last summer. Campbell yelled, cursed, cheated, and criticized both my play and etiquette. And wouldn't you know it, by the 12th hole, Campbell was bombed out of his mind. And on the 14th tee, he passed out drunk.

Now, I'll be the first to admit I wasn't a saint, and to this day, I still feel bad about what I did on the 14ᵗʰ. When I got home that night, I confessed to Kinsley, who's the closest person I knew to sainthood, and she reamed me out for a few minutes. Although Kinsley was pretty intoxicated herself. She told me it was inappropriate to continue golfing when my friend was ailing and unconscious. After thinking it over, I agreed with her.

But anyway, I laid Campbell on his side on the golf cart seat, and I finished the round as if nothing had happened. My old Hollandsworth pal slept as I continued hitting my drives and sinking my putts. Maidstone was the nicest course I'd ever played, and I didn't know if I'd have the opportunity to return. I shot a 92 and had more fun over those final five holes than the other 22 combined.

I drove Campbell home afterward, placed him on the white couch next to a passed-out Skye, and then joined Kinsley in the pool house. We had our brief, one-sided argument before she asked me to join her upstairs so we could reconcile properly.

When I went to the bathroom in the middle of the night, I found Kinsley working away on her iPad. It must've been 3:30 a.m., and I guess those spreadsheets and designs needed to be completed. My olfactory organs could also sense the acrid odor of sugar-free Red Bull that seemed to permeate the pool house's upstairs every day.

"Go back to bed, Kins," I said groggily. "And turn that blue light off. You're hurting your eyes."

"Why don't you c'mere and make me?"

I grabbed her iPad, tossed it onto the floor—which was a steep drop of nine inches from our boxspring-less mattress—and climbed on top of her. I didn't need eight hours of sleep every night. It was vacation after all.

JULY 4, 2018

THE SAILING TRIP

"This, ladies and gentleman, is *The Aeneid*," Campbell announced as we stepped off the dock and onto his boat.

"She's a 38-foot sailboat complete with a fully furnished bedroom, bathroom, and stocked kitchen below deck. Skye, get our pals here two life preservers, please."

As Campbell sailed us out of Montauk Marina and toward the Atlantic, it reminded me he was capable of impressing every now and then. My old Hollandsworth pal was surprisingly dexterous with the various sails and ropes, plus he'd always been an exceptional fabulist. And as I might've expected, he was wearing a white sea captain's hat.

"My father has had various boats occupy the marina for decades now, but this is the first one he's gifted. She's pretty, ain't she?"

"Why *The Aeneid*?" Kinsley asked, while seated next to me on the stern side.

"Not sure. I didn't name it. Book's good, though...Skye, break out the treats."

"Yessir, Cap'n Campbell."

Skye disappeared below deck and returned moments later with a picnic basket and a bottle of champagne.

"What do we have there, Skye?" I asked.

"Everything, Cashie. Chips, salsa, guac, chocolate truffles, strawberries, and Bellinis, my favorite."

"Jeff, this is all so magnificent," Kinsley said. "Thank you for bringing us here."

"Moreau, did I ever tell you 'bout the time I saved my baby cousin from a shark?"

"No...will I believe it?".

"'Course you will. I never lie."

Kinsley rolled her eyes but was still smiling.

"Keep your wits about you," he said, "We could catch a glimpse of a whale or shark out here—but anyway, where was I?"

"The shark story, J. You were gonna tell them the shark story." Skye turned to me and said: "It's high-key one of my favorite stories he tells."

Campbell jerked the tiller east, put on his black sunglasses, and cleared his throat.

"Would've been about six years ago—no seven. Everyone from the Campbell side of the family was sailing on *The Aeneid*'s predecessor. In fact, we were taking this exact route out of Montauk, and it was around this same time of day."

"Spooky, J."

"I was sailing when one of my cousins suggested we drop anchor and go for a quick dip. My father agreed, and we all dove in and swam and splashed for 40 minutes or so. Eventually, one by one, the group of seven Campbells filed back onto the boat until it was only me and little Darcy, who was three."

Campbell paused, leaned his head back, and allowed the sun to pierce through his pores.

"So then, in the distance, I saw a fin coming straight for little Darcy. She was giggling with her water wings and had no idea what was happening. My aunt screamed from the boat, but was paralyzed with fear."

"Come on," Kinsley interrupted. "This can't be true."

"Swear on Darcy's life it is. No more interruptions, please." Campbell continued, his voice rising above the heavy swell encircling the boat. "The fin came closer and closer and then the snout or whatever emerged from beneath the surface. It was a tiger shark. Massive teeth. Looked meaner and more vicious than anything I'd ever seen.

She headed straight for little Darcy, and just as it was about to open its mouth, I punched the thing right in the snout."

"No way," Kinsley said. "I'm calling b-s. You didn't punch a shark in the face."

"Skye, tell her."

"J's fist, like, temporarily paralyzed the shark. He grabbed Darcy, swam to the boat, and saved the day. That story leaves me shook every time."

"C'mere, kid."

Skye raced to the stern and essentially started licking Campbell's lips. And then she decided to wear the captain's hat the rest of the day.

"Hey, uh, Moreau. You and your girl come back here. I want to show you how to steer this thing."

Kinsley and I stood up, walked to the back of the boat, and watched Campbell demonstrate the proper usage of the tiller and how the ropes and sails came into play.

"So, Campbell, you have a lot of parties on this boat?" I asked, with the tiller in Kinsley's hand, and Captain Skye sensually massaging her beau's shoulder.

"I've only had her a year or two, so haven't had that massive 'dager' yet, but you can't imagine the girls I used to bring back here."

"C'mon Jeff, really?" Kinsley said.

"Don't be such a prude. It's not a good look," Campbell continued. "Anyway, before this one came along," he said, pointing at Skye, "I had every type of dime-piece you could imagine. We're talking MILFs, Instagram models, actresses, singers, every race and religion. Goddamn, man."

"I mean, Campbell," I said. "Isn't it awkward to say this stuff in front of Skye?"

"Skye, do you care?" Campbell asked.

"Not at all. It's actually making me a little horny."

"Oh, come on. Have some self-respect, girl," Kinsley said.

"You know," Skye began, "we don't all have to fit into your boxes of societal norms. There's millions of different kinds of loves and love stories, and J is mine and loves me for exactly who I am. Kins, you know I like you, girlfriend, but you should mind your own business and stop acting so basic."

Skye then began unbuttoning Campbell's white linen shirt and running her hand through his flowing, blond hair.

"Easy now, kid."

Skye then whispered, "I want you now," but it was loud enough for Kinsley and me to hear.

"Kid, head inside this instant. I'll join you in a minute."

The buxom, tattooed Skye turned around, skipped toward the bow, and disappeared below deck.

"Well, Moreau, duty calls." He gave me a salute and said, "Just point the damn thing straight. I'll be back."

Campbell slammed the door, which was undoubtedly not soundproof.

"I'm sorry, Kins. He can be difficult sometimes."

"I love being out on the water." She placed her hand on my cheek, saying, "And hearing the sounds of those seagulls and the waves hitting the boat."

"I'll talk to Campbell the next time we're alone. He's rough around the edges, but he means well, and Skye worships him."

"I'd love to get a sailboat like this and spend a month gallivanting around the Mediterranean. Just you and me. We'll start by staying with my grandparents in Tel Aviv and then go to Istanbul, Athens, Corsica, and Nice and dock in Mallorca or Ibiza. Wouldn't that be splendid?"

"Sounds heavenly."

Kinsley's voluminous hair blew into my face. I was steering the boat, and it was as if this life was ours. No jobs to worry about, no family or friends, just two soul mates sailing straight toward the horizon. And then the noises started.

Skye's playful moans crescendoed to orgastic yelps and cries. We heard "Oh yeah, daddy" and "Right there, daddy," but Kinsley seemed immune to the awkwardness.

"How 'bout a drink, Cash?"

Kinsley, the paragon, poured champagne and peach purée into two glasses and handed me one while I steered.

"Cheers," she said.

Kinsley and I continued chatting as if Skye's shrieks were nothing more than a playful dolphin in the distance. We spoke about how much better and more relaxing the Hamptons were than the scalding hot, smelly Manhattan summer streets. And then, after one final, blood-curdling squeal, Campbell and Skye joined us above deck.

Skye's hair was disheveled, and she was now wearing only her hot pink bikini, while Campbell seemed to have a smidge of drug residue spilling down his chin.

"Hey, Kins," he said. "You're next. Come on down."

"Campbell," I said, "that stuff isn't funny."

"Oh, come on, if she weren't here, you'd be dying of laughter."

I considered physically confronting my old Hollandsworth pal, but Kinsley restrained me. Instead, I repeated:

"That stuff isn't funny."

"Damn, man, chill out. You know my sense of humor. Nothing wrong with some meaningless jokes once in a while."

Skye then put her headphones on and skipped to the front of the boat.

"And while we're at it," Kinsley said to Campbell, "would it kill you to be sober for maybe 20 minutes this entire summer?"

"Easy, sweetheart. You drink more than I do. Passing out every night. You're no saint."

"Okay. Okay," I interjected. "Let's all dial it back. We're out on the ocean. We've all gotta enjoy ourselves. Okay?"

Kinsley and Campbell nodded. And after hearing the arguing subside, Skye came running back, kissed her boyfriend and said:

"Can we go swimming, J?"

"Of course, kid. Adjust the mainsail for me, will ya? And what are you listening to?"

"Bikinis and Bellinis."

"I love that song," Campbell said. "Moreau, you know that's Skye's song. She wrote and produced it. Threw it on her SoundCloud, and its stock has been rising for months. Didn't it hit 98 on the charts, kid?"

"94. Cashie, you should check it out. My DJ name is 'Skygreenii.' It's on SoundCloud, YouTube, and Apple Music. I gotta do a music vid ASAP. It'll be so lit, trust me."

By now, Kinsley and I were seated on the starboard side and downing our second Bellinis. Campbell was gripping the tiller, looking as laid-back as ever. His sunglasses hid what could've been any number of emotions. And there were still bits of coke jutting out from his scruff.

"Skye, adjust the sail now."

With her headphones and sea captain's hat still affixed, the famed DJ hopped to the loose rope and began twisting and untying it. Meanwhile, Kinsley's head was now perched comfortably atop my left shoulder, and I could smell her intoxicating, flowery shampoo. And then something happened to the boat.

The Aeneid jerked to the right, and the boom struck Skye, causing her to fall overboard.

"Jeff, stop the boat! Skye fell in and she doesn't have a life preserver. God, why isn't she wearing one?"

Campbell stood motionless as the boat continued onward with Skye howling from our wake.

"Campbell, man, turn the boat around. Skye's in the water."

My old Hollandsworth pal stood as cool as could be. If he'd been photographed, you'd think you were looking at a Brooks Brothers model. I'm not sure what was going through his mind, but he wasn't going to turn that boat around, so I ran over and started shaking him.

"Campbell man, Skye's overboard. We gotta turn around right now. Turn this thing around, man."

He didn't move a muscle, so I shoved him aside and attempted to operate the tiller myself.

"Kins, try to adjust the ropes or something. W-we have to move the sail in the other direction."

She ran to the cord Skye was handling earlier, but my Cincinnati girlfriend was helpless. Therefore, I chose to act. I ripped the shades from Campbell's nose and slapped him across the cheek.

"Turn us around. Now."

I was four or five inches shorter than him, but he was spindly and often not lucid, so a slap from me definitely affected him.

Campbell moved at a glacial pace, but did as he was told. Kinsley, on the other hand, was striding back and forth like a caged lion.

"Skye, honey," she shouted, "we'll be right there."

After a few minutes, we were within 50 feet of Skye, and Kinsley was too anxious to wait anymore, so she ripped off her shawl, put her life jacket back on, and dove into the mighty Atlantic to rescue one of the Hamptons' preeminent DJs.

My heroic girlfriend saved Skye, pushing her back aboard the ship.

The poor girl was breathing heavily and shivering as Kinsley rubbed her arms and repeated, "Everything's fine now." Skye kept nodding, clearly shaken.

"My phone and headphones are gone."

"Don't worry," Kinsley said. "We'll get you new ones. Everything's fine."

"But I'll have to add, like, new contacts and apps and stuff. I literally need to start my life over."

By now, Campbell was back below deck, and he let out a loud moan before poking his head from the doorway.

"Skye dearest, come join me, will you?"

"Don't move," Kinsley whispered to her. "Cash, go grab us the towels there."

"J's calling. I should see what he needs."

A still visibly trembling Skye leaped from Kinsley's lap, skipped below deck, and slammed the door.

Kinsley looked at me, shook her head, and laid down.

"Keep me warm, please. That water's freezing."

Her wild and wet black mane sprawled out in my lap. I placed a white shawl over her body like a blanket and noticed Campbell must've dropped the anchor or stopped the boat somehow because we were no longer moving. Kinsley and I heard the clink of glasses, the shaking of pill bottles, and the removal of clothing. Groans and creaks soon followed.

"What are we going to do?" the gravelly voice in my lap said.

"I mean, as I'm sure you've seen, he has good and bad days."

"Well, there's a direct correlation to his drug intake," she said while twisting the Star of David around her neck.

"So maybe we spend less time with them, and more time just the two of us."

"I'd like that."

I leaned over and kissed the upside-down face in my lap.

"Kins, he's a flawed person like all of us. You know his mom ran off when he was eight. He never talks about her."

"No, I had no idea."

"It doesn't excuse the bad stuff he's done and will do, but I promise he means well and would do anything for me...and for you, by the transitive property."

"I trust you, Cash."

"Thank you. And listen, the second I feel even an ounce of concern for your well-being, we'll be out of that pool house in an instant. And I'd beat him senseless. I'd never let anyone hurt you."

"I love you."

The shouts continued at an allegro tempo, and even a gliding seagull joined in overhead. The water was choppy, and the sky was grey, but I adored being out on the Atlantic. It was so freeing. No responsibilities. No schoolwork. No job. And I had the smartest, prettiest woman in the world snuggled in my lap.

Then Kinsley interrupted and said:

"Do you think Jeff did it on purpose?"

"Did what? Whaddya mean?"

At that moment, Campbell and Skye exited their non-soundproof love nest and joined us back by the tiller.

"Why the looks, guys?" Campbell said, with his blond locks still neatly coiffed.

I knew Kinsley wanted to excoriate my old Hollandsworth pal, but perhaps for my sake, she held her tongue.

"J, can I have your iPhone? I wanna play music."

"Of course you can, princess. Play anything you like. Play Bikinis and Bellinis. You know how much I love that one."

The 20-year-old bikini-clad girl, covered in eight to 10 visible and colorful tattoos, beamed. She grabbed the iPhone from her boyfriend's hand and blasted the music on the boat's Bluetooth speakers.

Kinsley stood up, walked toward the bow, and gazed out at the shore as Campbell steered us home.

JULY 21, 2018

A Brief Trade

I'M NOT SURE WHOSE IDEA this was. I *can* say for sure it wasn't Kinsley's. Earlier that week, Campbell and Skye had been discussing swapping companions for a day "just to shake things up." Skye could get to know me better and same with Campbell and Kinsley. My old Hollandsworth pal had been on his best behavior for the previous two weeks or so and subconsciously must've felt bad for his comportment on *The Aeneid*.

Kinsley needed a bit of convincing, but after I explained that I imagined both she and Campbell being significant people in my life for years to come, Kinsley changed her tune.

I, on the other hand, was content spending a day with Skye. She was a bit of an enigma to me. After almost two months living on the same property, all I knew was music was a huge part of her life, both of her parents had tragically passed, and she clearly worked out regularly.

Skye melodically knocked on the pool house door at around 10 a.m.

"Kins, I'm taking off now. We'll be home in the afternoon."

"Come here."

I walked over as she was furiously typing away on her iPad, and said:

"Yes?"

"I love you." She leaned up and flashed her dimples.

I answered the door and found a particularly scantily clad Skye standing before me. She was wearing black bike shorts and a neon green sports bra that probably displayed too much underboob, and her brown-and-blonde hair was tied in a messy ponytail.

"Be safe, you two," Kinsley shouted from the couch.

"We won't, grandma," my athletic friend chirped.

The day before, Skye had mentioned wanting to take her bike out for a long trip, but Campbell somehow never learned to ride, so she asked me. I felt it'd be a nice change of pace, and I'd been a little light on the cardio that summer, so I obliged.

Campbell paid for an Uber to pick Skye and me up and take us to the Pellegrini family clothing store in East Hampton. And once we arrived in town, I learned two new facts about the bewildering "Bikinis and Bellinis" artist. First, she took her grandmother's last name. And second, there was a dorm-room-sized boutique in an alleyway in East Hampton called "Pellegrini," where they sold European-imported tween and teen clothing and accessories.

"How long has your family had the store?"

"Long time. I have two bikes out back. I'll ride the smaller one from back when I was a chubby little virgin. You can ride the one I use now."

"Should I go inside and meet your grandma?"

"Why would you do that? Let's get going."

Skye and I hopped on our respective bikes and started circling in the parking lot.

"Do you have helmets inside?"

"What are you, like, four?"

"Or a responsible adult," I muttered. "But whatever."

Skye rode out in front and shouted:

"Follow me."

We spent the first leg of the 12 to 15-mile ride on the congested Route 27 until we passed Georgica Pond to the south, and Skye led us onto Wainscott Stone Road.

That's where the ride became palatable as we flew past winding, scenic roads with the most viridescent foliage I'd ever witnessed. The houses we rode past were magnificent both in size and splendor. All the hedges were immaculately trimmed; the grass was cut to a turf-like length; the driveways were paved so not a single pebble was out of place; the mansions were spaced out so no one would ever have to worry about waking a neighbor, and the hedges were often so high, one could only dream about what was occurring in these paradisal palaces.

We then breezed past Wainscott Main Street, Townline Road, and Hedges Lane. Skye, who'd been riding in front, drifted back next to me on the near-empty Sagaponack Road.

"Getting tired there, Cashie?"

Her raspy voice wasn't as deep as Kinsley's, but they were similar enough to make me wonder if there was some Pavlovian reason why Hollandsworth males fell for raspy-voiced females. Perhaps there was an attractive first-grade teacher who'd had a particularly hoarse voice?

"No, I'm taking in the views."

"Breathing pretty heavy there."

"So are you."

"Don't be salty."

Despite Skye's relaxed demeanor, I could tell she was working hard due to what appeared to be Audrey Hepburn crying on her upper arm and her left wrist's sea lion swimming in sweat.

"If it's chill with you," she said. "let's hop back on 27. It'll be faster."

"Cool."

By the time we parked our bikes on Hampton Road and headed into La Parmigiana, we were both drenched. And my sweaty limbs were accompanied by a beet-red face and clammy body. Skye, on the other hand, in part due to her Mediterranean-Caribbean background, had glistening skin the sun seemed to coddle and massage. Kinsley had the same remarkable trait.

"Whaddya want?" Skye said as she sat in a booth and picked up a menu.

"Gimme a sec, please."

"'Scuse me, babe," Skye said to a passing waitress. "We're ready to order."

"What can I get you?"

"You got cash, Cash?"

"Yeah, yeah."

"What's your problem?"

"Exhausted."

"Sorry about that, miss," Skye said. "It's his time of the month."

"Right. What can I get you two?"

"Cash, order for me."

"What? Why? You can order for yourself."

"Just order for me and don't get something basic."

Skye took the tie out of her hair and shook out her messy, sweaty ponytail.

"We'll share a, I don't know, Hawaiian pie. And two pitchers of water, please."

The waitress left the two of us alone, and Skye seemed more gregarious than even her boisterous beau.

"Hawaiian? What are you, some kind of freak?"

"Next time, order your own food like an adult."

"Whoa, shots fired. You're high-key miserable right now, aren't you, babe?"

"No, still catching my breath. That was fun."

"I'm sweaty a-f here. I must look so ugly, right?"

"No, you look okay."

"Just okay? Ever since I had my glo up and worked out like hell to get this thigh gap and Toblerone tunnel, no one has called me just 'okay.'"

"Yeah, you look good. Relax."

Skye took out her phone and started texting or swiping while I guzzled a glass of water.

"What do you think J and Kins are up to right now? You think they're having more fun than us?"

"I sincerely doubt that."

"Yeah, your girl's pretty basic."

"Jesus."

"It's true."

"Nope."

"Eh."

"Let's change the subject...how'd you get into making music?"

Skye rolled her head in a circle, loudly cracking her neck.

"I-d-k, dude. I played sax and violin growing up 'cause I got bored easily. My grammy told me I had talent. Believed in me. I started making beats in high school. Was really good at it. By 16, I was being hired for, like, people's Bat Mitzvahs and Sweet Sixteens out here. And a year later, I was like headlining the hottest clubs in Montauk, Amagansett, and Sag."

"That's really cool. Impressive for a person your age. Well, a person of any age, I guess."

"I don't think J and Kins will vibe as well as us. He's such a live life to the fullest guy, and she's, well, you know."

I loudly cleared my throat.

"Right, we won't talk about your friend anymore," Skye said.

"Do you wish you were going to college?"

"Hell no. I get to live and breathe music, stay rent-free, and make 10K a show. What the hell do I need college for? My life is literal perfection. I make great money and have crazy talent."

The waitress came by and dropped off our Hawaiian pizza. There were too many pineapple pieces on the pie, so I took some of the slivers off and placed them on my plate while Skye stared.

"I don't wanna throw shade," she said, "but your eating habits are super weak."

"Thank you," I said as I took my first bite.

"You're a nice guy."

I looked around the restaurant and felt it was like an Italian equivalent of an American diner. Skye and I were the worst dressed people in the place, but it was lunchtime and reasonably empty. A few La Parmigiana-goers wore elegant bathing suits and shawls, and a toddler was running around unsupervised, but it was a nice spot.

Skye brought out her phone again, took a quick selfie with me in the background, typed a message, and then put her device away.

"Aren't you gonna eat anything?" I asked.

"Not hungry. Especially not for pineapple and ham pizza. I mean, w-t-f."

"So, uh, you take a lot of pictures for your Instagram, right?"

"Do you follow me yet?"

"I don't have one."

"O-m-g, are you serious? We should make one for you today. But you'll need to shower and get cleaned up before we post a pic."

"I don't want one."

Skye rubbed her numbers' tattoo on her upper right arm.

"What does that mean?" I asked.

"Just my tat. You know I have 75K followers?"

"So?"

"So? Companies pay me to wear their stuff. I get dope free clothes and make a ton of cash. You can appreciate that, can't ya, Cash?"

I finished my third slice after abandoning the pineapples altogether on slice two.

"What's your end goal, career-wise?"

"Can you be a little less serious? Not gonna lie, it's high-key a major turnoff."

"Will you eat something, please?"

"No. But can we get me a bubble tea after?"

"Who'd you most want to collaborate with, musically?"

"Ugh, Billie Eilish. I-d-k man." She looked at my body and said, "You'd do really well on Insta. Muscular. Nice guy. I don't love your hair, but that's an easy fix. Take a few shirtless shots with me at the beach."

"Check, please," I said to the passing waitress.

"You should party more. You'd be a huge catch. I want you to meet my friends Brooklynn and Astrid later this summer. They'd fall in love with you. It's rare to find nice, good-looking, mature guys."

"I love Kinsley so much," I said. "I mean, such an awesome personality, looks great, has such beautiful hair, smells like sunflower fields, very refined—"

"Stop. Stop. T-m-i, dude. You're making me gag. And not in a good way."

"Let's get outta here."

"Wow, Cashie. That's so sudden, but if you want to. I've got a great, hidden spot around here. J won't mind."

"What? No. What are you talking about? I meant, let's leave the restaurant."

"I know what you meant. Just messin' around."

"Campbell's rubbed off on you."

"Yeah, he gets it in my eyes sometimes, but I mostly like it."

"Christ. Don't say that stuff to me. Jesus."

"L-m-a-o. One of these days, I'll get you to loosen up...What the hell do you think J and Kins are talking about? I'm getting major FOMO."

We walked around Southampton for a bit, and I bought Skye her mango oolong bubble tea. The weather started to cool down, and her glistening skin lost its shimmer as we sat on a shaded town bench. Despite Skye's extremely revealing outfit and her unusual way of conversing, I found her company quite pleasant. And she was right about one thing, I'd rather be a fly-on-the-wall at the Campbell-Kinsley day than ours.

JULY 31, 2018

CAMPBELL'S 23ᴿᴰ

"CASH MOREAU, YOU INCANDESCENT RAY of sunshine. Climb aboard," a pure, newscaster-type voice said, "And if it isn't The Gambler. How you doin', birthday boy?"

"Mathewson, my guy," Campbell said. "Boat's lookin' sleek as hell. Moreau, you been on a boat this big before?"

"Nope. Great to see you, Mathewson." Our hands clasped together and our chests touched in the always awkward but increasingly popular bro-hug.

"What's on the agenda, Mathewson? Gonna kill some sharks or something? Harpoon a marlin?" Campbell asked.

"Oh, will I get to witness Hollandsworth's very own shark killer in action? But nah, man. I do that stuff on the speedboat. *Tranquility* is my 65-foot lady. Meant for parties, long nights on the water, and endless debauchery."

"Your boat's named *Tranquility?*" I asked.

"Yeah, she brings me more peace and enjoyment than anything else in the world."

Mathewson started walking us around the boat and showing us her exterior. His inveterate confidence was his most noticeable trait, and he was quite forthright after a few whiskeys, but there was one image I couldn't get out of my mind.

In first grade, Mathewson was one of my best friends, and we frequently went to each other's houses after school. Mathewson had this middle-aged Filipina housekeeper, as many Hollandsworth families did, and she was quite diligent. On one particular playdate, Mathewson went to use the bathroom, and then he called for Darna. The babysitter scurried to the bathroom and forgot to close the door. Being a curious seven-year-old, I peered through the crack, and to this day, I still haven't forgotten that image. Apparently, after particularly aggressive bowel movements, Mathewson would have his housekeeper pour water on his behind and clean it for him. Anytime I saw TR after that, I thought of poor Darna with that magenta bowl dumping a quart of water onto his behind.

"Am I to understand we have Dollar Moreau and Gamble Campbell on board today?" a new voice shouted.

Mathewson, Campbell, and I walked to the stern and saw the old, familiar face of Dean O'Reilly.

"Whaddup Dollar? Been a while," he said to me.

"Hey, O'Reilly. How's it hangin'?"

I went well past my quota for bro-hugs in a day.

"And T-Rex Mathewson? Mi amigo. Great to see you all. We should get together more often. Gambler, we've got a hell of a surprise for you."

Campbell, Mathewson, and O'Reilly all looked relatively similar. They were between five-foot-eleven and six-foot-two; each had a chiseled jaw; all three had that European soccer player build; they wore slip-on shoes without socks; black or tortoiseshell brown sunglasses; and bright pastel shorts with short-sleeve button-downs barely buttoned.

However, the key differences were Campbell's long, flowing blond hair always perked up with some gel-based serum; Mathewson's six days of dark-brown scruff and a corporal's haircut; and O'Reilly's stringy, strawberry-blond strands he was frequently pushing out of his face. If they all dyed their hair and adjusted their eye colors, you'd be looking at three brothers.

While the four of us were standing around the deck and the boat's driver was guiding us out into the Atlantic, Kinsley texted me:

"Is it nuts? I miss you."

"No, pretty tame. Me, Campbell, two other Hollandsworth guys on a very nice yacht."

"Oh, that sounds lovely."

"I'm sure there will be drinking and drugs involved, and I may be home late, but good to see old friends. How 'bout you?"

"Of course. I understand. And I'm lounging by the pool. Skye has some surprise for Jeff in the big house and told me to stay out."

"Can't imagine what that could be."

"Anyway, have fun!"

"Love you."

"Love you too."

The group and I began by spending five minutes catching up. All of us were unemployed but were extremely confident we'd be employed by Labor Day. There was a toxic amount of self-aggrandizement in the air—enough to create unhealthy breathing conditions. I've always found these Hollandsworth guys to be fascinating, though. Specifically, how you could go five to 10 years without seeing one, and their personalities never changed. I've found that's not often the case with other men and women, but these Hollandsworth guys were older clones of their 12-year-old selves. If one was annoying at 10, he'd be just as irritating at 22, and if someone was immature at six, they were exactly the same way at 19.

"T-Rex," O'Reilly said, "you haven't spoiled our little surprise, have you?"

"'Course not. I don't even think my driver knows."

"Guys," Campbell said. "Whaddya got?"

"So," O'Reilly continued, "since T-Rex was kind enough to let us use the boat, and he paid for alcohol, I felt the need to chip in."

"Campbell, I got some Bérénice Louise rosés, my 1941 World War II Soviet red my great-granddaddy swiped back in his heyday, a few bottles of Dom, and limitless drams of the most expensive scotch Scotland was able to export."

"Not bad, gents. Moreau, feeling like a mooch yet?"

"I traded you Tommy Pham for pennies in fantasy last year. That inadvertently won you several thousand dollars, so that's my contribution."

"Hmmm, I'll allow it."

"And my girlfriend saved Skye's life."

"Well, then maybe you do owe him something," Mathewson chirped.

He then ran to the bow, presumably gave the driver some longitudinal direction, and came to meet us at the foot of the door to the cabin.

"Can't wait to see the look on both your faces," O'Reilly said.

Mathewson opened the door to the five-star hotel-suite-sized cabin whose cynosures were three objectively attractive females wearing minimal clothing.

"Well done, O'Reilly. Well done," Campbell said as we all stood awkwardly in the doorway. "Where'd you find these beauties?" He began to stalk his willing prey.

"These...what's the appropriate euphemism...courtesans...are the finest the Hamptons has to offer. Supremely expensive, but I spared no cost and specifically picked them out myself."

I was creeped out by the whole atmosphere, and the fact that O'Reilly and Campbell were talking as if the women couldn't hear them. But it was Campbell's 23rd, and I wanted to be there to celebrate the milestone. I thought worst-case scenario, if things got out of hand, I could potentially step in and assuage the issue while it was still in an early stage.

Mathewson went to the kitchenette and began pouring drinks, cutting out lines of coke, and organizing some pills into piles. Campbell and O'Reilly sat on the foot of the king-sized bed and began to talk to the girls, while I found a wooden chair a comfortable distance from the bed.

"Let me toss on some music," O'Reilly said. "I got just the playlist."

He leaped up, connected his iPhone to Bluetooth, and played:

"Blowin' Money Fast" — Rick Ross
"G.O.M.D." — J. Cole

"Stay Schemin'" — Rick Ross
"Mr. Carter" — Lil Wayne
"Blessings" — Big Sean ft. Drake and Kanye West
"Bedrock" — Young Money
"Steady Mobbin'" — Young Money
"Bikinis and Bellinis" — Skygreenii
"Up" — Loverance
"Just a Lil Bit" — 50 Cent
"W.T.P." — Eminem

Mathewson handed me, the guys, and the girls glasses of Dom Perignon, and we all clinked and sipped.

"So, what are your names, ladies?" Campbell asked.

"I'm Felony," the buxom, biracial twenty-something said.

"Peony." She was an elegantly dressed blonde college-aged girl who looked like she could've gone to an Upper East Side school, maybe Cordelia, before her life took an exciting turn.

"Lucille," the third, familiar-looking one added softly from the corner.

"So, where are you from, birthday boy?" Peony asked.

"We're all Upper East Siders. Went to Hollandsworth together. I went to Yale after."

"Wow, so you're smart, handsome, and rich. The whole package."

"I do alright," Campbell responded as Peony ran her hand through her hair.

Felony and O'Reilly went to join Mathewson at the bar area, and they each snorted two lines. I was probably at a 9.1 out of 10 on my uncomfortability scale.

Peony whispered something in Campbell's ear, while O'Reilly went and spoke softly to Lucille.

"You guys, I might need two of these girls," Campbell shouted while laughing.

Lucille approached me and knelt to my eye level.

"You shy, darling?"

And that's when it hit me. When Lucille was hidden behind her friends on the bed and the lighting was dim, I didn't notice it, but right when she said that, I understood.

"Whaddya think of Lucille?" O'Reilly shouted with a wily grin.

"That's not even remotely funny," I said.

"Jesus," Campbell shouted. "What's the problem now, Moreau?" Then he turned to Peony and said, "Always something with this guy."

"Lucille, is it? May you please walk to my friend Campbell."

"Of course."

The skinny, demure black-haired woman approached Campbell, and when she was under the light and directly in front of him, he burst out laughing.

"O'Reilly, you son of a gun. This is incredible. Lucille, you're absolutely gorgeous. Take a seat next to Peony and me."

"If you want two girls, I'll happily donate mine," Mathewson said. "It's a worthy cause."

"Thank God *you* said so," O'Reilly added. "I wasn't donating mine. And it doesn't seem like Dollar wants one. We're all good then."

I stood and walked toward the door of the deck.

"You guys," Lucille said in the most saccharine voice she possessed, "did I do something wrong? Why do you all keep laughing at me?"

"Dollar, you wanna tell her?"

"No, man. That's really creepy."

"You guys," Lucille raised her now, raspier voice. "What did I do?"

"Kid, you're a carbon copy, a near-exact twin, of the love of that man's life," Campbell pointed at me. "O'Reilly, where'd you find this one? Kid, where are you from?"

Before she could answer, Felony interrupted and said:

"Do y'all want to talk all night or have some fun?" And then she removed her top and bra.

"And...I'm out," I said. "I'll go chill with the driver. Happy birthday, Campbell."

I heard a few derogatory shouts as I left to wander around the deck of *Tranquility*. It was a nice boat, and the water was fast and choppy, and transformed from royal blue to navy the farther we ventured.

From the starboard side, I could still hear jovial laughter, glasses clinking, heavy inhales, and the distinct mix of accents.

After 45 minutes or so, O'Reilly, Mathewson, and Felony exited and joined me on a few chairs near the bow. We all sat in silence; staring out at the impossibly blue sky and the fading orange sun. I must've dozed off for a bit but was woken later by the birthday boy and his two girls diving into the perilous Atlantic, where my old Hollandsworth pal had once defeated a tiger shark.

I then thought about what O'Reilly's motive was in choosing a girl that looked like Kinsley. Had Campbell mentioned something about her in the past? I supposed O'Reilly had given his guy whatever pictures of Kinsley he could find online. It bothered me, but it was Campbell's birthday, and I felt the need to keep quiet.

I dove in and saw O'Reilly and Mathewson playfully fighting like a pair of pups or calves casually attempting to assert dominance. Felony looked on, amused. I supposed none of them were of sound mind or body considering the various elixirs they drank, snorted, or injected. Everyone seemed to be having fun.

Campbell was the one outlier. He had Peony and Lucille by his side the entire time, but they barely touched my old Hollandsworth pal. The three of them prated on about their childhoods, the best spots in the Hamptons, and Campbell's thrilling tales of academic and social prowess. He had this vacant look in his eyes and kept twitching, glancing around, and then gazing off in the distance. Campbell didn't seem to be present, but rather appeared to be treading water in a lucid dream from which he couldn't wake.

Tranquility carried us back to the docks around 8:15 p.m. I thanked O'Reilly and Mathewson for their hospitality and waved goodbye to the escorts from a distance. The always perplexing Campbell hugged his friends and then gave Felony and Peony handshakes before whispering something in Lucille's ear.

"Moreau, catch," Campbell shouted as he tossed me the keys to the convertible.

We were approaching the parked car when I noticed Lucille was trailing Campbell.

"What's going on?" I whispered to him as the boat and our other friends were out of sight.

"Easy does it, man. Just get us home."

I didn't see the need to delve into the arcana of Campbell's bizarre actions, so I kept my mouth shut and drove.

My old Hollandsworth pal opened the passenger door, and the petite Lucille squeezed into the open space between the two front seats.

"Are you sure this is safe?" I asked as Campbell closed his door.

"Relax, man. Drive the speed limit. Lucille, you're comfortable enough, right?"

"Enough, I guess," she said in her raspy, slightly accented voice. "Maybe get a four-seater next time. You've got the money."

"Thanks, kid. I'll consider that."

The ride was incredibly awkward for me, perhaps more so given the fact that Campbell never once touched the black-haired beauty. We all sat in silence as the sky darkened. If I were feeling uncomfortable, I couldn't even imagine how the escort felt. Then again, maybe she handled way more tricky situations in her line of work. Although she looked only 21 or so. This could've potentially been her first job. I didn't know anything. I desperately wanted to return to Kinsley and the pool house.

When we arrived, I stayed in the driver's seat, waiting for Campbell to direct me.

"Moreau, you can leave now. Lucille, come with me."

For whatever reason, I started sprinting to the pool house. I suppose I wanted Kinsley to be privy to absolutely everything. I mean, when you love someone and something significant happens, that event almost doesn't feel real until you tell your love about it.

I slammed the pool house door and called out:

"Kinsley, wait until you hear this. Kins?"

The first floor was empty, although there were two cans of sugar-free Red Bull lying on the TV table next to her Nikon and Vogue. I started to walk up the flight of 10 steps to the unfurnished second floor, where that hard mattress was sprawled out like a rug. But then I stopped. Serenity was seductively winking at me.

She must've been freezing as she stood on top of a snowy peak with her arms outstretched like Jesus Christ himself. The word "Serenity" was painted in black with the "S" beginning at her long, thin neck and the "Y" leading to her pelvis. The shoeless six-foot-tall woman had a cheeky smile as if she'd just thought of doing something inappropriate in a public setting. Her wink was almost hidden by several long strands of hair that broke her face's symmetry. And then I heard:

"Cash?" a sleepy Kinsley mumbled from the top of the stairs. "What are you doing?"

"Just, um, nothing. I don't know. You won't believe what happened or what's happening."

"Do I need to take those pictures down so you stop drooling?"

"They're kind of a cool idea."

"What's happening right now? You came in shouting, remember?"

"Wait."

I ran upstairs and lifted Kinsley off the ground.

"I missed you, Kins. You look so pretty right now."

"Stop, I was just sleeping, and I'm wearing your old football jersey."

"I don't know. I think you look stunning. I hope you had a nice nap and a relaxing day."

"I did. Thank you." And then while embracing, I said:

"Campbell brought a girl home."

"What do you mean? Here, come sit on the bed with me."

"Well, I can't."

"Oh, the dirty clothes thing. Whatever. Let's go downstairs. I need a Red Bull, and I'll make you a protein shake."

"You're perfect," I said as we walked hand in hand downstairs.

"So, Dean O'Reilly hired escorts as a surprise when we were on TR Mathewson's yacht."

Kinsley and I stood around the kitchenette. I watched her meticulously putter around as I continued:

"And Campbell brought one of the escorts back to the big house. She's inside and Skye's there, right?"

"Yes, she definitely is."

"I wonder what they're doing."

"They're a weird couple. I don't think they're gonna last."

"Maybe, but Campbell will never stop surprising you."

Kinsley handed me a Nalgene bottle with a homemade chocolate and peanut butter protein shake and then walked me to the couch.

"Wanna watch a movie?" I said.

"Absolutely. I need a good cuddle."

That's basically how our night ended. Kinsley was aware of everything. Well, almost everything. I intentionally left out the girl looking virtually identical to her. The Lucille-Kinsley comparison was creepy enough, and I felt everyone's lives would be better off if Kinsley didn't find out.

AUGUST 31, 2018

UNDOUBTEDLY THE BEST NIGHT OF THE SUMMER

GROWING UP, KINSLEY USED TO ride horses at some stable outside of Cincinnati. She had spent seven years on the backs of cantering stallions—casually riding, racing, and even delving into dressage before quitting for some reason. This piece of nostalgia reared its head during our Hamptons summer.

Throughout my life, I'd always found people are particularly grateful when one remembers some throwaway comment and brings it up months or even years later. Therefore, when I was contemplating how to wrap that summer, I plunged into the recesses of my mind and found a memory of Kinsley discussing her childhood ponies many months prior.

So, about a week earlier, I told Campbell about this, and he set me up with a friend of his father's, who had horses stabled on his property south of the highway.

I called the middle-aged man, described my request, and asked how much it would cost, but he told me it was on the house since he adores the Campbells and loves love in general.

"Can you please tell me where we're going?" Kinsley said from the passenger seat of her Prius.

"No way, but it's not far."

I was cruising down 27 with the radio softly playing and the soothing Hamptons air blowing in from the cracked windows. Kinsley then startled me by cranking the music, shouting "Offset" out of nowhere, and then rapping his verse on the song "Taste."

"Wow, impressive," I said after she dropped a mimed mic.

"I'm getting better, right?"

"Your 'Offset' scared the hell out of me."

"I need you to work on your Quavo verses."

"I'm still trying to nail my part on 'Closer.'"

"Oh, we crush that song together. Don't worry about that one."

"How are your Nicki Minaj solos going?"

"I practiced yesterday when you weren't home. We'll sing 'High School' together. You gotta work on your Weezy part."

After another 15 minutes, we arrived at a mansion near Georgica Pond. The snooty driveway had never had a car this cheap driving on it. I think the pavement felt disappointed.

"Where are we? Which Oscar winner lives here?"

I stepped out of the car, opened the door for Kinsley, and led her to the front of the massive house with eight white pillars introducing us to the front patio. A maid answered the door and then called down Mr. Wilkinson.

"Hello, sir. It's a pleasure to meet you in person." I gave him the ultra-firm handshake I'd learned in my Hollandsworth days.

"Same to you, dear boy. And you must be the lovely girl he won't stop gushing about. And my are you lovely."

"Cash, what's happening?"

"All in due time," the host answered for me.

Kinsley and I walked behind the barrel-chested Mr. Wilkinson, whose defining feature was his matching salt-and-pepper hair and mustache.

"Oh my gosh. Cash, you didn't?" Kinsley said when she saw the stable from afar.

Her dark eyes lit up, and she raced toward two saddled horses posturing outside their barn.

"Dear boy," Mr. Wilkinson said, "we may have just made that young lady's day."

The three of us stood by the horses as Mr. Wilkinson described the path we should follow. He wasn't particularly concerned about safety.

He simply handed us black felt helmets and told us to take them out as long as we wished.

"What are their names?" Kinsley asked while stroking the white thoroughbred's nose.

"You seem to be acquainted with Portia, so I suppose Cash will be riding the great Octavius."

"Thank you so much, Mr. Wilkinson."

"And Cash, you're not supposed to ride them on the beach, but if you remain on my property and are only there for a few minutes, it shan't be a problem."

Two minutes later, we were trotting along the 10-acre property on our very own thoroughbreds—Kinsley, on the cloud-white Portia, and me on the chestnut Octavius.

"Cash," she said, stopping her horse. "this is just, I mean, like, how did you? This is so magnificent. I can't even…"

"I love you, Kinsley. So much."

We looked out over the property. The massive two-story house was the centerpiece, but even more impressive were the rolling green fields with perfectly trimmed hedges and trees. Everything was symmetrical from the backdoor of the house down to the wooden boardwalk leading to snowy-white sand. Out of everything on the property, though, I was most beguiled by this simplistic pool encompassed by a wall of lavender.

"I'm going to get us a place just like this one day," I said.

"Oh, Cash. Absolutely."

"All this," I said with my finger spanning the area, "this is all gonna be ours one day."

Kinsley smiled and then held my hand as our horses trotted. I turned to her and saw tears starting to form.

"What? It's the embers from the fire, remember?" she laughed.

I eventually had Octavius stop to eat some grass while Kinsley cantered from one end of the property to the other. Her black waves bounced in the wind. The entire experience simply enraptured Kinsley. The love of my life had been infected with nostalgia; by thoughts of roaming, leaping, and laughing while her mother clapped and cheered from a distance. And memories of her typically jockish brothers actually standing still for several minutes simply to watch their only sister create sheer synergy with a 1,200-pound behemoth.

After an hour or so, Kinsley and I convinced the thoroughbreds to walk down the wooden boardwalk and onto the sand, where we stopped to take in the view of the ensorcelling Atlantic.

We held onto our respective reins as the low waves tickled the alabaster sand. Tears streamed down her tanned cheeks, past her black birthmark, and onto her billowing beige blouse.

"Jeez, Cash," she whimpered. "How are you ever going to top this?"

We returned the horses, thanked Mr. Wilkinson, and drove back to Campbell's pool house for a bit. Instantly after entering our enclave, the lascivious Kinsley tore off my clothes and guided me to our upstairs mattress. She was simply the most special woman in the world. From her ambrosial lips to her irrepressible desire to make me as happy as possible. Kinsley was the most exceptional beauty I'd ever seen.

I woke to a nude Kinsley tiptoeing around the room.

"Oh, I didn't mean to wake you," she said.

"You look fantastic...What time is it?"

"Eight, I think?"

"Oh, damn. We gotta get ready."

"What? Where are we going? Oh, don't tell me, it's..."

"A surprise," I chuckled.

"What should I wear?"

"The nicest dress you have."

"Cash Moreau, you're quite the inscrutable boyfriend."

"Come downstairs with me. Let's hop in the shower."

Kinsley lifted me from under the covers and held my hand past Serenity and down to the first floor.

Less than 30 minutes later, I was driving Kinsley's car, while she flailed her arms and mimicked Halsey's voice on the radio. Then, as we turned off 27, Kinsley froze and said:

"I figured you out. I know where we're going."

"You do?"

"The Crow's Nest, right?"

"Good memory. Yeah, it's my favorite steak in the world."

"It's going to be so romantic this time of night. With the lights and the moon and the beach and stars and fire and everything. You spoil me, Cash."

After arriving, the maître d' led us to our table. I pulled out Kinsley's chair and took my seat.

"Any other surprises I should be aware of?"

"Nope. I'm all out of ideas. You want the Bérénice Louise rosé?"

"Sounds delectable."

I asked the passing waitress to bring us a bottle and then couldn't stop staring at Kinsley.

"I can't believe I'm starting work on Tuesday," I said.

"We're too young to live in heaven, Cash."

"Aren't you gonna miss it out here?"

"Of course, but I miss the city. I love the convenience and not having to drive everywhere all the time. I think we've spent the ideal amount of time out here."

"It's crazy to think about. I'm gonna be a real adult with a boring job in four days. 8:00 a.m. to 6:00 p.m. five times a week. Working for my father."

"You're gonna have fun, and you'll be great at whatever's put on your plate. I'm sure of it."

"What if I don't like it?"

"We'll find you a job. You and I can do anything together."

The waitress came by, poured our rosé, and took our orders.

"The rib eye, please. Medium rare."

"And may I please have the scallops with pistachio and lemon orzo? But may I please have the honey roasted baby carrots instead of the arugula?"

"Sure."

She left us alone again in our back corner. The buzzy hotspot was probably loud, but I guess I was able to block out everything that wasn't Kinsley's low, gravelly voice.

"You know which day I simply adored," she said.

"The sailing trip?"

"Good one. No. When we went out to *Tetra* in Sag Harbor. Remember that?"

"'Course I do."

"And we danced for hours right on the water. Remember the DJ played all my faves: Drake and The Chainsmokers and 'Bailando.' And then we got drunk and got ice cream, and we were just silly and giggly. And I had ice cream all over my face. I loved that night."

"So much fun."

"How 'bout you?"

"When we went out to Montauk alone, and you almost beat me in mini-golf, and then we went out on that little catamaran by ourselves, remember?"

"Of course. How could I forget you getting us stuck?"

"Oh, c'mon. It wasn't my fault. The wind picked up the second we were trying to head back. And you weren't the star first mate I thought you'd be."

"You wanted *me* to jump into that water and push us out of the sand."

"You've got strong arms. You could've done it. Also, what's tacking?"

Kinsley laughed and then reached her tanned hand across the table and held mine.

"Gosh, and then there was the snorkeling. That was so cool. We saw those sea turtles."

"And that creepy flounder too."

"Let's maybe not talk about fish when I'm about to eat some poor, innocent scallops."

The waitress brought out our food a few minutes later, and I happily gave Kinsley a few bites of my sapid steak.

"So, Cash, do you have our next trip in mind?"

"Maybe we'll go to Costa Rica? Remember I told you my parents took me there when I was young?"

"I'm up for that. The holidays, maybe?"

"Maybe Thanksgiving? I'd like to be in the city with you around Hanukkah and New Year's. We could watch *It's A Wonderful Life* again and sing along to 'Auld Lang Syne' a million times, and light the candles together on your zebra menorah."

Kinsley and I finished our meals; I paid the check, and we walked hand in hand down toward the restaurant's famed beach bar. I ordered us two glasses of champagne, and we sat around the fire overlooking the water. It was a pleasant night, a little chillier than usual, but I hardly noticed as I was focused on other things.

"Cash, ow, I'm getting these embers in my eyes again. Give me your sunglasses."

"Switch seats with me."

Kinsley stood and proceeded to sit on my lap.

"All better," she said. "Actually, I wanna wear your shades anyway. They look good on me."

"You're not tipsy, are you?"

"Not even a bit."

We sat around the fire, finished our glasses, and gazed out toward the horizon in silence.

"Your heart's beating really fast," she said.

"You ready to go?"

Kinsley nodded, put down her glass, and held my hand as we walked back toward the restaurant. But before guiding her up the incline to the parking lot, I led her to the left—to a secluded area where the cattails and grass met the shores of Lake Montauk and gave us the ideal view of the waning gibbous moon and the navy, star-filled sky.

Kinsley walked out ahead of me, took off her shoes, and held them in her hands.

"What are we doing here?" she asked while facing the water. "Is this some fantasy of yours we haven't discussed? Sex in a public place?"

And then she turned around to find my left knee sunken in the sand.

"Holy...oh my God...what's happening?"

"Kinsley Avital, from the minute you approached my mom and me on that hill 460 days ago, I knew I wanted to do this."

Tears began flowing down her olive cheeks, and she started fanning her face.

"The past 460 days have been the most magical of my entire life and have made me realize something is always missing whenever you're not right by my side. I love absolutely every part of you, from your convivial nature to your unmatched fashion sense to your supremely knowledgeable brain, and the fact that your pearly white smile and cute little dimples infect me like a drug every time."

"I'm not crying. It's these damn embers from the fire."

"You've proved to be an affectionate optimist and more cultured and refined than any person I've ever met. And you're so damn likable and energetic and romantic. Listen, I know I'm only 22 and a half, but I've never been this sure about anything in my life. The thing I love most about us is we can turn absolutely anything into the most fun activity in the world. Whether it's a four-hour congested car ride, trotting on thoroughbreds in a stranger's backyard, snorkeling, kayaking, swimming, staying in a pool house for three months, and every other small and large moment we've ever faced together."

Kinsley, wearing a daffodil-yellow summer dress, her Star of David necklace, and carrying her black heels in her hand, wiped the tears from her face with her inner arm and said:

"I must look so ugly right now."

"Kinsley, you're the most beautiful crier I've ever seen. I'd be so happy if I could watch you cry tears of joy for the rest of our lives. Will you marry me?"

I then took out a diamond ring from Harry Winston I had no business buying. Although thankfully, my father said he'd loan me the money and take cash out of my paycheck for my first six months on the job to help me.

"Cash Moreau, of course I will."

Kinsley wrapped her arms around my shoulders and kissed me with such fervor I knew I'd made the right decision.

"Although next time, maybe try to be a little more concise," she said.

"I love you so much."

I scooped her off her feet and delivered my slender, slightly tipsy fiancée to the passenger seat of her Prius.

SEPTEMBER 1, 2018

THE NEXT DAY AND OUR LAST
NIGHT OF THE SUMMER

THE NEXT MORNING, I WOKE to the sound of Kinsley's shrieks from downstairs. She was on the phone with her mom.

I put on a pair of joggers and walked to the first floor, which led to Kinsley putting the phone down and leaping into my arms.

"I love you."

"I love you too, Kins."

"I want us to call all our family and friends. I'm so excited."

"I'll call my parents right now."

But before Kinsley and I could make our next phone calls, there was a knock at the pool house door.

"Moreau…notice I'm knocking this time," Campbell yelled from outside. "Like you asked."

I opened the door, and he stood there in a black bathing suit and sunglasses.

"Moreau, your girlfriend's still here?"

"Why wouldn't I be?" Kinsley said as she followed me to the door.

"Just assumed my prepubescent friend's proposal would've scared you off."

"Just the opposite. You're gonna see me for many more summers."

"Next summer, you two can have the big house. Congrats, kids. That's all I wanted to say. Mazel tov."

"Thank you, Jefferson," I said. "For everything."

"Don't get all sappy on me, Moreau. Also, I'm throwing you guys a sort of engagement party tonight."

"What do you mean 'sort of'?" Kinsley said.

"Meaning, I was already throwing a party for everyone's last Saturday out here, and I invited 300 of my closest friends, and it just happens to coincide with this thrilling news."

"Wow, so thoughtful."

"Thanks, sweetheart. Welcome to the family. Now, party starts at 8:30 p.m. It may go till 5:00 a.m. All white party. Don't you dare try to be a rebel and wear something other than white." He turned to jump in the pool but shouted back, "I love you guys."

Kinsley and I spent the next 10 hours calling family and friends and packing for our drive back to Manhattan the next day. While we could've stayed until Labor Day, I wanted to beat the holiday traffic and prepare for day one at Moreau & Associates on Tuesday.

By 8:30 p.m., about 80 guests had arrived, and another 150 or so wound up joining or merely passing through this party that was either the most fabulous twenty-somethings gathering the Hamptons had ever seen, or the definition of organized chaos. I, for one, fell comfortably in the latter group.

Campbell did make two intelligent party-planning decisions, though. The first was allowing us to keep the pool house locked and telling all the attendees it was off-limits. And the second was requiring all attendees to take a taxi upon leaving to avoid any drunken mishaps. The other essential Campbell commandments were:

-The only food allowed at the party was that which was catered by The Pratincole

-The hired bouncers must maintain a two-to-one girl-to-guy ratio at all times

-The only two people allowed to DJ are: Skygreenii and celebrity DJ and Instagram model, DJ Cree Mashun

-Out by the pool, bottomless alcohol for bottomless girls, otherwise, women have a three-drink maximum (this rule didn't apply to Kinsley, Skye, or any of the female celebrities)

"You want to check out the party with me?" I asked Kinsley.

"I'll stay here for another hour or two. I have to get a little more work done before Tuesday. I'll come find you."

"Cool, love you."

"Love you too. Be careful out there."

I started by taking a lap around the backyard where several bottomless girls were swimming in the pool and Jacuzzi, while the few Yale or Hollandsworth males that were there had no desire to wet their best whites.

Toward the edge of the backyard, there was an Instagram station where a professional photographer was taking pictures of people either on the newly-assembled hammock or the private beach just past Campbell's property. The sand also had a few stragglers lounging, but the majority of attendees were inside the big house.

Campbell himself was seated on the pool's recently installed diving board chugging from the silver and ivory flask his father had bought him. His white pants were rolled up, and his linen shirt was fully unbuttoned while his favorite accoutrement, his pricey black sunglasses, stayed glued to his face.

When he saw me, he lifted his flask, nodded, and went back to gazing at no one in particular, but rather, at the madness he'd created.

As I moved closer to the house, there was a moshpit of drunken partygoers grinding and fist-pumping to Skye's set. Her music was typically too loud and atonal for my liking, but it was the right sound for this party—beachy, tropical drums, claps and snaps, and the occasional saxophone or violin.

I spotted a sweaty, possibly drunk, probably wired on something Skye, with one headphone in her ear, one hand on her laptop, and one hand fist-pumping to the raucous crowd's delight. Campbell had, quite ingeniously, placed her DJ booth in the large doorway that opened to the backyard. One-half was in the house and the other outside. Even though there must've been 15 speakers throughout the party, this spot made one feel like they were close to Skye's music no matter where they were. I waved at her, but she was too focused to notice, so I continued to the indoor section of the soirée.

As I passed the kitchen, I noticed all The Pratincole caterers were women, and all were objectively quite attractive, which was almost certainly not an accident. Next came the living room, where all the furniture had been cleared out, and a crowd of 50 danced without rhythm. However, Bliss was still left in the room to watch the exuberant partygoers.

Bliss was standing atop a nondescript skyscraper, silently shouting with her fists clenched. The word was written in black across her collarbones, like a necklace. Aside from her nude body, Bliss' unusually large canine teeth stood out. It was nighttime, and her athletic frame probably could've used a sweater or jean jacket.

I then marched up the stairs and heard a lot of moans, groans, and guttural sounds coming from one of the bedrooms, so I immediately headed downstairs to check out the basement.

The innovative Campbell had split his furnished basement into three sections: one was a video game area where Super Smash Bros. and Mario Kart were being played on an N64. Then there was the poker segment where four tables were being used for sit'n'go's—and naturally, the dealers were all sub-30-year-old pneumatic women. Finally, came the section with the infamous pole Campbell had once told me was just for show. In this instance, two strippers were dancing to their routines while an all-male cabal threw dollar bills at them. So, all in all, it was a hodgepodge of disarray.

Despite my qualms as a newly engaged man, every single person at that party seemed ecstatic from the moment they walked in until the moment they left.

By about 10:30 p.m., after a few sliders and pigs in a blanket, I went to rescue the love of my life from the perils of hard work.

"Kins, you look, just...wow."

"Thank you." She kissed me gently, without smudging her lipstick.

My fiancée was wearing a loose, white garment that stopped no more than halfway down her thighs. It showed off her defined and scintillating legs while also leaving plenty to the imagination. Kinsley was a fashion all-star and really an overall genius.

"Let's go dance until our legs fall off," she said.

We jogged hand in hand from the pool house to the dance area in front of the patio. We stopped and waved at Campbell, who was still sitting on the diving board drinking from his flask, but he ignored us. As far as I knew, he hadn't said a word to anybody in two hours. Just meditating.

Kinsley and I then jumped, grinded, and gyrated to Skye's inspiring set-list that seemed to get much better after we had had our second drinks brought over by a busty cater waitress.

After about an hour of dancing, Kinsley and I went to the side of the patio to rest and finger some appetizers. And following five minutes of loudly talking over the music, devouring fatty foods, and kissing with distillery-smelling breath, we spotted Campbell leaving his post and sauntering toward the DJ booth.

"Wait, Kins, watch him," I said, pointing at him. "That's the first time he's moved tonight. Keep your eyes peeled."

"Yes sir, Mr. Moreau." She fed me a fry.

My old Hollandsworth pal walked to the source of the cacophonous electronic music and whispered something in his nodding girlfriend's free ear. Then, he disappeared inside and returned seconds later with an exotic-looking six-foot-tall woman who I believed to be DJ Cree Mashun. Campbell brought her to the booth, where the famed professional took over for Skye.

After our hosts vanished inside, DJ Cree Mashun began playing a much more ferocious, hardcore dubstep set. I didn't love the loud banging and aggressive drops, but the rest of the crowd seemed more than content.

"You wanna go to the beach?" I asked.

"Always."

Kinsley and I ran past the outdoor dancing moshpit, the pool with bottomless women, the Jacuzzi, the pool house, and the Instagram station until we found ourselves removing our shoes and gliding across the snowy-white sand as the clock approached midnight.

She then bent down, rolled up the bottom of my pants, and held my hand as we strode into the water.

"So, what do we do when we get back?" she asked.

"I hadn't thought that far ahead."

"Oh, stop. Yes, you have. You can't fool me. You plan everything."

"Honestly?"

"Always."

"I want to move in with you ASAP. And I'll pay for as much rent as you want, or we'll get a new place if you want to move out. I want to be with you all the time."

Kinsley leaned over and said:

"We'll start apartment hunting as soon as you get settled into your new job. I've been wanting to decorate a larger place."

"I'll give you free rein. Consider our first apartment your empty canvas."

"I'm really excited…for everything."

Kinsley then reached into my left pocket, grabbed my phone, and tossed it onto the nearby sand.

"Jesus. Why'd you do that? My phone's gonna be filthy."

Without a word, she held onto both of my hands and yanked me under the water with her. We wound up swimming around the pitch-black Atlantic for almost an hour, hearing the distant sounds of dub-step and manic millennials engaging in every hedonistic behavior imaginable.

The next day, I woke before a hungover Kinsley and went outside to assess the damage. I was surprised no one was sleeping on the lawn, and the whole property was eerily silent.

I strolled toward the back patio, wearing only joggers and a white t-shirt, and opened the door to the living room. I noticed Skye passed out on the couch with what looked like a journal or diary, opened to a specific page, on the table next to her. I then walked toward the kitchen, peered into the basement, and trudged up the stairs to find any stragglers. Yet somehow, the entire place was empty and oddly spotless. Not even Campbell was around, although his car was.

As I walked back downstairs, Skye rose like a reanimated creature and immediately began crying inconsolably. I ran to her and said:

"What's wrong? Are you hurt?"

"Hi, Cashie."

Skye rubbed her eyes as tears started to flow.

"What? Why are you crying?"

"J's gone."

She was wearing only an untied, navy, oversized men's robe.

"Well, where'd he go?"

Skye let out this disturbing half-yawn, half-howl.

"Hold me?" Her tears were steady now.

I backed away from her. She was clearly under the influence of a lot of stuff.

"J's not coming back."

"I think you need to sleep this off. How are you feeling?"

She didn't respond. Skye stood up, walked to the kitchen, and picked up this fancy steak knife. I didn't have great eyesight, but could tell the sharp edge was wet and red. Skye started humming "Memories," the Guetta and Cudi song.

"Skye, what's on that knife?"

But then I watched her dip it into a jar of raspberry jam and felt mildly better.

"Skye, where's Campbell?"

She kept humming and licking this steak knife covered in jam. Skye then hopped up on Campbell's kitchen counter and sat there. She stopped crying.

"Where did Campbell go, Skye? His car's still here. Are you sure he's gone?"

No response. I didn't know how to feel. Was she off her meds? High? Drunk? Manic? Admittedly, I hadn't done a great job of connecting with her that summer. After three months together, I still wasn't sure what status quo Skye behavior was.

I walked over to her, took the knife from her hand, and said in the sweetest voice I possessed:

"Skye, what's going on? You can tell me."

"J went poof." She blew onto her palm, "Bye-bye."

"Skye, please. It's me, Cash, your friend. You can talk to me. What happened to Campbell? His car's still here. Is he in the house? Did he go for a run? Did he sleep at Mathewson's place?"

"Gone. Gone. Gone." She did a cackle-growl. Bizarre guttural sounds.

"Do you want me to get Kins? Could she be helpful?"

Skye grabbed the steak knife from my hands, dunked it back in her jam, licked the tip, and continued humming the opening to "Memories."

"Skye, look at me, who cleaned the house? It's freakin' spotless. There were 300 people here eight hours ago. Where'd they all go?"

"I dunno." She started to tear up again. "He disappeared. Vanished. Poof."

"Skye, please. You can tell me anything. I need a little info here. Where's Campbell? How'd the place get so clean? Where'd security go? How did you manage to kick out every last person?"

"J's not coming back," she said in a sing-songy tone.

"Should I call your gramma? Do you need help?"

"How'd you like my set last night, cookie? I saw you grinding on your girl. Low-key hot."

I was sweating. Everything felt off. My hands were shaking a bit. I needed Kinsley. We had to get out of there.

"Listen," I said, "Kinsley and I are leaving soon. We're all packed. But we'll wait here with you until Campbell returns. Everything will be just fine. Otherwise, we'll call Campbell from the road and get this all sorted out."

"No, you won't. You can't."

Then, in a last-ditch effort, I called out:

"Campbell? Campbell, you here? Hello?" I kept shouting, my voice echoing throughout the immaculate, modern home. "Is anyone here?"

"Shush, dude." Skye covered her ears and went to lie back down on the couch.

"Do you want to come back to the city with us? Might make you feel better. Kinsley's got some great pipes, and she needs a girl to duet with in the car."

"I'm going back to sleep."

"Can you give me a hint where Campbell went? We can make a game out of it. Hide and seek? Clue?"

"Good night, Cashie. Love ya."

Skye closed her eyes and started humming again.

I wandered back to the pool house with a dumbfounded look on my face and a desire to drive back to Manhattan as quickly as possible. Upon entering and bringing my bags to the front door, Strength greeted me with a disappointed look; Sedation warned me about my future; Serenity told me never to leave this paradise, and Tranquility said my best days were behind me. And yet, I ignored them all and woke Kinsley.

"We gotta get going. It's late."

Her pretty face shook slowly.

"10 more minutes."

"Skye and Campbell are a mess. There's something weird going on. We gotta leave. It's an emergency."

Kinsley heard that word and instantly leaped out of bed, found her clothes, and handed me her packed bag to bring downstairs.

"What's going on? What do you mean emergency? Is anyone hurt?"

"No. Nothing like that. I think."

"Well, what's the problem? Why are we leaving so suddenly? I wanted to swim a bit and go to the beach."

"Kinsley, I'm sensing something bad is going to happen, and my senses are telling me we need to leave. Do you trust me?"

"Of course." She gave me a swift peck on the lips.

"I'll tell you everything in the car."

"Well, should I run inside and say goodbye to them?"

"Campbell's not home and Skye's asleep. I said bye for you. Let's go."

Within 10 minutes, we packed up, shoved our bags into the Prius, and Kinsley honked the horn melodically as we sped out of the driveway toward 27.

"Okay, crazy," she said. "What's going on?"

"Campbell's gone."

"Cool, so he went to the supermarket or went to smoke or something."

"Not the way it seemed. Skye's words were 'vanished' and 'disappeared.'"

"Well, then let's turn the car around and help her find him. What are we doing?"

"Kinsley, I don't have any concrete evidence. But I'll say something I've never said to you before: I'm scared."

My fiancée, looking striking as ever in black leggings and a white Under Armour top, rubbed my thigh.

"Now, why are you scared? And I'd never judge you because I trust your instincts completely."

"There are so many bad things that either could've happened or are about to happen, and I don't want to be a party to any of it."

"Like what? We spent three months with them, and there were never any...well, significant problems."

"I may be crazy or hungover, but I think there's maybe a five percent chance either Skye hurt him or Campbell is coming back to do something to her. Or someone kidnapped Campbell last night. Something like felony-level bad."

"To be honest, that sounds pretty insane. Like loony. And you're basing this off of the fact that Campbell didn't wake up at home, and Skye said he vanished?"

"There was something spooky going on at that house. Why was no one around at 10 in the morning after, like, 300 people were there last night?"

"They taxied home."

"The place was spotless aside from a whiskey bottle near Skye… and a diary."

"He paid the cater waitresses and bouncers extra to clean up?"

"Where do you think he is?"

"Have you tried calling him?"

"Uh, no."

"Jesus, Cash."

I picked up my phone and called Campbell three times. Straight to voicemail.

"Everything's fine, Cash. He went on some drunken bender and wound up at some Hollandsworth friend's house. Text TR. Text Dean. Facebook message any of his Yale friends you know. We'll call Skye tomorrow."

"By tomorrow," I said, "the cops are gonna find someone facedown in their pool."

"Is that a *Sunset Boulevard* reference or a Fitzgerald reference?"

"I'm really glad I have you."

I then texted Campbell, TR, and Dean while Kinsley put on a playlist, and we headed back to our new adult lives.

"Young and Wild and Free" — Wiz Khalifa
"Burn (Remix)" — Meek Mill, Big Sean, Lil Wayne, and Rick Ross
"Often" — The Weeknd
"The Hills" — The Weeknd
"Real Estate" — Wiz Khalifa
"Candy Shop" — 50 Cent
"Landslide" — The Dixie Chicks
"Soak Up the Sun" — Sheryl Crow
"Bleeding Love" — Leona Lewis
"Pinocchio Story" — Kanye West
"Power" — Kanye West
"Blank Space" — Taylor Swift

I was told to stop telling this story during the car ride home for whatever reason, so I guess that's all I have to say about that summer for now.

It's funny, despite everything that happened, I bet if you polled the four of us on who had the best time, my happiness score would be the highest. I was loose and relaxed throughout, and my soul mate accepted my proposal. For me, the Hamptons has always been a euphoric wonderland, but I know not everyone feels that way.

Skye Pellegrini

So I haven't figured out how to tell this whole thing. I think I'm just gonna start from when Jeff and I met and just like see where my mind takes me. I'll give you as much of the tea as I can remember.

But anyway Surf Lodge in I guess like 2017. Yeah must've been. Must've been Labor Day weekend. That was back when I was super thirsty just finna get anyone important to listen to my music. And back then my SoundCloud was getting mad hype and my music side hustle had literally become like full-time. I'd performed at Surf earlier in the summer and honestly I was dope so I knew they'd invite me back for another set and they did.

So I was at Surf which is *the* spot for DJing in the Hamptons imo... actually gotta pause again...so here's the deal: I'm not gonna be able to type some like huge thing with similes and metaphors and w/e unless I can speak the way I speak and type the way I text. You know? So I'm gonna give you what I gave my grandma when I started high school. I know. Don't hate me. I'll explain.

See when I started going out in high school I had to teach my gramma how to text. And I was using all these abbreviations and words she didn't know and she was literally always calling me and needing me to explain stuff. So I wrote this little chart/translator thingy for her to keep by her celly. And it low key worked perfectly. My gramma learned all the words and phrases and stuff. So anyway here it is and I may need to add to it as I go:

-amirite - am I right?
-brb - be right back
-btw - by the way
-bff - best friends forever
-besties - best friends
-cas - casual
-cya - see you later
-fwiw - for what it's worth
-gucci - great
-ily - I love you
-iykyk – if you know you know
-iso - in search of
-jk - just kidding
-lol - laugh out loud
-lmfao - laughing my fucking ass off
-lmao - laughing my ass off
-omg - oh my god
-ootd - outfit of the day
-s2s - sucks to suck
-ttyl - talk to you later
-tyvm - thank you very much

-tyfys - thank you for your service
-bde - big dick energy
-wtf - what the fuck
-s-o - significant other
-sus - suspicious, weird
-fomo - fear of missing out
-af - as fuck
-nsfw - not safe for work
-thot - slut
-GOAT - greatest of all-time
-bae - boyfriend/girlfriend
-thicc - big in a sexy way
;) - winky face
:P - tongue out
<3 - heart
-bpm - beats per minute
-otp - one true pairing
-w/e - whatever
-imo - in my opinion
-IG - Instagram
-ngl - not gonna lie

So that should help if anyone older reads this...Anyway I'm on stage with my laptop and I'm playing my set. It was like some remixes of whatever was dope at that time and then the six songs from my EP I dropped earlier that summer. Again ngl I was getting mad hype on SoundCloud and actually I might as well tell you about the songs since there aren't that many.

-Bikinis and Bellinis - By the time you're reading this I'm sure you'll know this song but for the older people it's sorta like M.I.A.'s "Paper Planes" meets Avicii's "Levels." It's got this classic beat, sits at like 128 BPM and then has some weird everyday sounds cut in...like keys jangling, school kids chatting outside at recess, seagulls squawking and then the hook is this really jappy girl saying "Sup, betches? You know what it's time for? Bikinis and Bellinis." And then the beat drops... HARD.

-Tranquility - I experimented with tempo a lot here. It starts really slow. Fingers snapping, hands clapping, me playing electric violin. Picture like going up a rollercoaster. You're literally so close to the drop but like you're not quite there yet you know? And Tranquility is that feeling. Peaceful beach resort music and then all of a sudden it's like this Skrillex kinda drop and that calming feeling is gone and it literally goes nuts.

-East Hampton Vibes - This song is like super near and dear to my heart. It opens with my gramma dropping knowledge. Not rapping but just talking. Like "Skye it's your time. When you set your mind to something there's nothing you can't accomplish. No one can stop my sunny Skye." And then you get this "In for the Kill" La Roux-type sound. I cut the bass. BPM goes way slow. Then gradual build-up.

-Your Juul Baby - I high key love this song. It's like super experimentational. My bff Astrid is singing vocals and does this like Lana Del Rey crooning, you know? And I play sax and violin on this one and it's got like this Kygo "Firestone" beat.

-Die for You, Daddy - I made this like intentionally depressing. Picture The Weeknd's "Beauty Behind the Madness" album. I cried all night when I mixed this. I swear I was draking hard. Mad feels. I got this girl from my high school who's like a total thot but has dope pipes to sing this. I swear she sounds like Amy Winehouse. It's about a girl whose boyfriend breaks up with her and she's lost and can't look at other guys cause the wounds are so fresh.

-Bliss - The last song is really happy and peppy. Imagine Kygo's remix of Seinabo Sey's "Younger" mixed with Avicii's "Wake Me Up." I added my own flair so it's like kinda trippy and psychedelic but it finishes on a high note and everyone always smiles and fist pumps to this one. Puts me in a trance every time.

Sorry for that detour. Just had to self-promote. Always gotta plug and look out for #1, you know? So now to the point. I'm banging "Bikinis and Bellinis." It's still early and no one's really dancing and there aren't many people paying attention to me which is chill because Surf's crowd can be super picky. But then as I'm scanning the room trying to see who might like truly engage with my sound... I see him.

It was this guy and he was kinda just staring right through my soul. He was freakin gorgeous. Long blonde hair, but styled. Kinda like when Chris Hemsworth's hair looks really blonde and goes to his collar. And this guy had on a silver rollie but the rest of his outfit was mad cas. Skinny white jeans rolled at the bottoms, Ferragamo suede loafers without socks, and then this navy short-sleeve button-down with little birds flying around his pecs and abs. I actually got a little nervous cause he kept staring at me and wouldn't look away. Have you ever had that happen to you before? When like a guy or girl, like you know this person's your future and you don't want to say or do anything to mess it up before you even introduce yourself?

I was also kinda not too confident because A. While my outfit was legit fire and my hair was on fleek a few hours ago, after a long sweaty set I was looking like actual street garbage. And B. The blonde guy was surrounded by literally six knockouts. So pretty. My first thought was he was some famous celebrity cause that man was hot af.

I'm embarrassed to admit this but I felt this weird need to impress him. And I know that's a terrible thing to say and that's the wrong mind-set but think back to when you were 19 and an older guy seemed interested in you. How would you have felt? I just wanted him to love me.

Okay so then the other girls were upset cause he wasn't paying attention to them and they followed his eyes and they all started staring at me and I was trying to focus on Tranquility. And meanwhile these girls then got up cause they wanted to show this blonde guy their sexiest dance moves. I mean lemme tell ya this guy just had so much swag and I was just drooling. But fast forward.

My set ended and people seemed to like it. I desperately needed to get my tequila on so I walked to the bar. Again I'm like sweaty and was wearing this outfit with like a lot, and I mean a lot of skin showing.

Within 10 seconds of me standing at the bar the super hot blonde dude approached me. And wow. His hair up close was like a blonde cloud. Fluffs on fluffs dude. When he ran his hand through his hair I just wanted to be like "Okay, marry me now." But instead I squeaked:

"Hi."

"Sweet set kid."

"Uh thanks dude." I was then staring at his chiseled jawline.

"I know you don't I?" He said and then turned to the bartender "two more tequila shots. Prima Adoncia."

"Yessir Mr. Campbell."

After hearing the bartender call him by name I thought this guy was like a huge deal.

"You're a townie, aren't you?" The dude said to me.

"Well that's not what I'd call myself."

"Whatever that's where I know you from. You're a store chick right?"

"Wow. You stalking me?"

"Skye right? You worked in Pellegrini?"

"Dude weird."

"No not weird. You're well-known kid."

"Why do you keep calling me kid?"

"You don't like it and I'll stop."

"Whatever. But why am I well-known? You listen to my SoundCloud?"

"Nah but my friends and I have talked about you before."

I swear he looked like a male model and I was a sweaty dumpster fire. That's happened to all of us I'm sure.

"Dude. How. Do. You. Know. Me?"

"Skye I've been summering in the Hamptons every year for my whole life you don't think I'd remember the cutest shop-girl out here? Tenet then Henry Lehr then Pellegrini right?"

"You are my stalker. Wow."

We knocked back our shots and smiled.

"What'd your friends say about me?"

"Back when we were younger and immature...no I shouldn't be telling you this."

"Oh come on. Tell me anything." I looked right into his leafy-green eyes.

"My friends and I had this unwritten list of the cutest townies. Back when we were in high school I told my friends you were the cutest. Some of them argued for this Sag Harbor townie but her personality sucked. Hot though."

"Yeah I think I know who you mean. Stay away. And I'm still not loving this townie word. But thank you."

"Your set was solid. That Bikinis and Bellinis is awesome. Had some young Avicii vibes to it."

"What's your name?"

"Jefferson Campbell the third. But call me anything you want."

"Okay. JC3." I smiled.

"Not that."

He ordered two more tequila shots and we just kinda stood there awkwardly.

"Let's get outta here. I wanna take you somewhere special."

"Anywhere."

And there I was—walking outside with Jefferson Campbell III. This legit male model who remembered me and seemed almost high key thirsty.

I was low key shook when the valet pulled up in a brand-new Merc. My heart wanted me to be like "Jeff literally impregnate me right now." But I kept my cool and he drove me to some sus beach nearby. He opened the car door for me and we were the only two people there. My mind was like "Skye baby what are you doing? This guy could literally murder you and no one would ever know." But I would've followed him anywhere. I was like such a loser.

We sat on the beach. Him in his skinny jeans and suede Ferragamos and me in my booty shorts and neon tank. Both slightly drunk. At that point he hadn't even touched my hand yet and I was like—what's this guy's game? He'd been dead silent for the past five mins.

"So uh what's your sign?" I asked.

"I dunno."

"When's your birthday?"

"July 31st."

He was just staring out at the water. Watching waves crash against the shore.

"What time were you born? And what city? And year?"

"I dunno like just past midnight I think. New York 1995."

"So then you're a Leo with a Virgo moon sign."

"I love secluded beaches at night. They seem to tame me."

"I'm an Aquarius but also a Virgo moon sign. So we both have like very analytical ways of thinking. See, we need to know moon signs cause sun signs only show the way you appear to the world. Moon signs show like deeper stuff and inner feelings."

"I like your voice. It's...different."

"Different how? And yeah so Virgo Moons love to be helpful and are fulfilled when contributing in practical ways. Like we're directed by logic. I mean it's like how when the sun acts, the moon reacts. You know?"

"It's darker."

"What is?"

"Your voice. Discreet and sleek."

"Thanks."

I'll say I never used to get nervous around guys, but I was in that moment. And I shouldn't have been. I'd seen hundreds of rich kids vacationing in the Hamptons. But he was just so different from any of the other dudes.

"Sorry I'm all sweaty and gross. I need a shower or maybe to just like jump in the water quickly."

He just sat there with his legs out. Didn't really look at or touch me. It was the strangest date.

"So what are you waiting for? Hop in."

"Good one."

"I'm serious." He said. "Go jump in the water."

"It's...I'm not gonna do that."

"Huh. So the tatted-up DJ girl happens to back down to challenges? Funny. Wouldn't have guessed that."

"I don't have a bathing suit."

"So?"

"Will you join me?"

"No. I like watching."

Now I literally don't know what was running through my mind. I guess it was like he was so rare, you know? I mean I really wanted him. More than any other guy I met that summer. Was he hot af? Yeah. But I'm telling you it was his personality and this like, mystery behind him. He wasn't some basic frat bro trying to drunkenly finger me on the beach. There was a mystical kind of connection, you know? So I didn't wanna disappoint him. I wanted to make sure he wanted to see me again after that night.

I literally just started walking down the beach with my back turned to him. I threw my shoes over my head then took off my top and threw it backwards. He could probably see some side boob but nothing else. I turned my head, winked at him, and then waded into the water before diving under.

He was just kinda like studying me. His eyes stayed on me the whole time but he didn't seem to like…idk, worship me like other guys did. Anyway I wanted to make sure he'd see me again so when I was fully underwater I took off my shorts and threw them to the edge of the shore. At that point I was fully nude cause I always go commando when I perform. But also I was completely hidden underwater so he could only imagine what I looked like.

Jeff started walking toward the water.

"Come on in. Join me J." I shouted.

He didn't say anything but picked up my shorts, tank, and shoes and then turned around and walked away. He also did turn his head and wink at me which I thought was so hot.

"Jeff? Where are you going? What are you doing?"

He just kept walking up the beach and eventually made it to his car. Obviously I was shook. I mean, what should I have done? Should I have gotten out and chased him? Even though then he'd see me completely naked. Or I could've just like cut my losses and hoped he'd leave my phone in the sand. I could've called a friend to pick me up I guess.

I dunked my head under the water and screamed. I was trying to figure out where I screwed up. Like where'd I lose him? I remember thinking like "Skye you're such a goddamn idiot."

And when I lifted my head out of the water he was running back toward the coastline with two towels in his hand—my friggin hero.

"Did I get you?" He said.

"Nope. I'm not afraid of anything."

"I can see that Skygreenii."

I loved hearing him say my DJ name out loud.

"How many girls have you tried this on?"

"Not sure." He shouted as I swam toward the shore.

"C'mon. You know. You're a smart guy."

"Oh, I know the answer. But I'm trying to figure out what answer you *want* to hear. Come here. Dry yourself off. I won't look."

"I'm not falling for it. You'll just pull the towels away or throw them or run or something."

"No I won't. This is gonna be step one on the road to gaining your trust."

I liked his voice too. It was like Capri Sun on a hot day. He spoke like very quickly and was proper. His voice was kinda like those detectives in those old movies my gramma always watched. Just filled with like depth and mystery. And so with that voice and then after watching him come back with those towels, for whatever reason I trusted him completely.

Jeff turned his back to the water and held his arms out straight to his sides making a T-shape.

"Why don't you come in and join me? It's beautiful."

"Maybe next time."

"What would you do if I pulled you in?"

"Probably send you a five-figure bill to pay for a new watch and clothes."

"You're funny."

I rose out of the water, grabbed the first towel, and wrapped it around my body, and then the second for my hair. Jeff was true to his word and never turned around to look. That was important.

We then walked back to his Merc and he opened the door for me before starting the car.

"So uh what now?" I said.

"I'll take you home. Or I'll happily drop you off a few houses from your place in case you don't want me to know where you live."

"God you have done this before. Haven't you?"

"You're cute kid."

And that was pretty much it. I directed him to my gramma's place on 18th Street just off Gardiner Ave. and we pretty much drove in silence. When he parked in front of my gramma's house I said:

"So why didn't you want to take me back to your place? I might've said yes."

"What's your number."

I gave him my digits and then kinda frowned when he got out and opened the door for me.

"I'm going back to NYC Monday and then to Yale in a bit but the next time you're in Manhattan, text me."

"So you're in New Haven?"

"I only have classes four days a week and am in NYC like every other weekend. Just text me if you want to. If not no big deal."

So given how impatient I was obvi I went into NYC the next weekend. I took the Jitney, told my gramma I had a show, and I texted him this when I was like an hour away:

"Hey it's Skye from Surf. I'm gonna be in the city tonight and tomorrow."

"Who?"

That's probably the worst response I could've received but my gramma taught me to be persistent. So then I messaged:

"Skygreenii. The DJ who skinny-dipped in front of you. I doubt you'd forget that quickly."

"Haha. Chill out kid. Just messing with you. Meet me at The Frying Pan in 90 minutes."

"Kk."

Okay so idk. Now what? That's how we met and we hung out a bunch all the way until we decided to live together off Townline Rd. that next summer. He told me about his plan to have this couple stay with us in his pool house. He said they were super tight and I was like 'fine...gucci... I'm in.'

But actually before I get to the start of last summer I think I wanna just like go backwards. My memory can be kinda hazy sometimes.

Drugs amirite? Lemme start at the end and skip around some. Not gonna lie I may get lost or forget stuff, but I promise it'll be worth it.

So okay. I'm gonna talk about the massive white party for a bit. I DJ'd so you know it was lit. What happened was…well actually lemme tell you about who was there. So first Jeff invited all his super-rich, preppy, dressed-in-all-whites friends from like literally every elite prep school and Ivy possible. J's goal was to make this the ultimate summer bash where like anyone who didn't show up would just die from fomo.

Cause like, it wasn't just some party with a bunch of Wall Street analyst douchebags. Jeff invited alotta influencers he'd met over the years at all the Hamptons hotspots. And then he let me invite any girls I wanted. That low key made me feel special cause I was the only other person who had unlimited invites to that sick night. From the way he described it I thought it'd be like a classy rich-kid *Project X*, you know?

Anywho, J made sure the ratio was two girls for every guy. Which I low key liked. Cause think about when you go to a party. If the host said "hey would you rather chill with four guys and two girls or two guys and four girls?" I'd want the more girls side. Let's be real: girls, at least the ones I know out here are pretty and super fun and love to party. And like they may get too drunk or high once in a while and Lord knows I've done some idiotic stuff, BUT most guys suck. Like before J and I started dating, guys I'd meet at clubs would like grind on me without my permission, spank me, like not subtly try to rub their junk against me. Idk. What else? Guys get in fistfights and brawls. I've had like random guys just walk by and like "accidentally" grab my tits. So listen. Point is, some guys are great. I'm not like some man-hater. I love the right kind of guy. I've just met a ton of pigs. So I was one thousand percent all for J's two-to-one ratio.

Cool. So I was starting to DJ at maybe 8:30. I had this mad tight booth right in between inside and outside. I was gonna be able to see my crowds dancing everywhere. I like to catch my audience vibes. Like I literally need to see if they like what I'm putting down. I'll adapt. I'm all about improv and just shifting the beat, tempo, bass and treble around to please people. I'm a one hundred percent audience-first DJ. And fwiw, no shade at all but not all DJs are like that.

I remember playing this new song I'd been working on in the garage studio. You probably know it by now: "D-U-Fly." I definitely composed it with Marshmello in mind. "Keep It Mello" has been a massive inspiration on my work and so "D-U-Fly" has a bunch of the same elements. The opening is pretty similar. It's got that boun...boun-boun... boun-boun...boun-boun...buh-buh-buh-buh-buhwha-uh-uh   sound. But mine has a heavier bass, harder drop, and a female on vocals.

So anyway I was playing that. The furniture was out of the living room and I got a great view of everything. Dude I was like the center of the party. The heart of it, you know?

But what else? So there was J's bottomless alcohol for bottomless girls at the pool...which truthfully I kinda dug the idea. Vibewise Jeff wanted to avoid the stuffy like old person/Baby Boomer Hamptons party and so this certainly did that—as did the baskets of drugs at the door which were monitored and labeled. Jeff was always just this super creative guy. Always stayed on-brand and didn't care what people thought of him or his decision-making. I envied him hard.

Let's see though. The other party thing I'm sure gave people fomo was the cater waiters. Look any Hamptons vet knows and loves The Pratincole cause they have food for any occasion and if they don't have the food you're looking for, they'll find it. Sorry I sound like a micro-influencer. But seriously The Pratincole is like one thousand percent goals. Iykyk. And somehow J got these mad hot girls to wait on people. We're talking like big boobs, flat abs, hair, and makeup on fleek. I may or may not have seen one of them making out with one of Jeff's Yale friends. But I'll never tell. And fwiw the great thing about J was—he didn't discriminate. The party had skinny rich waspy girls, thin exotic-looking up-and-coming Insta models, then all the super trim but busty cater waitresses, and then maybe a few deer-in-headlights mad petite rising college freshmen.

Idk what else? There was this massive cum-one-cum-all orgy in one of the upstairs bedrooms. People were snorting coke everywhere and then there was the Insta pic guy taking ootd shots by the beach.

Oh last thing. Celebs. Now I can't guarantee any of these people were there or there publicists will slit my throat but I'm pretty sure I saw a One Direction guy, a Fifth Harmony girl and that hot actress with the eyes that were essentially ear distance apart. Oh. And I really wanted Billie Eilish to come cause I'm high key obsessed with her but she/her people never got back to me.

But anyway I don't want to talk about this night and how it ended yet. That comes later hehehe. If you're reading this, just remember… white party = important.

brooklynn and astrid

They're my two bffs. Astrid and I grew up together. We're legit sisters. Like shared bdays. The works. Brooklynn I met...idk a few years ago when I first starting DJing. She is/was a DJ. Met her at her show in Williamsburg in I guess 2016? But I gotta paint a picture for you so here's the boring stuff:

Astrid's my age and I've been telling her for years she looks just like Zoë Kravitz. She doesn't see it and gets insulted when I say that. She always says "Zoë Kravitz wishes she looked like me. She's so old." Astrid is this like future world-class singer. She's got this dope Banks-type sound. After that summer she was going on tour and performing at like Spring Flings and colleges. Totally on the come-up. But yeah she's like skinny and kinda dark with long stringy black hair she's always styling in cool ways. One day it's like basic white girl style, next it's dreadlocks. She'll dye her hair. She'll do cornrows. She wears well I guess I'd call it frat guy clothing. Like her Iverson jersey, Pennington #10 green jersey, and an East Hampton High varsity football letterman jacket with nothing underneath. Idk dude her fit was always hard.

Sorry. I know I need to literally get to the point already. Bear with me. RAWR. I always think about a bear growling when I type bear lol. Sorry. Just wanted to tell you about my almost legit sister Brooklynn. She's also got this really dope unique look. I'm sure you won't know this actress when I mention her but Hannah John-Kamen. She was in like three blockbusters last year. Brooklynn looks like a more thicc version of HJK. B's got those sweet Insta-thot thighs. She's high key putting out thirst traps on the reg. I met Brooklynn at The Clean Dumpster in Williamsburg. She played this unreal trippy set. It was almost like a

David Guetta with maybe some Gregorian Chants or like rock opera voiceovers. That combined with the lights—best show I'd ever seen live. I introduced myself. We hung out for literally the next 24 hours. I'm literally in love with her <3. She has this loft in SoHo. So lit. She's legit a Peruvian/Norwegian pansexual. Wait. Pause. She could be from Pretoria not Peru. I think her dad's from South Africa? Why is Peru stuck in my head? W/e. I could text her now and find out, but that'd be awk. Let's just say she's Peruvian/Norwegian. Damn I'm a bad friend... Point is our personalities are legit the same. Whatever. Iykyk.

Okay. They came out to visit me together sometime in August. Idk when. I hadn't seen Astrid in months cause she was crashing at this big-time music producer's place in Malibu until her college tour in September. So they were both gonna stay in the two downstairs bedrooms in the mansion where Jeff and I were living in Sagaponack.

Good. You're all caught up now. Actually now that I mention it, neither one came to the Labor Day all-white party a few weeks after this. I remembered being pissed cause I really wanted them to see my set. They wouldn't respond to my texts or calls and had lame excuses. We all made up a few months later but I remembered by like September I was annoyed at them. But anyway we're in August 2018 now. Focus Skye.

Me, Astrid and Brooklynn all went out to La Fondita on a Friday night. And look, from the outside the place doesn't look like much. But realistically it's this low key Hamptons hotspot in Amagansett. Great place for drinks and Mexican appies. Astrid and I have gone there maybe 100 times in our lives. Un-fucking-believable.

So we sit outside and they've got the lights on at night. There's flowers and grass and it's mad cas.

"Guys I'm so happy you're here. I've missed you two like anything."

"Of course babe" Astrid said in her super high-pitched voice. "It's been waaaay too long."

"How's your *very* impressive bae?" Brooklynn's Peruvian/Norwegian accent was like eating Skippy peanut butter and drinking champagne at the same time. It didn't make sense, but it just worked. Idk.

"He's good."

"What's wrong?" Astrid said.

"Nothing. Everything's fine. I want to hear about you two. Asty, how's LA girl?"

"Honestly it's so tight. The weather's dope. The parties are lit. Me and these two other girls are crashing with Rodrigo, but it's just short-term."

"What's his place like?" B asked.

"Omg you guys. For starters it has legit my favorite thing in the world—an infinity pool. And it like overlooks the ocean. He's got like a real red Ferrari. The house is three floors. The girls and I sleep on the bottom and Rodrigo sleeps in the master up top. But we're always out clubbing and partying and I'm singing so we're almost never all in the house at the same time."

"Not gonna lie, that sounds a little extra." Brooklynn said.

"Oh don't get me wrong. It can be tough some times but he keeps plenty of party favors around and I never have to pay for anything. But enough about me. Brooklynn we don't talk enough. How are you?"

"Wait." I said. "Shots. Tequila. Now."

I ordered six shots of Avion all on my card. Opened a tab. What can I say? I was low key rich thanks to my music and IG. And then we ordered shrimp tacos and carnitas tacos. Damn I'm getting hungry just thinking about La Fondita. Pico de Gallo just dripping down my fingers. Licking guacamole off the chips. Ugh. Memories.

"Things are going great." Brooklynn said. "I've been playing around Williamsburg, Bushwick, and Bedstuy. I just hit 30K followers on Insta and sponsor a few start-up beauty products and athletic gear. I'm paying the bills."

"You meet anyone cool recently?" I asked.

"Mmhmm." she grinned and raised her eyebrows which were on point as per ushe. "Skye I was playin' around with this Upper East Side princess for the last month or two. You've for sure seen her in my stories. Totally prim and proper brunette girl. No tats, skinny, Jewish. Dresses like a nun."

"You're into that?" Astrid asked.

"What can I say? Opposites attract. But June and July were lit cause I'd play a show at like 1 am in Bushwick. Come home at 4. Sleep at the loft. Then wake to a 12:30 pm text from Rachel saying she's horny and wants to come for her lunch break. So she'd show up and I'd be basically still asleep. And you know I never wear anything when I sleep—left the door unlocked. She'd come join me in bed. I'd low key make this girl ska-wheel and SCREAM bloody murder. I'm a hundred percent sure her parents don't know she's a lesbian and she's got like a lifetime's worth of sexual frustrations pent up, you know?"

"Sounds like a dream." I said. "Are you still hanging out?"

"Nah. She told me she's 'not gay' and 'needs to find herself.' Hate girls like that—a legit embarrassment. But I met this guy on Bumble two weeks ago. Some super uptight UESer. Just trying to get over a messy breakup."

"Not gonna lie." I said. "Your life right now is goals. Actually you'd probably really like Jeff's friend, Cash."

"Let's get more shots." Astrid said.

So I ordered another six shots for the table and then Brooklynn and Astrid each got a round. So from what I remember we literally had anywhere from two to nine shots each. And I wasn't that hungry so I barely ate. Just nibbled a bit. But they loved the tacos. Wolfed them down (are you picturing a wolf right now? Cause I am lol).

You know what I used to do? Thinking about tacos reminded me of this. And I can admit this now since I don't do it anymore. But back when I was first starting out as a DJ and would take trips to NYC I found this cool hack on getting awesome free meals. I'd walk into any place doing mobile orders—Chipotle or Chop't for example. These corporate idiots would just place bags of completed orders out front. Like full meals in bags unmonitored. They had peoples names on them but if Chipotle is gonna be so idiotic and not have an employee watch the mobile orders, they deserve some stolen meals. And truthfully when the customer comes in and finds there meal not there/stolen, Chipotle just makes them a new one. So who really loses here? Not me. Not the customer. Just the corporate giants...but I stopped doing that cause I'm mature now. Just thought it was kinda funny. Felt like a bad girl.

Also I know I brought up the fact Brooklynn had 30K followers and had some like low-level sponsors. Well back then I had 75K followers and wore Golden Goose and Oliver Peoples. I'm not trying to throw shade at my girl. I just wanted y'all to have a better idea of where I was at. See I have/had this pair of red Golden Goose sneakers that I am/was high key obsessed with. I wear them anywhere. ANYWHERE. Obvi they're awesome like walking around town shoes and beach shoes and like even athletic shoes but I've worn them to weddings and dinner with Jeff's dad. If I could have a lifetime supply of any piece of apparel it'd be Golden Goose kicks. Always plug.

And I also shouldn't leave out Oliver Peoples cause they have these super dope shades. Like if I wanna look like literally the flyest girl in the room at all times I wear their Marianela blue square sunglasses and the pale pink ones. And these aren't some run-of-the-mill-Warby Parker-middle schooler glasses. Like Jennifer Aniston wears Oliver Peoples. Best sunglasses in the world. Always plug. And that's literally the last thing I'll say. I've got a story to tell. Sorry not sorry.

So anyway. We'd all had a lot to drink. I was basically blackout. We thankfully took an Uber home (DON'T DRINK AND DRIVE KIDDIES). And so I have a few final memories of that night. The first was when Astrid and Brooklynn asked me about Jeff again in the Uber.

"Guys. We're fine."

"Things have been better though right?" Astrid said. Words slurred.

"Sure. Whatever. Does it feel great to spend a night with you guys and away from him? Sure. But no humans should spend literally 24/7 with the same person. I think I just need like maybe a little more alone time in my day-to-day."

"Aww poor cloudy Skye. Trouble in paradise?" Brooklynn said.

"Rude. Don't call me that. You know I hate it. And there's no trouble. I love him so much and he loves me so much. We're relationship goals. No doubt. On his best days he's the love of my life and on his worst days he's the love of my life but also a teeny bit controlling and smothering and says or does gross stuff. But this dude is the love of my life. Get used to him."

"Idk girl. I think he's bad news." Brooklynn said.

"But Brooklynn," A said "admit that he's like one of the hottest guys our age. Like anywhere in the world. That dude's a big-time catch."

"Actually driver" Brooklynn said, "Can you take us into East Hampton...guys we're gonna go dancing. Asty, do you know a place?"

"I know maybe 30 places. Please beeotch."

"Cloudy Skye, that okay with you?"

"Idk. I'm gonna sleep now. Night night." And then I fell asleep/blacked out.

Anyway, so the three of us somehow got home in one piece. And my memory picks up again. My boyfriend the angel saw us arrive in an Uber, and he literally came outside and picked me up like a baby and carried me inside. I remembered him bringing me up the stairs, changing me out of my dirty clothes, helping me put on clean underwear, and then tucking me into bed. He kissed me on the forehead and said:

"I love you Skye."

And then he left and went downstairs.

Also. Now that I'm picturing Astrid and Brooklynn, there's another thing I forgot to mention. So you know how Astrid is like I guess they would call her biracial? And then Brooklynn is Peruvian/Norwegian (probably?), which may be the dopest combo imaginable. Well so my gramma is Puerto Rican and the rest of my family is Italian. I mean my parents were born in America, but three of my grandparents were Italian and my gramma is Puerto Rican. Just wanted to give you a general idea of my background and what I look like. Just picture like the hottest girl you've ever seen and...jk, jk.

Where was I? Um the next day. Saturday. I probably slept till noon, and the girls slept till 2 pm. I guess they were hungover cause they were like not themselves and not super talkative. The rest of their three day trip was actually kind of boring. No offense guys if you wind up reading this somehow. ily

We just went to Jeff's private beach by ourselves. Jeff, Cash (Jeff's friend), and Kins (Cash's girl) left us alone that day. The three of us just laid out and worked on our tans for hours. Swam a bit. Ordered a pizza for dinner and watched re-runs of *The Office*.

And actually I'm forced to jump in and go off again. So, *The Office*. Everyone knows the show. You know what I think? It's the worst best show ever made. The first time I watched it, I was like everyone else. Oh wow Jim and Pam are like totes relationship goals. Oh wow Michael's so funny and kooky. And that girl Cathy who goes to Florida with Jim is super-hot. I'd low key let her eat me out. But my point is, everyone talks so much about how great *The Office* is. It's so mainstream and basic now. Anytime someone tells me *The Office* is their favorite show I'm like 'okay cool, nice to meet you. Let's never speak again'. The same goes for guys who say their favorite movie is *The Wolf of Wall Street* or girls who say they love *The Notebook*. There's nothing I hate more than unoriginal people. Like I support and love most people in the world. I don't care about ethnicity, religion, sexual orientation. Those shouldn't matter to anyone. Where I draw the line though is unoriginality. Sorry rant over.

So finally the next morning, Brooklynn said she was feeling sick. Astrid offered to take her home, and they both just left at like 9 am on Sunday. I was high key bummed but people get sick. It happens. I was more upset they didn't come to my big show at Jeff's white party. But anyway the three of us, The Tan Queens are all still besties to this day.

another random summer section! aka idk i'm just trying to do what I was told

Jefferson Campbell III true love dude seriously. But before I tell this cool story I'll say, idk if they're having Cash write a section or Kinsley write one. I don't really know what's going on and why I'm doing this. I mean when REDACTED sends you a check for $REDACTED and all you have to do is write 100 or so pages about last summer. You do it. I was told: no questions asked. I don't know who's gonna read this or why or anything. I'm writing and just trying to spice it up and make it interesting. I'm worried that if Kinsley has a section you guys might get bored to death so I gotta liven up your days. Surprise you. All I know is I'm not supposed to reveal anything important early on so hopefully I haven't. I don't know if I'm supposed to write this descriptive paragraph but w/e. They'll just take it out if not. On to the story.

I LOVED, LOVED when Jeff took me out jetskiing. I mean dude let me paint a picture for you. J has a private beach leading to the Atlantic behind his backyard. The sand is super soft and hot and pretty. He has his sailboat in Montauk Marina but on his private beach, JCIII has a jetski. A mad sexy, unbelievably sleek, all-black jetski. I don't know if you're supposed to name jetskis but his says "Skygreenii" on the side in my favorite color hunter green. I loved that man.

"Where's my baby?" Jeff called out from the backyard.

"Be right there daddy."

I raced downstairs, ran out to the yard, and jumped into his arms. My bathing suit was fire. J's hair was on point and his linen game was strong. Idc what age you are if you spotted the two of us together, you'd instantly ship us. We just had this like cosmic connection. Two people just meant to be together, you know?

But anyway I was wearing this mad skimpy neon pink bikini that was def too small for me. But Jeff loved it and I wanted to make him happy. And I swear to you when J saw my thigh gap in the front and Toblerone tunnel in the back, I could just sense his bathing suit stretching.

He held my hand down to the water. We were both walking barefoot.

"Carry me daddy." I said.

He lifted me up, kept me dry from the crashing waves, and then placed me ever so gently on the back of his jetski. Then J kissed me and gave my lip a nice bite before climbing in front of me. I still remember him in that all-white Vilebrequin suit and his baby blue linen shirt he never buttoned. I wrapped my arms around his waist and he literally just revved that baby full throttle.

I will say I got low key turned on anytime he went fast or we were wild. Whether J was gunning it over 100 in his convertible or going full speed on the jet, oh boy I was literally dead.

"How's that feel baby?" He shouted.

"Soooo nice daddy." I felt the vibrations as we sped up and hit the bumps.

Then J had this little slot where you could put like valuables and stuff. So my iPhone was in there and I reached into my bikini and grabbed my AirPods and put on some music for myself. I played "Jubel" by Klingande which not gonna lie is one of the 10 best summer songs ever made. I was shaking my head and totally flowing to the beat. J kept speeding and we were way out into the ocean and basically couldn't see the shore anymore. It was so tight.

"Skye baby how you doing?" He said and I pretended I couldn't hear him.

It was just like complete and utter bliss. Best guy ever. Best song ever. Speeding in the water. Memories man. But anyway he kinda stopped suddenly and so I took my headphones out.

"What's going on daddy?"

He didn't say anything but instead took out a baggie of coke and looked right into my eyes—one of those super deep soul-piercing stares.

"Daddy?"

He then unhooked my bikini, leaned me down a bit, and poured some coke on my tits. I felt the heat from Jeff's nostrils as they sped over my skin. He made a deep "ah" sound, closed his eyes, and said:

"You know I could kill you right now and no one would ever know."

"I bet you could. How would you do it daddy?"

I undressed fully and started rubbing my boobs in his face.

"I'd choke you out."

"Yeah daddy? Choke me." He started doing it lightly.

"I'd lay you down like this and take out my Swiss Army knife."

"Whip it out and choke me harder."

I was fully naked and laying out on his jetski and poof, he was inside me.

"What's next?" I said. And I'm like yelping and screeching at that point.

"I could slit your throat." He held the knife to my neck. "And then cut up your whole body. Gotta attract the threshers kid."

And then he got that wild look in his eyes. He only gets that specific insane stare when we're in the water. Something about the water dude: mi amor was a deranged animal. Total nut.

Actually lemme skip any more X-rated deets. J will tell you those. J's better at describing that stuff anyway. You should see how wild his sexts get. Legit psycho but I love it.

Right afterward he just faceplanted into my boobs and we're both breathing super heavy, and it just felt like super intense. That was real love to me. It's life and death. It's savage. It's drama and sex and power and just like following your animal instincts. Knowing exactly how to make your S-O tick...and finish. I knew Jeff better than I knew myself. No girl could do to him what I could. None. Period.

He licked some leftover coke off my body and then started licking my face. Just cleaning me like a cat. And I got into it too. I was licking his nipples and his belly button and his eyelids. That man just did something to me. Turned on a different side of me. I mean, it's so insane to think about.

Yet after we started riding back and were totally speechless, my sick mind started to wander. First I started thinking about what Jeff would do after he killed me and dumped me in the ocean. I knew he'd never hurt me. But I just imagined him frantically returning to shore and yelling to Cash and Kins. Mi amor—the actor, freaking out and telling some crazy tale about how his arch-nemesis shark sank its teeth into my legs and wouldn't let go. He punched it and stabbed it and eventually killed it but I was dead too. RIP Skye. He'd be legit crying and screaming when he called the police. And he'd go to my gramma's, looking like the saddest dude who ever lived. He'd dress in his dirtiest outfit and weep into her lap. And then idk—he'd call that girl from his birthday or that high school senior he had a thing for. And in a week he'd forget about me. But w/e. We got back to the house and I thought about wanting to grow old with him and have his children.

I mean that wasn't like a typical day but it wasn't that far from one. You see the thing with J was, more than anything he was so considerate back then. Every time before we had sex he'd ask me "are you sure you want to do this?" Every. Single. Time. Day or night. At first I was weirded out cause like who does that? But after a while it made me love him more. He just cared so much. My answer was always yes. Not once did I say no. But I'll never forget that about him for as long as I live.

any guy would be lucky to have a girlfriend like me, seriously

This night I'm gonna talk about is def not for everyone but if there's one thing I learned about J it was to always just go with the flow. That dude was a buckin bronco. Like a bull in Spain or something. Or actually better yet a pit bull. My gramma has two pit bulls. Dahlia's six and mean but can be nice sometimes, and Grecia's one and mainly nice. So what I'm trying to say is: mi amor was so cute and great to look at but he could get wild and crazy. Tough and sexy, but could be laid-back and chill. Never a friggin dull moment. What girl doesn't want to feel alive ALL the time? Find that girl for me and I'll call her a liar to her face.

Okay. So. Jefferson Campbell III's 23rd birthday. July 31st. Mi amor—the Leo with a Virgo Moon Sign had his plan for his big day and I had mine. J was going out on his Hollandsworth's friend's boat. Cute Cashie was going. And I think there were two others. Four hot rich guys on a super expensive boat. Oh and Hollandsworth is some prep school in Manhattan I guess.

Before he left I gave Jeff a little surprise in the bedroom...and then another later in the garage studio ;). But I'm getting sidetracked. Skipping ahead. J and cutie Cash left. Kins went God knows where. Probably hanging out in Quogue or West Hampton lmao. Or maybe a library cause she thought she was miss smarty nerd bookworm workaholic. Point is I was alone in the big house. Wanted to make J's night special when he returned.

So what did I do? I drove into EH and did some heavy-duty shopping. I literally bought all the birthday stuff I could find. White balloons. His fave color. Black-and-white streamers. Silver "Happy Birthday Jefferson" signs—custom-made. I prepped the red room. And I also bought two cards and wrote like super heartfelt messages in them. "Oh J you're my sun and stars and moon and sky. Last person I want to see at night, first person I want to see in the morning." Cheesy, but meaningful stuff. J loves loyalty more than anything. I told him I'd always stick by him and love him until the day I died...and in the afterlife.

I bought four big juicy steaks I could grill up. Also snagged some mad classy champagne. It was already gonna be so lit but I knew my J and he needed profiteroles and chocolate-covered strawberries too. So that's what I got.

Then...I feel like I should make this known. Earlier that week Jeff's friend Dean called me and asked my permission about the girls on the boat. Dean said:

"Skye if it's alright with you I was planning on obtaining several escorts for our boat ride on Campbell's birthday."

"Yeah that's chill."

"That's it? You're cool with that? No questions asked?"

"Yeah. J and I trust each other 100%. We have some unwritten understandings."

"Okay well just so you know it'll be three young women. Very classy expensive ladies. These are not your five-and-dime AIDS-infected street harlots."

"Dean it's fine. It's not sus. I get it. Guys need a little adventure. He'd never get too out of hand."

"Right. Well I just wanted to inform you. It felt like the admirable thing to do. We'll all take care of Campbell. He's our brother. We'll swim a bit, drink a bit, maybe partake in some frivolous South American games and then have him home tonight."

"No worries dude. Have him home before nine and don't let him eat too much. I have a few surprises of my own."

And that was that. So I did work around our house. Hung streamers, blew up balloons, and even broke out the motherfucking Swiffer. I was basically low key a 1950s housewife at that point. The big house was spotless and then I went to the kitchen to start making food. I was marinating the steaks and setting the table when Jeff sent me the first text. All it said was: "Your thoughts? Xoxo." At first I didn't know what he meant but then the pictures started coming through.

The first one was of two fully nude girls standing side by side below deck on the boat. Girl on the left was shorter than me—had long thick black hair, eyebrows on fleek, tiny brown nipples on kinda small tits, and then these really trim/athletic legs. She was probably 21 and had like Middle Eastern skin.

Girl numero dos was like every rich NYC boy's fantasy. We're talking long blonde hair, perky boobs, flat abs, big blue eyes, pale skin, and this innocent look on her face. DSLs too. She was like one of the girls who'd summered in the Hamptons with her mommy and daddy and played tennis and sailed and went to pool dartys. (Oh sorry. DSLs= "dick-sucking-lips" and dartys/dagers are daytime parties/ragers).

"It's your birthday baby. I've got plenty of ideas for either of them ;)."

"That's my girl. I'll surprise you."

I don't know what that guy did to me that summer. Everything J did was the sexiest thing I'd ever heard of. I remembered just shaking my head and practically giggling. I was like a widdle schoolgirl. I couldn't wait for him to come home. He was gonna be so happy with me and as I thought about all the moments we shared together it had me all up in my feels.

Okay. Next I went and got changed. My lingerie game was always on fleek. I was wearing black lace garters motherfucker. No robe. No shirt on top. Just lingerie. And at that point I was blasting songs from my SoundCloud all throughout the house while grilling steaks. J and his little thot were gonna walk through the door any second and I was high key prepped and ready to go.

The timing was perfect—like a movie. Right when I heard the car pull up the driveway I took the steaks off the grill (medium-rare, c'mon) and put them on plates. Then I filled the champagne flutes, lit candles everywhere, and poured a bunch of frites on a big plate for the table.

"Kid I'm home" J shouted. "And I brought company."

I stood in the center of the dining room in nothing but my lingerie: had my hands crossed in front of my waist and my hair was tied in a nice, tight pony.

"Good evening Mr. Campbell." I said in the sexiest voice I had.

"Jesus Skye. This all looks amazing."

"Does it really Mr. Campbell? I did a good job? You mean it?"

"Are you kidding? Spectacular. Steak frites, champagne, and I love the decorations. Goddamn baby you look so hot. Jesus Christ."

He gave me a long hard kiss before introducing his quiet companion who was just standing nervously and watching us.

"Lucille this is the famed DJ Skygreenii."

Jeff had chosen the petite black-haired girl. And like a switch flipped and she sprinted over to me.

"Skye it's such an honor. I love your music so much. Is this 'Bikinis and Bellinis' playing right now?"

I nodded.

"You're my absolute favorite DJ. I follow you on Insta. Although my real name isn't Lucille."

"That's really sweet of you to say. You look so pretty. I love your dress."

"Ladies? Ready to eat?" he smiled.

The three of us sat at the table, ate our steak frites, and drank champagne. Lucille kept obsessing over my music which like I didn't blame her. And then J carried the conversation and told Lucille about my background and told me about her background. Not gonna lie it was cute. Like if you were there in person you'd be like: 'oh this looks lit. I'd wanna be friends with all of them'. And then Jeff finished his meal.

"Kid this was fantastic. Truly. You're a star in the kitchen."

I stood up, kissed him, and cleared everyone's plates.

"You don't happen to have a dessert prepared do you?"

"Come on daddy. Do I ever leave you unsatisfied?"

"Never Skye."

I brought out the profiteroles and then poured Jeff a glass of scotch.

"Profiteroles Skye? Did you make these yourself?"

"Of course mi amor."

I didn't make them myself. I bought them. I wasn't like a Michelin chef. C'mon.

So the three of us just sat there eating like a happy family. We're talking ethical non-monogamy at its finest. At least that's how I'd describe it. But then the tone changed mad quickly. I mean like while the thot was munching on her profiterole J said:

"Lucille. Stand up."

That girl did exactly as she was told and stood there. Silent. I was just watching. I loved this side of Jeff.

"Walk to the center of the room there." He pointed.

And that shy little girl just did whatever he said. Lucille was standing literally five feet from the table in a fire all-black dress with her hands together.

"Lucille. From now on I'll address you as Kinsley and only Kinsley. Do you understand Kinsley?"

"Whoa Jeff," I said. "What's going on? You didn't. I mean like I didn't know this was part of the equation. What's happening?"

"Relax baby you look stunning. I'm just having a little birthday fun."

I then stood up, wrapped my arms around his shoulders, and said:

"You know I'm down for anything daddy but like why this? I mean I didn't know you liked Cash's girlfriend."

Lucille just stood there motionless like barely even blinking. Honestly she did look like Kinsley but hotter I guess.

"Daddy I'm not so sure about this."

"Kid you say the word and I'll drive Lucille home and never see her again." He turned to the girl and said: "you'll get your money no matter what."

"How do I look?" I said.

"Prettiest girl in the world." He kissed me and touched my thigh. That man made me swoon every day I swear to God...Swoon? C'mon Skye. You don't say swoon. You don't swoon. Sus. But w/e.

Lucille was still awkwardly standing there. I thought about being like "yo gtfo" but it was J's birthday.

"You can call her whatever you want. Just don't forget I'm here too."

"How could I ever forget the sexiest girl I know?" he kissed me again.

Then J started feeding me a chocolate-covered strawberry but I didn't want the whole thing so I fed the other half to him.

"Skye baby put some music on. And Kinsley start stripping for us."

I grabbed my iPhone, hooked it up to Bluetooth, and started playing this new beat I was experimenting with. You probably know it by now. It was "Roasted or Ghosted." It's kinda like Fatboy Slim's "The Rockafeller Skank" meets Whethan's "Savage." But also it's got like this sweet groovy bass. Kinda sexy. Perfect song choice imo.

I'll give props to Lucille. That girl could shake it. She was taking off her dress (again her drip was insane, not gonna lie) like hiding her nips for a while and twisting and twerking to the beat. By then Jeff and I turned our chairs toward her and just watched. High key impressed (And drip means like swag. Like an outfit or jewelry or something).

"You got some moves sweetheart." I shouted to our guest.

Jeff and I started making out. Like hard making out. And then when the song ended Lucille stood perfectly still again. Only now like legit naked. Hands at her sides.

"Skye dearest" he rubbed his nose against mine "would you be so kind as to grab our video camera from the bedside table, unlock our little hideaway upstairs and Kinsley and I will meet you there momentarily."

He started kissing me again. J was always so passionate—especially around company. And then he was making his way to my neck before I stopped him.

"Uh-uh. Not yet. See you in a few daddy."

I ran to our bedroom high key pumped for what was about to go down. I found the camcorder behind his scotch and that book he had with the neon lighting on the cover. I always used to say to him 'why do we need a camera? Your iPhone is a better camera than this thing'. And J's reason made sense I guess. He wanted to use a camera that didn't have internet access and wasn't involved with Apple or iCloud. Jeff was super paranoid about getting hacked. Everything we did in the room was shot on this old-style *Blair Witch Project* camera. Sounds sus I know but thinking about it from his POV, it makes total sense.

So I unlocked the door to our red room and positioned myself in one of my fave spots and waited.

"Baby we're coming in" Jeff said from behind the door.

"Ready daddy" I said in my cutest baby voice.

And then J barged in and said:

"Kinsley go over to my angelic girlfriend."

"That's me." I was full-blown 100% baby voice at all times in that room.

The tanned naked girl walked over to me. Like super serious.

"Lighten up girlfriend," I said. She laughed.

I started to kiss Lucille and then handed the recorder to Jeff after he closed the door.

"Kinsley if you feel uncomfortable or aren't having fun we'll stop immediately. I mean that."

I don't wanna talk about the red room or what goes on in there. I trusted J completely. He trusted me completely. J's better at dirty talk anyway. I don't wanna embarrass myself. Let's just say Jeff, Lucille and I had a good time and end with that ;)

cashie da cutie

Ugh okay. This is the issue with going in some weird reverse chronological order. I haven't really talked about Cashie and Kins—more importantly Cashie though. See J was like my evil sexy devil and Cashie was the good. You know like the angel-type.

So he and I decided to go on a long bike ride together. I may have planted the idea in everyone's heads we should all get to know each other. Like alone. Everyone agreed.

Kinsley and J spent that day alone together which now that I mention it he may have found her to be sexy and I didn't realize at the time. W/e. He wouldn't dream of touching her. Or he'd tell me he wanted to and invite her back later. We were always so honest and straightforward with each other. I loved us.

So bike ride. Cashie rode behind me and not gonna lie I wore basically nothing. I was literally nude. I had on this way-too-small neon sports bra and these tiny little booty shorts. Idk if I wanted to show Cashie what he was missing or to make him jealous or to see how he'd react or if he'd make a move. Idk. W/e. I just...that's what I wore okay?

I definitely stood on the bike and leaned over more than I needed to. Gotta give Jeff's oldest friend a good view, you know?

But anyway we're riding. At some point we're biking next to each other and idk. I'm low key feeling something. I mean he just had this like power about him, you know? It kinda hit me. I mean I'm sure I always knew but I just liked really strong guys. And I don't mean like massive Hulks. I'm talking like emotional or psychological power. Like the way they speak and walk and dress. Dude Cashie was just power. That was him. He was peddling with like his broad shoulders and he had this short hair. I know Cashie wasn't but he felt like an Army guy. So strict. He never did drugs or cursed in front of ladies. Fuck.

See I'll be the first to admit I had fantasies about Cashie. And I can say that and I know Jeff would be gucci if he heard me say that cause he was always open and honest with me about girls he thought were hot.

I had this dream the night after our bike trip. It was black-and-white cause I always dream in black-and-white. I'm special like that. And so in the dream J had like a huge party and he kicked me out of the house cause I was being rude or something (that would never happen but w/e it was a dream). So I went out to the patio and Cashie was just sitting there waiting for me. And Dream Cashie said:

"Let's go for a ride."

"But there aren't any cars for miles."

"Hop on my back."

We flew. But then it was more sexual. We were making out and then he jumped off one roof and ran through the air to the ocean. Cashie was kissing me the whole time and his shirt flew off and we dove into the water and were floating, touching, and kissing. And dolphins and sea turtles were swirling around us and we were soaking wet. Then I woke up.

Where was I? Okay. So then we got to South and went to La Parmigiana.

I would've been so down for Sip N Soda though. It's like an og spot that doesn't have the same uptight Hamptons vibe. Sip N Soda has high key the best turkey club and peach ice cream out there. Food = amazing. Waitresses are local high schoolers. Totally different energy. The Fudge Company is dank too. But w/e we wound up at La Parmigiana. It's aight.

Now inside. We were both so hot and sweaty and I could see right through his shirt. He looked really sexy tbh. And of course Cashie still felt like powerful and intimidating. Again not physically cause these Hollandsworth guys never even hurt flies but like psychologically daunting. And actually let's be real for a sec.

I DON'T GET INTIMIDATED BY GUYS. I'm the one that intimidates them. In high school all the boys were scared to talk to me. I was too hot and too far out of their leagues. Later when I first started DJing I noticed these dudes were like afraid to approach me. I was powerful and was running the show and was like 17, 18, 19. Shout out independent women. The boys must've been like 'goddamn how am I supposed to talk to her? What's a guy like me say to a girl like that?' So the point is in my whole life no boy or man ever intimidated me psychologically, emotionally, or physically. But then I met Jeff. And I was just literally transformed. Less than a year later I met Cashie and felt the same feelings. It was crazy. Like something about their school or the way they were raised I guess. Cashie's parents and J's dad may have had an impact? Strangest thing. Point is: no guys ever intimidate/intimidated me except for the two dudes I spent that whole summer with.

Okay cool. Moving on. Cashie ordered waters and Hawaiian pizza. Which like, gross. If I were with J that day it would've been...well idk what it would've been. He does the ordering. But it would've been better than what Cashie did. See that's the funny thing. The two of them were literally the same person and brought out the same side of me and yet they were also like polar opposites. Legit contradictions. Goddamn.

"So Skye what do you think about Kinsley?" He said after ordering.

"She's fine. She's cool. Whatevs."

"You don't like her?"

"I didn't say that."

"What's the problem?"

"No problem Cashie. You looked like quite the cyclist. Tour de France-like. Great stamina."

"You should see Kinsley ride. She can do a wheelie and go no hands. I guess that's what you get when you grow up in a suburb."

Btw Kins grew up in Cincinnati. J and Cashie were Upper East Siders. I grew up in East Hampton.

"Mmhmm."

The food came in a bit and I watched Cashie take a little bottle of Purell from his pocket and squirt it onto his hands.

"You always carry that thing with you?"

"I mean don't you feel dirty?"

"I wish I did."

Then he literally spent an hour taking apart his food. Pineapple went on one side of the plate, ham on the other, and then the picked apart pizza slice sat in the leftover spot on the plate. And Cashie ate all the pineapple slices before moving on to the ham and then the pizza. And dude drank water like a camel. It was a super bizarre experience watching him eat tbh.

"Did you know Kinsley used to play softball and ride horses? You like the outdoors right? I think you two have a lot in common."

I swear every time he mentioned her I just dried up like a desert.

"You know Cashie I had this crazy dream about you two nights ago."

"Really? What happened?"

"Well it's super weird. Maybe I shouldn't tell you."

"No come on. You can tell me."

"Okay but don't judge."

"Never."

He was still munching on his ham and I was too grossed out to eat anything.

"Okay. So. You, Jeff and I were sailing all over the world. The wind was always blowing in our direction and we were just like flying across the water. And we're all like laughing and having fun and then Jeff makes fun of me."

"Interesting..."

"Shush. So. Dream J says something like 'you'll never be good enough for me. You know I could get any girl in the world. This isn't gonna last'."

"Jesus. Well it was just a dream right? Or nightmare, I should say."

"Yeah but no, I'm not at the good part yet. Stop interrupting. Rude."

"Sorry."

"So then you hear Jeff being mean to me and insulting my figure and stuff and you stepped in. My Scorpio superhero. You started punching him in the face and he was bleeding. The love of my life was just gushing blood. And he was laughing and I was laughing and you were laughing. And then I said 'throw him overboard.' You listened. And we left him behind and all the blood magically disappeared from the boat."

He was done with the pineapple and ham sections and was now eating the naked pizza. Cashie was fascinated by me. I mean ever since Cashie first met me he'd mentally swiped right. Facts.

"Goddamn Skye. What the hell kind of nightmare was that?"

"I'm not done. Then the boat steered itself and it started floating out of the water and we were literally gliding through the sky in our very own sailboat. And that's when you told me how great I was and we went below deck to sleep. Then a big wave crashed on board and there was water everywhere and I woke up."

He was just staring at me with those remarkable blue eyes of his. Totally weirded out.

"I know" I said. "I'm such a loser right? I have the craziest dreams."

"Kinsley texted me that she and Jeff are going to a polo match."

"Isn't she too uptight for you? I mean you're such a sweet and sensitive guy and have so much depth. And she's great and all but like super basic, you know?"

"No I don't" and then he said to the waitress "can we get the check please?"

Idk I guess he seemed uncomfortable. But that's kinda who Cashie was. Sweet, sensitive, muscular, smart, uncomfortable, awkward, goody-two-shoes, powerful guy.

"Why don't we get out of here?" he said.

"Wow Cashie. That's so sudden but if you want to. I've got a spot around here. J won't mind."

"What? No. What are you talking about? I meant leave the restaurant."

"I know. I'm just playing around."

"Campbell's rubbed off on you."

"Yeah he gets it in my eyes sometimes, but I mostly like it."

"Christ. Don't say that stuff to me. Jesus."

"Lmao…What the hell do you think J and Kins are doing? I'm getting major fomo."

So yeah I guess you could say I was breaking down the walls between us.

Anyway we grabbed me a bubble tea cause I wasn't gonna eat pineapple pizza. Then I asked him if he wanted to go to this underground hookah place but Cashie didn't want to. However he did agree to go into this like little pop-up boutique where they had the special healing crystals I legit loved. I may have begged and pleaded a bit but he could've said no.

He was sweet enough to buy me a blue lace agate for insight, aventurine for emotional tranquility, pyrite for power, and rose quartz for unconditional love. Those crystals were actually so lit I still keep them with me when I'm feeling uneasy. I know I sound like a total freak but I think they legit work. Also I'm not trying to flex about all this it's just like interesting that Cashie bought me $50 worth of healing crystals. Makes you think, doesn't it?

the water does crazy things to my bf

For starters let's get this out of the way cause I know if Cashie and Kins are writing they'll bring it up at some point. During this sailing trip I'm boutta describe the boat's boom hit me and knocked me into the water. Was it funny? No. Did I enjoy it? No. Did I believe the fucked theory that Jeff did it on purpose with no motive whatsoever? Absolutely not. It was nbd. The boom hit my shoulder more than anything. Maybe grazed my face. Nothing a little makeup couldn't fix lol. Okay? Are we good now?

The four of us left Montauk Marina. July. I was juuling at the beginning (mango pod duh), and J was steering, and Cashie and Kins were like holding hands or something. Not a great couple imo.

Jeff starts teaching them stuff about boating but really I knew more than he did. I used to ride catamarans, speed boats, canoes, kayaks, everything. I think the thing people forget is I grew up in East Hampton. I mean…sure the dudes summered out here once in a while but I'd take me over them in any outdoor activity.

Sorry anyway I gotta paint a picture for ya. Big white sailboat (although I've been on bigger) and it had a below deck bed and bathroom, plus mini fridge, plates, and glasses. You could one hundred percent live on that thing for the rest of your life, tbh.

"Go get the snacks baby and the drinks too please?" Jeff said to me. "Brb."

So I went below deck and brought out champagne for Bellinis and then all the chocolate truffles and strawberries and like chips, guac, and salsa. It was a dope picnic on the water for real. Oh and then I put on an EDM playlist. Not like trap remixes but cool laid-back stuff. It was Kygo, early Avicii, and then some of my early work.

Although J made me turn it off pretty quickly cause he liked to hear the sounds of the ocean and seagulls and that shit. Which I sorta get but also not really.

"So Campbell you have a lot of parties on this boat?" Sweet Cashie asked.

All four of us were around the tiller and I had one headphone in and just felt like super chill. I must've been feeding J truffles or something.

"I've only had her a year or two so haven't had that massive dager yet but you can't imagine the girls I used to bring back here."

"C'mon Jeff really?" Kinsley said.

"Don't be such a prude. It's not a good look." Jeff said.

J was right about her. I typically stayed quiet cause I never liked to escalate fights but I had to speak up that time especially after she involved Cashie.

"Cash you want to say something here?" Kinsley barked.

"Yeah Campbell isn't it awkward to say this stuff with Skye here?"

"Skye do you mind?" Campbell asked.

"Nah it's actually making me horny a-f."

"Have some self-respect girlfriend." Kinsley said.

"You know" I said "we don't all have to fit into what society tells us a relationship should look like. There's millions of different kinds of loves and J and I have our own unique love story. Kins you know I like you but you should mind your own business and not talk about shit you know nothing about."

I then began kissing J aggressively. I wanted to show Kinsley what real love looked like. That was true passion, you know? I then started unbuttoning his white linen shirt and running my hand through his flowing, blonde hair.

"Easy now kid."

I then whispered "I want you now" but it was intentionally loud enough for Kins and Cashie to hear.

"Kid head inside this instant."

So I did. Needless to say Jeff and I had no issues with our sex life. Goddamn. Dude knew how to rock my world. His stroke game was fire. Jesus Christ. The absolute GOAT. Actually I gotta go off on a bit of a tangent here cause this is important.

I thought about it back then and I still wonder from time to time. I mean how many girls had Jeff slept with in his life? Like he and I started dating when he was 22 and I was 19 and a half. I don't want to get into my past but J's body count could've been anywhere from 0 to 100 before me. See the reason it could be really low is cause of how picky he was. Jeff would only go for either like super-wealthy old-money girls or wealthy models/self-employed girls. He never wanted to mess around with women who didn't have money cause he was worried they'd manipulate or turkey baste. Ngl, any girl my age who's been dealing with nothing but Splenda daddies since hitting 18 would be obsessed with J and his generosity for real. So I get it.

But anyway I know this body count shit about J because A. he told me bits and pieces mainly when drunk or high and B. Because I listened to every word he said and truly wanted to get a better understanding of my beautiful and powerful soulmate. So he'd only be with rich girls who were like 9s or 10 outta 10s. And I mean how many of those girls exist in Manhattan and the Hamptons for real? More than like Kansas but still there can't be *that* many. Maybe a few thousand? Plus I'd never heard him talk about being with a girl older than him and he wouldn't mess around with underage girls cause of his family's name and image. So like realistically how many girls really fit these standards between the ages of 18 and 21? I don't know dude. J was a total mystery to me sometimes. (Oh sorry. Turkey basters are girls who take semen outta condoms and secretly try to impregnate themselves. Pro athletes know what I'm talkin' bout ;)).

Jeff and I rejoined our crew by the stern and then Kinsley said:

"You guys this is really nice. These views are incredible."

She took out her phone and was taking a zillion pics and vids while we were all trying to enjoy ourselves. I remembered thinking like 'what does she know about water?'. Kinsley couldn't even stand up straight on the boat without like falling over herself. Truthfully she was like a dainty little thing. Kinsley was all stressed out about life jackets and it's like 'sweetheart, I've been on boats my whole life. I could swim circles around anyone'.

"No way" Kinsley said. "I'm calling b-s. You didn't punch a shark in the face."

I zoned out for a bit but I guessed J was talking about the time he punched a real-life shark to save his cousin. I loved that story—my boyfriend the hero.

"Skye tell her."

"I wasn't there but J's fist like paralyzed the shark. He grabbed Darcy, swam to the boat, and saved the day."

Jeff and I started making out and he was just so passionate. Especially round the water. I loved that ferocious side of him. Kissing and biting my neck and shoulders, yanking on my hair, spanking me just for the hell of it. Idk dude the smell of saltwater just always got me and J going. Memories <3

Okay then at some point J did a few lines and popped some shit. Cashie was steering the boat and Kins was like sleeping I think. I will say ngl Cashie looked like a sexy pirate behind the wheel of the boat. Oh and I was wearing J's sea captain's hat cause I'm fly like that.

I had this dream last summer about Cashie and me on a super old pirate ship blowing up nearby schooners with our cannonballs. He was wearing an eyepatch and had his sleeves cut off to reveal those like big biceps of his. He kept saying 'argh' and calling me his 'wench.' There must've been a parrot somewhere and I was like singing shanties for him. Idk I'm a huge dork right?

Kinsley seemed uneasy the whole time. I wanted to be like:

"It's just a boat sweetie."

Too bad little Cincy girl isn't much of a swimmer or like water sporty. Just a basic bitch slash maybe brainiac nerd or some shit.

But I kept my mouth shut. She was our houseguest after all. J always told me to be kind to our guests. Hosting company and parties is an integral part of our world, you know?

Um. So then I'm snapchatting Brooklynn and Astrid. Brooklynn was somewhere in SoHo and Astrid was in LA. That was fun for a bit but I got bored and wanted to jump in the water.

"J, can we go swimming now? Please?" I shouted.

"Sure, baby. Just adjust the mainsail. We'll go in five minutes. I got a good spot nearby."

Not only did I want to go swimming but...and I'm not trying to flex...my abs were on fleek back then. I kinda sorta wanted to show off. I mean my body was sooo tight. Seriously. Like when J and Cashie saw me next to Kinsley they'd be like 'fuck.' I also maybe wanted to see Cashie shirtless and to show him the tattoos he hadn't seen yet ;). Back then I was doing hot yoga, Pilates, biking, and kick-boxing kinda frequently. And I was doing so well with sticking to my diet (J deserves an assist there too).

Then the boom thing happened and I flew into the water. See I've adjusted his sails like 50 times before and never had any issue. And there was no way he'd ever hurt me. That wasn't Jeff. He never did anything bad to me. Ever. So J wouldn't intentionally put me at risk. The wind may have shifted at the last second or we hit a wave or sandbar or something. No motive anyway. He loved me and I loved him. We were back on his bed like 15 minutes later—end of story.

Realistically though J was just like *really* high. I've seen him zone out before. He'll mix pills he prob shouldn't. He'll be like completely dead for minutes and then he'll snap out of it. So point is: I'm in the water but it's all good. I wasn't unconscious. I told you it hit my shoulder more than anything. I wasn't screaming or worried. Kins was the only one panicking. She was legit shrieking.

J eventually turned the boat around and I remembered thinking how chic he looked. The sun was hitting him at literally the perfect angle. Black Fendi shades, unbuttoned linen shirt, barefoot. My freakin' model boyfriend was glowing—like a knight in shining Italian linen.

"Skye honey we'll be right there." Kinsley said.

"I'm fine. Just a bruise," I shouted back.

Tbh I was most pissed about my phone and headphones drowning but J got me new ones the next day so nbd.

I treaded water for like five to 10 mins before Kinsley pulled me onto the boat. J wasn't there to greet me but he did call for me from below deck.

"Don't go. Stay still." Kinsley said.

"Yeah Skye" Cash said. "We'll take care of you. Just breathe."

They were treating me like I was dying which I hated...so I sprinted below deck and found Jeff relaxing shirtless on the bed.

"Are you okay baby?"

"Yes daddy. Thanks for saving me!"

"Yeah sorry for the turbulence. Rarely happens to me but I'm glad you're all...oh you've got a little bump." He touched my cheek and then shoulder.

"Is it bad? Do you have a mirror?"

"Nothing a little makeup can't buff out."

"Am I still pretty daddy?" I said in my baby voice.

"Prettiest damn girl in the world."

Then I started unstrapping my too tight bikini.

"How 'bout now daddy?" My voice was super high-pitched just how daddy liked it.

And he couldn't stop staring and touching and complimenting me. I'm gonna skip ahead but I just wanna say he was such a good dude. Always an adventure and never a dull moment. Goddamn.

"Why the looks guys?" J said as we walked back outside hand in hand. "Kick back and relax."

Okay. Kinsley was really getting on my nerves. She kept giving all these pompous looks and eye rolls. I'm not about that life. Seriously I was the bruised one and now she's pouting by herself near the bow? Rude.

"Mi amor" I said. "Can I play music on your phone?"

"Of course sunny Skye. Play anything you want as loud as you want."

I smiled and quickly compiled this playlist from his Spotify:

"Lullaby" - R3HAB X Mike Williams
"Remind Me to Forget" - Kygo ft. Miguel
"Keep it Mello" - Marshmello ft. Omar LinX
"Feel So Close" - Calvin Harris
"Summertime Sadness (Remix)" - Lana Del Rey & Cedric Gervais
"Into the Past" - Nero
"In for the Kill (Remix)" - La Roux ft. Skrillex
"Desire (Remix)" - Years and Years ft. Gryffin
"Groove" - Oiki
"Sexual" - NEIKED ft. Dyo
"I Took a Pill in Ibiza (Remix)" - Mike Posner ft. Seeb
"Surface" - Aero Chord

Also. Last thing. I wanted to tell you about the other activity J and I used to do when we were alone on the sailboat: fly the drone. Jeff had this super expensive drone and he taught me how to like steer the thing. Some people would probably think this was extra but I thought it was mad dope. I'd send the thing like 100 feet in the air and then search for other boats and spy on them. I once spotted another couple legit fucking on the deck of their boat hehehe. I've been a huge drone girl ever since.

So I guess what I'm trying to say is all-in-all, it was a weirdly fun day. Which seemed to be the case every time the four of us chilled together.

anyone can be besties when wine's involved

Idk now. I guess I'm going back to June of last year? There are probably a few more things I wanna talk about before I head back to that last night of the 2018 summer.

Here I think it's important to show I certainly tried to like Kins.

So here's the deal: J wanted a guys day with Cashie so apparently that meant Kins and I needed to have a girls day. I didn't really see why it worked like that since I would've been more than happy spending a day alone in my studio but w/e.

Also. Pause. I should mention I was still performing at Hamptons clubs literally every two weeks last summer. But idk how to write about me DJing for three hours straight and like not bore you...fwiw, J would come occasionally. But he stuck out. I mean when it comes to my shows the best way I can describe them is just...it's a vibe...And J's aesthetic was off. Didn't match the vibe.

Okay wine. I knew Kins liked wine. In fact after a few weeks into the summer anyone who partied in EH or Montauk knew she liked wine. So where'd I take her on our good old-fashioned girls day? A vineyard. Duh.

By now if you hadn't figured it out already I am/was pretty well-liked. I never had any problem making friends and still talk to like a million people from high school. I guess I should add I didn't make any guy friends until after my glo up but by last summer I was like J. We both had a ton of friends/connections and if we ever needed anything no matter what activity/topic, one of us had the hook-up.

So. wine. I grew up with this French girl Bérénice Louise. Her family had a vineyard in Alsace I visited when I was younger. And probably 15 years ago they got a spot in the Hamptons. It is/was a family-owned spot. It's called Bérénice Louise Vineyard because that's also the gramma's name. The mom's name is Lulu. Point is the three generations run the spot outta Water Mill. They make a zillion bottles of rosé and last I checked it was the fifth best-selling vineyard in the Hamptons. We took Kins' car.

"I really appreciate you taking me here Skye."

"Of course dude. Should be fun. Just don't embarrass me." I smiled at her.

"So what's it like there? I've never been to a Hamptons vineyard."

"Dude. It's lit. Tasting room, winery, great spot for Insta stories. Really it'll just be you, me, and my friend Bérénice walking through the rows of vines downing glasses."

"Okay...well...should we have ubered here?"

"Relax girl. You and your boy are always so uptight. Life just works out if you chill and don't stress all the time."

"Right."

Kins was wearing this light pink summer dress that went past her knees. It was for sure Zara. Super basic. And this thing had an ultra-high neckline and it basically went to her feet. She looked like a bubblegum nun...eh I gotta say though her hair was on fleek as per ushe. Killer long black waves. Looked great with her olive skin. Facts.

So we get there. Park. Berni runs to me. We hug and kiss and then she says:

"Dude you look so cute."

"Thanks B. So do you. Love the dress. Zimmermann right?"

"You know it...you look so skinny. Wow. What's your secret?"

"Idk. I juul a lot. Work out a ton."

"I've seen your stories. It's like gym and studio all day every day."

"True dat. This is Kins by the way." I pointed at the bubblegum nun.

"Hi Bérénice. I'm Kinsley Avital. It's a pleasure." She actually stuck out her hand for a handshake. Like a legit 50 year old.

B hugged her and then said:

"We're gonna have so much fun today. Skye I wanna hear all the tea on Jeff and the girls...ah I'm just so happy to see you babes."

We hugged again and she looked mad sexy as always. I was low key scared to bring her around Jeff. He'd pounce in a second. See Jeff would never cheat on me but I did get this like insecure feeling that if he met someone smarter and skinnier and sexiest and just more perfect, he could've dumped me. And not gonna lie Bérénice was goals.

See she had this super sexy French accent that could just make any guy hard in one sentence. I mean if any straight males or gay/queer females read this, I wanna paint a picture. Supermodel skinny French girl comes up to you. She's wearing Dior from head to toe, has the body of a Bond girl, is like six feet tall in heels, has this short French-girl bob haircut and then...then she comes up to you at a bar or club or museum or wherever and says in her French accent:

"I fink...may-bee you should...buy me a dlink."

How many guys would need to change their pants right then and there? I mean seriously. I love how B tells me I look skinny and cute. It's like stfu lol. I know this is so bad to say but literally Bérénice and I would be bffs if she wasn't so friggin hot.

"Let's head inside. Kins you can meet my gramma."

"Is Lulu around?"

"She's out with a buyer for a few hours so you may miss her."

"Well def give her my best."

Anyway we went inside. The place had this dope vibe cause it wasn't too like uppity. It was like nice imported French furniture, an old fountain and then bottles of wine all over the place. I'd say the vibe was chill but chic.

"Hello girls" the OG Bérénice said. "B your friends are gorgeous. Where'd you get your dress?" She asked Kins.

"Thank you so much. And this? It's just Zara. I'm afraid I might spill something today." Kins laughed at her joke. (Was it a joke?)

"And sunny Skye you need to put some meat on those bones. You look like a twig."

"Thank you Bérénice."

"Seriously Skye...B we should have a baguette in the kitchen. Bring out some bread and cheese and one of the 2008 rosés."

"No I'm totally cool. We already ate." I said.

"Gramma I wanna give them a tour first...we'll take two bottles though. A bientot."

B grabbed some bottles and then we started walking around the outside. She handed both me and Kins bottles of rosé she just uncorked. And lemme tell you Kins and I didn't let a drop go to waste.

So we're walking through the rows and it's as gorgeous as you'd expect—just a zillion rows of perfectly aligned vines and grapes. The whole area was green and pretty. And the weather was sun with more sun.

"Dude" B said. "This is my fave spot for stories. I'll take one of each of you if you take one for me."

"Absolutely B. You know I've got 75K now."

"My my. Little Skye is growing up fast."

I was trying a few different poses in front of and around the vines and grapes.

Bérénice took literally a thousand pics and vids of me and eventually we made our choices.

"I wanna use an Audrey caption" I said. "B do you have service here? Google her best quotes. This low key has the potential to be one of my five best stories."

"I think you're wearing too much clothing for that" Kins said.

Anywho. We spent like 30 mins taking pics and vids and 15 mins figuring out the best caption. It was like me kinda hiding under one of the plants like peeking out. And I had this super low-cut top. And we edited out some of my excess arm and stomach flab. Oh and Kins gave me her sun hat. I was the one that discovered this Audrey caption:

"There are shades of limelight that can wreck a girl's complexion." In the end I think the story got like almost 30K views—no joke dude.

Then we kept walking along the rows and Kins was mostly quiet and observing but crushing her drink. B started vlogging and she included us in it and tagged us later. It was sweet. She was always a sweetie. But anyway, B's vlogging, and she's like:

"Out among the grapes. Another beautiful day in Water Mill. The rosé has been so wonderful this summer and just wanted to give a shoutout to all our fans. Bérénice Louise would be nothing without you guys blah blah blah." Boring shit. I don't remember what else.

I kissed her on the cheek and then Bérénice ended her vlog with: "Bisous. Bisous."

Last part of the day the three of us went to this dining room area back at the main place and just sat around drinking. Kins and I already finished are first bottles and were splitting a second. See she and I don't mess around. We're pros—for real. But not like alchy's.

"Gosh" Kins said. "you guys have known each other since you were five? Do you keep like a ton of deep dark secrets?"

"Idk about dark" B said.

"Well. There might be a few we can't share" I winked at B.

"Spooky. What *can* you share? I wanna know everything! You two are so cool."

"You know" B said. "I took Skye to prom. Remember babe? My beautiful prom date."

"Of course. How could I forget."

"Oh." Kins looked shocked. "Skye I had no idea. I didn't know."

"Know what? We were just like two besties without dates so we went together."

I swear Kins looked relieved or embarrassed or uncomfortable—such a weirdo.

"I don't understand" she said. "You two are so cute. You must've had 30 guys begging you to go with them."

"There were no like fun and cool guys at our high school" I said. "The school was great but the guys were all either super lame or like hyper douchebags. So I asked B to go with me."

"It was the right decision" she said in her sexy French accent.

"We both wore these black dresses. Absolute fire."

"Skye your boobs were basically on the floor."

"Oh stop you were the one with the dress that legit ended at your waist."

"I still think I dance better than you" she said.

"Oh we're not even in the same league sis. Maybe you can waltz better but if we're talking club dancing—like grinding, fist-pumping, twerking, it's me by a mile. I got that Puerto Rican blood."

Kins couldn't stop laughing and she actually did spill on her cheap Zara dress. I thought that was funny. Really we were all giggly and just super happy. Stress-free. Tranquility. I should hit B up soon. I'm getting major feels just thinking about that day and like prom and us snorkeling together when we were kids. Dude I hate getting old.

throw it all the way back to day two of that summer

I was sleeping in the middle of J's Cali King and he woke me up. And it was the special wake-up call he sometimes did when he needed me to do something for him. See we had this super-secret code. If he woke up first he'd kiss my right eyelid and say:

"It's gonna be a great day kid."

Every time he did that I knew he wanted me to kick the other girl out of our bed and help her find her way to the door.

That morning. Received the eyelid kiss and the code phrase. So. Action time. Grabbed the girl snoring next to me while J broke out his fave flask and then fell back to sleep.

I grabbed the girl's things, thanked her, hug and kiss. And then she was gone. J and I had probably done that morning routine like 10 times. J and I were always so in sync, you know?

Anywho. I toss on a sports bra and shorts so Kins and I could head into town for spin. Oh and a drawstring too. With a change of clothes cause we were hitting Babette's for brunch. I didn't wanna waltz in there and have both the staff and wives be pissed at me. Been there done that.

Kins and I hopped in her car and drove to EH for spin. And the first thing I noticed was how she was essentially wearing a burka.

"Dude what are you wearing?" I said while she drove.

"What do you mean? Workout clothes."

"But like long-sleeve Under Armour and full-length leggings? Does Cash dress you so guys won't hit on you?"

"What? No way. I just don't feel entirely comfortable wearing a sports bra in public. Especially since I'm..."

"Flat?"

"What? No. Jesus. That was mean. I was gonna say: someone's guest."

"Whatever. Suit yourself. I'm just trying to help you out."

"Okay well maybe I should return the favor."

"Go for it."

"Insulting the figure of someone who's staying with you for three months isn't the way to start off on the right foot."

"No need to get all teary-eyed about it. I legit have no idea what you look like. You wear these like eskimo clothes. You could be the hottest 95-pound woman in the world or a 250-pound beast. I have no clue."

"Let's just change topics. Please?"

"Damn dude. Okay. But you'll be hearing a lot worse this summer around our house, so you gotta chill."

Cool. So it was our second day together and Kins was hypersensitive and I was gonna have to walk on eggshells all summer. Great.

She parked. We were basically silent. I think she hated me. W/e. I did a Harlem Cross to get to spin. Kins waited for traffic to pass. Then we took a nice long spin. Sweated out the toxins and just chilled (Oh and Harlem Cross is a term Jeff taught me. It's like extreme J-walking. You try to get as close to a moving car as possible without it hitting you).

Spin's done. Bathroom to change then walked to Babette's for brunch. We were basically still not talking but I knew I could get her to loosen up. If were being real, I can get anyone to loosen up ;).

"I like your outfit." I said basically kissing her ass to save the summer.

"Thanks."

She had on a white tee and white jean jacket. Idk. Cute brunch fit. White was her best color. And I had on my white Supreme hoodie and my red Golden Gooses. Or would they be Golden Geese? Fuck if I know.

"What should I get?" She asked.

"If you don't care about calories get the cinnamon swirl French toast. It's the GOAT."

"Eh I'll just get an omelet. You?"

"They have great juices here. I'm gonna get a watermelon lime juice. I'm technically on a cleanse, you know?"

So. We were sitting at one of the best outdoor tables and the waitress took our orders and went away. Still mad awk. I texted Astrid about how much I hated Kins and was pissed we'd be spending so much time together. But Asty gave me an idea.

"'Scuse me ma'am," I said to the waitress. "Can we get two mimosas ASAP?"

Astrid said we needed a little relaxation juice.

"That cool witchu?"

"Sure thanks."

It was low key working cause after Kins finished mimosa numero uno she felt like a non-robot. Food came and the second drinks came and things finally livened up.

"So Cash tells me you have quite the following on Instagram. How'd you do that?"

"Well you heard I make music so that certainly helps. And then I guess I just try to flaunt my body. Take some nice beach pics. It's not hard to figure out. The less clothes I have on the more likes I get."

"I think there are other ways to get a lot of likes. I told you I do this for a living right? I'm a social media manager."

"Yeah but it's definitely like different for a company versus one person."

"Hundred percent true but there's plenty of tips and tricks that work great for both. For example those first nine pictures on your page are crucial. And it's great if there's a theme or pattern, you know? Always ask yourself: how can I make this more aesthetically pleasing?"

"Sure..."

I'd finished my juice and we both downed our second mimosas. But now Kins was so locked in and engaged I could've put any food or drink in front of her and she would've drained it. Tbh when someone is talking about their passions there's not much that can slow them down.

"Some tricks I've seen work are color themes or even patterns. For example maybe you have a pattern of blue picture, white picture, red picture. And you keep rotating."

"Right. I know that. But like won't that look boring?"

"Not at all." Kins said. "You just need to experiment. You have baby blue and lighter shades in your first blue pic and maybe your reds and whites are faded or lighter colors. Then you get to the middle row and there moderate blues, whites, and reds. By the bottom your looking at navy, an almost grey-white and then perhaps a deep red/burnt sienna as your picture backgrounds."

"Seems like a lot of work and I don't think the results are gonna change."

"I'm sure they'll change. I've seen it hundreds of times. The other thing I like is if the outer pictures are all vertical but each middle picture in every row is horizontal. It's all about experimentation and what works for you but I could give you a ton of ideas if you're interested?"

"Yeah totally. I mean I'm all about my music and like staying in shape but if there's little tweaks that can help me get more followers and sponsors, I'm like let's fuckin go."

And that was basically it for brunch—mimosas/social media engagement. I paid cause I'd seen J do that a zillion times and you always seem like such a baller when you pay.

We drove back. Our two bfs lounging on *my* flamingo floats.

"Ladies bathing suits on." J yelled. "Hop in. We miss you."

"Be right there bae" I shouted.

I just sprinted right in. I had my sports bra and bike shorts on underneath. Idgaf. And to tell you the truth Cashie was definitely staring at my body. I just got back from the gym and had no food or water so I was looking tight. Why wouldn't he look? His gf just had a feast and definitely didn't burn off as many cals as I did. There was just no comparison.

"I'm gonna change into my suit." Kins said.

I think she was embarrassed. Kins must've known if you put us side by side in bikinis what guy would choose her? That's why she threw on her big ugly one-piece. It wouldn't draw attention. I mean after she walked outside when the three of us were in the pool, J just started laughing and said:

"Give us a twirl sweetheart."

Imo he had the best sense of humor. See Jeff had this great way about him. He just knew how to lighten the mood no matter what, where or when. Cashie and Kins—always uptight and anxious—just came across uncomfortable alotta the time. I typically wouldn't know what to do around people like that. But mi amor just always found the perfect thing to say. Sometimes our guests would laugh, sometimes they'd fight him or be pissed, but every time he'd get his reaction. That's what humor's all about tbh.

Kins was a good sport at the beginning of the summer. Like not gonna lie she got roasted plenty but fought back—tough Ohio girl.

Like here she pushed J off his flamingo float and we all got into chicken fights and just like that we were all loosened up and having fun. That's what summer's all about man. The vibes.

We even did swimming contests which I won most of and we did a who could hold their breath the longest contest. That happens to be an expertise of mine ;). I won by like 45 seconds. No cap.

Cool. So then we changed, drove into town and grabbed like a mid-afternoon lunch at Golden Pear. And it was funny that guy from that CW show was there. You know the tall one with the blue eyes. I'm bad with names. You'd know him if you saw him. He low key winked at me (And no cap means like I'm not lying fwiw).

Anyway I didn't get any food cause I was gonna do an IG post at the beach later and would be in my bikini so I didn't wanna look bloated. See getting and maintaining an Insta prof with 75K followers is no joke. It's a lot of hard work and not everyone is up for it. Point is I just got a Core Coconut Water and they all stuffed their faces with challah French toast, eggs, and then Cashie's whole...situation. I'll never forget it cause it was the least attractive thing about a very hot guy.

So Cashie got this monster sandwich right? Wasn't on the menu but he and his gf wouldn't order something from the menu if you gave them a zillion dollars. Their always needed to be something. No onions. No cheese. No tomatoes. Can I get that with baby carrots instead of asparagus?...but anyway that's not the point. The point is Cashie gets a huge gross meaty sandwich. He picks it apart instantly. Grilled chicken on the left side of the plate, bacon on the right, bread on a napkin next to his plate and then lettuce at the bottom of this mess. And he got a Core Peach Mango.

So. He eats the lettuce first and after every bite he must take a sip of his drink. And then he ate the bread. Again drinking like an ounce after every bite. Then he literally ate all the bacon and finally all the chicken. And NOBODY SAID A WORD ABOUT IT. EVER. It was the strangest thing. I must've eaten legit a zillion meals with him and it was like I was the only one who noticed. It was super gross and interesting at the same time. Like watching zit popping vids on YouTube. Maybe that's why he always orders steak with no sides at fancy places? Idk. W/e. Got sidetracked.

We go to Atlantic Ave Beach. Kins and I split this bottle filled with leftover mimosa—although let's be honest she essentially drank the whole thing while reading like "Social Media for Idiots." Sorry...W/e. I'll be nicer.

Realistically it felt cool being the youngest of the crew. Like here I am sipping Veuve mimosas and juuling hard with like basically full-grown adults. They clearly felt I was mature enough to handle whatever they did. And c'mon what's cooler than when cool people think you're cool? I mean it's not like I needed them to tell me I was dope cause I knew I was. But like it's nice to get...you know, validation?

It's funny. I drank all the time and was not 21 but like Hamptons police officers and the rich summer crowd get more upset when some Nassau County idiots are blasting their music at full volume on Main

Street while driving their Corollas then some 20-year-old sipping champagne.

Okay so I'm jc'ing. Kins and I were pretty drunk at that point. I was working on my tan. I snapchatted Brooklynn and Astrid. I posted a story on Insta #beachlife #betchlife. They're all reading and being boring. I think eventually J went into the water but I didn't join cause I just washed my hair after the pool and didn't wanna get salt in it (jc'ing—just chillin').

Eventually we went home and changed. Idk. Nothing else exciting happened. I was mixing in my studio when we got back. My stuff never sounds as good when I'm drunk. I played the sax a bit but I got motion sickness I think—idk dude. We got Cittanuova for dinner and then came home and Jeff and I had a little fun in the jacuzzi ;)

maybe it all could've gone differently

J and I sat at Navy Beach. I wanted to sit across from him and face the water but he told me our guests get the good seat. Although that sounded like bullshit to me. Anywho. My mood changed super-fast when "Jubel" by Klingande started playing over the speakers. I don't wanna ruffle feathers but that song may be the GOAT. Great vocals, awesome use of sax, super chill beat, love it every time.

Okay. So they show up. And as you might've expected I wasn't very impressed with Kins at first glance and was kinda dtf Cashie on site. See she was wearing one of her long flowy dresses. Super loose and baggy. No skin showing. I do remember her black hair being on fleek though. Meanwhile Cashie walked super straight and had these big strong shoulders and these nice biceps. Idk. I just thought there was so much power coming from him. You know, like his aura.

Next thing I remember is Kins immediately being freezing. I was like this basic thot can't remember to do the simplest thing? Hey sweetheart bring an extra layer when you're by the water. I knew that when I was in kindergarten. Cute Cashie instantly gave her his cashmere sweater that was choking his biceps. This made his super high maintenance gf smiley for like a hot sec.

What's next? Food orders I guess. They're all sitting there awkwardly looking at menus and I didn't even need to look. See J and I had literally the same taste buds and he always knew the best things to get on every menu. I let him order for me and tbh it kinda made me feel like a princess or something. It's silly. I know. But we were mf'ing relationship goals.

Look I don't wanna gush or anything but let's be real: Jefferson Campbell III and I were super cute together. I mean ever since my glo up at like 16, guys started looking at me differently. And if we're being real before I met J, I was with a lot of guys, girls and even a trans person I dug. But I realized Jeff was the only person I wanted to both chill with at like any hour and also just like rip their clothes off at any second. See mi amor was like a ferocious tiger and I was his sweet little puppy...actually wait...he was like a great white shark. The water did something to him dude. He had bde no doubt about it. And I was his super chill and playful dolphin. I guess what I'm trying to say is most importantly every single day I woke up next to Jefferson Campbell III I never knew who I was waking up next to. On a Monday he might be the sweetest, kindest, most loving S-O in history. Then by Thursday he'd be distant and wouldn't talk to anyone but me. Maybe Saturday he's in a yelling and screaming mood but never at me always at the world or something. And I loved every version of him the same, you know?

I'm sorry. Where was I? Cashie got a steak with nothing on it and nothing near it. And I still remember that night was when I first noticed he was taking a sip after EVERY. SINGLE. BITE—like a legit psycho. I also feel like I need to say this: I always get criticized for having my phone out when I shouldn't, you know? But just cause I had my phone out didn't mean I wasn't paying attention. Like I was pretending to text while watching Cashie eat. If I were just staring at him everyone would think *that's* weird. My phone gave me like invisibility.

Cool. So Kins was super annoying with her ordering. I wanted to be like: "sweetheart do you need attention that badly?" I remember she was meeting me and J for the first time that summer and was always like:

"Can I have a lime on the side and not in the drink?" And "Can I have the bearnaise on the side?" And "Can you not bring out the fish with the head still on?" And "Can you take out the crab meat? I don't want to have to break the thing apart." And "Can you peel the shrimp in the kitchen please?"

She was such a little brat. J was like:

"So I guess I can't take you guys to nice places can I?"

I will say J could have a harsh sense of humor but he was always right.

But I remember the whole dinner started awkwardly cause like no one was asking each other questions. So I decided to take on the starring role as per ushe.

"So Kins whaddya do for a living? You seem older."

"I'm 24." she laughed. "I work at a beauty start-up. I manage their social media. So I'm on Instagram, Facebook, LinkedIn, YouTube and Twitter every day. And I'm analyzing statistics and trends."

"That's your job? Sounds more like a hobby."

"Yeah. It's a lot of fun." She was all laughy and smiley the whole night. The world's brightest happiest gift. Ew.

I immediately thought she was a basic prissy princess—a spoiled little brat. But you know, and this should be a lesson to whoever reads this if you're gonna spend a zillion hours with someone put the claws away—for real.

So we talk for a bit but then everyone's silent again. And I'm thinking to myself: why is it my job to entertain everyone? Sooo not chill. Summer starting out with bad vibes.

"Cash how'd you and J reconnect?"

"Good question." He said. "We met up at the five-year Hollandsworth reunion and blah blah blah whatever." I don't remember what else he said.

He went off on some tangent and then started talking to Jeff about fantasy sports. Kins was just sitting there like a cult follower sipping her Kool-Aid and I was snapchatting Brooklynn.

This is a brief note but I think I should mention it before I forget. J always used to tell me:

"Nobody understands the intricacies of a relationship like the two people living in it."

I thought that was so powerful and true. Cause like I could literally spend tons of hours and pages describing Jefferson Campbell III and how deep our love was last summer but you still wouldn't get it. Any outsider would like nitpick and criticize every little thing. But to anyone like that who reads this: GTFO. J and I were rock solid. Two souls that were meant for each other. So if anyone doesn't like our love that means they just don't understand it or maybe they don't understand what love is in general. RANT OVER.

Jeff and Cashie talked about flag football or squash or whatever for literally 20 minutes. And I think something I realized when I first had my glo up...and girls this is a super important lesson...so LISTEN UP. The hottest guys...the dudes with the muscular bodies...are gonna talk about sports. They're gonna wanna watch football and play basketball and go to baseball games and there gonna spend hours talking about fantasy. You know what my advice is? Don't be the little thot that tells them to stop talking about their passions. Listen to them (or don't). Learn (or don't). Whatever you do, DON'T CRITICIZE THEM. J taught me sports bring everyone together. And he's right. I swear I started pulling hotter guys the second I became more chill and sportier.

"Skye who's this?" J asked about the background music.

"Flume."

"You guys Skye is an incredibly talented musician. She knows every EDM song. My girl is gonna be the greatest DJ in the world one day. She taught herself to play the sax, piano, and violin as a little girl. Ain't that right kid?"

"Stop. You're embarrassing me." Jk. I loved it. hehe. In my head I was like...Facts. All facts.

Lemme say something else. When you're a 20-year-old musician or actress or writer, it means the world when someone is praising you like Jeff was. He told me like every day how awesome my music was and how talented I was. Having someone outside of your family who just believes in you every step of the way…is just like, everything. Family, friends, and like true stans are all I really care about in the world. Like I don't need 50 Gucci purses and six cars (although I'd like a dope motorcycle one day. I told J that). I just need love. You know?

J and I were so cute together. Who would've thought? A Leo—element of fire. And an Aquarius—a love child. Cashie and Kins were both Scorpios. But truthfully she acted more like an Aries which is the worst star sign by far. Don't @ me. I bet she was an Aries Moon.

Ugh. Sorry. Back to Navy Beach. The waitress and manager were always coming to the table to check on J. They'd call him Mr. Campbell or sir. It low key turned me on. We were literally Hamptons celeb status.

Food arrived. We're all chewing away. J was telling them everything we're gonna do that summer. Not sure why they didn't ask me for ideas since I'd lived out there for 20 years straight but w/e.

Then I almost gagged watching Kins and Cashie feed each other. It's like grow up. You're not even cute together. But I didn't say anything. It was their first night and J needed me to be a good little host.

"J, I just want a quick bite of your…"

He gently held my hand and placed it on his lap. I guessed that was his way of refusing. Which was funny cause I was only trying to share ironically. I wanted Jeff to push me away. It showed we thought exactly the same. Relationship goals.

And after dinner I was craving chocolate cause I barely ate my fish. I high key needed chocolate in my life at all times. And tbh dessert at night is fine cause I'm not going to the beach or taking shirtless pics.

"J can I pwease have a widdle chocolate cake?" I'm guilty of using the baby voice to get what I want. He was obsessed with it.

"We don't need dessert, Skye."

He was right. Honestly I wouldn't be in the shape I am today without J. He motivated me all the time and I bet I'd have fewer Insta followers if he hadn't helped me with my figure.

So J gets up to "secretly" pay the bill which I always thought was so considerate. I mean he paid for legit everything last summer. And I make/made PLENTY of money but he always wanted to pay for me— my chivalrous bf.

We started playing cornhole which is def not my fave game because there isn't enough action. Like ping-pong is a much better party game cause you're moving around a lot and always involved. Cornhole is kinda tight depending on who you play with but tbh it can def get boring. Although actually I will say, watching J do anything was fun.

Sometimes he'd bring me to watch him play poker and he was just so intoxicating. You know? So focused and powerful whenever he did anything competitive.

Sorry. So Kins and I were next to each other and we just started chatting like legit sisters.

"So what's with this Hollandsworth place they went to?" I asked. "Are all the guys like them?"

"Do you think Cash and Jeff are similar?" Our dudes couldn't hear us.

"Oh totally. Both have got that like super proper/kinda spoiled vibe about them. They both seem super smart. They dress well. Treat girls nicely."

"*Really*? You think all that's true?"

"Idk. So what do you think it was like growing up on the Upper East Side? Must've been so sick."

"Not sure about that. You should ask Cash."

Kins and I were taking turns throwing our sandbags into the hole at the other end. I was better than her. That was clear to everyone.

"Your dress is really pretty btw." I said.

And that was no joke. See. I'd never have worn the clothes she wore last summer but I'd totally wear them at some point in my life. See if I hadn't painted enough of a picture yet, Kins dressed like I'd want to if I were a 35-year-old with two kids (not that I'd ever do that— shoutout birth control). And that's not necessarily an insult. I mean

Jeff leaned over, kissed me and I started rubbing his thigh. He and I never fought. We knew how to cool each other off. Not a lot of couples are like that.

We got to Talkhouse but there were literally a zillion people waiting in line. J turned to me and said:

"Nothing President Grant can't solve kid." He was so fucking dope dude.

He handed the bouncer cash and we were in. Unfortunately the venue sucked. Super crowded. Music wasn't even good and the surroundings were meh. W/e. I was turnt and started juuling into my purse while J went to find Orca: his Hamptons coke hookup.

Then some other stuff happened and eventually, I was in the bathroom and ran into some girl doing her makeup. Such a cutie and 100% mine and J's type. 18-year-old white girl. Tall, skinny, not too made up—a natural beauty. She was the type of girl who could dunk her head underwater and not be concerned about her makeup or showing her face, you know?

Okay so let's say her name was Amanda. She and I chatted. We were both like a little tipsy but again, she's high key super pretty.

"Your hair is literal perfection." I think I said.

"Thanks." She was so innocent and smiley. I knew J would love her.

"You should totally come meet my friend Jefferson. You two will for sure hit it off."

"Okay...um...cool."

I brought her to J who was probably coked out.

He was all hyper and we went up to him and he gave me a wink. J and I knew each other so well. Honestly his winks and our little secret codes were more meaningful than any bracelet or dress. Seriously I was the only girl in the world who was in on these codes.

So. He chatted with her and I don't remember what he said that night but he was so sharp—like flirty but not creepy, confident but not cocky. Within literally a minute I'm thinking she's dtf. And J noticed it too cause then came this part which is unusual for other people, I guess.

"Hey Amanda. I'd love for you to come and see my place in Sagaponack. Would that interest you?"

"Mmhmm."

"I have one question though because I care about you and your safety."

"Okay..." aWkWaRd.

"May you please show me some form of identification?" MAD AWKWARD.

The tall blonde girl had that same confused look on her face that all the girls got and so J continued:

"I just want to make sure you're safe and I'm safe. Cause safety's what's most important."

She handed him her driver's license and J inspected like it was one of Orca's coke bags. And then after he okayed it, he held both our hands and brought us to the bar.

Listen. I will say it was super embarrassing he did this. However when I tried to put myself in his mind and soul, I understood it. He didn't wanna do anything inappropriate and also like didn't want a younger girl to have any dirt on him. The Campbells were a super-wealthy, well-known family. Made total sense.

The funniest times were when the girl didn't even have a license. Sometimes it'd be a state ID, sometimes even like a college student ID or even them pulling up their Facebook account and showing their age there.

Anyway. I don't remember much else for a while. We drank more and sweated and did drugs and then were starving and got pizza. Legit I always wanted either pizza or chocolate at 1 am on weekends. It was a literal addiction. Plus the A/C was broken wherever we were. Idk. I was ready to leave a lot earlier. But after pizza J called an Uber Black to take us home.

See for anyone who doesn't agree with Jeff's lifestyle keep in mind how many other guys wouldn't do the stuff he does to stay safe. The carding girls and then leaving your car parked overnight because you realize you're too drunk to drive. Not many 22-year-olds do stuff like that. Gotta give him mad props, right?

We're in the Uber Black and X may have been involved at some point cause I just had this weird mood. I was staring at Jeff. Our eyes were 100% locked but neither of us leaned forward. And instead I decided I wanted to kiss Amanda. I wanted to see what she tasted like.

But so I ran my hand through her hair and she tasted like lemons.

We got to J's place and even at night the girl could see how massive it was.

"Jefferson, this is so huge." That girl was low key wet.

But then she got this surprised look cause J headed for the pool house first.

"Wait don't tell me you live in this itty-bitty place?" Amanda said. "Who lives in the big house? Your parents?"

"Chill kid." J said.

And then we just burst in on Cashie and Kins. I thought maybe we'd catch them having like missionary sex but they were basically just like asleep on the couch.

Actually now that I'm remembering, that Amanda's eyebrows were on fleek. She was super cute. Maybe I should look her up somehow. She seemed wealthy too.

"Cashie come on. Let's go swimming." I said. "Join us."

"Guys we're trying to sleep here. Some other night." He said.

But if we're being realistic, I bet if Kins weren't there he would've joined us. He probably would've brought Amanda back to the 2nd floor of the pool house tbh. I never blamed Cashie.

"Skye seriously. Get out. Let us sleep." Kins shouted from the couch.

I had no problems with her at the beginning but she just seemed to get offended by everything Jeff and I did. Dude. It was summer. Chill da fuck out.

"Jefferson let's go swimming." Amanda shouted and took her top off.

And then we all got into it. Me, J and Amanda took everything off but our underwear and dove backwards into the pool. Although I got out right away and started blasting a playlist from my Spotify.

"Turn that off please." Kins opened the front door of the pool house and shouted.

"No can do, sweetheart. House rules." Jeff said.

She slammed the door shut—her loss.

Although in the end we only swam for like 10 mins cause I felt bad for Cashie. I just whispered in J's ear:

"I need you now."

And that's all it took. He and I raced back to the patio and Amanda was jogging behind us carrying her clothes.

"Ladies I'm gonna pour us some drinks. Skye, toss on some music. Something beachy. You two should have a dance-off."

He mixed me my amaretto sour. He drank Bushmills straight and then he brought out some cheap Svedka he had all our girl guests drink. Then Jeff told me to set up the room while he spent a few minutes alone with Amanda.

I skipped up the stairs, changed out of my wet clothes, grabbed the camera, positioned myself in the red room and waited.

Obvi I'm gonna fast-forward past what happened in there but I do wanna quickly discuss something else you've probably been wondering about: OUR HOUSEGUESTS.

See a few weeks after J and I met back in 2017 we talked about exclusivity. It was something like this:

"J you're the only guy I want. I'm not interested in other guys right now. I hope that's okay?"

"That's really sweet of you to say kid." He kissed me so gently but passionately.

"How do you feel?"

"Well kid I've never been a one woman guy before. We're so young and have so many options at our disposal."

"Don't you think we're special together?"

"Of course baby." He kissed me again.

"Well maybe we can come up with some kind of agreement? Cause I'll literally die if I can't be your girlfriend."

"Jesus. Don't be so dark. You're wonderful and I love you. You know that."

"You do?"

"Of course I do kid."

"Well I have an idea then." SEE. IT WAS MY IDEA.

"Shoot. I'm always open to suggestions."

"So I know I'm only 19 but I've been with girls before."

"Um...what?"

"You heard me. Lots of 'em."

"What's happening?" I rarely caught him off guard so this was a huge surprising twist.

"What if we...Idk what I'm even saying...but like what if we kinda did stuff with other girls...together. You know?"

"How do you mean?"

"We'll be official boyfriend and girlfriend right?"

"Okay..."

"But if we see some super sexy girl we could bring her back to your place...and you know...share her?"

"Wow. This is...I mean..."

"I've got the great Jefferson Campbell III speechless?"

"A lil bit yeah." He laughed and kissed me again.

"We'll just test it out and see what happens okay?"

"That's totally fine with me as long as you're comfortable. I don't want you doing anything that makes you feel uneasy."

"This is my idea J."

"You know what? This could be a lot of fun."

He and I kissed and were madly in love. I don't think he'd ever been happier with a girl than he was with me on that night. And that's all it really took to snatch up one of Manhattan's most eligible bachelors.

the moment you've all been waiting for

So. We're back at the Labor Day white party now. Remember from earlier? It was all about creating a fomo atmosphere with great music, celebs, cool activities and just the chillest people.

I wound up DJing for maybe two and a half hours. I played a bunch of my new hits and then some of my all-time faves. The first 60 minutes looked something like:

"D-U-Fly" — Skygreenii
"Bikinis and Bellinis" — Skygreenii
"Tranquility" —Skygreenii
"East Hampton Vibes" — Skygreenii
"Your Juul Baby" — Skygreenii
"Die for You, Daddy" — Skygreenii
"Bliss" — Skygreenii
"Thigh Gap" — Skygreenii
"The Ocean" — Mike Perry ft. Shy Martin
"Remind Me to Forget" — Kygo ft. Miguel
"Krishna" — Dropgun
"Hey" — Fäis ft. Afrojack
"Jubel" — Klingande
"Here for You" — Kygo ft. Ella Henderson

And so I'm killin it. And when I have the audience on my side I feel truly blessed and I can legit go all night. That evening was weird though. I just entered into these like five-minute trances, you know? I disappeared into my own world and the music. I remember focusing on like one of the dancing girls and just locking eyes and zoning out.

There was this one girl who had a pacifier in her mouth and she just kept rooting for me and cheering me on. She was the only person who was able to dance nonstop for my entire set. I don't know anything about her but as a DJ having the full support of your fans is absolutely everything.

Anyway J's just chilling on the new diving board he put in. Just sitting there with his legs hanging down, sipping on his flask. This man was the definition of too cool for words. He must've just been there for like 90 mins. The dude was hanging back and watching everything that happened—like a God. He seemed so at peace. Almost like a corpse.

But then all of a sudden he got up. And I was startled at first. I almost stopped my set and stared because it was just like SNAP, and he was up and had a purpose. He literally jogged somewhere and found DJ Cree Mashun and had her walking beside him and toward me.

Quick stop here though. Not gonna lie DJ Cree Mashun was really good. She had this exotic super unique look. Had way more followers than I did and her music was strange and great. It was this mad fierce hardcore dubstep style. HUGE drops. Some occasional out-of-nowhere heavy metal riffs, crazy experimentations with tempo and rhythm, and dude she was six-feet-tall. Cree and I haven't produced anything together yet. But I'd one hundred percent be down. Although our styles are so different I'm not sure how we'd mesh. But she's a high key genius. Idk. Maybe I'll reach out to her one day.

"Hey kid." He shouted as he took one headphone out of my ear. "Cree here is gonna tag in for you. That cool?"

I nodded and DJ Cree Mashun smiled. Then J held my hand and escorted me through the moshpit and up to the master.

He unlocked the door, we went inside the soundproof room and then he locked it again.

"Are you okay daddy? You seem off."

He didn't say a word but started kissing me. It was weird though. He was super gentle and sensual. Kissing my lips ever so softly. Everything was in slow-motion. I was kinda taken aback. It was just so…romantic. He wasn't acting like a Leo at all.

"I love you." He said.

"I love you too. Are you okay?"

He took off his shirt. Revealing that super-hot body.

"Are you okay with this? You consent?"

"Yes. Yes. Of course. But please talk to me."

"Shh." He put his finger to my lips. "I love you so much."

And so fast-forward and then we were lying in bed together. My head was resting on his chest. And he was fast asleep in seconds. I felt his heart beating like mad quickly. The whole scene was mad eerie dude. I mean it was really romantic and beautiful and loving but it just wasn't like him or us, you know? He kept telling me how pretty I was and how beautiful my hair was and how sexy my body was and how my boobs were perfect and everything about me was exceptional. I was the sexiest girl in the world he said.

"I love you so much Jefferson Campbell III." I said. Although he was still fast asleep.

I decided to leave him alone and let him unwind. I wanted to go and join the party for a bit to hear Cree's set. I was gonna check on him later.

So I went downstairs, grabbed a handful of pills from the monitored pill station (don't remember which lol) and went to the moshpit.

I guess I was just fist-pumping the rest of the night. I felt so happy. The music was sick. I had the best boyfriend in the world. My life was just so perfect. Unfortunately I don't remember anything else that well. I probably went to join J by 3 am. Passed out next to him while the party was still going on.

the morning after the party

Jefferson Campbell III died in his sleep that night. I guess he OD'd on some pills or bad coke or something. But when I found him lifeless at 7 am I completely and totally lost it. Panicked. Screamed. Slapped him across the face. Poured water on him. He was gone. Grey as the October sky dude. So then I needed to act. Idk why I thought I needed to hide his body but that was my first thought.

I'd seen so many movies and TV shows where people get blamed and arrested for stuff they didn't do. So I just freaked out and entered into SVU mode. I was a famed DJ with 75K followers and made somewhere in the six figures that year. I wasn't gonna let this ruin my career before it had truly taken off. I know I sound like such a psycho and looking back on it, I was acting totally psycho but I'm just reporting what happened.

I grabbed dead Jeff by his legs and yanked him off the bed and onto the floor. He was super heavy and I knew I couldn't lift him so I acted quickly and decided to bring him to the red room which was super secure.

I took a few sips of his scotch and then pulled him by the legs from our master to the red room. I dragged him into that crazy hideout. I wasn't even thinking. I was in full-on ferocious tigress mode.

So I don't wanna go into like too many details but we had these big rings or hoops where people could hang. And the first thought that came to my mind was to drag J to that area. Then I tied a bedsheet around his neck. And I just sort of had him hang there. I was bawling my eyes out, no lie. I then locked the soundproof room and went downstairs to sleep on the couch for a bit. And I may have taken a Valium...or two...or six.

Then Cashie came by and woke me up.

"Skye what's going on? Are you okay? Where is everyone?"

"They're all gone. J too."

"What do you mean?"

I was crying hysterically and super groggy.

"J left. He's not coming back."

"Of course, he is. Take a deep breath. Did you take anything?"

He sat next to me and put his arm around my shoulder. That's when I saw my out. Cashie was such a nice person. A beautiful human. He could've been my savior.

"Cashie I want you now." I took off Jeff's robe that I was wearing and was totally nude.

He got this weird look on his face but then took off his shirt and said:

"Finally. I've been waiting so long for this."

"You have?"

And he started kissing me so deeply and with so much passion I thought I might die.

"Skye you're the sexiest girl I've ever seen."

"But what about Kinsley?"

He and I were both fully naked, and we couldn't stop making out.

"Fuck her." He said. "She's so basic. I've just been waiting for you to make a move. To show me you wanted me too."

He just railed me on the couch and it was literally the best sex of my life. So romantic, but also we were like animals. We couldn't keep our hands and lips off each other. And when it was over, I asked:

"What are we gonna do about Kinsley?"

Cashie was stroking my hair and licking my nipples while I ran my fingers along his big biceps.

"I know what you and Jeff do."

"You do?"

"Of course. I'm not an idiot."

"So what?"

"So I think you're both high key so sexy." He said. "You're the two hottest girls in the world...you're number one, of course."

"Duh."

"So I told Kinsley to wait 30 minutes and then come join us in here."

"How'd you know Jeff would be gone?"

"I just did."

Cashie and I started kissing again.

"You know I don't like Kinsley." I said.

"Neither do I. We'll put up with her for a few months and then I'll dump her and it'll be the two of us for the rest of our lives. How's that sound?"

"Heaven."

Then Kinsley started walking from the pool house to the back patio. And just as she opened the door and saw us kissing on the couch, she ripped off her clothes and pounced on Cashie and me...

OKAY. OKAY. I'm sorry lol. I can't do this anymore. Jk. Jk. None of that stuff happened. Did I fool everyone reading this? Sorry not sorry. I just thought everyone else's sections must be super serious and blah blah blah. I just wanted to lighten things up a bit. Hope you enjoyed that but now to the real ending...

the real ending. this is what really happened. I promise.

I woke up alone on the couch the night after the party. Some nude caterer was sleeping on the floor near me. Could've been anywhere from 6 am to 10:30 am. But right when I got up I felt something was wrong.

See anytime I fell asleep before Jeff or slept later than him he'd always place a blanket over me and a pillow under me and kiss me goodnight. This was the first time that summer he didn't do that. So, idk. The whole day's vibe was off. I had this psychic feeling in my heart Jeff was having a problem.

I kicked out the last few stragglers. Had the house to myself.

I called out for Jeff and even tried like dialing his cell but he wouldn't answer. His car was still there so I now was incredibly freaked out. I checked every room. Dude vanished. No note. No text. Nothing. So I took two Valium which I chased with some scotch. Fell asleep.

"Skye are you okay?" Cashie shook me awake.

"What? Yeah. I'm fine."

"What's going on? Where's Campbell?"

"Gone."

"What do you mean gone? His car's still here."

"Nope. He disappeared. He's not coming back. Ever."

"How? How do you know? I'm gonna get Kinsley. I'll be—"

"Don't."

I covered up and took a few deep breaths cause I was high key worried.

"Have you been drinking this morning?"

"No."

174

"Listen Kinsley and I are leaving soon. We're all packed. But we'll wait here with you until Campbell returns."

Cashie came over, hugged me tightly and placed my head on his shoulder. Such a sweetheart.

"Everything will be just fine. If you want us to stay, we will. Otherwise we'll call Jeff from the road and get this sorted out."

"No you won't. You can't."

"Do you want to come back to the city with us? Might make you feel better. Kinsley's got some dope pipes, and she needs a girl duet partner."

"I'm going back to sleep."

I exhaled as he walked outside to leave.

"J and I will be together in some way or another."

Cashie and Kins left and I was all alone. I was scared. My first thought was I needed to take my mind off things. J loved me and would get back to me as soon as he could. So I decided to put on my bikini and go to his beach to sunbathe and think.

But as you may have guessed as soon as I got there I saw "Skygreenii" the jetski flying across the waves. There was the love of my life.

"Hey kid." He shouted from the water. "I'll come in in a sec. You can drive today."

I was beaming. He was completely fine and I was completely fine. We were madly in love and nothing bad would ever happen to us.

He returned to shore, kissed me as hard and deep as ever and then wrapped his arms around me as I drove us out.

"That was sus." I said.

"What? There are only maybe four places I could've been if my car was here."

"True."

"Jesus Skye. You're shaking. You take something?"

"Yeah."

"Well slow down. I drank a little too much and don't want to be throwing up on you."

I drove us in circles. He wasn't missing but I felt kinda empty. And maybe a little bit horny. See. Jeff was the love of my life but maybe I wasn't ready to be with my soulmate yet, you know? I can't be the only girl who's had that feeling before right? Idk dude. I wasn't feeling like myself. Not sure if I was high or drunk or just insane.

I decided to stop the jetski in the middle of the water. We were all alone and too far from shore to be seen. I ripped off my bikini and started kissing him.

"Wow kid. So aggressive today."

We started having sex but stopped for a moment so I could take the letter opener I'd hidden in my hair.

"Skye baby? What's going on?"

"What?"

I kept riding him while running my fingers along the letter opener I snagged from his kitchen. I was scared.

"Easy now Skye."

I held the thing up to his cheek and then his neck.

"How's that feel? I'm in control now."

"Maybe put that...oh that feels so good...away."

"Make me."

He took his hands off my boobs and reached over to grab the letter opener, but I was too quick. I shoved it into his neck and got blood everywhere.

"Et tu, Skye?" J said.

There was blood gushing down his body and he was shaking. I was calm though—for the first time in a while. I stood on the jetski and felt the tranquility wash over me. There was no need to stress. Everything would literally be one hundred percent great—like always. I never made mistakes. I'm an Aquarius, goddamn it.

I pushed his corpse into the water and then skied back to shore. I then wiped as much of the blood off of the boat as I could and ran back to the house.

I packed two bags: one with like all of my clothes and stuff and the other with things I stole from the house. It was a nice haul too. I got a rollie, a gold bracelet, a YSL wallet, a ton of cash from his safe, a special picture, the keys from the Audi and those black Fendi shades he loved so much.

Changed outta bloody bikini.

Then drove my new Audi literally 100 miles an hour to gramma's place. I was crying super hard but she squeezed and consoled me.

"Gramma. We were...jetskiing and then my darling Jeff fell in the water. And then I tried to lift him out but like there were four sharks literally surrounding us and they took a bite out of his leg. I was so scared. And they kept eating him."

"There there angel. It'll all be okay. I'll call the police. What an awful awful thing to happen to such a nice young man."

After a few days of talking to cops and answering questions, I decided I needed to pack my things and move. The Hamptons and really the East Coast weren't for me anymore. It was just like too stressful.

So I called Astrid and told her I was driving the Audi to LA and needed to stay with her. So...it was a pretty wild September for me.

Anywho. I can't tell you where I am now or who I'm with but if you follow me on social you probably know. My music career is as strong as ever and I'm truly very happy. I have my ride-or-dies, my music and my beautiful soul. I hope whoever is reading this is rooting for me. I'm rooting for you <3. At this point in my life the most important thing I've learned is there's nothing and no one who can stop me from reaching my dreams and achieving the fame I deserve. #blessed

Dude. I'm just fucking with you. I literally made that section up, too. I know. I know. You hate me lol. Jeff's alive. Just trying to have fun with you guys! You should know me well enough by now.

Jefferson Campbell III

DEAREST READER, FOR STARTERS, ALLOW me to assuage your concerns: I'm very much alive. I felt it important to begin on that note because I know Skye is penning one of these summer parables, and she has a vivid imagination. If I were in your position, dearest reader, I wouldn't believe a word she writes. However, I suppose the most valuable feedback I can give you, whoever you are, is please do keep an open mind. Nothing you read in any section should be treated as factual. Thoreau once wrote:

"Rather than love, than money, than fame, give me truth."

Now those are the words of a poor man. Because truth is nothing more than snake oil or pixie dust or love. It's a made-up word about a made-up thing. I'll take tangible goods and cash over non-existent ideals any day of the week. But alas, on to the matter at hand.

You see, this is an important story that needs to be told. And my goal here is not to posit that I'm the debonair hero of this tale or a modern-day Don Juan, but rather to weave a narrative with assiduous precision you shan't find in any of the other sections.

If Kinsley's section comes first, I may be seen as an onanistic brute. Or if Skye's assuredly pernicious ramblings precede mine, you'll have an entirely different view of Jefferson Campbell II's supposedly hedonistic son. All I ask, dearest reader, is you reserve your judgments until my bloviations have ceased.

Frankly, my writing of this story is long overdue, but not for the reasons you may extrapolate. If there's one unforeseen benefit to having your undivided attention for the next hundred or so pages, it's to present myself as an inimitable protagonist.

Now, before I drive myself to drink due to my self-proclaimed circumlocutory prose, my simple point is the clear plurality of protagonists in modern-day society—be it novels, films, or television shows are—for lack of a less truculent term, losers. Basic, unoriginal losers.

Dearest reader, I know you must be a sagacious, winsome, and inquisitive person, and that's why I implore you to think back to your favorite characters throughout the past decade or two. What percentage would you describe as say, introverted? Better yet, how many have a great deal of success with whatever gender they lust after? Of these protagonists, dearest reader, what fraction of them are truly happy to be where they are and when they are? My point is, I'm here to speak on behalf of the class of people of which your typically starry-eyed, rich in dreams but not in money leads are consistently ranting covetous thoughts.

7/4

HAVE YOU, DEAREST READER, EVER offered your mind the privilege of consuming Virgil's *The Aeneid*? Everyone can relate to the unassailable warrior, Aeneas, who sojourns throughout the Mediterranean in search of his destiny. However, the particular part that's been entrenched in my mind for some time is his exit from Carthage.

I apologize to the illustrious scholars reading my story who have devoured Virgil on a myriad of occasions and are reading my tale as an escape from their typical jaunts to ancient Rome. However, I'm requiring myself to bore you with my thesis before our deep dive into the debatably laborious summer.

The valorous Aeneas peregrinated to Queen Dido's Carthage. And upon meeting the woman, he found her to be quite alluring. Despite the fact he needed to found Rome, as per his destiny, Aeneas' ardent heart told him he could settle down and live an idyllic life with the lovely queen. However, despite the grapplings of his superego and id, our hero left his ambrosial love behind because his fate lay elsewhere.

And so that transitions us to me, the volcanic Skye Pellegrini, the loyal Cash Moreau, and the mystifying Kinsley Avital sailing out along the tempestuous Atlantic. The latter two were staying in the Campbell Manor pool house for the summer of 2018.

"Jeff," the black-haired beauty said, "this boat is unbelievable."

"Thank you, Kinsley, my dear. It's a 38-footer, gifted to me by the magnanimous Jefferson Campbell II."

"Campbell, what's the farthest you've ever taken her?"

"I don't consider her for thousand-mile excursions, but she's gotten me to Martha's Vineyard and Newport in the past. Have a peek below deck. *The Aeneid* has a bed, a little shower, toilet, kitchen, fridge, and microwave. I've spent a week aboard in the past. Love this lady."

Skye gave our guests the full tour, and of course, upon returning above deck, my frisky companion had our full picnic in hand.

"Campbell, this is awesome. You've really outdone yourself."

You see, dearest reader, I always aim to please. I'm part of a surprisingly select group of humans who are at their happiest whilst making others as ebullient as humanly possible. On this day, that meant chips, salsa, guacamole, truffles, strawberries, and Bellinis. I've always prided myself on understanding my friends' taste buds, and here I had erected a pristine picnic for all their peripatetic palates.

"J, can I play my music?"

"Not this moment, kid. I want our guests to obtain a true taste of the sounds of sailing on the same ocean Columbus, Vespucci, and Magellan once did."

Skye always had me call her "kid." It was a bit Neanderthalic as far as nicknames go, but I'd postulate the reason Skye loved it so much was because of her greatest fear: aging. My lovely girlfriend frequently spoke in her baby voice and enjoyed being referred to as "kid," and I may let you know about some of her bedroom quirks on a later page. She was a sui generis young lady to say the least.

"Isn't this positively stunning, sailors?" I said.

"Gosh, Jeff, I'd be out on the water every day if I could. This is such a dream."

"Yeah, Campbell, seriously. This is quite the life you've got."

"You two should come back here and man the tiller. I'll teach you some simple rope ties."

And so, the two of them joined me as the sultry Skye spun her hair around her index finger.

"Kinsley, you grab hold of the tiller and keep it straight."

"This is simple enough," she said while white-knuckling the mahogany.

"Moreau, grab this rope here. I'll teach you the bowline."

My loyal friend grasped the double-braid and was listening intently.

"This is the essential one, Moreau. We can use this to secure sheets to the clew of our headsail."

"Okay," he chuckled. "Just tell me what I gotta do."

A big, happy family. Skye was sunbathing and shooting me seductive looks, Cash was fumbling with the bowline knot, and Kinsley was running her olive hand through her lush locks.

Ms. Avital was a special young lady, and therefore, Moreau was supremely lucky. I saw this statuesque young woman steering my boat and felt fortunate. On that day, she wore rose-framed Aviators that matched her pale-pink one-piece and then encased her body in a white shawl topped by a straw hat and accessorized with a Miansai bone-faced watch. Ms. Avital never dressed too skimpy or tawdry. The young woman was dignified. As refined a 24-year-old as I'd ever encountered. However, her outfits were only the exordium of what was a magnificent young woman.

As you'll come to find, Kinsley was a brilliant person with a sparkling affability that could charm even the foulest curmudgeons. Her ineffaceable optimism made her a joy to be around, and I think she's the absolute apex when it comes to what can only be classified as "wife material." Moreau was a damn lucky man. Damn lucky. Sometimes I needed to beware of jealousy. It is the green-eyed monster, which doth mock the meat it feeds on. But I digress.

At that moment on the boat, I remember dealing with a brief fit of ennui, so I uttered the following day-shifting line:

"Skye baby, you want to join me below deck? I think our new first mates have the boat under control."

"Are you sure, Campbell?"

"Point the damn thing straight. You're surrounded by water with no impediments. Enjoy yourselves."

I closed the door behind us, and Skye's bikini immediately fell to the floor. But before I could take care of her, I needed a little help from my pal, Orca.

"Pop. Pop. Pop," Skye said as she skipped to the kitchen counter.

My girlfriend, like many of our nation's youth, was an ecstasy lover. She was an adventurous sort, and there was indeed no pill Skye wouldn't try. Skye was a master alchemist who frequently experimented with a plethora of pill combinations. On a near-daily basis, I'd hear phrases like:

"J, what happens when you take Advil with X?"

"Is it okay to chop Percocet and Adderall, mix 'em and snort 'em together?"

"What's something safe, but cool, to lace my weed with?"

And it was my old Hollandsworth running mate, Orca, who supplied our every need. He was a unique sort. A rarity who abandoned his genteel background and fell in with the iniquitous dregs of Nassau County society. So, dearest reader, if ever a person tells you that you can't change your place in life and nature far outweighs nurture, remember even those with everything will throw it all away. You see, dearest reader:

"Reputation is an idle and most false imposition, oft got without merit and lost without deserving."

After a quick line or two, I walked to the king-sized bed with the navy duvet and called to Skye:

"Kid, care to join me? You quite finished over there?"

She didn't hear me. *"Dans la lune,"* as the old Hollandsworth French teacher would say.

"Skye," I said louder.

"Oh. What's happening? What's going on, J?"

"You know, I'm worried about your ears. You must keep the volume down on your headphones."

"Make me."

"I'm concerned you're damaging them at such a young age."

"If you were so concerned, maybe you could stop shooting your loads in my ears? That probably doesn't help, right? I'm not a doctor, though."

"Someone looking to get spanked?"

"I thought you'd never ask, daddy."

The pneumatic Skye slithered over my lap and placed her ass in front of my face.

"Daddy, I've been a bad little girl, haven't I?" She spoke in that baby voice of hers.

Now, some men are perturbed or will even castigate their female companion upon hearing this type of voice for the first time. I wasn't one of those troglodytes. You see, I've found the most important dogma I'd pass down to the college-aged person has to do with not shaming someone for their kinks. It's not my job to quell Skye's spirit. I emboldened her. Constantly.

I'm quite abashed by this upcoming brief pilgrimage into my past, but I do believe this anecdote is imperative.

When I was just a fetching 11-year-old, I was at my friend TR Mathewson's Hamptons house. We'd spent the afternoon playing Wiffle Ball in the backyard with his father and then would be driven out for ice cream—your typical, jovial summer day in the closest approximation this world has to Eden.

Six of us hopped into his father's BMW. TR's parents were situated upfront, his older sister behind the driver, TR himself in the middle seat, and me on the right. However, TR's six-year-old sister needed a place to sit. She was a cute rambunctious kid with long blonde hair and a perdurable smile.

"I'll sit on Jeffy's lap," she shouted after discovering her limited options.

I laughed as she climbed aboard, and TR's father began driving down Breese Lane. An old Tom Chapin song started to play, and apparently, it was TR's sister's favorite. The little girl began jostling and bouncing on my lap. And that's when it happened. I achieved my first erection. I was mortified and have kept that story to myself for my entire life up until this sentence. I've always cerebrated how Freud, or better yet Laurence Sterne, would have felt about that old childhood tale.

Anyway, I spanked Skye several times; each one was progressively harder and achieved a forte reaction. And next came our unmatched aggression centered around choking, slapping, pinching, clawing, and biting.

"Daddy, you feel so good. Please, daddy. I *need* it."

My spunky girlfriend simply craved me.

"You're so fucking sexy, Skye. Jesus fucking Christ."

"Slap me, daddy," she commanded. "Harder."

"You like that, baby?"

"Tell me I'm your little whore."

She was riding on top of me. Her massive double-Ds flopped around like beached whales.

"How's that feel, you filthy whore?"

"Oh, daddy," she shouted. "Please. Harder. Oh my God. Right there. Fuck me, daddy. You're so fucking huge. I'm just an itty-bitty girl, but I can take it." I continued to choke her.

"Now, I wanna taste you, daddy."

We shifted positions, and after Skye swallowed, we cuddled for a bit and then rejoined our companions above deck. We were as blithe and refreshed as ever. Skye was awkwardly stumbling around toward the stern, basically toppling after a few steps. That's what ecstasy, Bellinis, great sex, and choppy waters will do to a person.

"Kinsley dear, mind if I take over?" I asked.

"Sure."

"Skye baby, adjust the mainsail, please?"

"Yes, daddy."

She wobbled to the rope and began twisting, but her balance was still off due to our below-deck tryst and her homemade concoction of Lord knows what. Poor Skye teetered off to the starboard side, and the boom nudged her into the turbulent Atlantic.

Truthfully, I didn't notice at first. I had my shades on, and my eyes may have been closed at that time. Skye and I had just had one of our many indelible capers, and neither of us was remotely lucid. However, all worked out fine. Moreau and Kinsley helped me, and Skye was lifted from the ocean and brought back on board in no time.

I went below deck again because I needed a little pick-me-up and wanted to inspect Skye's body for any previously unseen bruises or scrapes.

"Skye," I shouted from behind the closed door. "I need you."

She burst through the door, and her wet clothes were on the floor in seconds.

"Like this?" she asked.

"Let me get a better look at you."

My nude girlfriend strutted over, bent down, and kissed me.

"How do I look, J?"

"Sexiest girl in the world."

"Really? You mean it?"

"Of course. I beat out every guy for your love, and you beat out every girl for mine."

"I love you, daddy."

"Love you too, kid."

It didn't take long before I was doing a few more lines, and she was tossing back a few more pills. Skye was bent over the bed and taking it like a champ just a few minutes after her clumsy little spill. What a little trooper she was. And dearest reader, while I loved her sprightly personality and competitive spirit, Skye Pellegrini was a stunning physical specimen.

Her body could only be stratified as alien-like. This exceptional beauty had what I'd call a top hourglass figure. Skye was about 5'4" and weighed around 105 pounds and had not a single ounce of fat on her. She was quite buxom with supremely toned abs atop her thin waist, and then her ass jutted outward. It was tight and firm. And then there were the tattoos and piercings.

Before Skye met me, she had six tattoos: a dolphin, crown, diamond, the word "Unconscious," Audrey Hepburn's face, and then the longitude and latitude of where her mother was shot and killed in Puerto Rico. Then I came along, and she added:

-a lion wrapped in a heart on her arm, that supposedly symbolized me since I'm a Leo
-the letters J and C, my initials, one on each of her inner thighs
-the date we first met on her ankle
-a left nipple piercing
-a clit piercing

Despite both of our innumerable flaws, I loved the girl. Like no one else. And that July 4th was a typical day in the life of Skye Pellegrini and Jefferson Campbell III.

We soon exited our love-nest and rejoined our loyal compatriots.

"Daddy, can I play music on your iPhone since you broke mine?"

"Sure, kid."

I handed her my device, and she bit my lower lip.

"And you'll buy me a new one tomorrow, right?"

"Whatever I can do to make you happy, kid."

"And headphones?"

"Of course."

"And a Gucci bag?"

"Why not?"

I let Moreau and Kinsley steer us back toward Montauk as fireworks began to illuminate the sky. The iridescent reds, whites, and blues fulgurated in the navy blue, star-filled expanse. My frisky girlfriend and I continued to kiss as she ran her hand through my hair. I glanced over and saw my loyal friend making out with his Aphroditian lady. It was one of those unsurpassable nights of which those who summer in the Hamptons frequently dream.

9/1

MY FATHER HAS BEEN A man of extraordinary promise ever since the day he was carried out of Mt. Sinai Hospital in 1965. He followed in his father's prodigious footsteps. Both men attended Hollandsworth then Exdover Prep outside of Litchfield and finally Yale. From there, my father could've worked at Goldman Sachs under my grandfather, but his entrepreneurial spirit led him to start his hedge fund, WhiteLava. As of Q1 2018, it had a total AUM of $7 billion.

The man was well-respected and driven, and then had the inveterate gift of knowing when to be bloodthirsty and when to be nurturing. Now, to that end, one of the many lessons he instilled in me was how to behave in every type of party atmosphere. This included both as a guest and, more importantly, a host.

Mr. Campbell II elucidated it's the host's job to produce two distinct emotions from his or her guests: happiness and envy. Therefore, on the eve of the first, I vowed to construct the most glorious party Hamptons' youths had ever witnessed. And that all began with a strict set of rules.

My guests were to arrive wearing their best whites, and that was non-negotiable. You see, dearest reader, there are certain areas where a host should improvise and others where one must, if you'll excuse the aphorism, stick to the script. And when it came to Hamptons' Labor Day parties, the all-white dress code was intransigent. Side note, I despise when women wear blue jeans. I've never seen a young lady wear blue jeans and then thought, yeah that looks good on her. Doesn't matter the fit or shape. I hate the blue jeans look on women. But, moving on.

In addition, I was obdurate about the catering. In my eyes, it had to be The Pratincole. It was always my father's most-treasured eatery, and if he happened to read about my soirée in NY's greatest paper, *The Post*, I felt it'd put a smile on his face.

But after those two fixtures were set, it was then my turn to improvise. I jotted down several ideas in my spare time, but felt having a partner to bounce ideas off could only be beneficial. Therefore, the weekend prior, I invited the omniscient Skye to join me in the living room to brainstorm.

"What are you gonna do about drugs, daddy?"

"How do you figure?"

"Well, I mean, no party is complete without party favors."

"People will bring their own and use in the bathrooms, I suspect?"

Skye was wearing this white Supreme hoodie with nothing underneath.

"J, mi amor, be realistic. You want this to be legendary, right?"

"Yeah. I already have a lot of ideas."

"You do? Like what?"

"We're going to have bouncers and security and won't allow anyone to drive home."

She yawned.

"What?" I said.

"What happened to happiness and envy, daddy?" She laid her head on my lap.

"Well, I have a pool, Jacuzzi, and beach for anyone to use."

"Who doesn't have that stuff?"

"You should DJ. And I'll DM some other DJs so you won't have to work the whole night."

"Now that's a good idea. And I assume you can find good use for that pole in the basement?"

"I'll make a call."

"Good. And for drugs."

"You and the fucking drugs," I laughed.

"What? You're the same way. Don't front."

"People can play video games and poker in the basement. I'll hire some dealers...card dealers that is."

"Make sure they're hot. Every woman at the party should be hot."

"You want photo approval?"

"The drugs, J. What about the fucking drugs!?"

"You tell me."

"Here's what I'm thinking." She sat up and held my face in her tiny hands. "You know how strip club bathrooms have those mint and gum and cologne stations?"

"Sure."

"Let's have a drugs station. Molly, percs, addy, coke, weed."

"I'll need to have a bouncer watch it like a hawk. Can't have anyone O'D. Gotta talk to the bouncer about drug limits for guys and girls depending on approximate weight."

"What a team we are."

"You're a fucking genius. That's why."

"Yeah, daddy? You like my big brain?"

"Uh-huh."

"How about my big tits?" She took off her hoodie.

"Love 'em."

"Well, I like this, daddy." Skye removed my pants.

"What are you gonna do about it?"

And then she skipped away.

"Skye, what the fuck?"

She was whistling away in the kitchen but returned with a jar of Nutella.

"Kid?"

Skye didn't say a word. She tore off my boxers and covered me in Nutella.

"How's that feel, J?"

"Pretty good, but it'll feel better if you're hungry."

"Starving. Haven't eaten all day."

"Well then, get to work."

Skye guzzled her weekly Nutella and semen smoothie and then joined me in the bathroom for a quick shower.

A week later, on the night of the party, all of mine and Skye's preparations proved to be fruitful. There wasn't a downtrodden face at the event. Skye invited a bunch of influencers, DJs, dancers, and actresses, and I brought my old chums from Hollandsworth, Exdover, and Yale.

Everyone loved the food from The Pratincole. With the filet du boeuf bites, various ceviches, and the chateau wines garnering the meritorious praise they deserved. Then, down in the basement, my eclectic guests played the ever-popular Nintendo 64 games, along with some no-limit hold'em. And then the evening's dancers were supposedly top-notch.

Halfway through the evening, I deduced we'd achieved an ample amount of both happiness from the partygoers and envy from social media dullards who were unable to reach VIP status. Those who weren't invited were forced to attend the party virtually by clicking from Instagram story to Instagram story.

Skye's tip about attractive women proved to be rewarding as 50 different people, both at the party and online at a later date, commented on how it was as if the Playboy Mansion were in the Hamptons. You see, dearest reader, I had an old Hollandsworth friend doing some entry-level photography work at *The Post*, and I gave the kid exclusive press access. It helped his career and allowed my shindig to be plastered within those infamous pages of New York's most scandalous paper.

Throughout the early hours of the party, I was sitting on the diving board, the metaphorical crow's nest, monitoring the comings and goings of my guests. My goal was to make sure everyone was enjoying themselves, and if they weren't, I was in an excellent position to spring into action. Now, that being said, I was living a profligate lifestyle that involved a silver flask and the occasional line of Peru's finest.

However, despite my languid behavior, one moment I shan't forget was when I spotted Ivee Petrapoulos while I was leaving my spot for the first time that evening.

Although I'm afraid I must delay that female interaction until the end of my saga.

It started Memorial Day weekend.

5/25

MY FATHER DROVE ME TO Litchfield, Connecticut for my first day of prep school many moons ago. And during that drive, he told me:

"Jefferson, you've been blessed with many atavistic traits the Campbells have all had since they sailed over prior to the French-Indian War. But, and this is of paramount importance; there are two blatantly obvious traits that can aid you in a rise in popularity both amongst your fellow man and your various love interests. The first, dear boy, is to ooze confidence. Your connate confidence should contaminate each and every room you enter. And second, dear boy, you *must* remain mysterious. This is particularly effective with women, you see. Keep your internal thoughts to yourself and don't reveal anything furtive unless you're sure you're surrounded by loyal parties."

That was only an abbreviation of one of many fine speeches my father gave me. But now, on to our first encounter with Moreau and his girl.

"Ah, Mr. Campbell, what a pleasure to see you this evening. Table for four, right?"

"Yes, my good man. Is this your first night working? I don't recognize you."

"Second weekend on the job."

"How are my friends treating you? How are Fabrizio and François?"

The still wet-behind-the-ears waiter led Skye and me to an indoor table next to a family of five.

"Here you are, Mr. Campbell."

"What the fuck is this shit?"

"Is there a problem, sir?"

"I'm Jefferson Campbell III, and when I come to Navy Beach, I sit outside on the fucking beach."

"J, should I get François?"

"Go on, Skye."

"Mr. Campbell, I'm afraid this is the only available table."

"Do you know who my father is? Fucking imbecile. I'll get my own table."

I ventured outside and found an empty spot situated right in the center of the beach.

"Mr. Campbell," said the moron, scurrying over, "that table's reserved."

Luckily, Skye arrived with the manager because I was about to lose it.

"I'm so sorry, Mr. Campbell. Clark here is new."

"Well, make sure this doesn't happen again. Please do enlighten Clark as to who my father is. This is a special night for Skye and me."

"Yes, of course. My apologies."

"I want a new waiter, a complimentary bottle of rosé, and for my guests to be greeted like they're the fucking Duke and Duchess of Sussex, capisce?"

Moreau and Kinsley arrived right on time and joined us at the best table Navy Beach had to offer. And the second my friend sat down, my mind took me back to a turbid memory I'd forgotten until that very minute.

Every Friday afternoon, from first through third grade, Moreau and I would frolic together at the famed 84th and Fifth playground. Each week, the four of us were there together: me, Moreau, my house-keeper, and his. The latter two were *dans la lune*, speaking in Tagalog while toeing the line between neglect and indifference.

Meanwhile, Moreau and I would climb that prodigious slide the Parks Department has since amended. You see, dearest reader, back in the early-2000s, that specific park had a colossal pyramid-shaped structure at its nucleus. Then the cytoplasm was made entirely of sand, and various tire swings constituted the mitochondria of this playground cell. But again, most importantly, stood the pyramid slide.

It's no mystery why the park's design has since been altered. A decade ago, that 50-foot-high pyramid slide was made of metal. It was a shiny silvery material that seemed to have a sensual relationship with the sun. Moreau and I used to climb to the summit, and on those May and June afternoons, the infamous slide must've reached 120 degrees. The metal nearly burned through our designer shorts. My friend and I used to hold hands and glide toward the pool of sand, and we'd be screaming both in pain and joy.

Then, after what could've been anywhere from 30 minutes to six hours, Moreau and I begged our guardians to purchase ice cream for us from a local street vendor. My shorter, brown-haired companion would get a Chipwich, and I'd devour a SpongeBob popsicle.

And on the walk home, Moreau would give me his in-depth analysis on Donovan McNabb, Billy Volek, and Kyle Boller.

"Moreau, looks like I may be losing money on your Phillies tonight."

"Three-nothing Jays in the first, right?" he said as he pulled Kinsley's chair out for her.

"Remind me why I ever bet on Eflin? Guy's a grade-A bum. Kyle Kendrick reincarnated."

"Kinsley, how cool is this place? Campbell, Navy Beach is my favorite. Unbeatable views."

"You and your girl want a bottle of rosé?"

"No, I'm good, man. But lemme say, Kinsley and I are so appreciative of you hosting us this summer."

"Are you kidding?" I said. "You're one of my day ones. I'd take a bullet for you."

My childhood friend still hadn't developed a predilection for vino, but that was alright. The man had enough positives to make up for it. One of which was, of course, Ms. Avital.

She was, to use the parlance of our times, a smokeshow. Now, dearest reader, in case you were wondering what wealthy UES jerk-offs like me are interested in, it's a young lady like her. Ms. Avital was a woman from means who'd never embarrass herself in a public setting. She had a soupçon of snobbiness but had this convivial wonder about her that could impress any man or woman, regardless of age. And on top of her personality, there was the background.

Now, dearest reader, I don't want you to take this the wrong way. I need you to understand that you, like me, have personal preferences when it comes to members of the opposite (or same/different) sex. I, and I'm speaking for many of my dear friends from our old all-boys school, have an affinity for a certain type of foreign woman. I tend to lean toward ladies whose families come from Mediterranean backgrounds.

I believe we've all had that dream in our lives where we're able to build our ideal mate in a factory. And while I do have personality partialities, I'd probably end up molding her looks first. And in the end, my afflatus would have one-half of her family as fourth-generation Americans and the other as immigrants from a Mediterranean country. I'm a sucker for olive-colored skin. All Upper East Side guys are.

"This rosé is wonderful. Thank you, François," I said after a quick aeration.

"J, you should bring one back to the cellar."

"Now, Moreau, here's a crucial Hamptons lesson for you."

"Shoot."

"What types of new people do you think I enjoy befriending the most?"

"No clue."

"Well then, my friend, I'll tell you. I'm most happy when I have the pleasure of making the acquaintance of sommeliers, masseuses, club promoters, sports bettors and card sharks...oh, and fishermen."

"And DJs," Skye joyfully chimed in.

"You know, Jeff, I was wondering," Kinsley said, "why must people travel all the way to Montauk or Amagansett? Cash and I passed a bunch of lovely places in West Hampton and Quogue."

"OMG. J?" Skye looked as if she'd swallowed spoiled fish.

"You see, Kinsley," I said. "West Hampton and Quogue are like the Queens and Staten Island of Eastern Long Island. They may be driving distance from the true Hamptons, but nobody with even an atom of class or dignity would live there."

"Mmhmm. I see."

I ordered the hamachi ceviche for myself and the shrimp ceviche for Skye as appetizers and the soy-glazed tilefish and swordfish as entrées. I was genuinely proud of my girlfriend's diverse palate. By that time, I had a reasonably high success rate when it came to ordering something she'd enjoy.

Kinsley asked for the Atlantic salmon, which was also a razor-sharp play. Montauk had fabulous salmon and lobster. I'd put the town's fish and crustaceans against any on the East Coast.

But her ordering style left much to be desired. It was:

"May I please have the Atlantic salmon, but with asparagus on the side? Oh, you don't have asparagus? How about summer squash? You don't have that either? Huh. Capers then?"

It was like that everywhere we went. Even at The Golden Pear, she was adding and subtracting. I felt as though it was my place to tell her these were world-renowned chefs who knew our palates better than we knew them ourselves. However, I never wanted to put Moreau in a tough spot, so I kept my mouth shut. And anyway, that was an extremely minor foible. If I were Moreau, I would've given her absolutely anything she wanted. No matter what.

"So, Kinsley, what do your parents do?" I asked.

"Well, my father is a zoning lawyer in Cincinnati, and my mother's a homemaker."

"Brothers and sisters?"

"Two older and one younger. All boys."

"That'll toughen anyone up."

"They were always nice to me."

"And quite protective, I'd presume."

That was quite an enthralling night for me because I had to put on my best acting skills around Kinsley. You see, dearest reader, I learned from my father one couldn't have strangers stay in their home for months on end without knowing anything about them. While I trusted Moreau's judgment, I needed a smidgen of...additional comfort. Therefore, I had my father's guy do a background check on her a few weeks before the Navy Beach night. Anyone who comes from a name family and significant prosperity will understand my wariness.

As it turned out, one of her older brothers had an assault and battery charge, and the other older one had two DUIs to accompany his brief stay in a drug rehab facility. And while her father did have a net worth of $2.6 million, he had a penchant for African-American harlots. Kinsley checked out, though. So, overall, the Avital background check produced an eclectic amalgamation of facts I chose to keep to myself. In all seriousness, one may hate me and my uncouth processes, but it was the safe play. And in my opinion, 95 percent of humans are awful or evil in their own ways. We all have done horrible activities we're not proud of, and we all have disgusting and disturbing skeletons. Well, most of us do. I did wonder whether Kinsley or Moreau were in that saintly five percent.

"So, how'd you two, like, reconnect?" Skye asked Moreau.

"Well, Campbell and I met up at the Hollandsworth five-year reunion and were reminiscing about old times. He brought up his NL-Only fantasy baseball league he thought I'd be interested in, and that really reignited our friendship."

"Moreau, do you remember that time in first-grade when my father had four owner's box seats at Giants Stadium?"

"Oh, Jesus. Not this one."

"Cash, you never told me this," Kinsley said in her patented raspy voice.

"Moreau? You don't tell your girl everything? Shame on you."

"Go ahead," he said.

"So, ladies, I have four tickets. Sit in the owner's box. Can you imagine that? As a seven-year-old sports fanatic? Dream come true, right?"

Kinsley held Moreau's hand and smiled.

"Well," I continued. "As hopefully Kinsley knows at this point, Moreau hates all the New York teams. Some congenital hatred no one knows where or how it began."

Skye was scrolling through her phone at that point. Her elbows inappropriately planted on the table.

"My father called Moreau's father and extended the invite. His dad put mine on hold and asks little Moreau. You know what little Moreau responds? 'Who are the Giants playing?' Can you imagine that? Best seats in the house. Any child's dream come true. Moreau was a huge football fan. And yet, he has the gall to find out if it's a good matchup before accepting."

"Tell them the rest too," Moreau said with a coy smile.

"So, Moreau didn't want to see the Cowboys play. He said they sucked, and Quincy Carter and Chad Hutchinson were the worst QB tandem in the league. But his father convinced him, and they showed up. Unfortunately, Moreau was intent on rooting for the Cowboys, not because he liked them, but because he hated the Giants. So, there was a seven-year-old kid booing the Giants, sitting 10 feet away from the owner. I'll tell you, Old Man Mara lashed out at my father after that game."

Kinsley and Moreau started laughing, and then I heard an EDM song begin to play in the background.

"Skye, who's this? She knows every electronic song ever made" I had to involve my poor, ADHD-fueled girl.

"Flume. Duh. Sleepless."

"You like it?"

"Dull and repetitive."

"You know, you guys, Skye's an incredibly talented musician. Taught herself how to play the sax and violin as a child. Virtuoso. I'm so unbelievably proud of her."

"J, you're embarrassing me."

During that summer, I was particularly distressed about my future. My father wanted me to go to business school and then work for him, but aside from stocks, I had zero interest in finance. While it was unclear where I saw myself, I was often beguiled by Skye's music. She most certainly had talent and a solid following. Perhaps my calling was to help her? I thought there was a path to me becoming a music manager. I could've signed Skye and her friends. I had enough money to create my own management company. It would've been a compelling path with the added bonuses of money, being my own boss, and attending parties and events surrounded by beautiful people. But this all centered around the fact that I one hundred percent believed in her.

"Mr. Campbell," the manager said, "your food is arriving now. Will there be anything else?"

"Another bottle of rosé and an amaretto sour for Skye, please. Moreau, anything?"

"I'm all good."

We each began eating our food while I explained every single activity on tap for our next three months.

"You forgot about the ice cream at Scoop du Jour," Skye said after I finished. "Kins and I absolutely must go to the vineyard too. I have a friend that owns a winery place. So chic."

"Any other ideas I left out, Skye?"

"They should, like, ferry to Shelter. Sunset Beach is mad tight. J, tell them about all our favorite restaurants."

"Good idea. Well, there's Navy Beach, obviously. Then Sant Ambroeus, DOPO la Spiaggia, Tutto Il Giornio, The Crow's Nest, Lunch, Cittanuova, La Fondita, 75 Main, Coche Comedor, Solé, and, uh, Gosman's out by Montauk Point."

"That's a lot to take in," Kinsley said.

"Gonna be a hell of a summer, friends. Wait until you see the house."

Moreau and his girl then started feeding each other, which I'm vehemently against. It's one thing if you're alone in your own home, but if you order an exquisite meal from an opulent venue and then start shoving a porterhouse down your date's gullet, that's where I draw the line. But again, I kept my mouth shut. I wasn't going to mess with the evening's qi.

"Daddy, I want dessert."

"We don't need chocolate right now, Skye."

"Skye, do you want to play that cornhole game there?" Kinsley said. "Looks like fun."

"Sure." She leaped out of her seat, leaving me and my old friend alone.

The Skye dessert conversation was always a riveting one. We'd had discussions about it on countless evenings over our past year or so of dating, and I'd found it was a game I couldn't win. You see, dearest reader, after dinner, I had several options. First was to order Skye every dessert on the menu, but if she knew I was doing that, she'd never eat her immaculately prepared entrée. In addition, the following day, I'd get yelled at for allowing her to consume 2,500 calories of seven-layer chocolate cake and mint chocolate chip ice cream. Somehow, I was culpable. Second, I could ignore the conversation entirely and let her think for herself. However, this presented an issue because she'd spend 35 minutes figuring out what food to get and would whimper about how I wasn't helpful.

Thus, that summer, I frequently turned to option three: telling her we don't need dessert. This was the most advantageous route because she wound up smiling and thanking me for always thinking about her figure and Instagram following.

I paid for everyone's meals because my father raised a munificent gentleman.

Although, I will say, I never tip off the post-tax amount. Apparently, this has become a point of contention. But I find it rather ridiculous. You see, dearest reader, I always tip based upon merit. This can lead to an 80 percent addition or potentially a five percent tip if the service is dreadful and I have an inkling they spat in my food. But the waiter's performance has nothing to do with how much New York State is taxing me.

Anyway, Moreau and I joined our girlfriends by the cornhole game boards. Kinsley and Skye were tossing their sacks toward us, and we began playing a competitive game moments after a little chatter.

"So, you and Skye seem to be great for each other," Moreau said, now that we were out of earshot of our dates.

"I love her, man. What can I say?"

"I think that's awesome. You know, she's not the type of girl I would've pictured you with."

"Me too, but I finally found the type of relationship I want. Weirdly enough, it's a girl who's 80 percent Stepford wife and 20 percent spontaneous, ADHD, adventurous, model-type wild child."

"You've never had, like, an official relationship before her, right?"

"Yeah, but I sort of went with my father's advice on this. He always told me not to settle for a vituperative woman who'd fucking emasculate me in public. The dream should be someone who's loving, affectionate, and bubbly and keeps you young. You get that, right?"

Moreau tossed his bag toward the other end. He couldn't take his eyes off his black-haired beauty.

"The only thing I'm worried about," I continued, "is what if her music really blows up?"

"Well, wouldn't that be the dream?"

"Yes, but I keep thinking about all the creepy guys who'd DM her nudes and dick pics on her IG. Plus, dudes would be snapchatting her nude videos all the time. The more famous one gets, the more gross groupies—men and women."

"I think it'll all be fine. Relax. Enjoy her, man. She seems cool and...different."

"She'd never break up with me. We love the roles we play. I'm the powerful, controlling rich guy, and she's the fun, artsy socialite who wants to be told what to do. It's fascinating, man. You have any Kinsley complaints?"

"If I ever discover one, I'll let you know." He gave me that dimpled grin of his that hadn't changed in 20 years.

"You ever see *Baby Driver*?" I said as I tossed a bag into the hole at the other end.

"Yeah, sure."

"The protagonist has it all figured out. He robs banks and makes dirty money, and yet, his fucking smokeshow girl will go with him anywhere."

"I think occasional arguments and feistiness are a good thing," Moreau said.

"How'd that work out for your parents?"

"Good one." He continued to keep his eyes glued to his girlfriend.

"Loyalty is the number one thing for friendships and relationships. That's all there is to it."

After the game ended, my faithful Skye sprinted across the sand and leaped into my arms.

"I missed you, daddy." Her lips tasted like saltwater.

While my girlfriend's legs were wrapped around me, I thought about her lithe figure and indecorous outfit. Skye Pellegrini dressed in a style I'd classify as Instagram-model chic. It was a superfluity of garments no one would've worn in public even 10 years prior. My girl had two presets: endless neon with an abundance of cleavage and skin showing, or men's clothes worn in the way college girls adorn themselves with button-downs and jerseys at frat parties. Skye frequently wore outfits that showed off her tattoos, and then there was always a pair of sunglasses that could be found in her hair, on her sleeve, in her pant-loop, in her sock, backwards behind her head, or in her mouth. The girl was a stunner no matter what she wore.

Kinsley was clad in her best boating outfit with Sperrys, various navies and whites, and a straw hat. She was a classically conservative beach dresser and a stunning young woman.

"Would you all like to accompany me to one of those couches there?" I said to the group.

"Sounds fun," Kinsley said. "Cash, if you see the waiter, may you please get me something tropical?"

At that point, Skye was getting overly clinging. This happened once in a while, and I wouldn't be surprised if she had popped one of her little friends in the bathroom. My girl was licking and touching me, all while we were on the couch in public.

"Easy, tiger," I whispered.

"No." She pouted while biting my lip.

Her capricious behavior was often welcome, but I needed to unwind.

"Skye, go check how the water feels."

She left me to meditate amongst our companions. And truthfully, it was on the nights when she became overly obsessive, I'd try to bring a female companion home with us. Skye often enjoyed our polygamous eves. And I always gave her veto power.

She ran back toward the couch with soaked feet and a huge smile.

"Daddy, do you have my Juul?"

"Here you go."

She started smoking in front of me, and I certainly appreciated the phallic imagery.

"Moreau, want a cigar?"

"We're right next to the restaurant. You can't smoke here."

"I can smoke anywhere I want."

Kinsley had a few drinks and fell asleep on the outdoor couch, while Skye and I continued until we reached number four or five. I loved that about my girlfriend. She and I could wassail with Nattys at frat parties or imbibe an exceptional rosé or champagne with the Hamptons finest. Skye was a queen of all trades.

"Skye dearest, would you care to accompany me to Stephen Talkhouse this evening?"

"Ugh, I hate that fucking place. It's all old people and Brooklyn beanie weirdos."

"Orca will be there."

"Can we leave, like, ASAP?"

"That's my girl." She bit my lower lip again.

I think last summer I was getting that itch every night. I don't think I was able to fall asleep sober. It seemed as if I was paying for Orca's Hamptons mortgage.

Skye started bouncing on my lap and said:

"Can we leave yet, J? Please. Pretty please."

"Moreau, you don't want to go to Talkhouse, do you?"

"Nah, I gotta take Kinsley home."

"Your loss. Skye? Ready, dearest?"

"Do you love me, J?" she asked while rubbing her hands up my thighs.

"Doubt thou the stars are fire, doubt that the sun ought move, doubt truth to be a liar, but never doubt I love."

She raised her eyebrows and hugged me tightly.

"Ready when you are, daddy."

Skye and I hopped in the convertible, and I started to drive toward Amagansett. However, my mood shifted when I glanced at the floor to my right.

"Skye...what the hell is on the floor of my car?"

"Um, I dunno."

"*Skye?*"

"Sand."

"What is *sand* doing on the floor of my convertible?"

"I dunno."

"Fuck, Skye. How many times have I told you to wipe your feet before you get in my fucking car?"

"I'm really sorry, daddy." Out came the baby voice. "Sometimes, I don't think. Can you pwease forgive me? Pwetty pwease? It'll never happen again. I pwomise."

And then came part two. My tipsy girl unbuckled her seatbelt, leaned over, and started to massage my groin.

"Will you ever be able to forgive me? You don't want to see rainy Skye, do you?"

"No."

Then she unbuttoned my pants and unzipped my fly.

"Wait a minute. What's this? Are you...hard?"

"Maybe."

"So, I guess that means I'm forgiven?"

"Yes. You're forgiven."

"Well, I wanna get my prize for being such a good little girlfriend."

And just like that, my shaft was in her mouth, and I was struggling to drive straight. Skye always loved to add a hint of danger to our sexual escapades. And me, coked-up, tipsy, and supremely aroused, certainly fit the bill. I was dancing over the double yellow lines and may have even run over a few blades of grass on the right.

Her technique was flawless, although I believe she'd give me a significant amount of credit for that. When we first started dating, her oral technique was lacking. Skye's teeth would scrape against me. She'd stop after three minutes and complain of jaw fatigue. She seemed to entirely ignore my testicles. Couldn't deepthroat. And frequently, after a few minutes, Skye would give up and say, "Can you just move my head up and down on top? That'll be easier."

Then, after about two months of dating and 15 or so mediocre blowjobs, my girl realized I wasn't as thrilled as she'd like me to be. So, to her credit, she sat me down and asked, "How can I do better? Teach me everything you like. I wanna be the legit best." And so, thanks to honest communication, she became the savage she is today. I always loved that determined, competitive mindset of hers.

On this particular car ride, I was receiving another one of her 10 out of 10 blowjobs, and after I finished and Skye swallowed, she licked her lips and said:

"You taste so good, daddy."

Our sexual chemistry was unmatched.

We arrived at Stephen Talkhouse, which neither Skye nor I loved, but when it's nighttime, and we needed our fix, we went wherever Orca was.

"Hey, buddy," I said to my old friend in the cramped bathroom. "What's on the menu?"

My hairy, Jewish friend handed me two Ziploc bags and said:

"Let's hang out next week. Let's play nine in Sag sometime."

"Yeah, yeah. Text me."

Somehow, I was able to find Skye amongst an obstreperous crowd, and she subsequently dragged me into the women's bathroom.

"You can't be in here," some cretin screeched at me.

Skye hissed at her like a cat, and we started making out in an unoccupied stall. Her giraffe-like tongue glided from my teeth to my cheeks to my earlobes.

"Daddy, what do you have for me?"

I proudly displayed the bag of X to my recalcitrant 20-year-old girl-friend, and her eyes lit up so wide it was as if her dead parents had come back to life right in front of her.

"You spoil me, J. You gotta little of the coka for yourself?"

I unveiled bag number two, which made her giggle and rub her diminutive hands together.

I don't remember the next 30 minutes or so, but I imagine we danced and made out, and I'm sure I fingered her in the middle of the dance floor. But she vanished after a while, and I think I was distraught because I didn't like it when Skye and I were separated amidst a crowd.

Luckily, it was only for a short while because I recall Skye returning, her arm intertwined with a blonde knockout.

"Jefferson, I'd like you to meet my new friend," Skye said.

I thought the new girl's name was Delaney, but I had no fucking clue.

"Hi," she said and held out her porcelain hand.

Delaney was a tall, thin woman who appeared to be Skye's age, only much more fragile. She also seemed to be quite clean—her body devoid of any tattoos, freckles, or blemishes. Upon meeting this girl, I pinpointed her as a picture-perfect young lady, probably Ivy League material, and the apple of her father's eye. Yet, Delaney must've had some hidden rebellious streak too. I don't know how I knew that, but she did have these refulgent blue eyes that kept darting around the room and mine and Skye's bodies.

Anyway, the three of us must've flirted for a bit, and then once I'd gauged Delaney's interest level, I proposed she join us back at Campbell Manor.

An Uber Black picked us up, and I was pretty fucked up at that point, but I stuck my head out the window, and the cool Hamptons air relaxed me.

"You know, you're, like, really pretty," Skye said to our porcelain pixie.

"Thanks. So are you," she snickered awkwardly.

"Delaney, you're gonna love J's place. Huge pool and Jacuzzi. Big house. Beachfront. It's literally so epic."

"Oh, can we go swimming, Jefferson? I'd love to go swimming. I'm so hot."

"Of course," I said. "Skye and I are all about trying whatever you want."

Delaney grinned, clasped her hands on her lap, and looked at Skye's revealing outfit. My girl glanced over, and they locked eyes.

"You guys should kiss," I said.

I have no idea what the Uber driver was thinking or doing, but I'm sure he was looking in his rearview.

Skye, seated in the middle, leaned over, grabbed hold of Delaney's jocular blonde strands, and landed her succulent lips on our newcomer's. My girlfriend opened her eyes and gazed at me throughout and concluded with a piquant wink. I loved that girl's adventurous spirit. Jesus Christ.

We arrived in one piece and decided to make a quick pit-stop at the pool house. When Moreau and Kinsley didn't answer the door, though, I decided to use my key.

"Cashie, come swim with us," Skye shouted.

"Campbell, what are you doing? Get out. It's 1:30."

"Just a quick dip, man. It's vacation."

"Come on, you guys. The more, the merrier," Delaney added.

"Close the door and leave us alone, please," Kinsley said in her raspy voice.

"Your loss," the interloper added while slipping out of her dress.

Delaney, wearing only her underwear, dove into the pool, and I, still jacked up as ever, joined her.

"J, I'm gonna put on some music. Brb."

Skye blasted some of her own tracks and then went over to the deep end of the pool. She stripped down to that avant-garde runway figure of hers and dove into our chlorinated paradise.

"What's wrong, Delaney?" Skye said as she swam over.

"What do you mean?"

"I thought you were hot?"

"In what way?"

I loved watching Skye work her magic. She had become a champion flirter.

"Sorry, I mean, I thought you were like broiling hot earlier and sweaty? Remember?"

"Oh, that. I was. But the pool feels amazing." Delaney attempted to keep her eyes up, but couldn't help glancing underwater at her companion.

"Maybe," Skye continued, "you should take off that bulky bra of yours. You'll feel much cooler. I mean, look at me."

Delaney gulped as Skye's heart-thumping EDM blared in the background.

"Come here, baby." My girlfriend's voice rose an octave. "I really enjoyed our kiss earlier. You're so pretty."

I circled them like an eager film director, capturing every angle of this nascent romance. Skye, astutely realizing Delaney was one who required a gentle touch, rubbed our guest's pallid cheeks.

"Can I kiss you?" my baby asked our visitor.

"Yes."

Skye then ran her tender fingers across Delaney's face and sweetly pecked the porcelain lips.

"That feels good, right?"

Delaney nodded as her eyes remained closed. Skye then kissed her again. This time with the fervent comportment of which I knew all too well. My garrulous girl proceeded to add her tongue to the equation, and after 30 seconds of progressively affectionate kissing, Delaney removed her bra and placed Skye's hands on her perky breasts.

"I think we'd better get outta the water," I said. "Skye, turn the music off out here and switch it on in the house, please."

The girls followed me along the back patio and through the floor-to-ceiling doors that so often illuminated my living room and kitchen in the mornings. The two-story house was built within the past 20 years, and my father's interior decorator made sure there was plenty of open space. And while there was a dearth of furniture in the first-floor rooms, a surfeit of fine modern art was what any member of high society would instantly notice.

My most treasured set happened to be a series of black-and-white pieces I commissioned outside of Avignon during one of my palatable summer trips. You see, dearest reader, there's a photographer by the name of Delcourt who had an exquisite eye and immense influence in the underground European scene. I commissioned a series of 10 or so portraits of tremendously attractive young models posing in the nude. He and I brainstormed settings and poses and went through thousands of pictures of models. Then, I explained I wanted a singular word painted on their nude bodies. Now, I won't reveal why I chose these words, but I will tell you they were: Tranquility, Sedation, Strength, Serenity, Bliss, Ferocious, Savage, Sky, Death, and Loyal.

You see, throughout my childhood and teenage years, I was frequently venturing into museums and galleries and seeing tasteful collections of nude women from the 21st century back to ancient Greece.

I felt I wanted to be a part of this plenteous tradition, and figured out how I could add to the genre. Needless to say, Delcourt and I couldn't have been happier with the results.

Skye went upstairs to prep the red room while I had a little chat with our bewildered guest.

"So, Delaney, are you having fun?"

"Yes."

"If you'd like to leave, now would be the time. I'll call you an Uber, and it'll take you wherever you'd like."

"No, don't."

"It's no trouble at all."

"I wanna stay and see what happens."

"A curious little coquette, aren't you? Follow me." I led her upstairs and into the previously locked room.

Upon entering, we saw Skye standing naked in front of the king-sized bed.

"Baby, will you please loosen up our guest?"

"Yes, daddy."

Skye walked over, grabbed our visitor's hand, and led her to the foot of the bed.

"You're, like, so pretty, Delaney. Like a little model."

"Thank you. You are too."

"Can I kiss you again? You taste really good."

Delaney nodded, their lips pursed, and they began making out in what seemed like slow-motion. I picked up the old video recorder that was never connected to the Cloud, and started shooting.

"Delaney, feel free to say stop at any time," I whispered.

After a few minutes, Skye was removing her companion's clothing, folding it, and placing it by the door. Then once they were both entirely disrobed, Skye held her new friend's hand and stood next to her, as I continued shooting. They were both completely hairless from the eyebrows down.

"What happens now?" Delaney said.

"Shush," my devoted lover responded. "Speak when spoken to and fucking call him, sir."

"Yes, ma'am."

I panned the camera around the room to show the hardwood floors, the cherry-red curtains, four-poster king bed covered in a matching quilt, and the various floggers, whips, feathers, gags, blindfolds, cuffs, knives, butt plugs, and ropes. Directly above the bed was the always-crucial ceiling mirror. And finally, sitting atop the headboard stood my favorite Delcourt photograph: Sky.

This particular picture was of the glorious Skye Pellegrini. She was standing in front of my private beach with Beats by Dre headphones wrapped around her dyed hair. Both of Skye's hands were cupping her left and right ears, while her eyes were closed and she looked directly upward. The word "Sky" was painted in black across her throat. I took that one myself.

"Delaney, start touching yourself."

"Yes, sir," my bright-eyed guest said.

So, dearest reader, I started fucking my girlfriend, whose strident yelps certainly could've woken our neighbors if not for soundproof walls, while Delaney laid out on the bed, watching intently.

"Daddy, can I taste her?" Skye said.

"Of course."

Naturally, I filmed this event for a considerable amount of time until Skye said:

"Gimme the camera, daddy. Fuck Delaney's brains out."

And so, I obliged. Delaney was crying tears of joy for several minutes as Skye filmed.

The girls obeyed my every word. They each called out my name and yelled whatever I asked while the camera was placed in front of their youthful faces.

"Daddy," the panting Skye said during Delaney's turn, "if it's alright with you, I'd like to use the flogger on Delaney's tight little ass." She spanked her companion.

"Barring any objections from Delaney, so it shall be."

Our evening continued with multiple sessions taking us well into the early morning hours. However, eventually, my love and my lust were all tuckered out, and we retired to the master for a well-deserved slumber.

Love is heavy and light, bright and dark, hot and cold, sick and healthy, asleep and awake — it's everything except what it is!

8/17

DEAREST READER, SOME MONTHS PRIOR to this summer I'm chroni-cling, I was in Manhattan on a date with the lovely Skye. Simple enough eve. We had dinner at one of those pompous spots all the boomers love—Jean-Georges, Le Bernadin or Per Se maybe. Then afterward, I booked a hotel suite at The Standard. Nothing was par-ticularly unusual until Skye went to take a shower.

I knew Skye kept a diary, which seemed mildly childish, but who was I to judge? On that night, Skye left her book open at the foot of the bed while she sang Guetta's "Love Is Gone" under the water in the other room. I felt because Skye left it open face up to a specific page, that meant it was fair game. She wanted me to see that one entry. So yeah, I looked and was glad I did. It read:

I don't think I've ever ached for someone like this before. Maybe Bérénice or Georgia. Not Michael or Will. Definitely not Andrew. But God, Jefferson. I want him deep in my skin. Deep in my goddamn bones. Someday I'll make a map of my life that shows how each part connects to the other. I'll trace each deci-sion, each mistake, and each success back to the very beginning and see how I ended up here. Not that I know where here is just yet. But I have an idea. And I know it will be pretty great.

Now, fast-forward to the 17th, and I was thrilled to still be with this sexy and feral DJ. However, despite our epic love, even Skye and I needed occasional independent nights.

Ms. Pellegrini was having two guests stay at Campbell Manor. Her old friend, Astrid, and newer friend, Brooklynn, were going to be occupying the two downstairs bedrooms for that entire weekend. I, being the loving boyfriend I was, gave Skye as much space as she needed.

Therefore, on that particular eve, Skye, Astrid, and Brooklynn went to La Fondita, while I decided to spend a night at one of the Hamptons' finest speakeasies, Seagull's Beak. The place had been around for centuries. There were plaques dedicated to where John Tyler, Chester A. Arthur, and Jackie Bouvier once sat. It was the archetypal getaway for someone like me. Leather couches, dim lighting, one of the most well-stocked bars in the Hamptons, no tourists, and several superbly effervescent female employees.

I was wearing my violet Brioni window-pane blazer, a pair of bone-white pants, and my sunglasses. I typically dressed in my finest garments when I was out on the town. This was an eccentricity my father passed down to me. He explained even if I'm going out for a slice of pizza, there's no way of knowing who may be waiting around a particular turn. I could run into a potential business associate, celebrity, or wife.

Now, dearest reader, I sat in my usual spot on a corner couch and ordered my usual drink, which the menu referred to as "Tranquility." It was three ounces of champagne, one ounce of each Jackdaw coconut rum, Leningrad vodka, and half an apricot drowned at the flute's bottom. Delectable.

From there, I had no plans other than merely studying the room's patrons, new and old, and enjoying a night alone. Because while I loved the company of Skye, Moreau, and all others, once in a while, I needed a brief respite from the delirium.

After 90 minutes of silence and three units of Tranquility, I was debating never leaving. The live band was playing early Charlie Parker all night, and I was lost in my own world. And the waitress knew to leave me alone unless my drink was empty. Unfortunately, my idyllic recess was interrupted by a nosy partygoer.

"I've been watching you," a high-pitched voice emanating from a barely visible face said.

"Why would a nice girl like you be doing that?"

"Mind if I sit?"

"I have a girlfriend whom I love."

"And me asking to sit across from you on this leather couch impedes that love?"

"Honesty and loyalty are of paramount importance to me."

The young lady, dressed in a long, black evening dress with matching pumps and a white clutch, sat across from me.

"Let's cut to the chase," I said. "Why were you watching me, and why do you want to talk to me?"

"My, my. Are you always this brusque?"

"Seriously, kid, I've gotta get going soon. If you're not interested in me romantically, I'm assuming you want money? A job, maybe? You must know who I am."

"It's a shame when I find so many cynical guys your age."

"My age? You're younger than I am, aren't you?"

"Assuredly." She brushed the tendrils from her forehead using both hands.

"Nice dress. Doesn't look cheap."

"I'd expect a man with your level of refinement to know the dress is but the fourth most expensive item I'm wearing."

"Jefferson." I held out my hand, which she then shook.

"Ivee Petrapoulos."

"Do I know you from somewhere? Last name sounds familiar."

"The Petrapoulos is my father's hotel. It's near Hudson Yards."

"Huh. Is that right?"

"You know, you have quite the reputation, Mr. Campbell," Ivee said as she fondled her pearl necklace.

"I'd venture to say you know nothing about me."

"Quite frosty this evening. Wasn't what I was expecting."

"Look, I have a girlfriend. I don't like talking to girls when she's not around and doesn't know about it."

"The great Skygreenii. Her music's not very imaginative, is it? A little banal for my taste."

"How old are you?"

"I'm supposed to start at Princeton in three weeks, but I don't want to go. I'm probably gonna take a gap year."

"18, huh? You'll figure it out, I'm sure."

"Excuse me, miss," Ivee said to the passing waitress, "gin and tonic. Cambridge Seasonal with a lime. And then he'll have a dry martini with French vermouth, stirred with a twist."

The waitress nodded and walked away as a sax blared in the background.

"They don't card you?"

"I tip well. Very well."

"You come here alone?"

"Nope. Came with my friends from Cordelia. They're over in the corner. I told them I needed to speak with you. They understood."

"Cordelia? How'd you like being surrounded by nothing but x chromosomes for 13 years?"

"Somewhere between exhausting and nauseating. How's that?"

"If I were four years younger, I bet we would've hung out. Some debutante event, maybe."

"We'd have done more than hung out." Her bulging turquoise eyes remained fixated on me.

"You're a funny little girl."

"Aren't you embarrassed with the way little Skygreenii dresses? Flaunting her...opulent figure all over the Internet."

"I love my girlfriend."

"For now."

"All the high school guys from the brother schools must've drooled over you. Never had a guy say no to you?"

Our drinks arrived, and Ivee took a long sip while twiddling her symmetrical and undeviating, thin, blonde strands.

"On the contrary. I had plenty of suitors, sure, but I never found one..."

"Worthy," I interrupted.

"I'm glad you said it. I wasn't going to."

I sipped my martini, closed my eyes, and listened to the band play "Billie's Bounce."

"What do you do for fun aside from harassing uninterested clientele?"

"Promise you won't laugh?"

"Eh." I shrugged.

"Good enough. I want to be an actress. I want to wow audiences with my poise, diction, looks, and attitude."

"And you think Skye's dreams are trite?"

"I'm really good. I've taken classes at the New York Film Academy and played Iago in the Cordelia spring play."

"Good for you."

"Maybe you'll watch me perform sometime?"

"I doubt it. You seem like an intelligent lady. What's with this obsession with me?"

"I don't know where or when it started. My family's been summering in the Hamptons since I was a baby. I always used to see you out either with your family or friends. You were so intriguing. A cool, handsome older guy who didn't care what anybody thought of him. Dressed really well. Known family. Always surrounded by women."

"Did you know I was going to be here tonight?"

"Maybe. For years I've heard all these stories about the hedonistic, thrill-seeking Jefferson Campbell III. I wanted to see for myself. It just took a few drinks to build up the courage."

"I can only imagine what stories you've heard."

"Everything. When I get married one day, you're gonna be the one person on my celebrity list. The one person I'd use my hall pass on. God, this is so insane. Finally meeting the guy I've been crushing on since high school."

"Sorry to disappoint."

"You haven't. At all." She reached over and touched the back of my hand. "You've lived up to everything I could've imagined. Loyal, devastatingly handsome, sharp-witted, high tolerance."

"Well, thank you. I'm flattered."

"One of these days, Jeff. You'll see."

"Madam, you have bereft me of all words. Only my blood speaks to you in my veins."

Ivee brushed her hair behind her ears, stood up, and left. And five minutes, I headed to the bathroom, took out a $100 bill from my pocket, and left 10 minutes later.

I ubered back to Campbell Manor. I'd greatly enjoyed my night alone and found Ms. Petrapoulos to be an endearing enough comrade. That's part of the reason I went to those eclectic speakeasies and haughty parties; one meets such bewitching denizens.

"Jeff," a mildly familiar voice shouted from downstairs. "Can you, like, come get Skye out of the taxi?"

It was Astrid, sounding rather tight. I came downstairs, wearing lululemon shorts and no shirt, and greeted the whiny partygoers.

"Where's Skye?"

"She's still in the car," Brooklynn said. "We couldn't lift her."

"That's my girl."

I jogged outside, tipped the Uber driver, and lifted a groggy Skye.

"J, is that you? It has to be. Such soft skin."

I closed the front door behind me, carried Skye upstairs, and placed her on our king bed.

"Baby, I'm gonna get you out of these clothes. Let me grab you a clean t-shirt."

"I want you now, daddy. Pwetty pwease."

"Not like this. You know our rule. If one of us is blackout drunk, no sex."

"I'm not even, like, blackout...Okay, maybe just a bit."

I stripped off her dirty dress, placed her head through an over-sized shirt, and tucked her under the covers.

"I love you, daddy," she said.

"I love you too, kid." I gave her a peck on the forehead and turned toward the door.

"Take care of my friends. Finish their night off right."

I said, "Of course, starry Skye." And left the room.

"Brooklynn, Astrid, how about a beverage?" I called as I descended the stairs.

"Got anything good here?" Brooklynn asked.

"Please. I only keep good stuff in the house."

"What about that bottle of Svedka there?"

"That's for our...less-esteemed guests, of which you're not. Take a seat on the couch. I have something in mind."

I went to the kitchen, opened the locked cabinet filled with either high proof or particularly electrifying bottles, and began whipping up one of my famed concoctions.

"This is a nice lil place ya got here, Jeffy," Astrid said.

"I've seen bigger."

"When you have a place of your own, then you can insult mine."

"Is this yours?" Brooklynn asked.

"Wanna see the deed?"

"Ease up, girl," Astrid said. "What are we drinking, Jeffy?"

I dropped off their glasses and took a seat in the neighboring lounge chair while they huddled close on the couch.

Astrid, the one on the left, was Skye's longest-tenured friend. She looked like a younger, less refined version of Zoë Saldana. Every time I saw this girl, her hair looked vastly different. And on that eve, Astrid had the tips of her braided locks dyed grey.

Brooklynn was a newer friend and a worse influence. She hung around odious characters in the outer boroughs of New York City. Supposedly, she'd never found a human to whom she'd say no. This girl looked like the Brooklyn one from *Gossip Girl*, only with additional mass, most of which was located in her Michael Turner-like thighs and Nicki Minaj-esque behind.

"What's this spooky drink, Jeffy?" the high-pitched and clearly still intoxicated singer shouted at me.

"We have a champagne and absinthe mix. And then, try this."

"Party favors?" the one on the right shouted. "Now, you're fucking talking."

The girls winced after a sip or two of my bizarre amalgamation, and then each one wolfed down their pills with the delight of one whose fake successfully scanned at 1Oak.

"Why don't you two have boyfriends? I've got 50 friends that'd kill to date either of you. Wouldn't it be nice to have some guy wait on your every need?"

"I'm pan," Brooklynn said.

"Right, well, whatever the definition of that is, you can still have a guy or girl or someone to buy you dinner and make you smile, right?"

She rolled her eyes at me while Astrid giggled and said:

"You got any handsome friends for me? Anyone that looks like you will be fine."

"I might have a couple. What do you like?"

"Idk, it's weird to talk about."

"Fine, we can talk about anything you want."

Brooklynn finished her drink and laid her head down in Astrid's lap.

"Ugh, there's something about you," Astrid said to me. "I think it's your eyes. You have very trusting eyes. I think that's like a bad thing, though."

"We don't have to talk about you or me. Skye just wants me to be entertaining."

"I like white guys," Astrid said. "They need to have money. They should be in great shape, and how tall are you?"

"Six feet."

"They have to be six feet. And then, like, chill. Someone I can lay back and smoke a bowl with all day, and then they'll come see my shows."

"I can look through my Rolodex."

"Your what?"

"Nothing. I'll ask around. Do I follow you on Instagram?"

"Probably. Check your phone, though. I have 118K followers."

"How's the sex with Skye?" Brooklynn blurted out.

"Don't ask him that. You've had too much to drink, girl," Astrid said as she finished her beverage.

"It was hit or miss at the beginning, but these days, it's fantastic. Top five for me, for sure. She knows my body better than anyone."

Brooklynn sat up and said:

"What kinda things do you like?"

"Jeffy, I'm sorry about her. She's drunk." Astrid stretched her arms over her head and said, "You and I need some shots. We gotta catch up."

"That can be arranged."

I went to the kitchen, poured four shots of Prima Adoncia tequila, and returned to my simplistic living room, furnished with only white, modern pieces.

Astrid and I clinked our glasses and downed the first two, and then Brooklynn and I knocked back the others.

"I don't feel well," the latter said.

"No doy, idiot," her high-pitched friend said. "You shouldn't have taken a tequila shot. Not gonna lie, that was fucking dumb."

"I know. I know. Hold me."

Brooklynn laid facedown in her friend's lap while I was developing a mild buzz from the nearby chair.

"Can I get you two some Pepto Bismol? Always helps my stomach."

"Skye was right," Astrid said. "You're a sweetheart. A misunderstood one."

"Jeff," Brooklynn's dour voice whispered, "sit next to us, please. Rub my tummy."

"Okay."

I did as I was told. Unfortunately, I wasn't the five-star entertainer Skye would've hoped, but we were all so tipsy by that point it probably didn't matter.

Astrid began singing some improvised lullaby while Brooklynn laid in her lap, and I, for whatever reason, was rubbing her stomach. The more bilious one was given two tablets of Pepto Bismol.

But then, as the night was coming to a close and we were each about to doze off, Brooklynn turned onto her stomach and regurgitated absinthe, tequila, champagne, and chunks of tacos, all doused in a hot pink hue, upon Astrid's lap and dress and one of my couch cushions.

"I'm so sorry. I'm so sorry, Jeff. I didn't mean to."

"Don't worry. It's not your fault," I said. "Astrid, take her into the bathroom there. May you please clean her off and give her some water. I'll see what I can do about this couch...the housekeeper comes on Wednesdays."

The girls disappeared into what was acting as Brooklynn's room for the weekend. Meanwhile, I, a man with about 13 minutes of cleaning experience in my life, attempted to drunkenly clean two pounds of malodorous, hot pink lumps from my rather exorbitant couch.

"Jeffy," Astrid shouted from behind the closed door. "Please come help us."

I went into the bedroom and then knocked on the bathroom door.

"Hello? What's the problem?"

"The shower won't turn on."

"You have to pull the lever out and then twist it."

"Fuck. I've tried everything. It doesn't work."

"Are you using the rainfall head or the detachable?"

"Fuck, dude. How are we supposed to know?"

"Brooklynn, are you okay in there?"

"She's fine, cuddled by my feet. She's puked all the sickness out of her. But dude, help us turn this fucking thing on."

"Are you decent?"

"Just come the fuck in and help us. Jesus."

I entered the room to find them both stark naked.

"Christ, you should've warned me." I put my hand over my eyes.

"Grow up. They're just tits. From what Skye tells us, you've seen plenty."

With my hand over my eyes, I began fumbling for the showerhead.

"Jeffy, seriously, you're not gonna be able to turn it on like that. Open your fucking eyes."

I did as I was told and stepped into the marble shower area.

"Asty, why'd you let him in? I'm totally naked, dude."

"Relax, I've known him forever. He's like one of the girls."

"There, it's on. I'm gonna go up to bed. See you two tomorrow."

"Wait," Astrid said. "You've got Brooklynn's dinner on your shirt."

"I'll take care of it later. It's fine. I'm just a little fucking uncomfortable right now."

"Will you please chill, dude. We'll tell Skye how amazing and caring you were. Stop being a little bitch."

Every man's kryptonite is being called a bitch. So, I took off my shirt and handed it to the still-nude Astrid, who began washing it in the sink. Brooklynn then got off the floor and approached me.

"Wow, you're really hot. Skye made a good choice."

"Uh, thanks. I guess."

"What's wrong, stud?" she said. "You're shaking. Never seen a hot South African-Norwegian girl before?"

"Astrid, I think you got it all."

Brooklynn reached over and touched my chest.

"Oh, so firm," she said. "And I'm so horny right now."

At that point, I was getting annoyed.

"Please don't touch me. Only Skye can touch me. That's one of the rules."

"Oh, we know all about your rules, daddio," Brooklynn said.

"Astrid, are we all set there? The shower's running, and you're wasting water."

"Skye says you love to get other girls involved," the pansexual continued.

"Not like this. The rule is Skye and I can only be with other girls when our significant other is there and consenting."

"So, you gave us all this alcohol and all these pills, and we're not even gonna put them to good use?"

"Astrid, I'd like my shirt back. I'm leaving now."

"Jeffy, no one's stopping you. You outweigh me by 80 pounds and B by 65. If you wanted to leave that badly, you would've done so already."

I stood paralyzed in the corner of the white-and-gold bathroom.

"B, get under the water. I'll join you and get you all cleaned off."

"Asty, I'm so fucking horny right now."

"Do you guys want me to leave?" I said.

"No need...Come here, B."

Astrid joined Brooklynn under the cascading water.

"You wanna join, daddio?" The South African-Norwegian said.

"Do you mind if I just stand here and...watch?"

They both shook their heads and continued to embrace and make out. It was sloppy and aggressive. The duo didn't have complete control of their motor skills, so they were slipping and their limps were flailing.

It wasn't this infallibly beautiful scene in the traditional sense. I was viewing two undaunted, drunken friends acting as naturally as possible. Brooklynn's tongue licked Astrid's cheeks, the former's teeth bit into the latter's nipples, and shampoo and soap were entering into unsuspecting somnolent eyes.

"Enjoying the show, Jeffy?" Astrid said.

"Yeah I am, kid."

"Asty, get the showerhead. Hook a girl up."

Skye's oldest friend did as she was told and removed the detachable.

"Ladies, and feel free to say no, but would you mind if I grabbed my camera and filmed you?"

"We're hot enough for you?" Brooklynn said in a sardonic tone.

"I want to film you, show it to Skye, and use it later on. Would that be okay?"

"I don't give a fuck." Astrid said.

I sprinted out of the bathroom shirtless, raced upstairs, snatched my video recorder from the bedside table next to a cooing Skye, and returned to the first-floor restroom.

"We waited for you," the thinner one said.

"Asty, put it right here. I'm literally hornier than I've ever been."

I approached the girls, opened the sliding glass door of the shower, and filmed Skye's best friends.

Their sensual session began with Astrid massaging the pulsating showerhead against every inch of Brooklynn's body, but then the two seemed to share a visceral love as the purely carnal activity became romantic.

I zoomed in as Astrid's tongue circled. Fingers were soon inserted into every orifice. Moans and shrieks reverberated throughout the capacious first floor. And then after the final yelps had subsided, a sopping wet Brooklynn uttered:

"I love you so much, Asty."

Astrid was silent and continued to kiss her friend's inner thighs, while Brooklynn stroked and pulled at Astrid's drenched black-and-grey wisps. That 15-minute period was perhaps the most indelible one from that summer.

And in case you were wondering, dearest reader, Skye would have had no problem with my behavior. I handled it with appreciable aplomb.

You see, dearest reader, throughout our then 11-month relationship, Skye and I assented to 30 different rules involving what we could and couldn't do when exploring our sexual boundaries. It started with 10, and then ones were continually added as we saw fit. The most frequently recurring rules were:

-Skye and I can be with other girls sexually, but only in the presence of our counterpart

-Filming other women is permissible as long as your counterpart is shown the video at a later date
-No attending events with a plus one other than your counterpart
-Skye has full veto power on any and all girls I'm interested in
-Skye must consent to every sexual activity before proceeding
-Once the word "Serene" is uttered, all sexual activity ceases.
-Cheating is considered any type of kiss with another person or any person coming into direct contact with your breasts or genitalia. Oral, anal, and vaginal sex are obviously cheating (unless, of course, your counterpart is present and consenting).

6/15

"I THOUGHT OF TWO, DADDY. In a vineyard in a classy, white dress 69ing...and at the Thanksgiving dinner table while my gramma and your dad watched. Reverse cowgirl."

That's what Skye texted me as I exited the Audi. It was a gratifying game we'd been playing since we first met. I viewed it as a kind of modern-day Clue, only made by mine and Skye's demented minds and not Hasbro.

You see, dearest reader, given our hectic schedules, Skye and I needed to find ways to spice up our sex lives whilst not in the same zip code. It all began a while back when I was attending a rooftop event at The Viceroy. The top floor of the hotel had a bar overlooking Central Park, and when the weather was nice, one could examine 60 blocks worth of treetops from several hundred feet above ground. Naturally, there was a railing to prevent the drunkards from meeting Satan sooner than anticipated. So, I sent Skye a picture of my view and texted:

"The Viceroy/you bent over the railing/wearing a plaid skirt with no panties."

Now, any normal young lady would be rightfully terrified or disgusted by my line of thinking, but not the intrepid Skye. She responded with an image of her DJ booth at a club and texted:

"Me sitting on my turntables/legs spread/you fucking me raw while my audience watches."

This became one of a plethora of games Skye and I played.

"On the first tee box. Me skullfucking you while you use my putter to play with yourself. And you're wearing this hot golfing outfit." I sent

Wil Glavin

Skye an image of a lady wearing white short-shorts, a lime-green tube top, and a visor.

Skye responded with that drooling face emoji.

"Are you gonna hit, Campbell, or text your bookie all day?"

"Jesus, Moreau. Relax. Gotta lot more golf to be played. Don't tense up."

My loyal friend and I teed off on the first at Poxabogue. Now, dearest reader, I don't want you to get the wrong idea. I'm well aware Poxabogue is no place for an experienced golfer with a five handicap. However, I prided myself on my desirable hosting abilities, and this is the course my old Hollandsworth pal wanted to play.

"Hey, Moreau," I said to him on the first green, "how about you not step in my line?"

"Relax. Don't tense up," he smirked.

We continued to the second tee, where he was unable to reach the 120-yard green on his first shot.

"Watch and learn, Moreau."

I took a sip from my silver and ivory flask and then plastered the ball with my pitching wedge. It was an impeccable swing, and my Titleist landed a mere foot from the hole.

My father taught me how to play back when I was the cutest young boy Hollandsworth had ever accepted. He was a phenomenal teacher. My father knew precisely when encouragement was required and when wrath and a raised voice were necessary.

"The heart in my breast is balanced between two ways as I ponder, whether I should snatch him out of the sorrowful battle and set him down still alive in the rich country of Lykia, or beat him under at the hands of the sun of Menoitios."

My father also always had a pricey flask and a Cuban cigar while golfing, so I followed in his footsteps.

"You're gonna start drinking at 11:00 a.m.? What are the odds of you making it through 27 holes, Campbell?"

230

We strolled to the third tee with our bags slung over our shoulders. It was as if no time had passed from our seventh-grade outings at the illustrious nine-hole Poxabogue course. He still walked straight-legged and bizarrely never moved his torso as his legs stepped forward. Moreau walked like a first-generation android. But I never derided him. He was always there for me.

"Do you have any baseball futures?" he asked.

"Cubs over 95.5 wins, Nationals over 91.5, Pirates under 82.5, and Braves over 75.5."

"I love the Nationals this year. And I'm saying this as a Phillies fan. How can a team with Scherzer, Strasburg, Rendon, and Harper not make it to the World Series? It's embarrassing."

I lit up a Cuban as we walked to the par-3 4th hole. I'd always thought Moreau would've been a more gregarious companion if he let loose once in a while.

"In a hospital bed, me in a nurse's outfit, you choking me with your stethoscope," Skye texted me.

"On *The Aeneid*. Me fucking you over the side of the boat. You flying the drone and filming us."

"Oh, daddy, that sounds so fucking hot. Let's do that. One zillion percent...hope you and Cashie are hittin birdies xoxoxo."

Moreau's tee shot landed short of the green and into the sand, but he remained stoic as per usual.

"Can I ask you a serious question?" he said as we walked to the green.

"Always, man."

"I think I wanna marry Kinsley."

"Fuck."

"What?"

"Nothing, man. I just wasn't prepared for that. Fucking Christ, Moreau. Marriage? You? Now?"

I pressed the ivory reed to my lips.

"I think I'd make a tremendous husband and father."

"Fuck, dude. Father? You went from college grad five minutes ago to husband five seconds ago to father? You're fucking 22."

"I turn 23 in a few months."

"I know when your birthday is. Been to four of Andrea Moreau's famed surprise parties."

We continued talking as I lined up my birdie putt and Moreau his par.

"Why shouldn't I?"

"I'd answer that, but I'm afraid the round'll be over by the time I'm quite finished."

"Gimme your top five reasons."

"The best elucidation I've got?"

"Lay it on me, Campbell. You won't change my mind."

"First, you're too young."

"Irrelevant. Next."

"Allow me to finish, please. And it's not irrelevant. You've had, what, two girlfriends before her? She's had what, one boyfriend before you? The whole point of early-20s relationships is to have fun and get all the mistakes out of your system. You and Kinsley will undoubtedly fuck up more than a couple married at 30 will."

"Next."

"Your sexual eroticisms, man. I won't ask you about Kinsley's performance, but are you sure whatever it is the two of you are doing will still be mind-blowing or at worst, adequate, 60 years from now?"

"Next."

"You don't have a fucking job, Moreau. No career path. No apartment. You're a Hollandsworth and Penn alum with not a single tangible skill to hang your hat on."

"Next."

We each teed off on that annoyingly short fifth hole before I continued:

"Look at our parents. Look at Kinsley's parents. Look at Skye's parents. Not together, divorced, divorced, dead. Which one of those has a happy ending? Which one of those makes you think, 'Gosh, I'd love to attach myself to this woman who will leave me one day?'"

"I think it's unfair to compare relationships. My parents' relationship has nothing to do with mine."

"Correct, but statistically, it matters. How many marriages consistently remain two standard deviations above the mean where your x and y values are number of years together and happiness levels?"

"You have one more reason why I shouldn't propose?"

"You need to walk around in Kinsley's skin. Why would she marry you? From what I gather, she has such a tremendous amount of ambition. She's a woman who always tackles everything head-on. Your girl's not only a drop-dead knockout but a future self-made millionaire. A fucking genius, it would seem. She has that type of personality that can rule the world. What are you? Why does she choose to stay with you? What do you think you bring to the table? Why would she say yes? Come on, Moreau. Sit down and think these questions through."

We didn't speak much for the next two holes aside from me scolding him on golf etiquette. He and I could read each other very well. Anytime my dear friend felt sad, disappointed, or angry, he'd shut down. I first noticed it when we played sports. If Moreau made an error on the baseball field, he wouldn't yell or pout, he'd become silent. Moreau wouldn't speak to anyone until either he turned his performance around or the game ended.

He was also that way for months, if not years, after his parents' divorce. Same with after his first girlfriend broke up with him. There's never any screaming, crying, or woe is me. He'll just stop speaking and turn on autopilot.

"Check out this pond," Skye texted me and then followed it up with an image from her vineyard trip.

"What about it?" I typed back.

"I want us to crawl in there late at night, and I want you to fuck me in that filthy water. I want like leeches sucking at our bodies and frogs ribbetting while they watch us. And then we'll leave the water covered in algae, mud, blood, and leeches."

"You're a savage."

"Too far, daddy?"

"Never, kid. I love how imaginative you are."

"Thanks, J. Kisses."

Moreau and I sat at the restaurant by the clubhouse after our round of nine. I was feeling a bit buzzed and decided to retire to the bathroom for a quick break before my omelet.

"I have responses," Moreau said as I sat back down.

"Lay 'em on me."

"Tons of couples succeed when married young. High school sweethearts exist for a reason."

"That's different. When someone is your first and only, that's a lifelong soul mate. If you're choosing to stick by someone without knowing what else is out there, that's true fucking love."

"That's basically what Kinsley and I have."

"Not even close. She's tasted other cock, man. She's felt other dicks inside of her. If she gets tired of you, she knows there are potentially other ways to be satisfied."

"That crossed about a thousand miles over the line."

"Duly noted. Retracted. I have a supreme level of envy toward those who immediately settle down and never taste another's lips or touch another's body. To know you were meant for someone even when you're teenagers is straight Biblical. That's what I meant."

"So saccharine, Campbell. Unlike you. Then, sexually speaking, I won't get into details with you, but I figure if there's ever any occasional boredom, there are a thousand books that can give us new ideas or positions. Or, worst-case scenario, I'll come to you," he laughed.

"You got a career path? A way to make money?"

"Nope, but I don't need to yet. Kinsley and I can discover and progress our passions together. That's part of what love is."

"You'd know better than I."

"And the parents' argument is irrelevant. Skye's mother was tragically shot, so remove that from the equation. My parents are still good friends and have lived a block away from each other, even after being divorced, for seven years."

"So, is your goal to get married, live together for 20 years, get divorced, and then move in next door?"

"No, but I believe I've learned from their mistakes."

"How so?" I said. "One example?"

"My father always put his work and money first. I won't do that."

"You'd sacrifice your entire career of sitting on the beach and not having a job for her? How virtuous of you."

"Then Kinsley's parents got divorced 20 years ago, but they never loved each other in the first place."

"That's a deceptive argument. I don't buy they never loved each other. There are only three instances people who don't love each other get married: green card, arranged, drunken mistake."

"You're always so sure about everything, aren't you?"

"I'm sure the Avitals loved each other."

"I won't bring up your parents. But you get my point. We're a new generation with new ideals and modern ways of thinking. You can't compare the two."

Moreau munched on his chocolate chip pancakes as he planned out his walk down the aisle.

"She and I have a mythic love. There's no one else I want to be with. I don't find any other girls attractive anymore. I don't feel whole unless she's near me. It's frightening stuff, man. I hope you experience it either with Skye or one day in the future."

"Right. Skye."

I paid for lunch, and Moreau offered to drive us to Maidstone. My lucidity was in rapid decline, but I wasn't going to let that hinder my performance on the nationally-renowned course.

"You gonna be good for 18?" Moreau asked as he parked the car at the club.

"This is nothing, man. I've removed someone's appendix when I was drunker than this."

Unfortunately, I have next to no recollection of our round, but I specifically remember shooting a 72 and being able to procure the phone number of the Maidstone cart girl. However, after I texted Skye the lady's IG handle, my scrupulous girlfriend said the woman wasn't up to our mountainous standards. Therefore, I had no further communication with the enigmatic soda server.

I remember waking on one of the lounge chairs beside my pool. Moreau had placed my Fendi shades over my eyes, and I must've been out for hours because the sun had set.

I knocked on the pool house door, but Moreau and his girl weren't home. And when I wandered into Campbell Manor, I found a nude Skye sprawled out on the kitchen floor like a sea star. Thanks to me, though, she soon had a pillow underneath her head, and a blanket draped over her sultry figure.

As I began to sober up, I remembered the older brother of one of my loyal Hollandsworth friends was hosting one of his special parties. In those days and circles, the brother went by Fillet.

I put on a black suit and tie, wrote Skye a note explaining my whereabouts and why I was leaving my phone at home, and called an Uber Black to take me to the mansion near Cooper's Beach.

I exited the taxi, put on my silver Il Dottore mask, and ventured to the front door of the mansion, which was held up by eight towering, marble columns.

"Escalus," I said to the masked security guard.

He opened the door and invited me into the grand foyer, where two unclad, pale Caucasian women greeted me. These young ladies then led me beyond the silk curtain and into the great hall that was glimmering in gold, courtesy of a colossal crystal chandelier.

My companions then led me to one of the off-white Baroque chairs situated in the corner of the great hall. They each sat on an arm of my seat, and the three of us watched as 25 masked men and women copulated in a boisterous Bacchanalia that featured thrashing limbs, excess pubic hair, a chorus of cacophonous shouts, and that unique sound of one human's skin thumping another. The exclusive scene was one of grotesque beauty.

I personally never wished to partake. Even prior to my relationship with Skye, I preferred to view these sequences from up close, but I never considered joining in on the debauchery. Ever since my first party of this nature, which took place off-campus in my college days, I'd become not just interested, but mesmerized by the female figure. These parties created a safe space where I could view the majesty of vaginas and breasts, but also understand what made certain women especially aroused and why. It was an immaculate confluence of science and art. I felt like a modern-day Niels Bohr mixed with a 21st century Titian.

The uneducated might deduce I was simply there for a gratis show as if it were a sexy cinema from yesteryear. However, I wasn't there for onanistic reasons. There was something particularly provocative about juxtaposing the mansion with 30-foot ceilings, $500,000 chandeliers, and golden Baroque furniture and paintings with the ostensibly mutilated scene of screaming women and unhinged men.

After 30 minutes of analyzing, I left with my two companions, who guided me up the carpet-covered stairs toward an empty bedroom. These young ladies had clearly recognized something about me and knew exactly the type of revelry in which I chose to partake. As I held their hands on the way to the bedroom, I imagined these girls could've been absolutely anyone from the wealthiest Cordelia and Verity Prep princesses to fortuitous detritus from the metaphorical swamps of Jericho, Roslyn, or Great Neck.

I closed the door behind me and turned to find the two girls kneeling with their hands situated on their pallid thighs.

"You," I said, pointing to the brunette on the left, "I'm going to call you Clarissa." I then turned to the blonde and said, "You're now Ivee."

They turned toward one another and nodded.

"If you don't want to do something, please let me know, and we'll stop immediately."

The girls agreed before I began pacing around the immense bedroom. The cynosure of our white-and-gold abode was the Victorian four-poster canopy bed with magnificent gold silk curtains. Aside from that, the room's accoutrements were tasteful but forgettable: an oak dresser, two wooden chairs, and several paintings that were either some of Klimt's lesser-known work or possibly Malani-Neri.

That evening's activities consisted of me asking Clarissa to pretend to be a cat, meowing at my command. And Ivee, a dog barking. Collars and leashes were involved. Then, some tickling with this feather...Eventually, the tone shifted. The two of them were breaking out baby voices and sucking their thumbs. Belt came out. They consented, of course. I whipped them until the tears started flowing. I stopped. Blonde and Brunette started licking each other's tears, per my request. I closed my eyes and luxuriated in my unmitigated control over other members of my species. We took some pills Fillet left for us on the dresser. They referred to me as "your majesty," which I adored. I watched Ivee eat out Clarissa. One of them broke out plush handcuffs. The other used her Womanizer toy. I had them sing Natalie Imbruglia's "Torn" to me. Then mauve anal beads, I think. I was arrantly aroused, but my clothes remained firmly attached to my body, and my hands never once touched my two angels.

At some point, whatever drugs we'd swallowed started to take effect. I was feeling loopy and tired but continued to study fake Ivee's cunnilingus technique. The last thing I remember were the nipple clamps.

I don't know when or how, but I exited the house and entered into a waiting taxi.

"Skye," I screamed at the top of my lungs upon returning home. "Red room. Now."

"Daddy?" She wiped her eyes and joined me at the top of the staircase. "Do you need me?"

"I always need you, and I'll always love you. Follow me, kiddo."

6/8

SKYE PELLEGRINI WAS MY FIRST exclusive girlfriend, but I'd had several schoolboy crushes and seasonal flings many years prior. And the first moderately successful one was with a young minx from The Quelea School for Girls: Clarissa Lockheed.

This scintillating seductress was the "It Girl" amongst Manhattan private schoolers circa 2009. She was an early-developing brunette with sharp facial features and twiggy legs that were always caressed by black leggings. Clarissa Lockheed was two years my senior, and I may have used some manipulatory tactics to breach her inner circle.

I was cognizant of Clarissa's existence through a combination of Facebook posts, debutante dances, word-of-mouth conversations, and a *New York Post* article or two. However, I was graduating from Hollandsworth in a month and would be moving to Litchfield, CT for boarding school at Exdover when autumn rolled around, so opportunities were in short supply.

I had had a healthy obsession with Clarissa for approximately two years and had since become progressively closer with her younger sister, Angelica. The latter and I were amongst a select group of 80 who spent our Wednesday evenings at the illustrious Boxington dance class.

I used to frequently ask Angelica to dance and learn about her austere mother and aloof father while slipping in a:

"And you have a sister, right?"

Or:

"How's that Christie doing? Or whatever your sibling's name is."

One day, Angelica, a Quelea girl like her sister, invited about a hundred rising freshmen high school students to her eighth-grade graduation party in June of 2009. And it was held at the Lockheed family's grandiose, five-story townhouse on 74th between First and York.

The event was rather docile—a bunch of pubescent tweens spitting out their first quaffs of alcohol followed by several unprepossessing public displays of affection. I, on the other hand, stood outside by the back-patio garden wearing my nicest Hickey Freeman suit and awaiting an appearance by the elder Lockheed sister. You see, dearest reader, I'd already confirmed with Angelica that the coquettish Clarissa would be in attendance. In fact, the rising high school junior was the party's only chaperone.

I briefly spoke with Angelica before pouring myself a tumbler of scotch and choosing to give myself an unattended tour of the townhouse, decorated astutely and exclusively with Renaissance-aged panache.

After briefly scrutinizing the second and third floors, I stomped up the staircase toward the famed fourth, admiring the oak baluster on my way. Once I reached the landing, I heard a mezzo-soprano voice confabulating with some lucky recipient on the other end of the phone.

"Hold on," my teen crush said, her door barely cracked open. "Someone's up here. I'll call you back."

There I stood, a brash 14-year-old, frozen on the fourth-floor landing with a tumbler in my hand and 50 different thoughts on what my next move should be. And then the door to the bedroom swung open, and I was finally able to lay eyes on the famed face that launched a thousand erections.

"Who the fuck are you?" Clarissa asked.

"Jefferson."

"What the fuck do you want?"

"Just trying to find an adult."

"Why? What the fuck did my fucking sister do now? I swear I can't get a second of fucking peace and quiet."

"She seems fine. No big problems other than some tipsy 14-year-olds swilling your father's finest Balvenie."

"Can I help you with something?"

"I'm sure you could, but I don't think you'd want to."

"You're kind of an unusual dude, aren't you?"

"I'm Jefferson Campbell III." I approached her and extended my hand.

"Oh. You're a Campbell? You look like your dad. Is that his tie?"

"No, it's mine. Brioni."

"You know B.o.B.? That's who I'm really into right now."

"No."

"Wanna hang out and listen to some music?"

"Sure."

An hour later, I had Clarissa Lockheed sticking her 16-year-old tongue in my 14-year-old mouth. And six weeks later, she and I were quasi non-exclusively dating.

Now, dearest reader, I know you're all agog to find out what happened on 6/8 during my cabal's previous summer, but I must plunge into one more vital vignette regarding my ephemeral tryst with the once-marvelous Clarissa Lockheed.

I was spending my final summer before boarding school in the Hamptons with my father. I'm sure there were seminal moments other than those spent with Miss Lockheed, but she was the sensual stimulus around which all other actions revolved.

During that July, Clarissa and I were locked in a steamy, clandestine affair that included zero public displays of affection and not a single orifice penetrated. She'd simply text me late at night, and I'd be driven to her usually adult-less house. And I'd often be carrying a treat, such as Tate's cookies. Then, Angelica would typically and awkwardly answer the door:

"Oh. You're only here to see my sister, right?"

"Yes, ma'am."

"You would think she could find someone her own age."

Then I'd run to Clarissa's bedroom, and we'd embrace and engage in blithe dry-humping for an hour or so. Our clothes always remained on, so I elected to wear athletic shorts or thin linen pants whenever possible. I was indeed a virgin and was silently querying whether she was too.

On one August day, Mr. and Mrs. Lockheed were scheduled to bring their daughters to a business associate's palatial estate for a hearty, backyard brunch. And for whatever reason, potentially to anger her taciturn father, Clarissa brought me along.

The Peppers were a young, nouveau-riche couple with two terrible twin toddlers.

"And who's this?" the male Pepper asked the contemptuous Clarissa.

"My husband, Jefferson Campbell III. A Hollandsworth boy." She held her deadpan expression.

"Ah. Mr. Campbell. I hear great things about your father. A philanthropic dynamo, isn't he?"

"I suppose."

"You know, our little Petey would just die to attend Hollandsworth," the mother said. "Would there be any way you could make a call? I'm sure it'd go a long way."

"Really?" Clarissa said. "Your two-year-old would die to go to Hollandsworth? You know it starts in kindergarten, right? You're years away."

"Clarissa. Enough," Mr. Lockheed growled.

My date then began holding my hand under the table while the adults argued about whether or not loud helicopters flying over the Hamptons were ruining the town's once world-renowned quietude.

After the chef served us mimosas and cinnamon rolls, the leggings-clad Clarissa said:

"Jefferson and I would like to retire somewhere. Perhaps we can watch the baby Peppers and Jefferson can make an honest assessment?"

"Ah yes. Good idea," the clueless Mr. Pepper said. "Grigri? May you please take these two to the basement? Let them watch the twins. Maybe show them how the basement theater works?"

The tiny housekeeper guided Clarissa and me past the Peppers' egregiously decorated first floor and down to the fully-carpeted basement. There, we were escorted into the Peppers' personal movie theater, which contained three rows of three plush, red leather seats.

"Jefferson, let's sit in the back row. Grigri, what are our choices?"

"The babies like *Grease*." The housekeeper whispered in an accented voice.

The two mini Peppers leaped with glee at what must've been their favorite word.

"*Grease*, it is," Clarissa said, as she planted her iconic figure in the middle seat of the back row.

Grigri put on the Travolta-Newton-John starrer and closed the door on her way out of the mini-theater. The baby Peppers sat on the floor with their eyes mere feet away from the prodigious projector screen.

"Psst, can I sit on your lap?" my semi-girlfriend whispered.

"Sure."

"*Took her bowling...*," Danny Zuko belted as Clarissa situated herself.

She then turned her body toward me and began kissing my innocent lips while the well-behaved thumb-suckers remained glued to the coruscating screen displaying the rumbustious Rydell High.

Clarissa's little pecks and nibbles soon turned into one of our raunchy dry-humping sessions, which always piqued my concupiscent curiosity.

"Jefferson, you're so fucking hot," she whispered in my ear.

"What are you doing? The babies are right there. Your parents are upstairs."

"I don't give a flying fuck," she frightened me in the best way possible.

The baby Peppers continued to sing along to the famed *Grease* soundtrack while Danny and Sandy frolicked on screen.

"I want to fuck you right now," Clarissa whispered in my ear.

"O, when she's angry, she is keen and shrewd!" I thought.

Clarissa unzipped my fly, grabbed my cheeks, and violently kissed me. And then, moments later, she shifted her leggings past her twiggy thighs and began grinding on top of my quivering lap. The toddlers never turned around. The adults never came downstairs. Danny and Sandy sang to us. And 15 minutes later, I was a virgin no more. And three weeks after, I went off to boarding school, and Clarissa stopped responding to my indefatigable BBMs and calls. I still become aroused every time I hear "Summer Nights" and "You're the One That I Want."

Now, dearest reader, on June 8th of last summer, my not-so-virtuous girlfriend and I went out for a night of drinks and flirtation at The Surf Lodge in Montauk. And following some sublime food and beverages, Skye and I were on the prowl at that lovely spot overlooking Fort Pond.

We sat on a bench in the corner of the outdoor patio. My hand warmed Skye's inner thigh while she smoked her Juul and drank an amaretto sour.

"Who's this playing, Skye?"

"Martin Garrix. He's solid."

"You see anyone who might play a nice third fiddle this eve?"

"Oh, that's what we're doing tonight? I can do, like, a bit of quick research. Hold my drink."

That's all it took for Skye and me to be up to our classically elegant subterfuge. And it took no more than five minutes for my little fox-hound to return with an orange-haired vixen.

"J, this is Danielle. She's a Gucci model. She walked the runway during NYFW last year."

And half an hour later, I was pulling up to Campbell Manor with Skye and Danielle hooking up in the backseat.

"Here we are," I announced while opening the car door for them.

"A little bumpy," Skye said. "You've had better drunken performances."

I opened the door to the big house while Danielle and Skye held hands behind me.

"Baby, I'm gonna head upstairs. Why don't you pour our guest a drink and meet me up there in five?"

"Yes, daddy."

I trudged up the stairs, stripped to my underwear, splashed some water on my placid face, picked up the camcorder, and entered the red room. I was leaning toward a discipline-filled night and started to plan out the next hour in my ever-racing mind.

"Daddy, it's us." Skye knocked on the door.

I turned the knob and led the two girls into my risqué sanctum.

"What. The. Fuck." Danielle shouted as the door closed behind her.

"What's the problem, kid?" Skye said.

"This is fucking insane. What's the matter with you guys?"

"Danielle, baby," Skye continued. "Don't you want to have a good time with us, baby?"

"Skye, down."

"Yes, daddy."

"Do you consent to this evening's events?" I asked Skye.

"Yes, daddy."

"Go stand in the corner, strip down, and begin touching yourself while saying my name. Loudly."

"Yes, daddy."

Skye went toward the back of the room, knelt in between the bed and the wall of pain, and sucked on her fingers.

"Fuck, dude," Danielle said. "What the fuck is happening? What's wrong with you two?"

Danielle and I stood across from one another next to the door while Skye pleasured herself to the medium shot of the redhead and me.

"Danielle, Skye and I have a rather, shall we say, outlandish relationship. However, we never move forward with any activities without mutual consent."

"This is so fucking weird. You just lure fucking girls to this fucking pleasure palace?"

"Only if they're interested and willing."

"Oh, Jeff. Oh, Jeff. Oh, Jeff." Skye's moans grew louder.

"You're a fucking mental patient, dude."

"Now, Danielle, you can leave whenever you like, and I'll of course pay for your Uber home. However, I'd greatly appreciate it if you don't insult my girlfriend and me. Everyone has their own inimitable sexual preferences, and no one should bully others for being different."

"I can't listen to this anymore. Strangest night of my fucking life."

"Oh, Jeff. Oh, Jefferson Campbell. Oh, daddy."

"No problem whatsoever. I'll escort you downstairs. Our evenings are not for everyone. You're not the first person to decline an invitation."

I led Danielle out of the red room, down the stairs, and to the grand foyer while wearing nothing but my silk boxers.

"What's your address? I'll call you an Uber."

"Nice try, freak. I'll call one myself."

"No need to be myopic, my dear. Not everyone must fit into your societal norms of what sex should be. And please allow me to give you some money for your taxi. You came all this way and are leaving disappointed. We can't have that."

I reached into a nearby drawer and handed the redhead two crisp hundred-dollar bills, which she of course took instantly.

"It was a pleasure meeting you. I wish you the best moving forward."

Danielle left without even a cordial goodbye. I didn't let it bother me too much, though. I had a howling girlfriend whose desire to orgasm came before any of my needs.

7/21

"YOU LOOK QUITE ALLURING THIS afternoon." I turned to my companion.

"Thank you."

"I think you have a great eye for fashion. You seem to have a wonderful sense of what complements your skin tone and hair."

"Thank you. So, what's this plan of yours?"

"Moreau mentioned you like horses, so I thought we'd check out a polo match. Is that alright with you?"

"What do you think Cash and Skye are doing?"

My R8 sped west down 27 on our way to Bridgehampton.

"She's taking good care of him. Of that I'm sure."

"You two make an interesting couple."

"You don't approve?" I said.

"I didn't say that. It's not my place to speak about others' relationships and friendships."

"Yellow looks quite sleek on you."

"You told me to wear my best Kentucky Derby-type outfit, and I listened."

Kinsley was wearing a flowy pale-yellow dress, black espadrilles, and a substantial sun hat that matched her shoes. She truly was a gorgeous young woman. Not sure if you ever viewed HBO's *Entourage*, but dearest reader, picture a younger version of the iconic Sloane from that program. One of the all-time beauties.

"You got a text from Skye."

"What's it say?"

"I don't think I should be reading your guys' texts."

"Loosen up. Will ya?"

"It says: 'cowboy and Indian on a ranch. Riding side-saddle'."

"Cool, thanks."

"What does that mean? Do you guys text in code or something?"

"It's like you said, we're an 'interesting couple.'"

I pulled into a crowded and lengthy driveway where a valet took the convertible and disappeared. I then led the Israeli-American beauty to the outdoor field.

"The sport of kings, Kinsley. Isn't it beautiful?"

"Oh wow. Look at that horse. She's so...regal-looking."

"That's a..."

"Criollo. I know," she interrupted.

"Okay, so I guess I'm watching with a true pro."

"Well, I know horses, but not polo."

We stood side by side, watching the players practice before the match started. The horses were either Criollos or thoroughbreds, mounted by Argentinian professionals.

"So, the game's divided into chukkas, which are like periods or quarters in other sports. Do you watch any sports regularly?"

"I watched a bit of football, baseball, and basketball with my brothers growing up, but I've started to get more into them since Cash and I started dating."

"Oh, that's splendid. So nice to have joint hobbies."

"Right? Cash has been showing me the ropes of fantasy sports, and it does make the games more fun. He'll talk about the statistics and analytics behind it. It's weirdly fascinating, and it brings him so much joy."

"If you want my advice, you should book a surprise trip to Vegas with him. He'd love that. You guys can watch sports and play poker, but also take in a *Britney* or *Backstreet Boys* show. And if you're feeling particularly adventurous, The Spearmint Rhino always promises to be a, what's that word you love, 'interesting' night."

"I could see us doing that...well, all except for the last part."

Kinsley responded with that hoarse voice of hers that often sounded like she had a bout of pharyngitis. At first, I oscillated between loving and hating her voice, but after a month or so, I couldn't get enough of it. Kinsley sounded like a failing actress pastiching a lifelong smoker.

The match started, and Moreau's lady was instantly immersed. Her irises darted from thoroughbred to rider to mallet.

"Why doesn't that guy on the navy team just..."

"He can't cross the line of the ball. The player who hits it has the right of way."

"Makes sense. I don't want to see any horses crashing."

"You see there, though. There will always be some bumping and body-checking."

"That was a nice steal by the white team."

"It's called 'hooking' in polo."

"This is exhilarating," she said. "Wow. Look at how brawny the horses are. Gosh, they're so big and fast."

"Have you ever seen the movie, *Equus*?"

"No, I think I've heard of it though."

"Movie about horses with Richard Burton. I think you'd like it. Good couple's movie."

"Cool, thanks."

The match continued, and the navy team was leading the white by a score of four to one at halftime.

"What's everyone doing?" she asked. "Where are they going?"

"It's halftime, so everyone in the crowd goes onto the field to stomp the divots. C'mon. It's fun. Follow me...If you want to."

"Sure."

I led Kinsley onto the middle of the field, and she pressed her black espadrilles into the worn-out grass.

"This is so bizarre," she said. "I can't believe this is a thing."

"Yeah, it's been around forever. The horses make a ton of divots from stopping and starting, so someone needs to clean this field. The crowd's like a human Zamboni."

Kinsley's copious black hair bounced and swayed as she gleefully stomped on the shabby field.

"This is so cool, Jeff."

"Yes. Yes, it is."

The horses and riders began making their way back onto the field, so the crowd scurried to the sidelines. Kinsley held the hem of her dress as she hared to safety. She was a superb young lady, and Moreau was a very lucky man.

"Julius Caesar and his poor little slave girl in an old mansion somewhere, with chains," Skye texted me.

"On horseback in American Revolutionary clothing. The horse's mane tickling your back," I responded.

"Dinner at The Pratincole. Two love eggs in each of my holes. You controlling them remotely. Making me moan and weep in public."

Kinsley and I continued to watch the next chukka, and unfortunately, it was a relatively tedious, low-scoring match. After the navy team held on for the win and guests started to clear out, I brought Kinsley to the stable area of the property.

"How do you know these people again?"

"Who knows? Friends of my father, probably. I know everyone. How'd you like to pet and feed one of the thoroughbreds?"

"Oh, Jeff, can we? I'd adore that."

I spoke to one of the stable boys who was previously told I'd want an audience with the finest horse on the property. He led me to a magnificent sorrel stud with an extremely sinewy frame.

"Wow, this brings me back," she said while brushing the horse's coat and feeding it a carrot. "I used to pet, brush, and feed horses my whole childhood. I missed this."

"What's his name?" I asked the stable boy.

"Serenity."

"No kidding. Kinsley, his name's Serenity. How old?"

"Two."

Kinsley rubbed her nose against a whinnying Serenity.

I took 30 or so pictures of the arresting young lady and her temporary best friend. Soon after, I drove Kinsley home. Moreau's lady's comparatively tense personality had loosened, and she seemed to enjoy my presence. And I should reiterate this young woman was an absolute rocket. Refined, fashionable, friendly, effervescent, Mensa-level intellect, and maybe slightly arcane. Kinsley was the type of girl Homer or Ovid would've deified. That impossibly infallible woman of whom you'd do anything to spend even an extra two or three moments.

But dearest reader, that was Moreau's lady.

8/30

ONE OF MY FAVORITE TIMES in any relationship is when you first discuss your masturbatory exploits. Most couples our age have that conversation at one point or another, and my adventures, especially in the early high school years, were quite atypical.

You see, dearest reader, I don't think all ladies realize the power of a Facebook or Instagram bikini photo. My meaning, of course, is any winsome woman who's confident enough in her body to post a swimsuit picture seems wholly unaware of how those photos are being used. But I'm afraid I'm bloviating again.

In the simplest terms, especially in high school and college whence males are at their peak horniness, all those sexually charged bikini pictures are being copied and pasted into teenagers' "special" folders. They're named something like: "New Folder," "Math Homework," "NFL Highlights," or "Extra Credit." And these abstruse folders contain not just girls' nude photos that have been passed around from guy to guy, but also the easily accessible Facebook and Instagram bikini pictures.

Now, some ladies may say, "'Why would guys jerk off to pictures of me when porn is everywhere?'" And that's the million-dollar question. The answer is simple: there's something particularly thrilling about knowing and having conversed with the person you're thinking of while indulging yourself.

Throughout high school, I much preferred pleasuring myself to the Bahamas bikini pictures of my Exdover classmates than to random, surgically altered MILFs on various pornographic sites. If a Hollandsworth friend happened to send me the latest nude photos of a Cordelia or Quelea girl we grew up with, fantastic. However, when those were unavailable, I was happy to scour my Facebook and Instagram feeds for a provocative procession of revealing pictures.

My libidinous curiosity typically peaked during March, the summer months, and Halloween. You see, dearest reader, when were the objects of my affection most likely to be posting their beach pictures and flaunting their seasonal abs? Spring break and summer break, of course. And then, it's a well-known certitude that women throughout the country adore posting their most seductively revealing outfits on the nights surrounding American children's greatest gorging.

I may have even taken this whole procedure further than my compatriots in that if my go-to girls hadn't posted in a while, I'd turn to rather eclectic sources. I'm most embarrassed to admit that a few particularly salacious female headshots on LinkedIn caused me to break out the lotion and enjoy some self-pleasuring on rare occasions. And yearbook photos, dating app profiles, and even my peers' YouTube channels have achieved the same indecorous results.

There was never anything malicious or sordid about my activities. Before these scathing paragraphs, I'd never shared these taboo excerpts. However, I believe all people delve into cringeworthy activities during their years of self-discovery. I will say, dearest reader, there's no right way to undergo puberty, and I'd never lambaste a teenager who's learning about their snowflakian sexual desires. So, I open this section not by repenting for my teenage actions, but rather by educating my dearest reader whilst also cautioning people about their social media content. For every bikini picture a popular high schooler/college student posts, I guarantee at least 30 of her classmates have pleasured themselves to said picture during their period of self-realization—a bit of food for thought.

Alas, we beat on to the only other day I was charged with the Sisyphean task of stimulating the young Miss Avital.

It was about 32 hours before what you'll find to be the proposal heard 'round the South Fork, and Moreau needed me to abscond with his inquisitive angel. He called me that morning and said:

"Campbell?"

"Where are you? What time is it?"

"I'm by the pool, and it's 9:32. I didn't wake you, did I?"

"What's up?" I said as I took a quick shot of scotch.

"Tomorrow's the big night. I'm doing it."

"Getting a job?"

"Stop. You know what I'm talking about."

"Whaddya need?"

"Two things. Can you give me the number of that horse guy? I wanna take her for a romantic ride."

"Done. I'll text you."

"And I need you to take Kinsley somewhere for a few hours. I gotta call her parents, call my parents, call the horse guy, call The Crow's Nest, and pick out an outfit. Formulate a plan. I dunno. A million things."

"Breathe, Moreau. I'll take care of everything you need. You know you're my boy."

"Thanks, man. Appreciate it, as always."

"What are you gonna tell the girl?"

"Do you need a suit?" he asked. "Or some fashion item?"

"Always."

"I'll tell her you don't trust Skye's advice and want her to help pick out some fall attire for you."

"Done."

We hung up, and I then told Skye about the potential proposal and asked her to spend the day however she liked, while I entertained Moreau's beauteous belle.

I then drove Kinsley in the convertible, parked it in the East Hampton lot, and walked with her down Newtown Lane.

"Where are we going?" she asked.

"I thought we'd hit up John Varvatos, Theory, and James Perse."

"Okay. And you need my help to shop? You dress fine."

"My father always taught me unless you're the best at something, ask for help. It's why I have The Pratincole cater my big events and why I have a pilot fly the family jet."

"Right. Well, thanks then."

"Of course. You're venerated as a new age Anna Wintour."

"By whom?" She laughed.

"Moreau. Guy worships you."

We went into John Varvatos and scanned the outerwear section, which was filled with various browns, blacks, and greys that time of year.

"So, are you looking for, like, a trench coat or a parka or vest? Please give me something to go off."

"Pretend I'm your mannequin. How would you dress me?"

"I work primarily in beauty products, not men's clothes."

"I've seen your lovely Instagram profile. I've scrutinized every dress and bikini picture with the goal of ameliorating my fashion acuity."

"Weird, but whatever. So, you're my mannequin?"

"Yes, ma'am."

"Stand still and close your mouth for once."

"A bit spicy today, aren't you?"

"Shush...let's see...how about, yeah, this seems like you."

The Mediterranean stunner pulled out a coat and wrapped it around my body.

"Black corduroy trench coat? This screams Jefferson Campbell III."

"Great, I'll take it. You're a genius. See anything else you like?"

"That's it? Not gonna try anything on?"

"Not how I shop. I'm an efficient man. I shop with intelligent experts and waste not a minute."

"Then you're missing the essence of shopping. You're not getting any true joy out of it."

"I get enough joy out of other pursuits."

"Whatever. Pay, and then let's check out James Perse."

Upon exiting John Varvatos, Kinsley and I walked outside to a perfectly tranquil Hamptons summer day. I closed my eyes and took in the sunlight while my companion looked in the window of our next store.

"Who's that dashing man in the seersucker suit?" a familiar voice crowed.

I turned and found Ivee Petrapoulos approaching Kinsley and me. The 18-year-old dynamo pinched my lapel and scanned both my body and my now-present friend's.

"Mr. Campbell, who's this dashing young lady? Things with your DJ girl didn't work out?"

"Skye's fine."

"I'm Kinsley," my suddenly riveted compatriot said.

"Kinsley, this is Ivee something or other."

"Petrapoulos, but you knew that. Mr. Campbell and I are old friends. I attended Cordelia. You're not from the Upper East Side, are you?"

"No, I'm not."

"Now, Mr. Campbell, I seemed to have overheard something about an intimate gathering you're having this Saturday eve?"

"Kinsley, why don't you head on in? I'll join you in a sec."

Moreau's lady gradually walked backwards into James Perse, attempting to unearth a non-existent history.

"It was nice meeting you, Ivee."

I was then left alone with the blue-blooded blonde.

"No Princeton for you?"

"I'm officially taking a gap year."

"Daddy must be thrilled."

"I'm my own woman. I make my own decisions."

She was wearing a floral Zimmermann frock and had her thin straight tendrils tied in a neat ponytail.

"So, was this a chance encounter?"

"I saw your car in the back parking lot. Figured if I stood outside long enough, I'd run into you."

"I appreciate honesty."

"I know you do."

"Well, you found me. Now, if you don't mind, I'm needed inside."

"That Kinsley's a fastidious dresser, isn't she?"

"I trust your ACTs went well?"

"What Upper East Sider can't throw out supercilious adjectives at the drop of a hat? Can we sit? I'm exhausted."

Ivee and I stepped toward a sidewalk bench and sat side by side for a moment, while Kinsley looked on, conspicuously, from the store's window.

"How can I help you?"

"I'd like to go to this exclusive summer bash of yours."

"We're at capacity."

"Guys my age don't say no to me, you know."

"I'm with Skye."

"What about that graceful older woman shooting me daggers from the James Perse interior?"

"She's 24."

"Here's the deal, Mr. Campbell: either you invite me to your soirée, or I'll be forced to accidentally show up at your address at a most inopportune time."

"Fine. Bring a few hot female friends of yours. I wanna show my boys a good time."

"Thank you so much. You won't regret this." Ivee wrapped her arms around my shoulders.

"Please don't touch me." I gently removed her arms from my body as if they were animal feces.

I stood and began to walk away, but she called out:

"One more thing."

Ivee stood no less than six inches from my face and said:

"I need advice."

"About?"

"I have around 360 days to find myself and my purpose. I don't know where or why to look."

"You're an astute young lady. You'll figure it out."

"Jefferson, I'm serious. I want your guidance. Only yours."

"You're toeing the line between infatuated and creepy."

"Oh, stop. You know you love me."

"You want my advice?"

"I'm dying to hear it. I've been waiting days to run into you again."

Ivee grasped her ponytail with both hands and began fiddling with it.

"Leave."

"What do you mean?"

"Leave here. Leave behind the Hamptons and the Upper East Side."

"Why would I do a silly thing like that?"

"'Cause I didn't...and I regret it."

"You went to Yale. Last time I checked, that's not in Manhattan."

"I came home every other weekend and spent my summers in the Hamptons. I'm so tired of nearly everyone I've ever met."

"So, Skye doesn't satisfy you?"

"Will you stop? That's not what I meant."

"Where do I go?"

"Leave the country. Bring a credit card, a passport, and a change of clothes. Nothing else."

"This sounds like your dream, not mine."

"Don't you want to just leave behind the pressures of school, your parents, your friends, and your career?"

"As long as there's a spa, a beach, and room service wherever I'm going."

"Do something spontaneous. That's my advice. Do something you never thought you'd do. Something that gives you an insane adrenaline rush and makes you forget about everyone and everything."

"You've clearly thought long and hard about this."

"I gotta go. Maybe I'll see you Saturday."

"Oh, I'll be there. The tall blonde in the linen Bottega Veneta."

I joined Kinsley back in the store, where she handed me three trendy blazers.

"You seem shaken," she said. "Who was that? What did she want?"

"Fucking Christ...excuse my language."

7/31

DEAREST READER, I'M NOT AWARE of your stock portfolio or your inheritance, but I have a hunch if we compared our net worths, mine would come out on top. Now I say this not to brag, but to introduce my next salient point.

Children that blossom whilst surrounded by dazzling opulence have an onerous future ahead of them. I bring this up not because I want or even expect a particle of sympathy, nay, this is a vital verity that'll aid in your understanding of why I am the way I am.

I assume it's not a bombshell if I say that as a stripling the word "no" wasn't in my caretakers' lexicon. If I wanted a GameCube, Giants tickets, a jet ski, a bustier au pair, an Audi, a helicopter ride to beat traffic, or my own house, I was given it. Now, the downside to this is as I progressed through my adolescence, I became harder to satisfy. Frivolous spending and trivial trips no longer stimulated my snobbish pheromones.

Throughout the past five years, I've needed to unearth new ways to reenergize my ossifying neurons. And throughout high school and college, while I found sky diving, swimming with sharks, canopy tours, and acro-paragliding to be suitable ways to quench my inextinguishable thirst, these weren't always readily available. Thus, my primary stimuli were frequent drug binges courtesy of my dealer, Orca, and increasingly deranged sexcapades. And for those reasons and several others, I loved Skye Pellegrini. She'd hang on me as if increase of appetite had grown by what fed on it.

Now dearest reader, on the 31st of July, my 23rd birthday, my loyal Hollandsworth friends—Cash Moreau, Dean O'Reilly, and TR Mathewson—joined me on the latter's boat for a presumed afternoon of debauchery while Skye was busy back at Campbell Manor. She was spending several hours of her day preparing to surprise me in a way only she could.

"Mathewson, you son of a bitch, I love your fucking boat."

"Thanks, Gambler," he called to me. "Happy birthday."

"T-Rex, we gotta take the fucking Gambler below deck. Huge surprise waiting."

"I know where this is going," Moreau said.

We opened the door to the palatial bedroom beneath Mathewson's deck and found three high-priced smokeshows waiting for us.

"Irish, you fucking dog," I said to my clever friend. "This is fucking awesome. Thanks a lot. Love getting together with the boys."

"Didn't get one for Dollar, though," O'Reilly said. "That uppity Israeli dime might get pissed."

"I appreciate your sentiment and candor. I wouldn't have partaken anyway."

"How 'bout some fucking lines first?" T-Rex Mathewson shouted. "Irish, invite the girls over."

Two of the young ladies remained situated on the bed, while the third joined Mathewson and me by the kitchenette.

"Moreau? Nothing for you, I presume?" I was always worried he felt lonely.

"All good, thanks. Enjoy, though."

After some toasting, birthday singing, and bountiful lines of South America's finest, I went and sat with the ladies on the bed.

"I'd like our three beguiling sirens to please introduce themselves," O'Reilly said.

"I'm Felony," a buxom, biracial twenty-something said.

"Peony," a blonde babe who looked like a Quelea dropout added.

"Lucille," an exotic, raspy-voiced one whispered.

"Moreau, you gonna sit by the door all night?" I asked my loyal friend.

"I'm more comfortable over here...and I may not stay long."

"You guys, I might need two of these girls," I laughed.

The shy one, Lucille, went to greet Moreau personally.

"You're quiet, handsome."

I didn't notice it at first because the lighting was dim, and she was hidden, but this escort, Lucille, looked like the long-lost twin of Kinsley Avital.

"Whaddya think of Lucille?" O'Reilly shouted to Moreau.

"That's not even remotely funny," he said.

"Jesus," I shouted. "What's the problem now, Moreau?"

I will say I couldn't stop laughing when I saw her up close. It was such an uncanny resemblance.

"O'Reilly, you son of a bitch, this is incredible. Lucille, take a seat next to Peony and me."

"If you want two girls, I'll happily donate mine," Mathewson said. "It's a worthy cause."

"Thank God you said so," O'Reilly added. "I'm not in an altruistic mood."

Felony interrupted and said:

"Do y'all want to talk all night or have some fun?" And then she removed her top and bra.

"And...I'm out," Moreau said while he instantly exited center stage. "Happy birthday, Campbell."

My loyal friend exited, and Mathewson soon followed him out the door with a baggie and a bottle.

"Irish, you gotta tell me the story behind this."

"Ladies, you don't mind a quick story, do ya?"

They all shook their heads and half-heartedly listened to O'Reilly.

"So, remember when you called me at the beginning of the summer, right after Dollar and his girl got out here?"

"Yeah..."

"Not sure if you remember, but it sounded like you had a crush on Dollar's girl."

"I don't remember saying anything of the sort."

"Fuck outta here. I think I'm quoting here. You said, 'Moreau's girl is an absolute goddess. She's got intelligence, looks, a sense of humor, and comes from considerable wealth and class. The girl's a taller version of the kid who sings that "Bad Things" song with MGK.'"

"That's some insane memory you've got there."

The three girls started chuckling at the peculiarity.

"After that call," O'Reilly continued, "I looked through Dollar's girlfriend's Instagram, pants down of course, and that led me to a moment of clarity."

"So, this plan was two months in the making?"

"Yes, sir. I called Algonquin the next weekend and asked him to send me pics and Insta handles of his roster."

"Jesus. I haven't spoken to him since the five-year reunion. You're quite resourceful. Papa O'Reilly would be proud."

"Algonquin sent me a bunch of Asian girls and some super-beat-looking white MILFs. Not your types. So, I filtered the search. Asked him if he had any Mediterranean girls. He came back with some big-titted Italian girls. Eventually, I sent him Kinsley's Instagram handle and said, 'Find me a girl that looks identical to her.'"

At that point, a topless Felony and bouncy Peony were laughing uproariously while Lucille sat there perplexed.

"Not sure where Algonquin found you," he said to our doppelgänger friend, "but you're an angel. Campbell'll treat you right...bro, you want Felony or Peony as girl number two?"

"You're both amazing young ladies, but I think Peony is more what I'm looking for."

"Fuck you, dude," Felony said, laughing. "Nah, I'm only playin'. Enjoy, girls."

She held Irish's hand and blew me a kiss as the two went back above deck.

"Well, ladies, it's just you and me."

"What do you want to do to us?" Peony said.

"Keep your clothes on for the time being. I have a proposition."

"I don't love where this is going," she said while her associate remained quiet.

"No, it's nothing bad. I have a girlfriend, you see, and I remain loyal to her. In fact, I'd appreciate it if you two don't touch me at all."

"This is off to a super weird start."

"I'd like to pay you additional cash right now if you'll allow me to film you."

"Doing what?" the blonde said.

"Anything I ask...within reason."

"I'm up for it," Lucille finally spoke.

"I'll give you $500 each if you do everything I say and don't hide your faces. Or I'll give you $250 if you do everything I say but do hide your faces. Finally, you may leave at any time, and I'd never ask you to do anything without your consent. So, what'll it be?"

"500."

"500."

"Feel free to stop or leave at any time. I'm taking out my phone camera now and am pressing record."

I never felt comfortable filming myself on an iPhone that's hooked up to the Cloud, but as long as my face wasn't in the video, it couldn't do me any harm. I was planning on auto-tuning or muting my voice and editing out certain parts later.

"Lucille, describe what Peony is wearing."

"Um, a leopard print dress and black heels."

"What's her most attractive feature?"

"Um, her hair."

"Looking at her now, what's the first thing you'd like to do with her...sexually?"

"Um, I dunno."

"Come on, kid. Indecisiveness is the only thing that won't work here."

"Um, okay. Lick her nipples."

"Proceed...Peony, feel free to say 'no' at any time."

Lucille gradually removed the silent Peony's knee-length garment along with her heels and proceeded to tongue the protuberant nipples. I zoomed in and became particularly aroused when I saw how much the two were enjoying themselves.

My camera then filmed Peony's lips venturing throughout her cohort's body as muted purrs emanated from the mouths of both my puppets. Over the next 30 minutes, I continued filming as Lucille blindfolded, bound, and gagged Peony. I had the former continue to compliment the latter. My goal was to create a loose, fun atmosphere.

I then went from panning around the room to show the décor to a mid-scene establishing shot, and eventually some over-the-shoulder and birds-eye view angles.

Lucille proved to be quite adroit in the bedroom as her partner's soft groans soon crescendoed into cacophonous screeches of joy. And after the epic climax, Peony could barely move.

"After you've cleaned up and settled down, I'd like you to stand side by side. I need to take a picture of you two for my girlfriend to see. Lucille, strip."

"Yes, sir," they both responded.

I turned the video off and proceeded to take several photos of my now exhausted companions.

"Skye, which do you prefer?" I texted her the most flattering image of the lascivious ladies.

"It's your birthday, baby. I've got plenty of ideas for either of them ;)."

"Peony, may you please leave Lucille and me alone. Go out and join the others...as soon as you feel up to it. No pressure."

After a few minutes, I was left alone with Lucille, so I explained my latest proposition.

"I'd like for you to come home and meet my amorous little girl-friend. Is that something you might be interested in?"

"I dunno."

"I'll give you $500 to meet her and have dinner with us, $2,000 to have sex with us in my red room. And $5,000 if you do everything I say and give somewhere between an A-minus and A-plus performance. And of course, you can so no and leave at absolutely any time. No pressure at all."

"I'll do it. Sounds like fun, Jefferson."

"Two other things, though. When you meet my girlfriend, I want you to approach her and say what an honor it is to meet the greatest young DJ in the country. Compliment her on her song 'Bikinis and Bellinis' and really ham it up. Her DJ name is Skygreenii, by the way."

"Simple enough."

"And then once we begin to get sexual, I'm gonna change your name to 'Kinsley.'"

"Is that that quiet guy's girlfriend?"

"Yes, it is…Are you judging me?"

"Of course not, sir. I appreciate any and all kinks."

"We're gonna have a good time…and don't touch me unless we're in the presence of Skye and she approves."

The rest of the boat outing was a congenial blur. My Hollandsworth friends and I went for a lengthy dip with our charming guests before eventually returning to shore and saying our hearty farewells. I then had Moreau drive Lucille and me back to Campbell Manor, where Skye was undoubtedly waiting with some surprises.

"Kid, I'm home. And I brought company."

I will say, dearest reader, Skye looked hotter than I'd ever seen her. Greeted us in nothing but a three-piece garter set. She was in a submissive position with a tight ponytail complementing her whole mien.

"Good evening, Mr. Campbell."

"Jesus, Skye. This all looks…fucking wow."

Skye actually thought to hang streamers, blow up balloons, and make me dinner. I never thought she had any type of maternal instinct, but that little minx was full of surprises.

"Does it really, daddy? I did a good job? You mean it?"

"Are you kidding? Fucking spectacular, baby. Come here." We engaged in a passionate kiss while our guest looked on with envy. "Is that steak frites I smell? And champagne? Goddamn baby, you look so hot. Goddamn. I love you so much."

"Lucille, this is the famed DJ Skygreenii."

"Skye, it's such an honor. I love your music so much. Is this 'Bikinis and Bellinis' playing right now?" Our guest was a natural sycophant. "You're my absolute favorite DJ. I follow you on Insta. Although my real name isn't Lucille."

"That's sweet of you to say. You look fucking sexy. I fucking love your dress."

"Ladies? Ready to eat?"

Lucille and Skye became quite chummy as I triturated my medium-rare steak and we all sipped glasses of champagne.

And once the three of us finished our dinners, wouldn't you know it, my newly domesticated girlfriend cleared everyone's plates. I was astounded by this side of her. We'd been together for 10 or 11 months, and I'd never seen it before.

"Baby, you're a fucking star in the kitchen. What are you going to surprise us with next?"

She wrapped her arms around me before retreating into the kitchen.

"Profiteroles?" I said as she delivered the dessert and accompanied that with a glass of scotch for me.

"Did you make these yourself?" I asked after chewing one of The Pratincole's succulent profiteroles.

"Of course, mi amor."

"Skye, take a seat. You're working too hard. Eat one."

"Do you two have...company often?" Lucille asked.

"We have the occasional bouts of ethical non-monogamy," Skye said.

"That's so cool you two have a system like that. I envy you. Monogamy is so antiquated, but also you need to have a certain amount of comfort with one person."

"J and I think it's all about trial and error. We've figured out some things work, and some don't, and we constantly adapt to, like, please each other."

"True relationship goals. I'm jealous of you guys."

"I'm sure you'll find the perfect relationship soon," Skye said. "I mean, with a body like that, you legit must have guys tearing the clothes off your body."

"That's not the issue. I want someone who will want my clothes left on for a few dates, and then we explore the other stuff later."

"Lucille, stand up." I interrupted.

And all of a sudden, I had complete control of the house.

"Walk to the center of the room."

Our submissive stood still in the middle of my lavish all-white dining room as Skye looked on.

"Lucille, from now on, I'll address you as Kinsley and only Kinsley. Do you understand, Kinsley?"

"Whoa, daddy." Skye turned her attention to me. "What's happening? I didn't know you were...I mean, why? I don't understand."

"Chill out, baby. Grab some stuff from our special drawer and offer it to our guest."

"Daddy, you know I'm down for anything, but I wanna know why? I mean, Kinsley?"

I gave her a warm embrace and rubbed the top of her head while Lucille looked on vacuously.

"Skye baby, you know our rule. If you don't want to do this, I'll send her home right now. No hard feelings. We're rock solid, baby. Tell me what you want to do, and I'll do it."

I held her cheeks as she responded:

"Well, I mean, I guess it's, like, your birthday. Okay. I consent. I'm up for anything. But let's make this the first and last Kinsley night."

"Of course, baby."

"Remind me, how do I look again?"

"You're the prettiest fucking girl in the world."

"You're okay too."

We embraced again while Lucille, presumably immune to any sexual oddities, stood motionless. She was a true professional.

"Daddy, I think I've got some stuff for us," Skye said after she returned from the drug drawer.

"Kinsley?"

"Sir, may I partake?"

"Of course. What's mine is yours."

Skye and I sat back at the dining room table and turned our chairs to face Kinsley.

"Skye baby, put on some music. And Kinsley, start stripping for us."

My girlfriend played one of her hits, and Kinsley proved she was a true veteran despite her younger age. I mean, dearest reader, this girl was gyrating left, twisting right, twerking her tight little ass, and she achieved the ideal amount of teasing without going overboard.

"You got some moves, sweetheart," Skye shouted to our guest.

When the song ended, Kinsley powered down and remained still and amenable. She was now entirely nude, and her hands were stationed at her sides. Our little doll.

Skye, now noticeably aroused, straddled my lap and aggressively bit my lip. It seemed as though Skye was trying to compete with our fucking knockout of a guest.

"Skye dearest," I said, rubbing my nose against hers, "would you be so kind as to grab our video camera from the bedside table, unlock our little hideaway upstairs, and wait for Kinsley and me?"

"See you in a few, daddy." She nodded.

After Skye scurried upstairs, I went to gauge Kinsley's comfort level.

"You okay so far?"

"Yes, sir."

"Is there anything you're not comfortable with?"

"No, sir. I wanna make you and Skye as happy as possible."

"You're a rocket, Kinsley. We're gonna have a lot of fun."

I led our guest upstairs to the red room door and knocked.

"Baby, we're coming in."

"Ready, daddy," she said, electing to speak in her top-notch baby voice for the rest of the evening.

We entered, and I said:

"Kinsley, go to Skye."

"That's me!"

"Lighten up, girlfriend," Skye said to her new black-haired partner.

My girl handed me the camcorder, and I opened with an establishing shot before circling the two of them and then zooming from a medium shot to an extreme close one.

"Kinsley, if you feel uncomfortable or aren't having fun, we'll stop immediately. I mean that."

Skye stripped out of her clothes and continued to touch and nibble at every part of Kinsley's athletic figure as they made their way onto the bed. The former had unmitigated control in this particular scene.

However, the lovely events began to take a turn when Skye started biting Kinsley's neck. Fake Kinsley, the consummate professional, moaned and shrieked and never once appeared out of her element.

Skye then grabbed our darker companion's ankles and dragged her to the foot of the bed.

"You've been a bad girl, Kinsley. It's time for a fucking spanking." Skye's voice shifted from her peppy baby to a punitive cuckquean.

By that point, Kinsley was splayed out at a 90-degree angle with her legs dangling off the California King while Skye stood over her and grabbed her ass-cheeks.

Our guest's behind was becoming rosier with each progressive slap.

"Tell me I'm fucking prettier than you," Skye shouted as I filmed Kinsley.

"You're prettier than me."

"Tell me I'm fucking skinnier than you, you fucking slut."

"You're skinnier than I am, mistress."

"Tell me you're my little bitch."

"I'm your bitch, Skye."

"That's enough," I thundered. "Skye, go sit in the corner. That's not how we treat our guests. This room is about fun, not vitriol."

As aroused as I was, I believed ebullient hospitality to be one of life's most important tenets. And Skye's performance was certainly not that. I turned the camcorder off and approached Kinsley.

"Are you okay? Your behind is redder than a pinot noir."

"I'm fine, sir. Have I been a good Kinsley?"

"Wonderful. But how are you feeling?"

"Horny, sir."

"You can leave at any time, and I'll pay you full price."

"No, sir. I wanna stay until everyone has been satisfied."

"You hear that, Skye? We have a true professional in our midst."

My girl sat alone in the corner of the room, snickering maniacally.

"Skye, we're going to get started here. I'd like you to sit the first few plays out and join us once you've become a bit less despicable.

"Yes, daddy."

"And naturally, you have every right to tell Kinsley and me to stop if you don't want us to do something."

"Yes, daddy." The baby voice had returned.

"Kinsley, head to the cabinet underneath the floggers. There's a hidden fridge and food drawer."

"Yes, sir."

"Now, from the drawer, you'll see jars of Skippy peanut butter, Nutella, and Speculoos. Choose whichever one you'd like."

"What's Speculoos, sir?"

"It's like a cookie butter spread with cinnamon flavor from Belgium. If you've never tried it, I implore you to choose that one."

"Yes, sir."

"Follow me," I said.

I walked over and stood directly in front of Skye in the corner of the room while Kinsley trailed a few steps behind.

"Kinsley, unzip my fly, remove my pants and boxers, and lather the area in Speculoos."

I leaned against the red leather wall, with Kinsley lathering and fondling while Skye sat five feet to our right with the camcorder in hand.

"Now, taste the Speculoos, angel."

Kinsley's tongue began pirouetting around in circles and diagonals, slurping the Speculoos spread out of every ridge and crevice. Skye could no longer sit out and watch the licentious activities.

"Daddy, may I please return?"

"Absolutely, love. Help our guest out. Show her how it's done."

A starving Skye spent the next five minutes gobbling down the Speculoos while Kinsley kissed her neck and shoulders.

"Now, kid, learn how to share with our guest," I said.

"Yes, daddy."

Skye and Kinsley then took turns caressing and inhaling while I stood against the wall in a euphoric state.

"Did my heart love till now?" I thought. "Forswear it, sight! For I ne'er saw true beauty till this night."

We eventually made our way onto the bed, where I railed Skye while she ate out Kinsley, and then the two of them switched places. There was ample yelping and some aggressive clawing, biting, and slapping. In the end, Lucille received a well-deserved $5,000 in cash along with a car to drive her home around 3:00 a.m. She was a phenomenal sport. What a fucking night.

9/3/17

AFTER ABOUT THREE MONTHS OF dating and a plethora of conversations about our various kinks, Skye and I agreed to spend a night at a strip club. I suppose this was around Christmas of 2017. I'll circle back to 9/3/17 shortly.

I had a tremendous amount of respect for Skye in general, but specifically for her inquisitiveness. The kid always wanted to learn more, whether it was about my life, my sexual quirks, or even how to become a more well-rounded person. And at the time, she was a 19-year-old permanent Hamptons-dweller who had limited experience with Manhattan's squalid underbelly.

Before entering this 34th Street staple, I handed Skye $300 and told her to use it wisely. The manager then directed us to a VIP table a considerable distance from the stage, but I told him we'd prefer to sit by the main attractions to achieve the most authentic experience for my first-time guest.

Skye tossed dollar bills with glee, squeezed the dancers' asses with fitting vivacity, and even skipped over to two of the terpsichoreans by the bar and brought them over to us. I watched as Skye's elation reached new heights after receiving her first-ever lap dance from an F-cupped MILF. And then, toward the end of the evening, she used some of "her money" to pay for several lap dances for me, sedulously taking mental notes.

Toward the end of the night, we sat in the corner of the club, and Skye had a friendly, tattooed Argentinian grinding on my thighs. However, the lap dances themselves weren't the highlight, but rather the way my girlfriend spoke to these ladies.

Skye was honest and affable, gregarious and empathic. These dancers wanted to hang around the two of us even after we'd paid for our dances, and there was no more money to be earned. My girl was able to be the highlight of many young ladies' nights, and she even gained enough of their trust that they opened up to her.

"You can't believe how many sickos we deal with in here," I remembered one of the dancers said. "You know there are dudes that come in here, and...do you know what 'docking' is?"

"No," we responded.

"Docking is when a stripper is giving a guy a lap dance, and then he tries to sneak his dick inside her vagina. It happened to me once. I was dancing on a dude, and my eyes were closed, so he quickly unzipped his fly, moved my panties to the side, and shoved it in. These animals will do stuff like that out in the open."

"Fuck. Why don't you quit?" Skye asked.

"The money can sometimes be huge. And I know it sounds lame, but I love to dance. I meet plenty of cool, nice guys who just want to escape. You know how good it feels to have people constantly complimenting your figure and your dancing? And I choose my hours and who I dance for. It's empowering."

"You're perfect and I love you," Skye said.

But, dearest reader, I meant to take you back to the beginning here—to when Skye and I first officially met. Apologies for darting all over the place, but continue to trust me, and it'll all be worth it in the end. I promise.

You see, I'd spent every summer in the Hamptons since I was a baby. And during my childhood and adolescent years, I'd attempt to explore every nook and cranny of the famed area either by myself or with my father, au pair, or Hollandsworth friends. And during my daily expeditions down Jobs or Newtown Lane, I'd meet a wide variety of people, nearly all wealthy.

However, my friends and I were always enchanted by the local girls; those who spent 12 months a year living with their mortgage-paying parents in $500,000 houses in Springs or Hampton Bays, as opposed to the typically multi-million-dollar summer mansions in Sagaponack, Wainscott, Water Mill, East Hampton, or Southampton.

So, you see, Skye had been one of a group of five to 10 girls my Hollandsworth friends and I would discuss as we coped with our daily bouts of boredom. I'd spoken to Skye about her favorite Hamptons hotspots a few times back when she worked at Henry Lehr and then Tenet. She was a fast-developing girl with a wild personal style and an inveterate principle that led her to treat everyone, from day-laborer to CEO, the exact same way.

The last weekend of the summer of '17, I went with some Chapin girls to The Surf Lodge. They were in the grade below me and essentially begged me to roll with them to improve their clout. However, I wasn't complaining because I always felt there's nothing hotter than a skinny, spoiled rich girl.

I knew these ladies, knew their families, and was planning on having sex with two of them that night, but at some point, my entire mentality shifted.

It happened whilst I was watching the local clothing store girl absolutely crushing her set. This DJ, whom I faintly remembered, was garbed in neon from head to toe. And she had a scintillating amount of skin showing.

Dearest reader, I'm sitting next to a coterie of passable mademoiselles whom I'd known forever, and yet, I couldn't take my under-the-influence eyes off this rainbow creature playing homicidally dulcet beats from behind her DJ booth.

The Chapin girls, wearing their best Labor Day whites, tried to nudge me and find some way to get my attention. However, I was entranced for what seemed like 30 minutes. Then the music stopped, and the polychromatic clothing-hawker was standing at the bar. I approached within seconds.

"That set was tight," I said.

"Thanks."

"I know you, don't I?" Then, "Two more tequila shots. Prima Adoncia," I said to the bartender.

"Yes, sir, Mr. Campbell."

That was a nice touch from the bartender. When a person at a hotspot calls you by your name, all the girls around you freeze, take out their phones, and try to figure out who you are.

"Uh, thanks dude."

"You're a townie, aren't you?"

"What?"

"That's where I know you from. You're a store chick, right?"

"I'm a DJ."

"You worked at Pellegrini."

"Dude, weird."

"No, not weird. You're well-known, kid."

"I don't know you."

"It's probably better that way."

In addition to her resplendent outfit, the DJ had some intoxicating aroma emanating from her pores. It was a mix of ocean water, sweat, and a faint, applied-two-days-ago floral perfume.

"Why am I well-known? You listen to my SoundCloud?"

"No. Skye, I summer out here every year, you don't think I'd remember the cutest shop-girl in East Hampton?"

"Stalker vibes." Her serrated edge disappeared, and a smile formed.

We took our shots and stared at each other.

"What'd your friends say about me?"

"Nothing much. I just thought you were the cutest townie."

"Appreciate it."

"There was this other shop-girl in Sag who was hot, but her personality sucked. Super dull.'"

I could see the Chapin girls out of my periphery. They were an amalgamation of seething anger and intense curiosity. None of them likely viewed the DJ as girlfriend material for a 21-year-old of my stature, but I was apathetic to that group's opinions.

"But anyway, you had some young Avicii vibes."

"What are you a producer or agent or something?"

"I'm someone who values talent."

"What do I call you? Stalker has a nice ring to it."

"Jefferson Campbell III."

We knocked back a few more shots, and then I said:

"Let's get outta here. I wanna take you somewhere special."

"You're, like, a total original. I'll give ya that."

Realistically, it isn't that hard to pull a girl like her. Skye was a DJ who was typically approached by drugged-out European hardos and the bridge and tunnel crowd going to her sets in Queens and Brooklyn. I'm a flawed human, but I'm not literal street trash.

I drove her to this secluded beach that girls always loved. Waves crashing, soft sand, no clamorous people around. That night, it was the brooding, well-dressed Yale student and the local store vendor slash DJ.

Unfortunately, she was immediately boring me by talking about signs and astrology bullshit. The combination of her dreary conversation, my earlier drug-and-alcohol cocktail, and the soothing waves crashing against the shore was causing me to fade. It was a miraculous human achievement that earlier I successfully drove my dad's Mercedes the three miles to the beach. Eventually, I interrupted because I couldn't take it anymore.

"I like your voice. It's...different." And that wasn't some mendacious line.

"How?"

"It's darker."

"What is?"

"Your voice."

"Are you saying it's not girly or, like, feminine?"

"It suits you well. I appreciate your whole aura. You're a non-conformist."

"Sorry I'm all sweaty and gross. I low-key need to jump in the water."

She definitely was still sweaty. While not quite a hot mess, Skye was a lukewarm one. I didn't care about her or anything, though. I was drunk and bored and whatever.

"So, go for a swim."

"Good one."

"I'm serious...What? The tatted-up DJ girl turns down adventure and fun. Not what I would've guessed. You seemed like the wild and crazy type."

"I literally am that type."

"You're zero for one in proving it to me."

"I don't have a bathing suit."

"So?"

"I see what you're doing. You think you're so smart. I'll go in if you do."

"I'm not going in. I'm nice and relaxed where I am."

"Fine. I'll go in myself. Not because you told me to, but because salt water's good for my skin."

"I'll watch over your stuff."

Skye began an exaggerated runway model strut toward the water. Her taut figure with that firm posterior livened me up again. She removed her shoes and bra while her front remained concealed, which I thought was extraordinarily sexy. That was when I officially decided I wanted to see her again. And then, she just continued to outdo herself.

Skye dove underwater and then threw her shorts onto the shore.

"Jefferson," she called out. "Help me. The waves washed away all my clothes."

"The stroke of death is as a lover's pinch which hurts and is desired," I thought.

I walked toward the crashing waves to get a better look, but everything beneath her neck was submerged.

"Is it cold?"

"See for yourself. Join me."

"I can't get these clothes wet."

"So, don't," she called out from the water. "Take 'em all off. Like I did."

I had three options. First, I could skinny-dip with her. Second, drive off and never speak to her again because she wasn't my usual type. Or third, steal her clothes, which would both make me laugh and test how she reacted to high-stress situations.

So, I picked up each one of her items, carried them to my car, and started the engine. Meanwhile, Skye was half-cackling, half-screaming from the water.

"Jefferson? J? Jeff? Please, I'm cold. Don't leave me."

And then she dove underwater. At that moment, and this rarely happened to me, I felt sympathy for her. My perfidious actions had left her in a relatively panicked state. I exited the car, jogged toward the water, and held out her clothes and a car towel.

"Did I get you?"

"Not funny at all," she laughed. "How many girls have you tried this on?"

"You called my bluff. A lot of other people would've run out of the water naked and chased me."

"I've dealt with a lot of douchebags before. I know the type."

"Careful now. I've got your towels and clothes."

"You're too nice to drive off."

"That's a word I never get called."

Skye grabbed two towels from my hands and stepped out of the water.

"My fucking hero," the DJ said. "I'm low-key pissed you didn't join me. Kind of a pussy move."

"Let me drive you home, kid."

We walked side by side back to the road where my convertible sat. I had no plans to kiss or even touch her. Throughout my life, I'd probably brought 30 girls to that beach spot to talk. The goal was to understand their personalities, learn how tolerable they were, and find out their intentions. And the trait I was most drawn to was a certain eccentricity. If I looked hard enough, could I find another girl like this one?

"So, uh, what now?" Skye asked as I opened the car door for her.

You see, dearest reader, if I touch, kiss, or fuck a beautiful woman the first time I meet her, how am I different from any other man? My goal is for the ladies I go out with to separate themselves from the pack, and I shall do the same.

"I'll take you home, or I'll happily drop you off a few houses from your place in case you don't want me to know where you live."

"God, you have done this before, haven't you?"

"Your hair looks good wet."

We then drove in silence to Springs, where Skye lived with her grandmother. I was a bit drunk, a bit high, and a bit taken by the perky Skye.

When we arrived at her grandmother's little two-bedroom cottage, I parked the car, and she said:

"So, why didn't you wanna take me back to your place? I might've said yes."

"Put your number in my phone."

Skye entered her name as "That Naked DJ."

"I'm going back to Manhattan in a day or two and then up to Yale in a bit, but the next time you're in the city, text me."

"Yale? Fancy boy."

"Eh. I'm in NYC like every other weekend. Text me if you want to. If not, no big deal."

Naturally, That Naked DJ texted me the very next weekend as she "happened" to be coming into the city. I wasn't remotely surprised at her ardor nor that she had no hotel and allegedly no place to stay. Thus, following drinks at The Frying Pan, I booked a hotel room, and she was nude and on her knees 60 seconds after we received the room key.

9/1-9/2 AND BEYOND

Now DEAREST READER, BEFORE I lead you into what I find to be a thrilling climax and denouement, I'd like to describe to you my ideal woman.

My Elysian muse would need to be loyal, inquisitive, humorous, effervescent, affectionate, and decisive and have a shade of Machiavellian tendencies. And I've always believed in a relationship with a foundation of mutual worship.

And in terms of her background, my Aphrodite should be born into great wealth. Not that I need any additional funds, but I've found it much easier to converse with those who grew up from means. Commonality is vital, you see. It's also paramount this spectered goddess be able to present me, or a dinner party full of people, with thought-provoking conversation. Because, while on many occasions I've acquiesced to spending time with the more vacuous members of high society, I'd love to be surrounded by someone who always knows how to pique my interest.

Now, dearest reader, if I can turn back to the valiant Aeneas once again. He who once had an ill-fated relationship with the mercurial Queen Dido. I am bringing this up because I'd like to believe he would've gladly remained in Carthage to live out the remainder of his days if the dazzling Queen Dido checked enough of his boxes. Aeneas could've attempted to alter his predestined track for the sake of love. However, he noticed enough issues early on, and the fact that she was so quick to end her life may have proven his choice was the correct one. And as I found on the night of September 1st of last year, my opinion of the similarly mutable Skye shifted quite quickly. And in the end, I chose to continue my never-ending search for my utopian muse, while Skye was left to a similar fate as her Carthaginian doppelgänger.

When I last discussed this future-altering eve, I was explaining how it began in a simple enough manner. I sat on the newly installed piscine perch monitoring my collection of posh guests, who, in my nebulous state, appeared to be one large cloud floating and twirling.

The relaxed tone of the evening shifted once I spotted the perpetually perplexing Petrapoulos leaned against the locked pool house with a drink in hand.

"Ivee?" I said as I left my crow's nest for the first time.

"Mr. Campbell, I was hoping you'd find a minute to entertain each of your party's guests."

"Can't say I'm surprised you came."

"Wouldn't have missed it for a funeral. How am I dressed?"

The rising college freshman was wearing some linen Bottega Veneta that cascaded down to her ankles. It obtained that divine fit where her figure was appropriately outlined, but it wasn't too revealing. And then her silver Alaïa pumps harmonized with the translucent earrings partially covered by blonde strands that rested perfectly on her nubile shoulders.

"Stunning, actually."

"You sound surprised...and intoxicated."

"Mildly. To both. You have everything you need? Drinks? Drugs? Entertainment?"

"Drink, yes. Drugs, no. Entertainment, not initially, but maybe now."

"What's your poison? I can satisfy you."

"It's a little difficult to snort drugs after watching first-hand as your mother plummets deeper and deeper into a zombified state. But I suppose all of us UES women eventually turn to drugs. You men become so insufferable after a while."

I spotted my DJing girlfriend zeroing in on this conversation from a hundred feet away, so I felt it was time to put a stop to it.

"Well, anyway, I should get going…more guests to entertain. Maybe I'll see you around. You do look great, though. You stick around long enough, and you may find the man of your dreams."

At some point, I think I approached DJ Cree Mashun and brought her up to play while removing Skye from her post. The former is that eclectic heavy metal EDM DJ who you'll occasionally see on the charts—Amazonian woman who knows how to work a crowd.

Skye and I then bolted to the master and engaged in what wound up being our final sexual act of that summer. It was merely tranquil missionary sex culminating with a half-hour nap that undoubtedly sobered me up.

Before dozing off, I whispered:

"Thank you for tonight. I love you."

And she beamed while her eyes remained closed, not knowing what events were about to transpire.

We had slipped into the early hours of September 2nd, and the party showed no signs of decelerating. During that 12:30 a.m. to 1:30 a.m. hour, I instigated what I'd view as a self-tracking shot of my party. It was part Scorsese shooting *Goodfellas* and part God looking upon his creation after six days of toiling.

I ventured past one of the upstairs bedrooms where a rather noisy orgy was taking place. I then made sure the red room door was still locked, walked downstairs, and chatted with security both out front and at the drugs station. I spent two minutes watching Cree and her set. I strolled outside and viewed some of the more intoxicated women skinny-dipping in my pool. I continued onward to the beach where I looked at my old friend, Moreau, and that utopian muse to which he clung. I headed back inside, went downstairs, and watched as the poker table, the miniature strip club, and the video game areas were all creating indelible memories for any partygoers who partook. And then I returned to the first floor.

DJ Cree was still playing her set while about 80 increasingly intoxicated twenty-somethings were gyrating and kissing both inside and outside the house. And unfortunately, one of the couples grinding and making out on my living room floor was my darling Skye and her old winery friend. That French girl, Bérénice. I stared from afar for several seconds. Perhaps it was a drug-and-alcohol-induced mistake. But they continued. 20 seconds. 60 seconds. 90 seconds. I chose not to confront them because my father always taught me the importance of keeping one's composure and not causing a scene, especially at my own soirée. So, not quite knowing the appropriate next steps, I simply sprinted outside.

I don't believe it mattered it was Bérénice. Nothing tells me she was Skye's one great love. It could've very well been her other friends, Brooklynn and Astrid. Skye has always had tendencies that led her to that particular gender. I do take some solace in the fact it was a woman she kissed and not a man. Had it been the latter, that may have signaled I wasn't an effective boyfriend, and her needs could've been fulfilled elsewhere. However, since it was a woman, I don't feel there was anything I could've altered in my comportment that wouldn't have led to the same conclusion. Skye had always believed in free love and would happily hook up with people of all genders. That's all well and good, but she and I had rules. One of which, she broke. Had she simply asked me to include Bérénice in the bedroom, I would've said yes. There needed to be some form of communication. So, my heart shifted from loving her dearly to despising her tremendously in a matter of seconds.

I was a rabid dog. I wanted to scream and yell and punch a wall and break everything in sight. Hell, if the opportunity had presented itself, maybe I would've drowned Skye in the pool. You see, dearest reader, had there not been nearly 200 people, my reaction would've been much different. But fucking Skye and Bérénice. It is thought abroad that twixt my sheets, she's done my office. At my fucking party. No wonder I'm so fucking fucked up.

I galloped past the dancers and the pool-goers before reaching the edge of my backyard where the grass met the sand. I turned around and viewed the glitzy, sybaritic celebration I'd caused. On such beauteous property in a town filled with palatial homes, I had been an accomplice to the current perdition before me. Once again, I felt like Milton's God after Adam and Eve had created the original sin. Skye was unfaithful and dishonest, yes, but I had molded her into the woman she'd become. Was I not as responsible as she? And just as God had felt such cosmic sorrow, I too had a difficult time contemplating my past actions.

And so, just as the Almighty had done, albeit several pages beyond Genesis, I elected to hit the reset button on everything I'd created.

While still not grounded in a salubrious state, I began searching for the then incomparable Ivee Petrapoulos. She was what I needed.

It didn't take long to unearth the Cordelia queen bee. She was sipping a cocktail on one of the many white pool chairs. Laying with her head tilted back at the stars as bottomless post-grads were running, splashing, and swimming around her.

"Hey." Was all I could muster.

"Rough night? Should've avoided the drugs, Mr. Campbell."

"You wanna get out of here?"

"I figured you might be strolling by. I saw your busty DJ's tongue somewhere outside her own mouth."

"Don't want to talk about it."

"Did you break up?"

"We're broken up. She doesn't know it yet."

"The first time we spoke, you preached loyalty. I figured that wouldn't fly with you."

"You've been right about a few things."

"Like, you shouldn't be guzzling, snorting, and injecting yourself with eight different types of drugs in one evening? Like that, Mr. Campbell?"

"Call me, Jefferson, please."

I held out my hand, which she used to aid in a rise to her feet.

"Where are we going?"

"I've thought a lot about what you said."

She held my hand as we walked past the back patio, around the side of the house, and toward the front yard.

"Which part?"

"Specifically, how Skye isn't the right type of girl for me. And about how you're not going to Princeton this year."

"Who's the right type of girl for Jefferson Campbell III?"

I brushed her symmetrical and undeviating thin strands behind her ears, stared into her hazel eyes, and kissed the famed Petrapoulos heir.

The first second of the kiss made me think of the disobedient Skygreenii, but then, as Ivee's lips danced in an unexpected direction and operated in a much primmer manner, I forgot about my DJ roommate.

Eventually, it was Ivee who pulled away and said:

"What now?"

"Let's run away together."

"You can't be serious."

"Look at my face. Let's leave everything behind this instant."

"I've met you three times."

"So what?"

"I don't know. People don't do things like this."

"Great. You sold me on the idea. The last thing I want to do is what everyone else does. If I stay here, I'll enter into this acrimonious and drug-fueled state. Let's travel the world. Venture somewhere. Anywhere. Anywhere other than Manhattan or the Hamptons."

"You're nuts."

"What if there's a nascent romance here? Your only tenable argument is no one else does stuff like this. That's drivel."

Ivee exhaled and ran her two index fingers along her hairline from the top of her forehead down. Several drunken partygoers stumbled out of the house toward the driveway where their Uber was waiting. I held Ivee's hands as her brain ostensibly ran 50 different permutations about her near future.

"If I did say yes, what would the plan be?"

"Well, the whole point of the idea is to escape without a plan."

"That's insane."

I kissed her again in an attempt to placate her vacillating feelings.

"Okay," I said. "I'll run upstairs and pack a backpack while you call the limo. I can give you my father's guy's number if you need one. Then, we stop at your place. It's late enough no one'll be awake. You pack a bag of essentials, and then we take the car to JFK."

"You expect me to go on a trip with a bag I spend five minutes packing?"

"I'm gonna grab my bag now. I really want you to go on this trip with me, but I'm going no matter what."

I ran back inside, desperately hoping I didn't encounter Skye— which of course would've led to her giving me some cockeyed exegesis. I found my old Prada backpack and tossed in three shirts, two shorts, two long pants, a button-down, workout clothes, Rolex, flask, wallet, passport, and all the cash I had in the safe.

I scanned the turbid throng one last time. Didn't spot Skye, Moreau, or Kinsley, so I went out to the driveway, inebriated with that feisty fusion of scotch, Adderall, ecstasy, zeal, and freedom.

With the bag wrapped around my shoulders, I sped down the driveway, hoping I had a companion waiting for me, but was by no means desperate for amity.

"I called a car. It'll be here in two minutes," Ivee yelled out from the edge of the driveway.

"So, you're going?"

"I think. Maybe. I figure I have at least an hour to decide between now and JFK."

We made a brief stop at Ivee's place in Southampton. I told her only to take five minutes and pack her essentials, but the glittering blonde took 12 and came down with both a carry-on and a checked bag.

"JFK, please," I said to the driver. And then to Ivee, "Are you sure you brought enough?"

"You know, I woke up this morning with one plan. To come to your party, make an impression on you and your friends, and maybe even be able to brag to my girls about how I made out with the unattainable Jefferson Campbell III."

"In the future, I'd recommend dreaming larger and more fantastical."

"I'm not sure I should be taking advice from you. Throwing away a life of privilege for a rash jaunt around the world."

"I believe in destiny. And mine will never be working a finance or real estate job for 50 years, five days a week."

"I respect that."

"And this current idea I have in my head is bringing me unbelievable joy."

"Care to elaborate on today's idea?"

"Fly somewhere. We'll land, google hotels and sleep together in the most fascinating suite the city has to offer. It could be a penthouse in Zurich, an igloo in Reykjavik, a villa in Costa Rica, or maybe a tent outside Nairobi. Then, we'll relax. Truly feel at ease for the first time in our lives. No parents, no pressures, responsibilities, or expectations, no friends, jobs, textbooks, or traffic. None of it."

"And then what, Jefferson?"

"We gain independence for the first time in our lives. We'll explore the area, visit every restaurant, every museum, maybe go sky diving or bungee jumping or heliskiing, or we'll hang-glide over a volcano. It'll be an exquisite union of quiet tourist exploration and death-defying extreme sports."

"And then what?"

"That's the best part. We'll go to the airport and fly somewhere else and do it all over again. We'll go to Istanbul or Beirut, Prague or Rome. Or, if you want beaches, we'll go to Santorini or Ibiza. Some Polynesian island?"

"What about money? Or our families?" She sounded worried, but the hypnotized smile remained.

"I've made a tremendous amount through the market, poker play-ing, and sports betting. Plus, my inheritance from my munificent grandparents. And we'll find ways to make money wherever we are. Two intelligent Upper East Siders with unrivaled charisma? I need you to stop thinking so much and leap with me."

"Fine. Tell me what I say to my parents, and then I won't worry anymore. Aloud at least."

"The only person I'm telling is my father. I'll tell him I'm looking into business opportunities abroad. And you should say you're going backpacking around Europe to find yourself. Tell them it's all about self-discovery and a non-linear, outside-the-box education. Do you speak any other languages?"

"Just French, Russian, and Italian."

"Jesus. That's amazing. So, we'll find an indie Moroccan film for you to do or an Italian play in Rome. I need you to trust me."

"I do. In a sort of, 'I know I'm following a future cult leader but don't really mind' type of trust."

She leaned her vestal face on my shoulder and said:

"I guess, worst-case scenario, I can hop on a flight home any time. Maybe Daddy will be thrilled if I get all of this free-thinking pensivity out of me at a young age."

"All I ask is that you give me and my...avant-garde ideas a try. Can you do that?"

"Yes."

And, dearest reader, that was that. Ivee Petrapoulos and I arrived at JFK, and we were on a flight to Milan shortly thereafter.

Nearly nine months after that fateful summer, I'm writing from overseas. I won't tell you precisely where I'm located or how much money I've made or even who I'm with, but I can express it's been the most sensational time of my young life. It was Milan in September, Stockholm in October and November, and Muscat in December, and I've split my time at two different locations here in 2019.

Unfortunately, I'm no closer to discovering my Aeneas-like destiny, nor have I figured out what the future holds. However, I've always been a man of action and adventure. Ivee helped me realize Skye never deserved the great Jefferson Campbell III.

After a few months abroad, I did reach out to Moreau to explain the entire situation, and he understood. The man's always been a loyal friend whom I can trust with any number of secrets. And boy, what a fucking fiancée he has.

Now, dearest reader, I leave you with a few final thoughts. The first being, no one should ever feel satisfied with who they are. Shakespeare's Caesar once said:

"Let me have men about me that are fat; sleek-headed men and such as sleep o' nights. Yond Cassius has a lean and hungry look; he thinks too much; such men are dangerous."

I need to be one of those dangerous men. The instant I become content with my girlfriends, finances, material goods, and in the future, parenting skills, that's when competitors will surpass me. And this sabbatical of mine has been more educational than anything.

Second, whatever you think your future holds, you're incorrect. As with Aeneas, Achilles, Hector, Adam, Eve, and Odysseus, their initial paths seemed clear. At one time, Aeneas could've settled down and ruled Carthage with the unstable Dido; Achilles could've remained in his tent and not fought the Trojans; Hector could've absconded from Troy with his family; Adam and Eve could've lived for eternity without experiencing carnal pleasure, and Odysseus could've remained with Calypso and never returned to Penelope.

The point being, dearest reader, no matter what you attempt to control, life will alter your plans. And your ever-wandering mind, your undersized superego, and oversized id will be engaged in a never-ending battle until the day you die.

"The evil that men do lives after them; the good is oft interred with their bones."

I don't consider myself to be a kind or forgiving young man. Despite everything I've been given in life, all I've found is the world is a barbarous hell watched over by a despotic God. Every single person I've ever encountered, beginning with the womb in which I once laid, is naturally evil. And this thought is not attempted to sway you, nor do I claim it to be my own. From Milton to Hobbes to Nietzsche to Campbell, all the most brilliant humans throughout history have understood this as a universal truth. Society corrupts everyone, and people make up society. So, who's causing the corruption? However, there's a way not necessarily to combat the endless wickedness of the world but to cope with it. And that is what I've always attempted to do.

From my teenage infatuation with Clarissa to my years as an Exdover and Yale Lothario and finally to those epicurean summers of late where I cavorted with Skye and the other vivacious Hamptons' beauties, the end goal was simply to have fun. How can we, as humans, distract ourselves from the daily ennui and iniquity? You, dearest reader, may disagree with my style or decision-making, but can you truly look at your own life and self and say that A) you're not an evil person? And B) you aren't frequently bored out of your mind?

While I'm not compassionate, I take solace in the fact I never pretend to be someone I'm not. I'm not a hypocritical human, and I *am* the antidote for many who can't find joie de vivre in their treacherous eighty or so years on this earth.

Thank you for your time, dearest reader. Hopefully, you gained something of value from listening to my tales of glory.

Kinsley Avital

OKAY. I THINK IT'S IMPORTANT I explain what the heck is going on before I start.

So, Cash and I each received these bizarre envelopes at our new apartment the day after we moved in. I didn't read his, but mine said:

Dear Ms. Kinsley Avital,

Enclosed please find a check for $1,000. If you agree to the upcoming proposal and complete the task within 150 days, you'll receive an additional check for $5,000.

The task is simple. Please write a detailed account of the events of last summer: from Memorial Day 2018 until Labor Day 2018. The piece should be between 75 and 200 pages and should be written however you'd like. All I ask is that you describe specific days' events along with your inner thoughts and feelings.

Please write in the first person and pretend as if you're writing to a group of friends, or perhaps it's a series of diary entries. Be creative and original. Break down specific days. Talk about first impressions, sailing, horses, last impressions, one-on-one interactions, etc.

If you're not interested in this task, feel free to deposit the check for $1,000 and forget you ever received this letter.

A stranger will be waiting for you at the Le Pain Quotidien on West 50th between Sixth and Seventh on June 16th at 11:00 a.m. It will be a man in a suit with a solid teal tie, knotted in a half-Windsor.

Please do not try to contact me.

Sincerely,
An Interested Party

Now, my first reaction was confusion. But then Cash told me about his letter, and we discussed it—because communication and honesty are absolutely non-negotiable for Cash and me.

"I'm gonna write one," he said.

"Why, though? Could this be some weird trap? Who wrote this anyway?"

"If someone offers me $5,000 to write a hundred pages, why wouldn't I do that? I could certainly use the money."

"Okay. But..."

"Kins, what's the worst-case scenario?"

"I don't want a bunch of strangers reading my thoughts."

"You're in complete control of what you write. And you and I don't have anything incriminating to say. Like the letter says, write a diary, and someone gives you $5,000."

"You're not at all freaked out by this? Seriously?"

"It's definitely bizarre, but where I grew up, strange requests aren't exactly unusual."

"Who do you think wrote it? And why?" I asked.

Cash was wearing some three-striped Adidas sweatpants and a football jersey. Sitting with me in our apartment was the only time I ever saw him dressed down. Ever since we started dating and Cash allowed me to sort of dress him, he always looked stylish.

"Probably Campbell, right?"

"Why would he want this? Have you heard from him recently?"

"It's been a little while, hasn't it? But this seems like a weird wedding present he'd give us. I dunno. Who else would care enough about that summer? And have the money?"

"Well...I mean...Skye?"

"Does she have the money?"

"Totally. I mean, come on. The girl probably makes 100K a year. Maybe she wants to start some defamation case against Jeff?"

"Campbell's father, maybe? Wants to get a better understanding of his son and his son's friends?"

Cash leaned over and began massaging my shoulders. Always the energetic and affectionate one, like a golden retriever puppy.

"Maybe one of Skye's friends or that Ivee girl? One of the Hollandsworth guys? Did you ever have a secret admirer? Maybe some girl from your past wants to learn about your life?"

"Who's Ivee again? And I only dated two girls before you, and I haven't spoken to either one in three years."

"That cute, creepy rich girl from last summer."

"Whatever. Maybe we'll figure it out, maybe we won't. What I do know is, we could for sure use $12,000 to plan a vacation."

"Maybe Vienna or Budapest?"

"We have some time to think about it. Yet another thing to look forward to after our wedding, Kins."

Cash kissed me. He had this natural tenderness, like a warm fur coat. Cash always wanted to make me smile. His parents raised him right.

"I love you so much," I said.

"I love you too. I'm sure we'll talk about this again. You wanna hop in the shower with me? And then maybe we'll go to Hillstone?"

"Sounds like a plan."

MY INTRO

I GUESS COMPARED TO SOME of these Manhattan people, my childhood wasn't that glamorous. We didn't have a private jet, houses in multiple cities, or a black card for every Avital kid. My dad was a zoning lawyer in Cincinnati, and my mom had a bunch of jobs. She taught high school English for a few years, was a law clerk, and has spent the past while working as a city councilwoman in Madeira, Ohio, where she's always lived. My parents got divorced when I was a baby, and so my three brothers and I had to commute to and from downtown Cincinnati and Madeira every weekend. It wasn't so bad, though. We were as close-knit as any siblings.

I went to an all-girls school from kindergarten through 12th grade called Adley Prep. And I honestly had an unbelievable experience from start to finish. I have so many lifelong friends, and without sounding too sappy, I cherish absolutely every memory from Adley, good and bad.

For example, every winter, like 10 of my friends would split a chalet in Utah, at Alta, and we'd all go skiing. And then there were the friends I made from the high school softball team. And I was close with some of the girls I took riding lessons with in Madeira. Truthfully, I absolutely adored my childhood and all my friends and family. I was and am truly blessed.

But anyway, I always did alright in school, and when college decisions rolled around, I was accepted at Duke. I was excited, but I remember feeling a little weird because all my friends were going to OSU or Ohio. I never thought of myself as any smarter than anyone else. We all have our strengths and weaknesses, and I happened to do well on my

SATs. But I think it was luck more than anything. And part of me was upset to leave my town and friends and everyone. Boarding that first flight to Raleigh-Durham was bittersweet for sure.

I will say, if I'm being candid, college wasn't as enjoyable. Don't get me wrong, it was still fun in its own way, but I have some not-so-sunny memories.

Unfortunately, whenever I think of Duke, I think of my ex-boy-friend. And I shouldn't do that because college was fun and I made a bunch of lifelong friends and had awesome sociology professors. But for whatever reason, the bad memories, of which there are few, always seem to pop up before the good ones.

The first 18 years of my life, I'd never kissed a boy. It wasn't some-thing I cared about. I went to an all-girls school, and all the extracur-ricular activities I did were with girls. I had the best friends a person could ask for, and we were always so preoccupied with other things. And it's funny because I'm super extroverted.

So, I have no idea why I never had a boyfriend or even a first kiss. Guys were never a priority to me. Schoolwork and friends took precedent.

My first week at Duke, I was definitely embarrassed by this. I knew nothing was wrong with me, but my first kiss was bound to be awk-ward. I wanted the internal fireworks but instead settled for a peck and a quizzical look from Jake.

I don't like thinking about him. He was a jerk, but I guess looking back on it, I must've liked something about him. Jake was gangly and dorky, but polite and kind at first. He didn't seem overly experienced with girls, and I guessed I liked that about him. We were boyfriend and girlfriend by mid-September of our freshmen years.

The next few months, Jake and I learned a lot about one another, and unfortunately, that was a negative. He smoked weed all the time, which I hated, and he skipped classes constantly. His GPA was never above three even though he had the intellect. Plus, Jake didn't dress well. He'd wear khaki shorts every day with a backwards hat.

I guess the reason I'm particularly bitter when talking about him is midway through our sophomore year, he cheated on me. I caught him with a sorority girl in his bed one night, and yet I stayed with him. Jake argued he was high and didn't remember anything. We talked it out, and he promised everything was going to change. And I fell for it. Always the forgiving type.

By junior year, I went with some of my Duke friends to Cartagena over spring break, and when I came back, I found a bra in his room that wasn't mine. And yet, I stayed with him. I didn't know what else was out there and was too scared to find out.

Eventually, my girls talked some sense into me, and by second-semester senior year, I broke up with him. I desperately wanted to move to New York and work in the beauty industry, and he was content to smoke and skateboard around Durham for the foreseeable future.

I moved to Manhattan with a few of my friends from Adley, and we rented this delightful loft near NYU. And shortly thereafter, I began working at a beauty start-up called Guépard. We were all super happy, and my career was going really well. But some nights, I did feel lonely.

To counteract this, my friends and I would go out to rooftop bars, and I was as sociable as ever, but I never met a serious guy my age who was looking to date exclusively.

Sometime around Valentine's Day of 2017, my roommates convinced me to try some dating apps. So, I signed up for Hinge, Bumble, Happn, and The League.

Hinge was the best because of their conversation prompts and well-organized interface, and it had guys who took the crafting of their profiles seriously. However, they could never carry out meaningful conversations. I don't know whether I was a dull texter, or everyone had ADHD those days. And Bumble and Happn were even worse.

On Bumble, the girls are required to message first, which I'm all for. I usually consider ice-breakers a strength of mine. But then the men would get belligerent and repulsive.

On Happn, I never even received a match. And The League was so restrictive. They only sent me three profiles a day, so I basically had only one match per month.

The whole process was infuriating, so I gave up on dating apps after about three months. I decided to stick with waiting for guys to approach me at rooftop bars, bookstores, coffee shops, or work events.

I don't want you to think finding a boyfriend was so important to me. It wasn't. My career took up almost all of my time. That was my focus from virtually 6:00 a.m. to midnight every day. However, no matter who you are, those bouts of loneliness always pop up. For some people, it's daily; for others, it's every few months; for me, it was on those rare occasions when I watched a super romantic movie at 2:00 a.m. I remember thinking, "'How many times can I watch *It Happened One Night* or *Marty* by myself?'" I loved my life, my job, and my friends and family. I was so grateful for everything I had, but I did feel kinda lonely sometimes.

MEMORIAL DAY WEEKEND 2017

"COULDN'T WE HAVE GONE TO a place that actually takes reservations?" my friend Jules said to me.

"We could've, but this is supposedly one of the hottest spots out here. It's super romantic, and look around, the views are exquisite. Yelp loves it, too."

"I didn't wanna wait 90 minutes for a table."

"Loosen up, girl. It's vacation. I can't remember the last time all of us were in the same place at the same time. Amy, what's in the Carmine Daisy? Can I try yours?" I asked my other friend.

"Pineapple, rum, and lemon. It's very tropical. You'd love it. Here." She handed it to me and continued, "What are you drinking?"

"Watermelon cooler. It has vodka, lemon, and mint."

"Cool, gimme."

We sipped each other's drinks and looked around the property before I announced to my friends:

"A toast. To the Adley girls back together at last. Let's make sure we don't wait another five years to meet like this."

All nine of my friends were circled around a fire outside this Montauk restaurant.

"Kins," Lucy said. "How's Guépard? You've told me, like, briefly what it's like, but gimme some details."

"Yeah, it is. I mean, there's only, like, 15 employees. Our office is this stylish one-floor spot in Chelsea. I like the essence of the place: open-floor plan, exposed brick, a lot of modern art. There's a Flicka painting right by reception and two Dochilla abstracts by the windows. Dahlia, the founder and CEO, is probably the most fashionable person I've ever met. I love her."

"And so, you're like, a social media manager? How'd you go from sociology major to that? I'm legit impressed."

"I know. It's nuts, right? So, Dahlia is only 28, and she founded Guépard during her senior year at Duke. And now, she goes to some of Duke's career events every year to find hot new prospects. Out of the 15 people, I think like, nine of Guépard's employees are Duke grads. I met Dahlia at a career fair, and all of her clothing was French. But not, like, super expensive, high-fashion stuff. I'm talking about cute little pieces you'd find at a flea market in Nimes or Arles."

"Oh, I thought it was just like a makeup place."

"It started as makeup and beauty products, but now Dahlia's importing French clothes to our Chelsea offices and we're trying to break into the fashion world as well. I'm in charge of finding influencers to market our new pieces, and if all goes well, Guépard may open an actual brick-and-mortar in the next year or so. Either in the Hamptons, Manhattan or Williamsburg."

"So cool. I'm so proud of you, Kins."

"Anyone else want another round on me? I'm heading inside now."

A few of my friends raised their hands, and I walked across the magnificent property toward the indoor portion of the restaurant.

To paint a picture for you: The Crow's Nest was both a restaurant and hotel north of the highway in Montauk. The property was situated right on the lake, nowhere near the bustling center of town. And once you pulled into the rock-covered parking lot, which I much preferred to cement or asphalt, you felt like you were transported from the rest of the South Fork to an island of sorts.

Once you left that lot, you walked toward this bucolic wooden building sitting atop a grassy acre, with absolutely stunning views. If you were seated at the restaurant and looked out, you saw perfectly groomed luscious green grass rolled down toward a sandy beach and, eventually, the lake itself. It was three different layers wrapped into one gorgeous view.

On my way back to the group of Adley Prep girls sitting by the fireplace, I spotted a guy around my age walking up the green hill. That wasn't the weird part. What was so unusual was his companion.

It wasn't some well-dressed Instagram influencer; it was his mother. She had a leg injury of some kind, so I found the whole scene to be super sweet. What college-aged guy is going to The Crow's Nest with his limping mom over Memorial Day weekend?

I walked back and took my seat in between Jules and Lucy and said:

"Look at that guy there."

"Which one?" Jules said.

"Coming up the top of the hill. Wearing all white."

"He's cute."

"Look at how sweet he is. Helping his mom up the hill."

"She seems drunk," Amy added.

"Do you think I should talk to him?"

"Sure, why not...wait, didn't we see that same duo at Sunset Beach last night?"

"When?"

"Outside the restaurant after dinner," Amy continued.

"Oh, definitely," said Lucy. "That's the mom who had us take pictures of her by the beach. The son was busy doing something else."

"You're a hundred percent right. That's them. What are the odds?"

"It's gotta be a sign," Amy said. "Go say something to them. You have your opener."

I stood up. I was cold and tipsy and wearing only a white t-shirt because I'd left my jacket in the car. I may have been sweaty too. But damnit, I was confident.

"'Scuse me," I said to the mother and son.

"Yes, how can I help you?" she said.

"Didn't I see you guys at Sunset Beach last night? You had us take pictures of you, right?"

"Oh, that's right. How funny. What a coincidence. I'm Andrea Moreau, and this is my son—"

"Cash."

"Well, anyway, I think you two are so cool. You're like a dynamic mother-son duo taking on the Hamptons. I love that. I'm Kinsley, by the way."

"You know, you're really pretty," Andrea said. "You could be a model. You've got all that hair and your makeup. Cash, isn't she pretty?"

I didn't leave him time to answer that.

"Do you guys wanna come and sit with my friends and me? We're waiting for our table outside by the fire. Isn't it chilly tonight?"

"Oh, absolutely. You know I have my own PR firm? Not sure if any of your friends are looking for public relations. What do they do?"

"Come on. Follow me. You'll find out."

So, there I was, guiding a handsome but quiet guy and his interesting mother back to our circle of wooden chairs.

The mom looked fashionable. She'd found a pleasant combination of a colorful but conservative outfit. Her dress was turquoise with a magenta floral pattern, and the hemline was about half an inch beyond her knees. The woman had three matching Aurélie Bidermann bracelets of turquoise, magenta, and white, and added a pair of ball stud earrings. She also had this smile that made me instantly want to like her.

The son was a bit shorter than average, but his white linen shirt hugged a muscly figure. He had this upside-down triangle body, with his skinny legs hidden by tight, bone-white pants rolled at the hem. And then his shoes were royal blue Rivieras, which I considered to be *the* beach shoe of that summer.

"Everyone, this is Cash and Andrea. Cash and Andrea, this is everyone."

My friends all waved and immediately started asking them a million questions while I sat back and watched.

"Cash, do you need a drink?" I finally interrupted.

"No, I'm good. I'm her designated driver."

"Aw, that's sweet. What a good son...so where are you guys from?"

"Manhattan," the mother said. "We live on the Upper East Side. You know, Cash went to Hollandsworth, and now he's at Penn. He just finished his junior year and loves it. My Cash has a *very* bright future."

"Are you cold, Kinsley?" he asked.

"A bit. I left my jacket in the car like an idiot."

"You know what? My mom has this nice snug coat in our car. I'll be right back."

He walked away, and Lucy gave me that OMG-he's-perfect look.

"You raised a caring son, Andrea."

"Well, I can assure you it was my doing and not my ex-husband's."

The early-summer wind was picking up, and the fire's embers kept blowing in my eyes, so I put on my black Beneventi shades and downed the rest of my drink.

"Here you go," Cash said as he wrapped the jacket around my shoulders. "This should keep you warm...and what's with the shades?"

"I appreciate it. And it's the fire. You'll see. It's brutal on your eyes."

His mom was chatting up my friends about Andrea Moreau PR, and by that point, I think I was sitting on the same chair as Cash.

"You wanna come with me? I'm gonna grab another drink," I said.

"Sure, love to."

Cash rose, and I immediately noticed him having a funny way of walking. His legs moved, but nothing else joined them. Cash's torso and arms were basically still. It was certainly odd. I was a bit tipsy by then, but I'll never forget the first time I saw that guy walk.

"So, where are you guys from?" he asked as we approached the bar in the restaurant.

"Well, we all grew up in Cincinnati." I had to shout over the raucous indoor crowd. "Then I wound up going to Duke, and the girls out there went to OSU, Ohio, and Miami. We've managed to stay close, though."

"Oh, sweet. So, what are you all doing here?"

"Sort of like a high school reunion. Five of them live in Ohio, and the rest of us are in Manhattan. I've been trying to arrange something like this for years. We're all cooped up in an Airbnb nearby. Ten girls, $1,000 a night for three nights. Not bad at all."

The bartender handed me my drink, and Cash gave him his credit card.

"You don't have to do that," I said.

"I want to. If I'm not drinking, at least I can live vicariously through you."

We returned to our outdoor circle and found Andrea arguing with some jerk who was hitting on my friends in front of his girl-friend. Our adoptive den mother, frothing at the mouth, shooed the guy away, and then we all calmed down and started chatting again. And at that point, Cash and I were still seated on the same chair for some reason.

"Oh, Kinsley," Andrea said. "May I please take a picture of you two. You look adorable. What a cute couple you'd make."

"Sure, go right ahead."

The mom took a bunch of shaky pictures and showed them to us.

"Wow, we look really happy," I said.

"I like that one the best. Mom, can you send that to me."

"What do you say?"

"May you *please* send that one to me? Thank you."

"Of course. Now, you two take a walk. Kinsley, I want to give your friends here some advice."

Cash led me around the property. He was kind of serious and mature for a 21-year-old, definitely an original.

"You know, I'm a real photography nut."

"Oh? What do you take pictures of?"

"I mean, everything. I'm a social media manager at this start-up called Guépard. Having a well-curated Instagram page is super impor-tant for both my company and me."

"Do you take pictures for fun, too?"

"Yeah, I'm a real animal lover, so I'll never turn down an opportu-nity for an animal photoshoot. And then, any unique landscapes. Oh, and fashion for sure. I'll sometimes stop strangers on the street and ask to take pictures of their clothes."

"It's cool you're so passionate. I envy you. You've truly turned a hobby into a job."

"Gosh, and I have a ton of hobbies. I love to ski. I played shortstop on Duke's club softball team, majored in sociology, love to exercise, and travel is a top priority too."

"Oh, wow. So, you're all over the place. Where have you traveled recently?"

"Everywhere. I've been so lucky. I went to Cartagena last summer. My friend's wedding was in Montenegro two years ago. I've gone on vacation with friends or family to Aruba, South Beach, Cancun, Newport Beach, and Punta Cana the past three years."

"Oh, so you're big on the beach—all those balmy places. No mountains? No cold?"

"Well, I ski all the time, remember? My friends and I go to Utah. Do you ski?"

"My family used to go to Jay Peak in Vermont, but I'm sure that doesn't compare to Utah or Colorado skiing."

"Kinsley," Amy called out, "they said our table will be ready in five minutes. Get back here."

Cash and I returned to our one chair and sat in front of the fire.

"You two getting along?" Andrea asked.

"Yes, Mom," he said, and then he continued after being introduced to the flames, "What's going on with this fire? This is bad. Jesus. It's blowing right in my eyes."

"You'll get used to it," Andrea said.

"Here, take my sunglasses," I said.

"No, then *your* eyes will get all itchy."

"Just take them," I said. "There are literally tears streaking down your face."

"Okay, okay." Cash laughed as he took the Beneventis.

Then the maître d' told us our table was ready. My friends immediately leaped up, and Cash's mom limped toward the parking lot, leaving us alone.

"You look cute in those. Like a prettier version of me."

We chatted for a few more minutes. I gave him my number, and then we ended our night with a hug. I could smell his spearminty breath as our cheeks grazed against each other. Then, Cash went and joined his nosy but well-meaning mother in the parking lot while I went inside to see nine friends who desperately needed details.

"Well...?" Ella said to me once all 10 of us were finally seated.

"What?"

The girls laughed and forced me to talk.

"Can we get a round of drinks first?"

It was like high school all over again. All the Adley girls drinking and laughing. It was marvelous.

"Guys, I don't know what to say. I feel super weird right now."

"He's cute," one of them said.

"Really handsome," another added.

"I mean, I'm for sure gonna see him again. He's nothing like Jake. Which is a good thing."

"A great thing," Amy said.

"And I look ugly right now."

"I have a good feeling about him," Ella said.

"And if you don't have an outfit ready for date numero uno," Lucy said, "I'll for sure go shopping with you. He shouldn't even recognize you."

MEMORIAL DAY WEEKEND 2018

"Get in. Hurry! While the light's red."

"Okay, okay. I'm coming."

He threw his green-and-black William J. Mills duffle into my Prius as we sped toward the Queens Midtown Tunnel.

"I brought you a Juice Gen smoothie. Coconut Colada with mangoes instead of bananas."

"You're such a sweetie, Cash. How'd you know?"

"You look really pretty, Kins."

He rubbed my thigh as Violet's tires skidded toward a frightening amount of traffic on 495 (And yes, I did name my car Violet.).

"Christ," he said.

"No worries. We saw this coming. We'll still be there on time."

"Campbell hates tardiness."

"Oh, damnit," I said.

"What's wrong? What'd you forget?"

"Nothing. But it looks like you packed one thing too many."

"What do you mean?" he said. "How do you know? My suitcase is zipped. You mean this sweatshirt?"

"No. I mean your stress."

"That was...not your best."

"I thought it was pretty clever," I said. "Have I ever told you how handsome I think you are?"

"About twice daily."

"Well, it's not enough."

"I love you."

"Love you too. And you'll be happy to know I made a stupendous playlist for what I thought would be a two-hour ride, but now seems like a four-hour ride."

He laughed and said, "Well, pass me your phone. How many vetoes do I get?"

"I'd say zero, but you're cute, so I'll give you one."

We played:

"Closer" — The Chainsmokers
"Motorsport" — Cardi B, Migos and Nicki Minaj
"Closer" — The Chainsmokers
"Cecilia and the Satellite" — Andrew McMahon
"Call Me Maybe" — Carly Rae Jepsen
"Spectrum" — Florence and the Machine
"Crazy on You" — Heart
"Layla" — Eric Clapton
"Sexual Healing" — Marvin Gaye (Kygo Remix)
"Palace" — A$AP Rocky
"Free Fallin'" — Tom Petty
"Over the Love" — Florence and the Machine
"Too Hotty" — Migos ft. Eurielle
"Walk It, Talk It" — Migos ft. Drake
"T-Shirt" — Migos
"HYFR" — Drake ft. Lil Wayne

Typically, it was my responsibility to memorize any female-sung lyrics in songs, and Cash was required to remember the male verses. So, "Closer" was good for us; "Motorsport" was fantastic; and then anytime Drake was on a song with another dude, I'd rap the Drake verse and Cash would, I wouldn't say butcher, but whatever a step above butcher is, that's what Cash would do to Lil Wayne and Rick Ross.

When we pulled onto Route 27, I may have been a bit awestruck by some of the houses. I mean, my family was very blessed, and I'm so appreciative of everything my parents were able to provide, but these Southampton and East Hampton palaces we saw that summer were unreal. If we drove down certain roads, every single house looked like an estate fit for Tom Buchanan. There were massive immaculately trimmed yards, pillars holding up houses, gigantic pools, two-story guest houses, and the greenest grass I'd ever seen.

"Ready for the greatest summer of your life?" I said as we drove through Montauk.

"Absolutely."

"Love you...oh, shoot. Look at the time. How close are we?"

"Five minutes. We'll be there basically on time. Don't stress, right?"

We arrived at this restaurant called Navy Beach, which along with The Crow's Nest, is the most scenic eatery on all of Long Island.

The outdoor portion of Navy Beach, where we were seated, was located directly on this beach. But instead of having sand, the ground was made entirely of these grey-and-white pebbles. And they led toward the bay, which was this sturdy Prussian blue from the shore to the horizon. The tables themselves were white, and a giant navy umbrella sheltered each one. And finally, by the edge of the water, were these white coastal couches with navy cushions and tiny tiki torches surrounding them. It was quintessential Hamptons.

"Hi, I'm Kins—"

"Ms. Avital. Pleasure," Cash's friend Jeff said before kissing my hand. "Moreau here has told me so much about you."

"I'm sure I'll never live up to the portrait my boyfriend painted."

"Well, leave the portraits to Oscar Wilde. What I will say is you're even more breathtaking than he described."

"I'm Skye," his slightly younger girlfriend chimed in.

Everyone exchanged hugs and took their seats with the late-May sun waning in the distance.

"Kins, I love your hair. What do you use?" Skye said.

I'd never seen a person show that much skin at a nice restaurant. Skye probably could've used a shawl.

She was wearing one of Jeff's business blue Brooks Brothers button-downs. However, I doubt he ever walked around with only one button fastened and a navy bra hanging out. And then, she wore these alabaster Zara short-shorts and baby blue flip-flops. But despite my light critiques, Skye was hot. No other way to phrase it. She had the big boobs and the firm tush that guys love and girls envy—credit to her for working out regularly and not being afraid to flaunt it.

"I'll try not to sell you an ad, but I use only Guépard products in my hair. Raw coconut oil, BB cream, a moisturizing shampoo, a moisturizing conditioner, and then some jojoba and alma oils. I get all my products from work. Do you know Guépard, Skye?"

"No. Dope hair, though."

"You should check out our IG page. We have a lot of great products for women our age."

"So that's, like, your job? You're, like, a beauty oil salesperson?"

"Not exactly. I'm a social media manager for Guépard. We're a small start-up, so I wind up taking on a few roles. And I also do some freelance graphic design to help pay for my apartment in the city. What do you do?"

"Skye's a phenomenal musician," Jeff interrupted. "Skye, what song's this? She knows every EDM song ever created."

"Sleepless by Flume. Duh."

Jeff was a good dresser. I guess when you have as much money as he did, buying stylish clothing isn't that difficult. That night, he was wearing white jeans, a navy short-sleeve button-down with pink flamingos, tortoiseshell shades, a Rolex, and navy Rivieras. I sound like such a freak for remembering what everyone wore, but I swear I have a photographic memory when it comes to clothes. Just clothes. Like, I absolutely wish my mind worked the same way with math or remembering dates or lists, but nope, just clothes.

"Skye, what kind of music do you perform?"

"Oh, she can do it all," her boyfriend interrupted. "Her focus is EDM right now. It's tropical and prismatic. Skye's blowing up on

IG and Soundcloud. Moreau, you and your girl should listen to her tonight. What are you all drinking?"

"Moscow Mule for me," Cash said.

"Some beachy drink. I think a piña colada for me."

Jeff ordered drinks for everyone, while Skye started to text, and Cash gave me those are-you-having-a-good-time eyes. I guess I was staring at Skye's tattoos. Don't get me wrong; they were pretty. But they were kind of frenzied. There was a whale here and numbers there and words here and Audrey Hepburn there. No pattern and a lack of organization. But she was undoubtedly an attractive girl, regardless—a natural brunette with blonde highlights.

"For appetizers," Jeff broke the table's silence, "I'll have the hama-chi ceviche, and Skye will get the shrimp. Then soy-glazed tilefish for me and swordfish for her."

"Very good, Mr. Campbell," the waitress said.

"May I please have the Atlantic salmon?" I said.

"Of course. It's excellent."

"New York strip for me. Medium rare. And fries. Kins, you can have some of mine."

"And salmon's on your do-not-eat list, right? Gosh, I feel bad. I'm gonna be eating your food, and you can't share mine."

"Moreau'll be fine. You know his parents used to take away dessert privileges as a punishment? Took away his cravings. He tell you that?"

"No," I said. "Cash, how many things do you think Jeff knows that I don't?"

"Probably zero significant memories and a few meaningless ones like that."

"Ease up, Moreau. We're on vacation. No stresses, please. The wait-ress is pretty hot, eh Skye?"

"Uh-huh."

"Skye, put the phone away at the table. Talk to our guests, please."

"You gonna make me?"

"I may have to...later."

"Promise?"

"You know, Moreau, I know the manager here, Jacques. Anything you and your girl want, I'll make it happen. Kinsley, if you want a seven-layer chocolate cake, it's yours. Moreau, you want one of your patented peanut butter-no jelly sandwiches for dinner, I got you."

"Cash, how'd you and J meet?" Skye piped up.

"Oh, you didn't tell her? Campbell and I went to Hollandsworth together. It's this haughty all-boys prep school in the city. I've known him for what, 15 years? We reconnected at the reunion over our love of fantasy sports. We've linked up a few times since then."

The dynamic duo then went on a lengthy fantasy baseball tangent before I interrupted.

"Cash darling, you and Jeff will have plenty of time to talk about Ross Stripling and Matt Carpenter. Let's focus on summer plans."

"True," he laughed that inaudible chuckle of his and said, "sorry, Kins. You're right. Like always. Campbell, do you have some idea of what this summer'll be like?"

"Some idea? Moreau, I've got the whole damn thing planned to a tittle. But first, you know Skye taught herself the violin and sax as a youth?"

"Is that right, Skye?" Cash said.

"J, stop. Don't be embarrassing."

"Just proud of you. That's all."

"Here are the ceviches, Mr. Campbell." The waitress delivered the food.

"Anyway, Jeff," I said, "Cash and I want to thank you so much for inviting us out here. Super generous of you. We're so appreciative."

"Moreau's been loyal to me my whole life. Not many like him. It's the least I can do."

"Thanks, man."

"But, my dearest apologies for keeping you all in suspense. Here are some of the illustrious ideas I had for our diminutive coterie."

"I've got ideas too, you guys," Skye said.

"Of course you do, Skye. But anyway, the house itself is a grand manor I decorated with the finest modern art and self-curated photographs. You'll love it all, I'm sure. But knowing Moreau's neurotic nature, I've decided to place you two in my fairly commodious pool house overlooking the Atlantic and my rather luxurious pool. The place has a bed, cable, WiFi, a couch, kitchen, shower, everything you'll need and more."

"Sounds good, Campbell. Thanks."

"As for the rest of the property," he continued, "I have a capacious garage with both a gym and Skye's new studio. There's a Jacuzzi and a wonderfully decorated stone patio, and then of course, my property has its own private beach at the edge of the backyard. You'll both adore the space."

"Jeff, it all sounds perfect."

"Kins, what about your job?" Skye asked.

"Oh, I'm going to be working remotely all summer. My boss, Dahlia, is super understanding of her employees' morale and social lives, so she's letting me take as much time as I need. I'll still be posting IG stories to Guépard's page every day, and I'll continue my never-ending search for additional followers and potential micro-influencers to market the products. The point is, I'll be working plenty while I'm out here, but a job doesn't feel like a job when you're doing it by the beach."

"Right," Jeff said. "Now, where was I? Oh, this summer. I'm thinking sailing, jet-skiing, polo matches, drinking rosé by the pool..."

"The food, J, and tell them about the ice cream."

"Oh well yeah. I'll take you to DOPO, Sant Ambroeus, The Crow's Nest, Sunset Beach, La Fondita, 75 Main, Tutto, Solé. All of the sleekest and swankiest spots this paradise has to offer."

"Kins, I'll take you to Scoop du Jour. Their ice cream is bomb."

"Kinsley loves ice cream," Cash said.

"Hang on now, Moreau. There's more. How'd you like a little Wiffle ball, some vino at the winery, a little golf here, some beach football there, clubbing, dancing. I swear to God, we're gonna do it all and more. I'm so freakin' pumped."

The food arrived, and it looked mouthwatering. It was such a magical night. Marvelous weather, delectable cuisine, stupendous cocktails, and one of the best views the Hamptons had to offer.

After dinner, Skye turned to me and said:

"Kins, wanna play cornhole? J, can we all play cornhole? Please?"

"Now, that's a fine idea. You and Kinsley go reserve our place. Moreau and I'll hang back and take care of the check."

I walked with a slightly tipsy Skye over the rocks toward the beach area where the cornhole game would take place. She picked up a few bags, handed them to me, and we stood next to each other while tossing them to the other end.

"Your Cashie is very handsome. You're lucky."

"Aw. Thank you. Jeff seems like a very mature person."

"Have you met any other Hollandsworth guys? I swear they're all literally so similar. Like, jacked, smart, mad polite, and generous. And they dress well and are sweet to girls. They're probs the coolest group of dudes I've ever met."

"Do you think Jeff and Cash are that similar?"

"I dunno Cash well, but, like, they don't seem that different. J no doubt parties harder. Cashie seems quieter. That's about it."

"Interesting."

Cash and Jeff then joined us at the other end, and we started the game.

"Ping-pong's better. Don't you think?" Skye said.

"Not sure. I mean, they take different skill sets. I love these little competitive games. Cash does too. We'll play Yahtzee and Scattergories and Cards Against Humanity. He and I love that stuff. We can both get a little intense, though."

"I can't get over your hair." She started running her hands along my ends while Jeff launched his bag toward our side.

"Thanks. I'm telling you, take a look at our products."

"Your hair is so smooth, so much volume. You're high-key lucky. Does Cashie tell you you're pretty?"

"Um, yeah. All the time."

"Thank God."

Jeff sunk a few bags into our hole. He'd definitely played before. I think Cash would agree his friend was the best, and Skye was the worst. But, of course, she also had a ton of other talents. Skye always kept everyone on their toes.

"How'd you and Cash meet?"

"Funny you should ask. I saw him at The Crow's Nest nearly a year ago today. He and his mom. They were so cute together. I asked them to sit with my friends and me. And the rest is history."

"The Crow's Nest is the absolute GOAT. Believe me. And what do you guys do for fun together?"

"Oh, um, a ton of stuff. We'll travel, see movies, go to a club once in a while, listen to music, read, play board games or video games, watch sports, go to restaurants, go to events. A little bit of everything."

"You watch sports with him? What a keeper you are."

"You're such a sweetheart. I truly believe it's super-imperative to take an interest in your partner's interests. And Cash agrees. He tries to learn about fashion, photography, and beauty and always asks me about work. I try to talk about fantasy sports and ask him a ton of questions so I can educate myself."

"You're like a saint," Skye said. "Who made you so perfect, beautiful?"

"I think Cash helps me grow, and I help him grow. We're constantly trying to improve each other. I think that's the hallmark of an amazing relationship. Don't you agree?"

"Is that what Cashie looks for in a gf?"

"I guess it is," I chuckled.

"What makes him laugh?"

"What are you girls gabbing about?" Jeff shouted from the other end.

"Nothing, daddy. Girl stuff."

"I sink this shot and me and Skye win," he called out.

"So...what does Cashie like in the bedroom?" Skye asked.

"What do you mean?"

"Is it like a lot of missionary, basic stuff? Do you think he appreciates you, or do you go, like, dead-fish style?"

"I don't really feel comfortable discussing that stuff."

Jeff made the shot, and Skye leaped in the air and raced toward him. She shoved her abnormally long tongue down his throat while Cash and I looked on.

"I missed you so much, daddy," she squealed.

"Would my little clique like to join me for a few more drinks by the water? Skye, I know you're down."

"Kins, you wanna go home or hang out for a bit?" Cash turned to me with those eager blue eyes of his.

"I'll have a few drinks."

Jeff guided us to a beach sofa with navy cushions a few feet from the collapsing tide. The sun was setting on the horizon and turned the entire landscape into rolling shades of coral with black silhouettes.

Cash stopped after two drinks, and I was planning on doing the same before Skye said:

"Loosen up, big sis. We're on vacation. Oh, and sorry I may be a bit drunk."

"Skye, go see what the water feels like," Jeff said.

After my third drink, I fell asleep on Cash's lap and that unbelievably cozy sofa.

"Kins, wake up." Cash nudged me after a while. "I'm gonna take you home."

He gave me a quick peck before I wiped my eyes and rose to my feet.

"Campbell, you mind blowing that cigar smoke anywhere but in mine and Kinsley's faces?"

"Your lungs should be so lucky as to ingest such an ambrosial vapor. Skye baby, get out of the water. You're getting your clothes wet."

Skye skipped toward us and said:

"Where's my Juul, daddy?"

"Right here."

The two of them blew smoke in each other's faces and continued loudly smooching. They were an eclectic couple, for sure. But who was I to judge?

"Moreau, wanna hit a club with the ladies and me?"

"Nah, I think we'll call it a night. Right, Kins?"

I was probably well-rested enough to go out, but Cash didn't have the energy.

"Yeah, we can head back. We'll throw on some Netflix and unwind. Been a long day."

Cash decided to drive home, which was probably a prudent decision.

"So, what'd you think?" he asked as we pulled onto 27.

"I mean, wow. Where do I begin?"

"Positive or negative first impression? Then again, I've never known you to have a negative thing to say about anyone."

"Very true," I laughed. "Jeff is super confident. Skye called him mature, which I agree with. He doesn't act like a 22-year-old. I don't think you two are similar. She disagreed."

"How'd you like Skye?"

"Well, for starters, I love her carefree attitude. She's so laid-back and relaxed. They're an interesting couple. Yin and Yang."

"Nothing negative to say whatsoever?"

"Well, I will say..."

"Finally. Here we go. Kins' claws are out."

"So, I love how Skye's super outgoing like I am. But I think we differ in that I'm reasonably self-aware and she's not as much. That's all I'll say, though. I don't wanna be mean."

"Oh, come on. That's not even an insult."

"I think I can guarantee none of us will ever be bored together."

We arrived at Jeff's place for the first time, but it was pitch-black, so I didn't get a look at the house or décor. Instead, Cash opened the passenger door, as he always did, and brought me back to the two-story pool house, which Jeff had left unlocked.

"Here you go, Kins. Our home for the next three months."

My first thought was it was surprisingly charming. The walls were alabaster and the floors limestone. A sand-colored sectional and a modern glass table sat on top of a black, herringbone rug, with a sizable flatscreen hanging. There was a four-seater dining room table and a quaint kitchen with marble countertops and a high-tech fridge. Other than that, the house was reasonably tame. It was really a guest house, not a pool house.

Unfortunately, the upstairs was just a queen-sized mattress sprawled out on the floor with some bedding folded at the foot and no box-spring or headboard. However, Jeff and Skye were so generous I wasn't going to complain for a second. It was all so magnificent. Well, I guess, there were the four massive nude black-and-white photographs hanging throughout the pool house. They certainly toed the line between tasteful and pornographic.

Each one had a gorgeous woman in some action pose with a word, possibly written in blood, across their necks, chests, or faces. These ladies had "Serenity," "Sedation," "Strength," and "Tranquility," covering their naked figures. I supposed it was odd, but not out of character from what I knew of Jeff. In the right setting, I think I could classify the black-and-whites as true artwork.

Anyway, Cash and I unpacked our clothes, toiletries, and what little food we brought and quickly changed out of the outfits we'd been stuck in for virtually the whole day.

"Kins, this place is awesome, right?"

"Oh, for sure. A pool right outside, and I can hear the waves crashing."

"I need a shower in the worst way. Wanna join me?"

"Of course."

After our shower, we got changed into comfy, clean clothes, made our way to the couch, and snuggled up under a Phillies blanket Cash brought from home.

"Wait, haven't I seen you wear those Penn shorts to the gym?" I asked.

"No, the navy Penn shorts are for outside of the house, and these red ones are inside ones. And when did I give you my Hollandsworth wrestling shirt?"

"I may have stolen it. It smells like you. Don't worry, I haven't worn it outdoors. It's solely a couch shirt."

Cash picked up the remote and scrolled through the titles before I said:

"Oh. There. *Stranger Things.*"

"Sounds good."

Cash put down the remote, sanitized his hands, and squeezed me against his chest.

"Wait. I want a Red Bull. I'm gonna get some work done after you fall asleep."

I went to the kitchen, picked a sugar-free one, and nestled into that always comfortable shoulder nook of his.

"All good? Anything else?"

"Just this." We kissed. And then he pressed play.

Cash always made sure to keep the TV's volume on a digit ending in zero or five, and after he settled on a number, we were locked in.

As always, he fell asleep before me, and since I didn't want to get too far ahead of him on *Stranger Things*, I switched shows. I put on season one of *The End of the F***ing World*, which Cash had finished during second semester and told me I'd love. Which I totally did.

But then I heard some cackling outside our door. I was naturally a bit nervous and had the Red Bull jitters, but then I remembered we were in the Hamptons, which Cash told me is probably the safest place on earth. And I always trusted him.

"Moreau and Avital? You guys decent? We're coming in."

"Fuck, Jeff. What are you doing?"

I guess I woke Cash because he said:

"Don't swear, Kins. C'mon."

"Sorry, but why is Jeff in our house at 1:30?"

Cash stood and walked toward the door.

"Campbell, man. What the heck? Get out."

"Moreau, come back to the big house. I wanna give you the tour."

"Get the hell out of here. And don't do this again."

"Come on, Kins," Skye said. "Swim with us. We brought a friend."

There was some high school-looking girl in her underwear standing behind them. She was absolutely on drugs.

"I'm okay. Thanks, though."

"Love you, sis." Skye whipped her hair around before turning back and whispering something to her friend.

I'm not sure what the hell that was all about. But then they closed the door and started blasting music, so I went outside and yelled:

"Turn that down. We're trying to sleep."

"House rules," Jeff responded.

I slammed the door and walked over to Cash, who was standing in the kitchen doing some deep breathing.

"Cash, you okay?"

He held up his index finger to me. He was doing his deep breathing exercises. Inhale for four, hold for seven, exhale for eight.

"All good now. Why don't we brush our teeth, head upstairs, and get ready for bed?"

"What have you gotten us into?" I smiled.

We finished making the bed and laid down. Cash sanitized his hands and then cuddled next to me.

"I'll talk to him tomorrow. I've known him for a long time. He just needs a little discipline."

"I trust you, Cash. We can handle anything."

"I love you."

"Love you too."

After he fell asleep, I took out my iPad. Cash had taken a few pictures of me at Navy Beach, and since I was in head-to-toe Guépard, I wanted to post a pic to the company's IG page. However, you can't post on Instagram at 2:00 a.m. on Saturday if you want maximum engagement. So, I was choosing the best picture and would post it around noon, which is an ideal time to post on Saturdays for B2C companies.

We took a lot of our inspiration from Yves Saint-Laurent's IG pages. Specifically, we had a Guépard page, which is where I'd post pictures of women wearing our outfits, and then the GuépardBeauty page, where I'd put up crisp images of various lipsticks, eyeliners, and foundations with interesting backdrops.

But I got distracted with this graphic design project I'd been mocking up images for. It was this start-up talent agency, Inspo, that wanted primary and secondary logos. They didn't have the money to hire some big-name, expensive place, so they posted on Indeed and gave me the first crack at the job.

I didn't fall asleep until around 4:30 a.m. and may have had a second Red Bull even though Cash frequently told me how bad it was for my heart and kidneys.

OUR ONE-YEAR ANNIVERSARY 2018

"KINSLEY AVITAL, I LOVE YOU more than anything else in the world."

"I love you too, but what time is it."

"10."

"You're so wired. My God. Was that all you woke me up to say? I mean, I appreciate it, but it probably could've waited until, I dunno, 11?"

"Happy One-Year Anniversary, you beautiful person."

He kissed me sweetly, but with even more passion than normal, which is saying a lot for him. And then, Cash went under the covers, removed my shirt and underwear, and we started making love.

"Come on. Let's go downstairs," he said afterward, a jackrabbit personified.

"Okay. Okay. Always in a rush in the mornings, aren't you?"

And then I saw what he did.

"Oh, fuck. Sorry, I didn't mean to curse. But what the hell, Cash? This is stunning. What did you do?"

"A little bit of everything." I kept picturing the White Rabbit from *Alice's Adventures in Wonderland* when he spoke.

"This is, oh God, I'm gonna cry. You're so sweet and caring. I love you so much."

Cash wiped my tears with his thumbs and held me tightly.

"I love you too."

"So, explain yourself. What's going on here? I want all the deets."

"Okay. Well...but sit down. Eat. Relax. Enjoy yourself."

"Okay. Okay. I'm sitting."

I sat at the kitchen table, my hair all frizzy from our morning activities.

"So, I went into town this morning. Campbell texted me some suggestions of places that'd be open. I bought the peonies and scattered petals around the floor at about 7:00 a.m. I bought the four-pack of sugar-free Red Bull 'cause they're your favorite. I bought the coffee and the lemon poppy seed muffin from The Pratincole. And then I whipped up some chocolate chip pancakes this morning before you woke up, but they may be cold now. And then there are mimosas in the kitchen."

"Cash, you didn't have to do all this."

"And today, we're going shopping. We'll walk around East Hampton and go into Brunello Cucinelli, Zimmermann, Clic, John Varvatos, Vilebrequin, lululemon, Henry Lehr, Tenet, and maybe even Pellegrini. But not Tory Burch. I know you hate her collection."

"You're the best."

"I wrote you three cards. They're on the table. Eat up and then we'll go out and I'll buy you whatever your heart desires."

"Also, how'd you find my two absolute favorite colors in the world? That's what those balloons are, right? Marigold and mint?"

"Yes, ma'am. You can find anything in the Hamptons. The trick was finding places that were open before 10. Also, we have a reservation at Sunset Beach tonight."

"Love you. Now c'mon. Eat with me."

"I'll heat the pancakes."

After I drove us into town, we walked hand in hand down the East Hampton main streets. We were kissing all throughout the day. Cash and I had this natural spark that never seemed to dissipate. I was always so attracted to him. And he thought of me like some goddess—which I appreciated—but he tended to ignore my flaws.

"So, Vogue Italia says lavender is the color that's gonna dominate the whole season. Keep your eyes peeled for any billowy lavender dresses. Dahlia's even marketing a lavender matte lipstick. Rapture rose is another hot color this season, and I think military green will pick up in a big way by the fall."

"Okay. I'm on the lookout. Purple, pink, and green."

"Not just any purple. Lavender."

"Isn't it blasphemous to wear other companies' clothes since you work in fashion?"

"No. Our inventory isn't large enough to fit a whole wardrobe. It's important to show that, like, this Zimmermann romper can work well with a Guépard fedora."

"Like the one you're wearing?"

"Exactly. This is our pecan floppy brim fedora. I think it works well with darker hair and olive skin."

"Looks cute on you."

"Thanks. I love these elegant but not too high-fashion hats. Like, you know the taupe night porter leather cap I wear?"

"Sure."

"That's one of my favorites."

"I also like the cheetah one."

"Oh, you mean my leopard print wool fedora? That was a great find. I got it at a flea market in South Beach if you can believe it."

Cash seemed very interested, so I continued.

"The hat is such an underrated part of women's fashion. Outside of the winter months, not enough people take advantage of it. I've heard a lot of women say they're not a hat person or it'll mess up their hair. But that's such a pessimistic mindset. Use hats to accentuate your outfit or wear them on particularly bad hair days, you know? Like, you've seen me wear your Phillies hat on days where I don't feel like doing my hair. They're so versatile."

"Right."

"Sorry for the rant."

"No, no. I love your passion."

"The backwards baseball cap at like, a rave, concert or bar will never go out of style."

"Okay, I'm sold. I'll buy you as many hats as you want."

We stopped next to James Perse and made out for a bit. Cash was wearing Jack Wills shorts with a rose, teal, and aegean checkered pattern along with a matching teal tee that hugged his biceps. And then he had on the classic Ray-Ban Clubmasters and royal-blue Rivieras. He looked comfy yet stylish. But realistically, I deserved the credit since that was an outfit I picked out.

By about one, Cash had bought me this super trendy latte sleeveless blazer from Brunello Cucinelli, an off-pink cashmere sweater from Henry Lehr, and of course, he *really* wanted to buy me a hat, so I now have a black leather beret from Zimmermann.

"Wanna grab some ice cream? Scoop du Jour is the absolute best," he said.

"Let's do it. And then let's swim afterward. We've been out here three days and haven't gone in the ocean yet. I feel guilty."

"It'll be kinda cold, but absolutely."

We walked into the quaint little ice cream shop, and I instantly wanted to try every flavor, partially because I loved ice cream and partially to get Cash to go on one of his many well-thought-out but ultimately meaningless rants.

"Excuse me, sir. May I please try the pistachio, the cookie dough, the cookies and cream, and the rocky road?"

"Certainly," the vendor said.

"Really, Kins? How many cookie doughs have you gotten since we started dating? 30 probably? Do you think you could tell any of them apart?"

"You're funny."

"Kins, you know..."

"I know. I know." I imitated him, "'Allow yourself to be surprised. Haven't you ever heard of spontaneity? Blah blah. You're 24. You know what pistachio tastes like, et cetera. et cetera."

"Wow, you got me."

"Oh, come on. You have the strangest pet peeves."

"Well, at least I don't always feel the need to speak up whenever someone pushes an already-lit elevator button."

"Good one. We're a match made in heaven."

I then decided to get two flavors that weren't among the ones I tried because I knew it'd make him roll his eyes. Anyone who's been in a long-term relationship knows what I'm talking about. Sometimes it's good to intentionally generate a little fake drama.

"Sir, we only accept cash," the vendor said to my boyfriend.

"Ugh, I only have cards."

"Cash, I've got it. Chill."

"It's our anniversary. I wanted to pay for everything."

"It's your anniversary?" the ice cream vendor said. "It's on the house."

"Seriously? You don't have to do that," Cash said, clearly not knowing how to accept free goods.

"Thank you very, very much, sir." And then I whispered to him: "Cash, this is my money we're talking about now. I want some free stuff."

My trusty boyfriend and I walked to the car, changed into our bathing suits, and took a long stroll to the main beach in East Hampton.

"Taste the s'mores," I said. "It's unreal."

"Oh, wow. That's incredible." And then we kissed with ice cream dripping down our lips and chins.

"Let's sit there where it's mostly empty," I said.

"I'll follow you. And I think I'm diving in right away because if I wait, I'll convince myself not to go in."

We laid down the towels in our secluded area a ways from the beach entrance. Sand stretched out limitlessly to the east and west like an Arabian desert, and the never-ending ocean met the horizon with matching cornflower blue. There weren't any children running around, and the beach's occupants were mostly fit teenagers, fit twenty-somethings, and fit thirty-somethings all wearing instantly identifiable Vilebrequin, lululemon, or Pesca swimwear.

Cash took off his shirt and said:

"Can you apply suntan lotion to my back, please?"

"Excuse me, sir," I said to him. "I don't normally do this, but I wanted to say, you have a great body. Are you, like, a model or an athlete?"

"Look, I appreciate it, but I'm just trying to enjoy some time off with my family."

"Oh, so you're married?"

"In the process of getting divorced."

"I'm sure she was in the wrong. No way a strapping but sensitive man like you would screw with a dame."

"She cheated on me. I caught her in the act and slugged the guy."

"Pity."

"For him or for me?"

"Pity that I wasn't there to watch."

"You got a screw loose or something? I like my women a little crazy."

"Then you're gonna love me."

"Do me a favor, will ya? Lotion up my back and join me in the water. You do that for me, I'll give you an autograph."

"But sir, I didn't bring any paper. What ever are we to do?"

"I haven't the slightest clue. But I do know my Northern European roots will leave me burnt to a crisp if you don't help me out."

"I suppose I can figure out a different place for you to sign. We'll get creative."

"What's your name, darling?"

"Kinsley Avital."

"Well, Ms. Avital, I think we're gonna be great friends."

And then, Cash laid on his towel, I applied the sunscreen, he sprinted into the water, and I joined him about five minutes later.

"Cash, it's freezing. Oh my God. I've got goosepimples."

"Ew."

"What?"

"Have I never noticed you say 'goosepimples'?"

"What am I supposed to say?"

"Goosebumps. Like a normal person."

"Since when do you like normal people? You love originality, right?"

"But naturally, pimples have a negative connotation, and bumps have a neutral connotation."

"Shush. Turn that pretty brain of yours off for a second."

We kissed for what felt like 20 minutes. I let my fingers dance around his muscles while he tickled me, and we just laughed together, our minds devoid of any stresses. Cash could always do that to me.

When we returned to the shore, his arms remained wrapped around my body to keep me warm. I felt like a cute little monkey that had stumbled into the wrong part of the jungle and was snared by a python.

"Kins, you're shivering. You okay?"

"I-I think s-so."

"Here, have my towel."

"T-thanks."

After some brief snuggling on our beach towels, Cash drove me home, we showered together, and then started to get ready for our anniversary dinner.

"Kinsley, you look so sexy. My God."

"Thank you, but can you tell me that again when I have clothes and makeup on?"

"Of course. Also, what should I wear?"

"Well, you know I think the white pants look great on you. You'll wear the Rivieras and then..."

"Either a linen shirt or a cashmere sweater."

"Wear that pale-pink linen one. Now shoo. I need to change, and you can't watch me this time."

He was waiting by the door when I did my pristine movie-walk down the stairs in my tangerine-and-azure paisley-print dress and matching blue pumps. They were both Guépard originals made by a designer in Saint-Jean-de-Luz Dahlia found about a year ago.

"Kinsley, you look so sexy. My God."

"Thanks, Cash. So do you. Now, as an anniversary present, can I drive to the restaurant and you drive home?"

"Of course. I'll do both if you'd like."

"Nope. I'm a fair lady. We're all about give-and-take."

I drove across 27 and through the woods north of the highway while we listened to this playlist:

"Walk It, Talk It" — Migos ft. Drake
"Plug Walk" — Rich the Kid
"Stir Fry" — Migos
"Ric Flair Drip" — Offset and Metro Boomin
"Powerglide" — Rae Sremmurd ft. Juicy J
"Bad at Love" — Halsey
"Hurt You" — The Weeknd ft. Gesaffelstein
"Changes" — XXXTentacion
"Tequila" — Dan & Shay
"Issues" — Julia Michaels
"I Get the Bag" — Gucci Mane ft. Migos
"Closer" — The Chainsmokers
"Good Old Days" — Macklemore ft. Kesha

"Must you drive 30 miles per hour faster every time a beat drops or Offset starts rapping? You almost hit that car when you were merging on 27."

Like any self-respecting person who listens to Migos, I knew exactly when to shout "Offset" and was able to shift between mumbling and screaming about 60 percent of the lyrics. Cash was obviously thrilled. And he was also ostensibly thrilled by my need to drive 15 miles per hour faster during Juicy J's verse in "Powerglide" and Gucci's verse on "I Get the Bag."

And then we took the ferry from I think Sag Harbor to Shelter Island, and I made Cash get out because the views were utter bliss. I needed him to step up and be an Instagram boyfriend once in a while. It was part of my job to gain followers, and showing the docile Peconic Bay, the yacht-filled Sag Harbor, and the tranquil shores of Shelter Island certainly did the trick. I also had Cash take a few (eh, maybe a hundred) pictures of me and the water. He was getting better at it.

"Just pull in here on the left," Cash said as we approached the restaurant.

"This is an adorable spot."

Sunset Beach was this uber-chic secluded spot where you could see anyone from Cash and me to Pippa Middleton and Christine Brinkley. We first walked into this boutique where they sold clothing and a lot of beach accessories, including some awesome rose-colored sunglasses I bought. And I convinced Cash to buy himself a second pair of Rivieras, this time in white.

At the restaurant, we were seated upstairs at a table overlooking the water with a series of wicker basket string lights shining above everyone's heads. The tablecloths were of a lighter material, designed with a large checkered pattern in honey and bone. And then the chairs were curved-back synthetic wicker.

"This is so pretty, Cash."

"I've always loved Sunset Beach. It's cool how it's both semi-formal and kid-friendly."

The waitress brought us menus, waters, and soon afterward, a bottle of champagne.

"Cheers, Cash. To the first of many magnificent years together."

"Cheers, Kins. I love you so much."

"You know what I think was an extraordinary moment?"

"What?"

"Your Penn graduation last December. You invited me, and I was a little nervous because your parents and aunts and uncles and cousins were gonna be there. But everyone instantly treated me like family. I mean, you know how much I love your mom, and she was as sweet and doting as ever, but also, your dad. He was boisterous and so funny and the life of the party. And then, when we played cards with your cousins back at the hotel, I never felt out of place."

"I'm so glad to hear that."

"Like, your cousin Mack told that story about how you saved his life using only a four-leaf-clover."

"Wait, he did?" Cash laughed. "What'd he tell you?"

"He said, I guess it was your aunt, uncle, and cousins with you and your family vacationing in the south of France, right?"

"Jesus. Yeah. I would've been maybe seven."

"So, Mack said he got salmonella from eating raw eggs and had to be hospitalized. Is this all true?"

"Shockingly yeah. He woulda been nine."

"And Mack said he remembers being in the hospital for three nights, and everyone was panicked because he wasn't improving. And your aunt and uncle didn't speak French, so this was a nightmare situation."

"That's right."

"And then, apparently, you decided to take matters into your own hands. Your uncle said you shouted, 'If the doctors can't fix Mack, then I'll have to do it.' Did you really say that?"

"I mean, I was seven, but that sounds like me, doesn't it?"

"Totally something you'd say. And you remember the rest?"

"I remember it, but I want to hear how he told it to you."

"Your uncle and Mack both said you went into the backyard of the house you were staying at and dug through a giant patch of clovers for nearly three hours—refusing to rest until you found a four-leafed one. And lo and behold, you found one. Your dad drove you to the hospital, you gave it to the deathly ill Mack, and the next day, he was all better and returned home."

"I remember." He laughed his inaudible laugh again.

"I thought that was so sweet. I think that story just encapsulates Cash Moreau."

Our food arrived, which we happily split, and at one point, two patrons who were leaving the restaurant, stopped by our table and said:

"You two make an adorable couple."

"Thank you," I said. "That's so sweet of you to say. It's our one-year anniversary."

"Well, have a wonderful evening."

That same middle-aged power couple sent us a bottle of super-expensive champagne, which Cash and I split. Although to be honest, I probably had 99 percent of it.

"Since we're talking family stories," Cash said, "you know what Ira told me?"

"What?"

"And you'd never told me this."

"When did you talk to him?"

"When he stayed with you over Christmas break. You went for a run along the East River, and he and I grabbed breakfast at the Jackson Hole in Murray Hill."

"Oh gosh, now I'm worried. What'd he tell you?"

"It wasn't any one thing. He said he'd never heard of anyone with a big sister like you. If he dropped his ice cream, you gave him yours. If he was frightened at night, you cuddled him back to sleep. When he first started high school, you convinced your friends to tell the freshmen girls how great of a catch he was, because no one would've believed it coming from you. And then, my favorite story was about some of your Saturday nights."

"What'd he say?"

"That when Ira was in the seventh to ninth-grade range, if he were ever alone on Saturday night, you'd invite a bunch of your friends and include him in whatever you were doing. Watching movies, talking about high school, texting boys, you never left him alone. I thought that was the sweetest thing."

"Thank you, Cash."

He looked really handsome in that pink linen shirt. I don't think he understood how attractive I thought he was. Inside and out. Just a good-looking, caring, dream of a man. Someone who always seemed to know what I was thinking.

"So, what does the future hold?" I asked him.

"You and I are perfect, but my job stuff sucks."

"What has your dad said?"

"I made him a promise I'd work for him if I didn't find a job by the end of this summer."

"He wants you to be happy. And so do I. Your dad gave you six months to find a job in Manhattan after graduating. What's another six months? It's better than doing something you're not passionate about."

"Kins, I'm scared to be like, a real adult human. I just, I don't want to age. I wanna stay right here."

"What are you most passionate about? If money didn't matter, what would you do? Ew wait, I sound like a college counselor. But you get my point."

"You and us. I'm happiest around you."

"What about when I'm at work? I'm gonna be working from the office in September."

"Let's change the subject. It's our anniversary. How's working remotely? Your boss is understanding?"

"Yeah, I love Dahlia like a sister. Such a great boss. If you had any beauty or fashion interest, I'd get her to hire you in a second. You can't beat the freedom I get. All anyone cares about is the work gets done. No one cares where or how you do it. That's super ideal."

"Sounds like a dream."

"Maybe you could create a start-up or join one?"

And then this little kid came sprinting over and crashed into my leg.

"You're pretty," the probably three-year-old said.

"Aw, you're such a cutie."

"Sorry about her," the mother said after racing over. "Christine, back to the table. You want chicken nuggets?"

They left, but that moment did cause me to briefly dream about my future kids.

"What's the right number of kids to have?" I asked.

"Three or four. They should all be similar ages. It's great for young kids to have natural playmates."

"Would you want twins?"

"Sure, why not? But I'd probably dot one of their hands with a permanent marker to tell them apart. I always think about what would happen if, for two years, I was raising Penelope and Marisa, and then one day, I couldn't tell the difference, and for the rest of their lives, Penelope was Marisa and Marisa was Penelope."

"Really? You *always* think about that? And those are your daughters' names?"

"You'll have plenty of input."

"Let's not grow up too fast," I said. "It wasn't so long ago you were probably a wild little kid who ran around killing bugs and catching frogs or whatever Manhattan boys do."

"I used to love hanging out by the creek on 88th and Park nabbing frogs and eating crickets."

Cash and I continued to talk while we finished our food and drinks. Mindlessly chatting about seemingly nothing.

"Is the bill paid?" I asked.

"Yeah, we're all good. Wanna go to the water?"

The sun was setting at the aptly named beach as I ran ahead and sunk my toes into the sand under the water.

"Cash, c'mon. Hurry! I need you."

"Everything okay?" he said, panting.

"Yeah, I just missed you. Those three seconds apart weren't easy."

"You were the one that ran up ahead."

"Just kiss me."

I then laid down on my back, looked up at Cash, and motioned for him to join me.

"If I could buy a plot of land on the moon, would you live there with me?"

"Wait," he said, "you want me to get down next to you? On the dirty sand? In my nice clothes?"

"Oh, stop." I grabbed his frequently Purell'd hands. "I'll wash your clothes, and we'll shower together at home. Now...to the moon."

He huddled next to me on a secluded portion of the beach.

"I'd move there with you, but there are conditions."

"Good. I need someone like you. I'm afraid without you holding the string, I'd float away."

"Is there electricity? Are we assuming there's oxygen and nitrogen, or must we have helmets on the whole time? Can we play outside? What year is this? Has the moon been colonized? Are there shops and tourist attractions? How do we import furniture? Buy clothes?"

"We'd improvise. Let's imagine we wake up tomorrow, and instead of being on that pool house mattress, we're in a house on the moon... that I decorated."

"Oh, so it's an extraordinarily elegant house? Shaker siding?"

"Right."

"Can we breathe outside?"

"It's my dream. You can do whatever your big heart desires."

"Then, absolutely. I'll live with you on the moon. I'd purchase a rover and drive you around every crack and crevice. You'd play Spotify playlists with eclectic mixes of rap, pop, and '70s ballads. We'd throw around a football on our moon yard that happened to have tiger-striped grass."

"Naturally. 'Cause that's how the moon works. I'm glad you're getting this game now."

"I'd want it to rain sugar-free Red Bull. I wouldn't have any, but I know you couldn't last without it."

"I'd cook dinner. I'd make you that jambalaya you love. Shrimp are bountiful in the sea about a mile from our property."

"You're a great cook, Kins. Although I don't think you could handle moon living."

"Why not? Of course I could. I'm offended."

"You need people around you. You're a gregarious, life-of-the-party extrovert. Someone like you wouldn't do as well stranded on an island or as one of two denizens on the moon."

"Oh, you think I'd go 'Hereeee's Johnny' on you?"

"Probably."

"You think I could beat you up, Cash?"

"Of course."

"No way. Really?

"I'd never hit you back."

"You could wrestle me to the ground, right?"

"But then I'd start kissing you. It'd be an illogical fight."

He held my hand on the way back to my Prius, and I fell asleep before we even made it to the ferry. And then, because he's the best, Cash carried me from the Campbell driveway to the pool house couch—although the landing could've been smoother.

"Ow, jeez."

"Sorry, I lost my grip. You have no fat to grab on to."

"Smooth."

"Wanna shower?"

"Yeah."

"Lemme guess, you're wide awake now?"

"Yeah."

After our shower, Cash and I put on clean clothes and he instantly fell asleep. I pulled out my iPad and spent time doing work for Dahlia. She had sent me a few images of various pumps, clutches, miniskirts, and blouses. I had to confirm the color combinations were on brand, and then I needed to select the pieces I felt would garner the most online engagement. Sometimes, I couldn't believe that was my job because it was absolutely what I loved doing.

I drank a Red Bull, worked for a few hours next to my unconscious lover, and then, for some reason, dreamed about Cash and I living on the moon.

ONE-ON-ONE WITH THE ONE-OF-A-KIND SKYE PELLEGRINI — JUNE 2018

"So, DO YOU HAVE ANY good music on this thing?"

"No, I only like bad music, sorry," I said.

"Dude, I'll just, like, hook up mine to the aux. I'll play some experimental stuff I've been working on. You'll for sure love it."

"Honey, we listen to your music all the time. I have a thousand songs from five different genres. I'm sure you can come up with a few you like."

She played the following on our drive to this adorable winery. Think of this as Skye's favorites of my favorite songs:

"Sure Thing" — Miguel
"The Morning" — The Weeknd
"Timmy Turner" — Desiigner
"Lucky" — Britney Spears
"Gimme More" — Britney Spears
"Novacane" — Frank Ocean
"Alone" — Marshmello
"21 Questions" — 50 Cent
"Ooouuu" — Young M.A
"Calling (Lose My Mind)" — Sebastian Ingrosso & Alessio
"Moment 4 Life" — Nicki Minaj ft. Drake

I should mention it was probably a 15-minute ride, and I think all of those songs played because Skye couldn't stay on one for more than two minutes.

"Wow, she's the most beautiful girl I've ever seen," I said after we arrived.

"Who? Bérénice? Dude, she's so effing hot. Wait until you see her up close."

Skye's French friend, easily six inches taller than either of us, skipped toward Violet.

"Skye, I can't believe this. You look so cute," Bérénice said in her thick French accent.

Our host was wearing this super eight frilled midi from Zimmermann. Hers was in blue meadow, and she wore a silver necklace with a gigantic sapphire. Skye's friend was thin from head to toe and had the most flawless skin I'd ever seen. Her chestnut hair was tied back, and she wore this ruby lipstick on her Jolie-esque lips.

"You must be Kinsley."

"Nice to meet you. I love your dress."

"Oh, thank you so much. You too. Where's that from? Pink is a great color for your complexion."

"It's Guépard. It's this beauty start-up I work for. Our founder imports all of our clothes from the south of France."

"Magnifique. Where?"

"All over, but I think Nimes, Avignon, Biarritz, and Toulouse."

"Tres, tres jolie."

"Okay, guys. Blah. Blah. Blah. B, where are we going?"

"I thought I'd take you guys on a tour around the vineyard. We drink. We dish. We dine."

"Perf. Kins, you know B's mother Lulu started this Hamptons spot, like, what, 15 years ago? And B's gramma is Bérénice too. Lotta rosé. B, your family must make bank."

"Yes, yes. Kins, have you met her bf? Jeff."

"Yes, I have."

Bérénice started puffing on a Juul as we entered the main house on the picturesque property.

"B, can we hit that inside, or will your mom get pissed?"

"She smokes more than I do. Lol."

"B, have you been working out more? You look so tight. I've seen your stories, and then I saw that post of you at the beach on your VSCO. I'm high-key impressed."

"Merci, amour."

The inside was super chic. It was an entirely open floor plan with floor-to-ceiling doorways that were all open to let in air and light. The furniture was imported from France, and there was even an old limestone fountain situated right in the center of the main greeting area. And then vines hugged the walls, and bottles of rosé were situated on every windowsill. I loved it.

"Hello, ladies," Bérénice's grandmother said. "Berni, you always bring the most beautiful friends. Where'd you get your dress?" she said to me.

"Oh, maman, Kinsley works for a French clothing start-up. They import from Provence."

"Well, our company's expertise is beauty products and makeup, but we're diving into fashion."

"Tres beau, ma fille. And sunny Skye, you're gorgeous as always, but you need to eat something. Mon Dieu. Berni, get the girls some brie and a baguette from the pantry."

"I don't want that," Skye said.

"I'm alright as well. I had a smoothie before we arrived."

"Maman, which rosé bottles can we take? I'm gonna tour the grounds."

"Pantry, the middle shelf. 2008 rosés. A bientot."

Bérénice kindly gave each of us our own bottle and then guided us outside toward the never-ending rows of the Bérénice Louise Vineyard.

The views were breathtaking. Aside from the countless rows of grapes, there were these rolling hills in the distance with the cloudless sky and an abnormally large sun beating down on the vineyard. The whole property was symmetrical and decorated with such a meticulous eye. There were trellises everywhere and loose vines constricting every piece of visible wood—an absolutely superb spot.

"So, Bérénice, which color is one supposed to taste first? Should I have white before rosé?"

"Kins," Skye interrupted. "Don't be so boring. Drink and take in the beauty, girl. B, pass me the Juul."

"Sorry, I just have so many questions. Like, should we have a spittoon for the wine?"

"B, you know I have 75K followers now."

"So proud of you, girl. That's huge news."

"B, let's come up with, like, some dank IG story no one else could do."

"Do you want funny or classy?"

"Both, obvi. Is my fit hard?"

"Always."

"Take my hat, Skye," I said. "And if you're going for classy, why don't you take a boomerang of you sipping the wine? The background will look so cool."

"Gross...B, should I lay down and you feed me grapes or pour wine down my throat or something?"

"I'm down for anything."

"I could double-fist two bottles. Caption it like: 'Do you think I can handle three?'"

"I mean, if you're solely doing it to add more followers, then you should be showing more skin," I said. "If you only care about your numbers and not the actual content and message, then sex it up."

"Now we're talking. Looks like someone decided to wake up. What should I do?"

"I mean, I wouldn't do this, but pull down your collar some more. Make your cleavage *very* visible. Flaunt your assets. Find a way to tuck your shirt up, so you have more midriff showing. And you have to display more leg than that. Some guys love thighs."

"Some guys love thighs. I feel that," Skye said. "How's this?"

At that point, she'd managed to turn her cute outfit into essentially a bikini, but I'm not one to judge. Skye was at a tough age and needed to figure out who she was. I totally supported that.

"Now, Skye," I continued. "Lay down in front of that vine there and have one leg outstretched and the other knee should be curled toward your chest. Lean forward. Clutch your left knee with your left hand. And then with your right hand, tilt the bottle back and very slowly pour a small stream into your mouth from as high up as you can. And stick your tongue out. You've got a nice, big tongue."

"That's so dope. I'm gonna do all that, 'cept B, why don't you pour it into my mouth instead. She legit adds way more sex appeal. Kins, you take it. Don't get my double chin, though. Take it from high up. And take a few. I'll change positions. And try slo-mo vids and boomerang."

After I spent about 20 minutes taking a ton of videos, I handed the phone back to Skye.

"I wanna use an Audrey caption," she said. "Kins, Google her best quotes. But they can't be too basic. Google like, 'Audrey Hepburn best subtle quotes.' No, wait. Google 'Audrey Hepburn quotes not common'…Actually, do 'Audrey Hepburn nature quotes' or 'Audrey Hepburn wine quotes.'"

Bérénice had walked away to inspect a few of the nearby grapes while Skye continued on her journey toward the chicest Insta story.

"Dude," Skye shouted. "I got it. I'm gonna caption it: 'There are shades of limelight that can wreck a girl's complexion.'"

"Great, can we get back to touring the property?"

"One more sec. I gotta edit out some of my excess arm and stomach flab. I look like a legit piglet."

"Skye, you know you're very thin and pretty," I said.

"Yeah, I know."

At that point, I desperately wanted to get back to the stunning views and the delicious rosé.

"So Bérénice, what makes these wines distinctive to others in the region? How do you concoct an original and specific taste?"

"Wait, Skye," Bérénice said, "since you got your story, I need your help with my vlog. I'll tag both of you."

Bérénice took out a special vlogging camera from her bag and started recording. Skye and I gushed about the wine and the unforgettable property, while Bérénice was her carefree, cheery self.

We went back inside after about two hours and sat in an ornately decorated room with four vintage French lounge chairs all in the forest green family. The matching curtains were drawn back to allow for tickling breezes to sweep around the gilded living room.

"Kins, gettin' drunk yet? You were kinda stumbling in here?" Skye said as she sat in one of the chairs.

"I'm fine. I can hold wine pretty easily. Not my first rodeo."

"You know, B was there when I had my first drink."

"Hopefully, it was only a year or two ago."

Bérénice stretched out her stick-figure arms and let out a lioness' yawn.

"We were both eight," Skye said.

"Oy. Was it just a tiny sip?"

"Not exactly," she cackled. "B was sleeping at my gramma's place, and my gramma forgot to, like, lock the cabinet one night."

"Oh, yes. I remember this vividly." Bérénice's eyes were glued to Skye.

"So, like, my gramma said, 'Skye, I'll be back in 10 minutes. Call 9-1-1 if there's any emergency.' And right when the door slammed, I sprinted to the wine cabinet and picked out a rosé."

"It wasn't a very good one, though. Your taste has improved since then."

"It was chill. Relax. So, I just tilted the bottle back and took a few gulps and told B to do the same."

"More like you forced me."

"Not even close. You were so down. You basically peer pressured me."

"Not how *I* remember it, girl."

"When my gramma got home, we both complained of tummy aches, and she gave us Pepto, and we were fine the next day. But I thought it was like, pretty fucking exhilarating."

"Oh, absolutely. We must've started sneaking wine like once a month after that. Our little secret."

"One of many," Skye laughed as some wine spilled down her chin.

"Gosh," I said. "My friends and I were still playing with Polly Pocket back then. That's crazy. But what are these other secrets you have? I'm curious...but feel free not to tell me if you don't want to."

"B, which should I tell her?"

"Oh, I don't care. Tell her anything."

"Don't worry about it. We can change subjects. So, what color wines do you have on the property other than rosé?" I asked. "I was researching wineries in the area, and they were talking about garnet and amber and topaz. It was fascinating."

"B and I were each other's first kisses. Right, B?"

"Something like that."

"But that doesn't really count," I said. I know a few of my friends practiced kissing on each other before like big dances or dates."

Skye pranced over, sat on Bérénice's lap, and started stroking her hair.

"It was more than that, right B?"

"I suppose so. Sunny Skye was always an adventurous sort."

"You guys don't have to tell me about this if you don't want to. Skye, we should probably leave soon anyway. Don't want the guys to get worried."

"Relax. Jeff knows he can't control me. No one can."

Bérénice took out her Juul, and she and Skye traded puffs while I suctioned the last few drops of wine from my second bottle.

"I'll tell it B, but stop me anytime if I'm telling it wrong."

Bérénice leaned her head back behind the chair and closed her eyes.

"So," Skye started, "B and I were probably 13, and neither of us had kissed a boy. We were like besties and told each other everything, and I didn't even like boys. B was always this hot, but back then, I was high-key an ugly duckling. Like, Kins, we're talking no lips, huge pores, no clue how to do makeup, um, what else? My hair was 95 percent split ends. I was living that no parent, no sibling life. Bunch of other stuff."

"I'm sure you weren't ugly. And even if you were, no one looks great when they're mid-puberty."

"She still had the nice, big boobs." Bérénice piped up with the Juul in her mouth. "Early developer, this one."

"Literally. But seriously, B and I rode our bikes to Mashashimuet Park in Sag. Remember we used to do that?"

Bérénice made a squeaky affirmation noise.

"Anyway, I'd say like, once a month, B and I would ride our bikes to that big park on Saturday nights. We'd post up on the basketball court at like 11. Idk if it was locked or not, but if it was, we snuck in. B would smoke cigs and let me bum one, and we'd just chat for like two hours. Catch up on life. Plan our futures."

"You guys smoked when you were 13?"

"Not the point," Skye said. "One night, we're smoking underneath the hoop and B says, 'You think Riley is hot?' And I was like 'No,' and she was like 'Well, who at school do you think is hot?' I said, 'Like, legit none of the guys are hot. They're all gross, really. For the most part. They talk about like sports and who takes the biggest dumps. I literally hate all of them.'"

"This isn't what happened, like at all," Bérénice interrupted.

"Yeah, it for sure is. What am I missing?"

"Sorry, continue. I totally want to hear your version."

At that point, Skye was lounging on the long chaise and Bérénice was lying at the other end, smoking her Juul, while their feet met in the middle. I was somewhere between drunk and fascinated.

"Then B said, 'There are some hot girls in our grade though,' and I was like 'Yeah, I guess,' and she was like 'Do you think if we were in Manhattan, everyone would be hotter?' And I said 'Totally, but maybe we're just like, looking in the wrong places,' and she said 'What about in the grades older than us? Or at like Southampton High?'"

Skye had started doing Bérénice's accent for each of her lines, and I was impossibly entertained.

"Then B started rubbing my hands and was like, 'Skye, you're freezing.' And I said, 'I've always thought you were hot.' And she blew smoke into my face and laughed. Then I just kissed her, and she was like, 'Dude, what was that?' And I was like, 'That was kinda nice.'"

"Bérénice, can I fact-check this with you?" I said. "I think this unfledged lustful story is delightful."

"None of this happened," she said with her eyes still closed. "Skye and I biked to the beach after school one day, went swimming, and were laughing about some nonsense. Then she pressed her lips against mine, and I was like wtf?"

"Nope," Skye said. "Didn't happen like that. We used to kiss on the basketball courts of Mashashimuet Park like every Saturday night for a year. Did that not happen?"

"It was, like, three times. You're, like, way too drunk right now."

"And we lost our virginities to each other in my gramma's store after closing hours. Remember that?"

"I'd clearly already had sex before that," Bérénice said.

I interrupted, "Let's talk about something else? Jeff maybe? Bérénice, you wanted to hear about Jeff?"

"That connard? Mon dieu."

Skye stood up, went to the bathroom, and returned to silence. She had a new pep in her step and said:

"B, tell Kins about how we went to prom together. You looked mad hot that night."

"Skye, your boobs were literally on the floor. Everyone was staring at us."

"That's certainly plausible," I said. "You're both really pretty and smart. I love talking to you guys. You're like a cool sitcom."

Skye sat on Bérénice's lap, and they recounted their memories from prom night until I fell asleep. It was surprisingly a fun day. I thought Skye was rough around the edges, but I absolutely adored her.

ONE OF MANY SPECIAL DATE NIGHTS WITH CASH — LATE-JUNE 2018

"WHAT ARE YOU IN THE mood for?"

"I'm feeling classical this morning." I said while starting Violet. "Find my summer classical playlist, please."

"Oh, but you can't sing to that stuff."

"Well, you know how to whistle, don't you, Cash? You just put your lips together and blow."

"Wow. A-plus Bacall quote."

"Thank you kindly," I smiled.

"7th Symphony, 2nd Movement" — Beethoven
"Piano Concerto Op. 18 No. 2" — Rachmaninoff
"Lacrimosa" — Mozart
"Clair de Lune" — Debussy
"Moonlight Sonata" — Beethoven
"In the Hall of the Mountain King" — Edvard Grieg
"Dance of the Little Swans" — Tchaikovsky
"Winter" — Vivaldi
"Romeo and Juliet Op. 64" — Prokofiev
"Jazz Suite No. 2: VII. Waltz No. 2" — Shostakovich

We walked into Sant Ambroeus in Southampton and ordered mimosas and some excellent prosciutto and then shared a tagliatelle bolognese. Cash and I sat outside in their courtyard surrounded by foliage, trellises, Italian olive-green chairs, and gigantic umbrellas with off-white fabric. The décor there was positively sublime.

"What'd you think of the movie last night?" he asked.

"Cash, and you know I don't say this often, it's one of the most profound experiences I've ever had watching a movie. And you'd never seen it before?"

"Nope."

"That's shocking to me. Every list I looked at had it as an all-time great, and you've seen basically everything."

"It's embarrassing, but it's the same reason I've never read Tolstoy's *War and Peace*. So lengthy. Whether it's a 1,000-page book or a 180-plus minute movie, I have a difficult time devoting my eyes and brain to something. Particularly if it winds up being some insipid piece."

"Well, have you learned your lesson after last night?"

"Kins, I kid you not, I could go home with you right now and replay *Lawrence of Arabia* from start to finish and not feel bored for a second. It's one of the few films that deserves and *needs* to be three hours long."

"I know, right?" I said. "What a character study. Lean does such an exquisite job of capturing Lawrence's descent into, well, I guess, madness. And O'Toole. Oh my gosh."

"Agreed. Weirdly enough, I can maybe see myself as T.E. Lawrence. Could you see me like that?"

"Which part specifically? As an egotist? As someone who could lead? As a traitor to his people?"

"All of it. I could see myself, in a different life maybe, exploring the desert lands in the Middle East, uniting cultures, wearing lustrous, foreign garb, leading an iconoclastic lifestyle, and being a hero to many."

"Well, he sees himself as a God. Do you want to play God? Is that what this is about? He also slaughters a ton of people."

"It's wartime, though. And yeah, I think anyone, even just out of curiosity, should want to either play God or be worshipped like one."

"Do you need me to compliment you more?"

He rolled his eyes and laughed.

"I dunno, Kins. There's something about that movie. I want to live his life. I think that'd be thrilling. I can picture myself riding a camel, leading an army, and being worshipped like a God. Is that a horrible image to conjure?"

"I'm gonna let you think on this one. Maybe if you beef up your resume in the next few years, you could become a T.E. Lawrence of sorts. It's not an entry-level position."

"This food's great. I want another mimosa."

"I think that's one of the reasons *Lawrence of Arabia* is so wonderful. I think there are so many matters to discuss and so many different ways to have a discourse about Lawrence as a character."

"Your turn to pick the movie tonight," he said.

"Tonight? No way. We're going to that new club, Tetra, remember? In Sag. I wanna see if your moves have improved at all or if you're still just copying what Will Smith taught Kevin James in *Hitch*."

"You'll find out tonight, I guess."

Cash paid for brunch, and then I paid for an Uber to the famed Cooper's Beach, because you can't park there without a town permit.

We laid out by the water, me a mere mortal, next to the great God, Cash Moreau. He fell asleep and undoubtedly dreamed of turning Cooper's Beach into his Arabian Desert, where he'd ride his camel, slaughter innocents, and bed thousands of women, or whatever that new fantasy of his entailed.

I read L'Ecole's new *2018 Guide to Succeeding on Social Media* while Cash's back started to burn. I laid my towel over him, but I suppose I neglected the backs of his legs because they looked like a matador's cape by mid-afternoon. God bless my dark Israeli skin.

I went down around the water and took a couple hundred pictures of the beach, along with a few shots of women's outfits I particularly adored. The Hamptons had a scarcity of many things, but fashionable women weren't one of them.

By about four, we hopped into the car and drove around various neighborhoods in South and Bridgehampton. I had Cash check out the Zillow prices of about 20 different homes.

"One of these is going to be ours someday," he announced as we pulled back onto 27.

"I dunno. With you off fighting infidels outside Damascus, I'm not sure if you'll still want me. Plus, I'm not sure I'm good enough for a God like you."

"Eh, that joke's getting stale."

"Oh, so now you're the God of Comedy, too?"

"Want BBQ for dinner? We can go to Townline right by Poxabogue. It's a bucolic little place that's fit for celebrities, kids, and everyone in between."

"Are you doing guerrilla marketing for them? You have to tell me if I ask. Otherwise, it's marketing entrapment."

"Duke teach you that?"

"Do you think if there was a tribe of Duke students and a tribe of UNC students in an Arabian desert, you could negotiate peace between them and convince them to join you as you storm Damascus? Maybe bed a few coeds on your journey?"

"Lawrence doesn't bed any women. Didn't you like the movie?"

"I loved it."

We shared ribs and burnt ends at Townline before going home, changing, ubering to Sag Harbor, and eventually entering this hot new nightclub, Tetra, near the Bay Street Theatre.

I was wearing this phenomenal Asos piece. It was a burnt-orange asymmetrical midi dress, and I decided to pair it with these white ankle-strap sandals. I'd always loved the orange-and-white look in the summertime. Highly recommend. And Cash wore different colored linen shirts with white chinos every night. I always found him to be so handsome. Always walking around duck-footed with impossibly erect posture and a goofy ear-to-ear grin. He made me smile every day. I mean, he genuinely cared about my happiness and well-being and continuously put me before him. Anyway, he dressed well. That's the point I was trying to make before I got all mushy.

"Cash, this place is amazing. How'd you find out about it?"

"Campbell's rec. He knows the owner. Said it was *the* can't-miss spot of the summer."

My boyfriend held my hand and led me toward the outskirts of the dance floor. Tetra was magnificent. It was an underwater nightclub right by the Sag Harbor docks. There was this shiny cyan water beneath all the dancing guests, and tropical fish were legitimately swimming underneath your feet. I'd never seen anything like it. And then the walls were made of an aquarium too. Sharks were swimming, like real-life sharks, circling the dance floor. I mean, come on. Cash and I were dancing to Jason Derulo while yellow tangs and Dory fish were fluttering in the water a few inches below us, and sharks were watching from the sides. It was truly awesome. Cash paid the cover, so I'm not sure what it was, but seriously, go to an aquarium nightclub if you can find one. Oh my gosh.

"Who's this, Cash?" I shouted.

"What?"

"What artist is this?"

"What?"

I pulled him in close and whispered in his ear:

"What song is this?"

He then pulled me in and said:

"'By Your Side' by Jonas Blue. But this DJ's butchering it big time."

"We need to learn sign language for nightclubs."

"What? Let's grab drinks."

Cash and I must've downed six Tetra Tackles between us. And I know that doesn't sound like a sexy name, but that was one stupendous drink. Red Bull, vodka, coconut purée, pineapple juice, and coconut flakes on top. Cash's choice. He still makes them for me at home to this day.

"You wanna get out of here?" he said after about two hours of sweaty, mostly silent dancing.

"Sure."

We walked a few blocks from the water and stumbled upon this other place that Jeff recommended: Sore-Bae.

"Cash, what's this place? Oy. It's too bright."

"It's sorbets, plus they have a liquor license."

"Oh, I'm so down for this."

"I thought it might appeal to you."

We approached the counter after a few drunken college kids left and Cash ordered:

"The dark chocolate sorbet and a piña colada please."

"Horrible mix, Cash." And then I turned to the scooper and said, "May I please taste the popcorn sorbet, the strawberry champagne sorbet, the sparkling pear and bourbon, and the Bellini sorbet?"

Cash took out his wallet and paid the cashier.

"No snarky comment?" I said.

"About what?"

"Me trying four sorbets."

"Nope. You've probably had nothing like these before. It makes sense to get tasting cups. Why? Were you looking for some drama? I could manufacture some anger. I've got a little buzz going."

"Would you, darling?"

Cash buttoned his almost entirely unbuttoned linen shirt and screamed:

"Kinsley Avital. You need to stop being so beautiful. You're embarrassing all the other women. It's practically repulsive, and it ends now."

"You're not the boss of me. I can do whatever I want."

"While I'm paying for your sorbet, you most certainly cannot."

"What are you gonna do about it? You want me to be uglier?"

And then, the normally restrained Cash took his dark chocolate sorbet and slowly moved it toward my face.

"Cash, stop." The cup kept creeping forward. "Cash, stop. Too close. Not funny anymore. Game over. Game over. I don't want drama. Be nice to me aga—"

But it was too late. He smushed his new sorbet onto my nose, lips, and cheeks and walked right out of the store.

"Cash," I shouted. "Get back here."

I stared at the person behind the counter, who wasn't quite sure what was happening. And then, five seconds later, Cash walked back into the store.

"Pardon me, miss." He walked past me, turned to the scooper, and said, "I'd like your finest dark chocolate sorbet, please."

I was still standing dumbfounded with sorbet dripping down my face and my mouth agape.

"'Scuse me, miss?" He turned to me. "Are you quite alright? You seem to have a little, well actually, a lot of chocolate all over your face."

"I'm not okay. My boyfriend and I got in a fight. He's such a brute."

"I'm so sorry to hear that." He then picked up some napkins and said, "Do you mind if I help clean you up?"

"Certainly not, sir. You're very kind."

"Your boyfriend must be feverishly handsome," Cash said as he cleaned my face.

"What makes you say that?"

"Well, if he's some uncouth lout, there must be some reason you're with him. Is he a dashing young fellow?"

"I suppose."

"Brown hair? Blue eyes? Barrel-chested? Big-armed? God complex?"

"That's him, alright. You know him?"

"Yes, ma'am. Saw him by the docks." Cash paid the cashier and said to me, "Follow me. I'll give him a piece of my mind. Here, take this."

He held out his hand, which I grabbed, and we walked side by side out of the store with a flabbergasted staff pondering what that audacious skit was all about.

"I'm drunk," Cash said as we plopped on the docks overlooking the harbor.

"I can tell."

I took a few pictures of Cash, then me, then the scenery. All very tasteful.

"Fun night?" he asked.

"That Tetra was nuts. Fish everywhere. Are you kidding me? Where else can you find that?"

He licked my nose.

"Ew. What was that for?"

"You had some chocolate. It was going to drip onto your dress."

"Thank you for slobbering on my nose, Cash. I really appreciate it."

He did it again. And then I did it to him. And then he did it to me. And then our tongues wound up in each other's mouths.

"Has my dancing gotten better?" he said.

"You can follow a beat. A little too conservative, though. Your legs are always moving, but you keep your arms tucked at all times."

"What should I do with them?"

"Lift them? Move them? You know, be a human instead of a robot."

"Oh, gotcha. That's what I was doing wrong. I always forget about that."

"You're a brilliant man, Cash Moreau."

I don't know if this sounds weird, but that was one of the best days of my life. That Uber ride home, while Cash was asleep, was the first time I thought about "soul mates." That was us. He could read me so well. Cash knew exactly how to behave around me in every situation. He was goofy, serious, intelligent, quirky, handsome, fashionable, so unbelievably considerate, honest, and forgiving. I remember thinking that I loved this guy, who at that moment was drooling on my shoulder, so goddamn much.

SAILING — INDEPENDENCE DAY 2018

"Wow, Kinsley. You look so hot. Sheesh."

"Campbell, don't say that in front of your girlfriend and me. It makes everyone feel awkward."

"That's about as light-hearted a compliment as I can give. I can be more grotesque if you'd prefer? Kinsley, would you prefer more details?"

"Enough," Cash said.

"Loosen up. Skye, pour him a drink."

"I'm good, Campbell. You've had enough for the both of us. What are the ocean rules on drinking while operating a boat?"

"No rules. You can drink and take drugs until you're comatose out here."

"You know, Campbell, I'm gonna go out on a limb and say that's untrue."

"Well, I know one can murder on the open water. You're not in any country's jurisdiction. Trust me."

"So, Jeff, why's it called *The Aeneid*?" I said.

"Well, Virgil was writing about Homer's character, Aeneas. You know, from the Trojan War."

"I know the book, Jeff. I meant your boat."

"I'm just messing with you. I know what you meant."

"How many drinks have you had, Campbell?"

"Skye, you're awfully quiet," Jeff said. "How many drinks have I had? Skye? Skye, are you listening to music? Take the headphones out, please. Enjoy the water and our company. Christ."

"Whatever." Skye took out her pods.

"Don't pout," Jeff said. "Why don't you make yourself useful and go below deck and grab the picnic basket we brought for our guests along with the Bellinis and other stuff. May you please do all that, kid?"

"Yes, daddy."

"And pop some fucking addy while you're at it. You seem down."

Jeff had a beautiful boat. Although I suppose most boats are beautiful. Just being able to be out on the water among the waves and the birds is so peaceful and liberating.

And Jeff surprisingly knew what he was doing. He was deft with the tiller and the ropes and knew all the lingo. If he were sober, I would've trusted him completely.

"Cap'n Campbell," Skye called him for some reason, "I'm hungry."

"My little first mate is hungry? Well, what are you telling me for? We packed the chips, guac, salsa, strawberries. Eat something."

"What should I eat? There are too many choices."

"Skye..."

"J..."

The two stared at each other, silently speaking in that secret couples' language every pair develops after being together for more than a few months.

"Moreau, take the tiller. Apparently, I'm needed for some reason."

"How do I do this?" Cash said.

"Christ, Moreau. You graduated from a goddamn Ivy. Point the damn thing straight."

Jeff was wearing a white linen shirt with one button fastened and these unmistakable Fendi sunglasses he wore that whole summer. His pale figure, bleach blond hair, and scruff glistened in the glowing sun.

He fed Skye a few chocolate-covered strawberries and then walked back to Cash.

"Kins, hop back here with us," Jeff said. "And might I say, I love the outfit. Your whole look just works. You were made to go boating."

I was wearing my rose-framed Aviators with a light pink one-piece and a white shawl. Then I accessorized with a simple, dusty dune straw hat and a bone-faced Miansai watch.

"Moreau, you and your girl need to hold the tiller like this and point it straight for now. I'll add more details later, but it's not that nippy out. Great sailing weather."

"Cap'n Campbell, you have to tell them about Cousin Darcy now."

"I've met Darcy before, right Campbell?" Cash said. "Younger cousin? Teenager?"

"Oh, Skye, I don't wanna bore them."

"Cap'n Campbell, it's, like, the most exhilarating story ever. How could you bore anyone?"

"Kinsley, would you like to hear it?" he asked me, and only me, for some reason.

"Sure."

Jeff then proceeded to tell the most nonsensical parable he could think of, and both his girlfriend and shockingly, my boyfriend, believed it. I'll save you the ridiculous details, but essentially, his five-year-old cousin was swimming in the Atlantic with him, and a gargantuan shark came to eat her. But Jeff punched it, and it swam away. He was turning himself into a Greek myth at that point.

"That story leaves me shook every time," Skye said.

"C'mere, kid."

Skye and Jeff then had a super aggressive, basically dry-humping session to celebrate a story well-told. By about 30 minutes into our boating trip, they were both drunk and high.

"So, Campbell, you have a lot of parties on this boat?" Cash asked while I steered, and Skye sensually massaged her beau's shoulders.

"Nah, haven't had any big dagers yet, but you can't imagine the girls I used to bring back here. Instagram models, Maxim girls, Miss Universe nominees, professional female golfers."

"C'mon Jeff, really?" I said.

"Loosen up, Kins," Jeff told me. "Anyway, before this one came along," he said, pointing at Skye, "you can't believe the roster."

Skye then brought Jeff two more lines of coke, which he snorted off the bench on the side of the boat.

"Daddy, can we go inside now? I need your help with something."

"Yeah, I think we'd better. Moreau, you got things here? Point it straight. Holler if you have any impediments."

And then Jeff and Skye vanished inside, and Cash and I were left alone at last.

"I'm sorry, Kins. He can be difficult sometimes."

"I love the water." I started playing with his hair. "The sounds of these birds and waves. This is just...wow. Thank you for bringing me, Cash."

"I'll talk to Campbell the next time we're alone. He has a ton of issues, but he's always been there for me, and Skye worships him."

"Cash, would you ever want to spend a few months out at sea with me?"

"Of course I would. That'd be a dream. Where would we go?"

"My grandparents in Tel Aviv, I think. Then maybe Beirut, Crete, Venice, Milan, Sardinia, and finally the French Riviera. Wouldn't that be marvelous?"

"Absolutely, except..."

"What is it?" I asked as I took off my hat and leaned my head on his shoulder.

"Well, I'm concerned we might encounter a *Life of Pi* situation."

"I'm quite certain we wouldn't..."

We started to hear yelping noises from underneath the deck, so Cash got up and walked over for some reason. He then attempted to peer through an opaque window and a crack in the door.

"Cash," I said. "How's the peepin'?" He turned toward me. "Cash," I repeated. "How's the peepin'?"

"What movie's that from again?"

"You don't know? I've stumped the brilliant Cash Moreau?"

"Gimme a second. You haven't won yet."

"Yes...I love watching your brain go to work. Lemme know if you need a hint."

"Uh, I'm picturing it now." He closed his eyes and stood in place. "The characters are sailing, right? And a young guy peers in on a couple having sex. Wow, that's a perfect reference."

"You sound surprised."

"Not that you could come up with it," he said. "You know I think you're a genius and the smartest person I know, but that such a perfect reference exists."

"Give up?"

"Actor who says it?"

"Philip Seymour Hoffman."

"*Talented Mr. Ripley.*"

"Well played, Mr. Moreau. Now get back here and stop being a little creeper."

He joined me by the tiller, and we kissed as the light breeze, filled with that instantly recognizable salty, fishy smell, pierced our nostrils.

"What do you think of Skye?" I asked.

"No comment."

"What do you mean? I'm your girlfriend. You're required by law to tell me everything on your mind."

"What's the punishment for that? I must've missed that question in Criminal Justice 101 at Penn."

"Me wearing my dirty outdoor clothes in our bed."

"That's a little harsh."

"So..."

"Well, you know, she has..."

"Why are you acting weird?"

"'Cause it's awkward talking about girls' looks in front of other girls."

"Jeff does it."

"But they're different than we are."

"I meant Skye's personality anyway, you silly boy. But now you have to tell me what you think about her looks since you made this so awkward."

"She's a winsome young lady, I suppose. If you're into that sort of thing."

"A winsome young lady? Who are you, Chaucer?"

"I mean, she has an objectively attractive figure, I guess. I don't like tattoos and piercings, though. And I think she dresses in a highly inappropriate manner about 85 percent of the time."

"Nice boobs, though," I said. "And she must do a lot of sit-ups and squats."

"Jesus. You sound like *you're* obsessed with her."

"Not at all. It's just, we should be able to have conversations about girls' looks without your forehead getting drenched."

"It's hot outside."

"Actually, you're getting burnt. Let me give you my sunscreen."

"What's the SPF?"

"30."

"I need minimum 55," he said. "And is it Helioplex?"

"No. It's $3 sunscreen from Duane Reade. You do realize Helioplex is one of those made-up branding words they use to make you think it's better. It allows them to charge $9 more. It's like using the word 'gourmet' on foods."

"I don't think you have any evidence to back that up."

"Here, stay still," I said. "Keep that pretty little mouth of yours shut."

I lathered his now-rosy face in lotion, while he squinted and made little groaning noises.

"What were we talking about?" I asked.

And then Skye and Jeff returned from their...recess.

"Ms. Avital, I see you haven't crashed the boat. Job well done."

Skye was now wearing only her hot-pink bikini with no cover-up, and they were both noticeably high on something.

"J, can we go swimming?"

"Five minutes, doll. Go adjust the mainsail for me, will ya?"

"Yes, daddy." She started playing her music on a speaker while fiddling with one of the ropes.

"Skye, do we need that music?"

"Yes," she shouted from the middle of the boat.

"You know, if you keep acting out, I might have to give you a spanking."

"Promise, daddy?" She gave an insidious snicker.

Cash and I were nestled next to each other by the back of the boat where the very intoxicated Jeff was navigating.

"You know, Moreau, Skye's song 'Bikinis and Bellinis' hit 98 on the Billboard charts."

"94," she shouted from the other end.

"Moreau, you and your girl should dance to her stuff. That's what she's always playing around the house."

"Jeff, sail's good now, right?" Skye shrieked.

He didn't respond right away. I think Jeff was staring at Cash and me, but he had his sunglasses on, so I couldn't tell.

"Jeff? Hello? Anyone home?"

The boat jerked and swerved, and the big metal rod that links the sail smashed into Skye, and she fell overboard.

"Jeff, stop the boat! Skye fell in, and she's not wearing her life preserver. God, why isn't she wearing one?"

He didn't move a muscle. Jeff was staring at the water, and the boat kept speeding onward.

"Campbell, man, what are you doing? Turn the boat around. We gotta get Skye."

I could hear Skye's increasingly faint moans from behind our boat. I was terrified for her. It wasn't dark yet, but if the sun went down, we'd never find her.

"Cash, do something!" I shouted.

He stood up, started shaking his friend, and then shoved him aside. My boyfriend then started turning us back toward Skye.

"Kins, adjust the ropes somehow. We have to move the sail that way."

The wind was stronger now, and even as I tried to alter the ropes, it was no use.

"Cash, I don't know what to do. Cash, she's gonna drown!"

My boyfriend, as determined and intense as I'd ever seen him, grabbed Jeff's sunglasses and started slapping him across the face.

"Wake the hell up, dude. Skye's in the water. We gotta grab her."

Jeff slowly emerged from his stupor and whispered something into Cash's ear. My boyfriend whispered back, and this went on for about 30 seconds until eventually, Jeff turned the boat around.

"Skye, honey," I shouted. "We'll be right there. Don't worry. Everything's gonna be fine."

I was genuinely petrified for her. I couldn't imagine what a panic I'd be in if I were in her shoes. Half an hour prior, Jeff was telling a story about how these are shark-infested waters. It's hard to even think about all the terrible things that could've happened. And despite there being two well-built men on board, I was the one who decided to jump in and save her.

I swam over, held out my hand, and pulled her back toward the boat. Skye felt very light. She was shivering and whimpering, and I remember repeating, 'It's okay. Everything's gonna be fine.'

Cash pulled us onto the ship, and as he was doing so, Jeff went below deck and slammed the door without a word.

"My phone and headphones are gone," Skye sniveled.

"Skye dearest," Jeff shouted from below deck. "I need you."

"Coming, J."

"Skye," I whispered. "Don't move. Stay here with us. We'll take care of you. Cash, grab some towels and drinking water."

But she stood and walked away. The door slammed behind her, and Cash and I, both stupefied and panting heavily, were left to steer the boat again.

Cash grabbed the tiller, aimed the boat straight, and wrapped two towels around my body.

"What the hell was that?" I said.

"Glad everyone's safe. You were so heroic. You saved Skye."

"Keep me warm, please. I'm so cold."

We snuggled by the back of the boat, both relieved.

"What are we gonna do?"

"What do you mean? We had a little accident. Everyone's fine now. No problem."

"Skye could've died. She had no life preserver on in supposedly dangerous waters."

"What do you want me to say?"

"What were you and Jeff whispering about?"

"Nothing." He turned his head away from me.

"Cash...what were you and Jeff whispering about?"

"Nothing. I said, 'We gotta grab her,' and that's what we did."

"Enough." I sat up. "Cash, I know you better than anyone. Don't hide things from me. We always tell each other the truth. No secrets. Ever."

"Yes. But are there exceptions if the secrets are really bad?"

"No exceptions. You know that. Tell me."

Cash took a deep breath, touched my cheek, ran his hand through my hair, and whispered:

"I said 'We gotta grab her,' and he whispered, 'Why?'"

"And then what?"

"'I said, 'She's your girlfriend and you love her,' and he said, 'I'll find someone else.' And I said, 'Did you do this on purpose?' And Jeff said, 'I don't remember,' and I said, 'Are you mad at her? Did she do something wrong?' And he said, 'Not yet, but I know she will.'"

"That's so bizarre."

"I swear to you that's every word that was said. Verbatim."

"I believe you. I believe you." We kissed, and then he continued.

"Kins, he's a great guy. I've known him my whole life. He's always been there for me.

But what do I do? What should *we* do?"

"To tell you the truth," I said, "I think he's a drug, alcohol, and sex addict. I think he needs help."

"An addict? Campbell's not an addict."

"Cash, I've seen stuff like this before. He has an addictive personality, and it's hurting the lives of those around him."

"He's a flawed person like everyone else. I have flaws. You have flaws. At least, I think you have flaws. I've never seen any before." He smiled painfully.

"I want you to talk to him about this. This is serious. Promise me."

"I promise."

"I know it's hard, but it's very important. I wanna help your friend."

"He's a loyal person. And magnanimous."

"I know, Cash. He says plenty of messed-up things, but early in the summer, I realized he's only disparaging when he's drunk or high. Which, unfortunately, is quite often. I let a lot of the things he says slide because I believe he has a serious mental health issue, and I'm not one to condemn someone with mental health problems."

"Of course."

"You know I love you and I want what's best for you and your friends. I feel bad for him more than anything. His mother disappearing when he was young, his distant father. He didn't have the nurturing households we did. My point is, I want to help you with Jeff."

"I appreciate that. And I'm sorry if he's said anything inappropriate around you."

"Water off a duck's back. I had three brothers. You can't imagine the things I've heard."

I grinned and put my arms around him.

"Just keep me warm now," I said.

Even after Jeff and Skye returned from another unhealthy binging, Cash and I remained curled up against each other—staying warm around the stunning scenery and taking in the eventual fireworks.

ONE-ON-ONE WITH JEFFERSON CAMPBELL III — MID-JULY 2018

"You look quite fetching this afternoon, Ms. Avital."

"Thank you."

"You do have a wonderful sense of style. An excellent idea of what complements your skin tone and hair. Quite refined."

"So, what's this grand plan of yours?"

"Moreau mentioned your nostalgic adoration for the equine species. I felt a polo match might beguile you. Have you attended one before?"

"No. But this is really pretty. Good idea."

It was a wide-open field of Kelly green grass with various Criollos cantering around the property. Their riders were practicing with their mallets as we found a spot to stand along the sidelines.

"Do you watch a lot of sports with Cash?" he asked as the game began.

"I try to. I think it's important in a relationship to learn to love what your boyfriend loves. Or at least make an effort. And vice versa."

"Quite wise."

"That's how you two reconnected, right?"

"Yes. He's quite the fantasy sports player. I think he's made a few stacks of high society the past few years."

"Oh, I'm sure. I don't have to tell you how intelligent Cash is. He just needs to find the right outlet to channel it. I don't want him to work for his father."

"Why's that? His father's a good man."

"Of course, but the most important thing in life is to do things you're passionate about with people you're passionate about."

"Was that Alcott?"

"No. That was me."

We continued to watch the game with Jeff explaining some of the more mundane rules now and again.

"You haven't had a drink today, have you?" I said.

"Just my morning scotch before brushing my teeth."

"You do that every day?"

"In the summertime, yes. Why? You're looking to alter your prosaic sunrise routine?"

"Not exactly."

"Why bring it up?" His tone altered.

"Just something Cash and I were discussing."

"And am I not to be privy to such fascinating discourse amongst two of the people I respect most in this world?"

"I'll tell you if you wanna hear it."

"Please do enlighten me."

Jeff was wearing a bluish-grey seersucker suit with his ever-present black Fendi sunglasses. His flowy yellow hair, which he frequently adjusted, shuffled in the light wind. And then, of course, his Rolex was fastened to his wrist.

Admittedly, he could be an intimidating man to some, but not to me. No one intimidates me. Realistically, I either felt frightened he'd attack someone or felt sorry for him. He was a caged leopard in a way. I would've loved to watch the movie of his life starting from his early childhood years.

"Cash and I are worried about you."

"Is that so?"

"Yes, it is."

"And did Cash mention to you he thinks *you* drink too much?"

"No, because there's a difference. I drink at night with dinner or out at parties. I don't have a morning scotch before brushing my teeth. Nor do I carry around a flask with me at all times."

"Okay. You've clearly had this on your mind for some time. Please do retch out any pent-up thoughts. I'd simply *love* to hear them."

The horses raced by us as the small crowd of people cheered.

"Cash and I both think you have some problems with alcohol and drugs. I don't know you well enough, and I'm not one to judge others so swiftly, but I may even use the word, 'addiction,' in this case."

"You do have such a beautiful voice. I'm sure Cash tells you that."

"Jeff, I'm serious."

"Yeah, Cash ambushed me with your little hypothesis two weeks ago. I'm an adult. I make my own choices."

"You're putting Skye at risk."

"She makes her own choices too. I never do anything without her consent."

The muscular Criollos galloped by our spot as the crowd cheered.

"You know, Kinsley, I wasn't aware you were the true apex of humanity. A noble saint whose words demand to be heeded."

"I only ever try to help people. If you don't want to listen to me, that's your prerogative. Cash and I were just a bit nervous when your drugged-up self tried to abandon your girlfriend in the Atlantic."

"That's not what happened."

"Then what happened? Cash and I were sober. We'd know."

"Any other life advice you can give me, oh wise soothsayer?"

"Do you have a job lined up for the fall? I know Cash has ideas brewing."

"Nope. And how about you? Do you have a job lined up?"

"I have a job."

"Oh, is posting pictures of cappuccino foam or matcha lattes while 'accidentally' leaving your Chanel bag in the background a job?"

"Sure. For some. That's not what I do, though. And you should know for the future—so you don't come off as ignorant—posts with cappuccino foam, pizza, flaming desserts, or anything with the caption, 'The 'gram eats first' are overdone. No one knowledgeable does those anymore."

"There's no getting a rise out of you, is there? The world's finest little Pollyanna."

"It's hard to stay mad when there's so much beauty in the world," I said.

"*American Beauty*. One of Moreau's favorites. Speaking of food, you ever cook for him?"

"Sometimes. I love to cook. And he started cooking for me recently. Trying to take an interest in my interests."

"What do you make for my inimitable old friend?"

"A ton of stuff. Jambalaya, chocolate chip pancakes, chocolate soufflé, sautéed kale grain bowls, baby back ribs, veal Milanese, French toast, macaroons, a lot of delicious things."

"He must be hard to cook for."

"Well, he's certainly picky, but it makes my life simple," I said. "It's pretty easy to memorize everything he likes."

"That's not what I meant."

"What did you mean?"

"His OCD."

"Oh, that."

"Isn't it a daily struggle? Kid's kinda high maintenance."

"I love him. I'm always glad to make his life easier."

"How bad is it? I know he brings the Purell squirter everywhere, and he separates his food by color. And then he has indoor and outdoor clothes and has to shower before getting into bed. Anything I missed?"

"I mean, it's not something he likes talking about. He's embarrassed by it."

"You and I can discuss it. I mean, you and Moreau are more than happy to go on about my alleged addiction behind my back."

"Well, it boils down to keeping three things clean: the bed, the cell phone, and the laptop. He always sanitizes his hands before touching all three. And yeah, he showers before going into bed. But once you know those things, it's not that bad. I've gotten used to it. I don't even notice it."

"You're a sweetheart. Does he tell you that?"

At halftime, everyone ran onto the middle of the field and stomped on the divots for some reason. I'll admit it was a lot of fun. Therapeutic even. The crowd was a little tipsy from the champagne. They were all giggling and stomping on grass. It was quite strange. A bunch of extremely fashionable people jumping on dirt and grass.

Anyway, the second half started, and Jeff was mostly silent aside from a few quips about the horses and riders.

"Do you hate me?" he asked after a long silence.

"No. I don't hate anyone. I believe everyone has positives and negatives."

"What are Skye's positives?"

"She's fearless and confident. Skye does things, says things, and wears things I'd never dream of. There's never a dull moment around her."

"You like her?"

"She's a marvelously unique young woman trying to find herself."

"Do you have any friends that would like me?" Jeff said. "Preferably someone extremely similar to you?"

"How do you know all these people here? Like, how'd you score this invite?"

"Just gonna ignore that? Okay then. Fair enough. And I mean, who knows? Friends of my father's, I guess. I've seen all these people forever. Not intimately. I couldn't tell you 70 percent of their names, but we're all part of the same glossy circle."

"And what about your mother? Does she come from these circles?"

"She doesn't get discussed."

His mood and tone shifted instantly from blithe apathy to humiliated toddler.

"But why not, Jeff? You never have any problem delving into others' pasts and asking extremely personal questions, right?"

"Why do you need to know about my mother? What do you gain from learning anything about her? There are certain lines even I won't cross."

"It might help you to talk about it with someone. Maybe Cash? Your addiction may stem from these issues with your mother."

"I'd appreciate it if the communications major who takes pictures of cloth for a living gets off her high horse and doesn't tell me how to live my life."

"Sociology. And I'm saying therapy might help you. I think therapy can do wonders for almost anyone. I'm not one to be mean. I wanna help."

"You wanna feed and pet one of the ponies after the match is over?"

"We really can have civil conversations when you're not high and drunk."

"You're not as nice as you think you are," he said.

"And yes, I'd love to meet some of the horses, if that's possible."

We went back to standing in silence for a little while. Jeff was texting Skye, presumably about the match or what she and Cash were up to.

"Jeff, there's a girl staring at you."

"So?" He didn't lift his head from his phone.

"I think she likes you."

"A lot of marchionesses look at me and a lot of them like me. Doesn't concern me. I love Skye."

"You do?"

"What does the girl look like?"

"Stop looking at your phone, and I'll point her out."

"Describe her to me."

"What? Why? You're so strange."

"I love hearing the sound of your voice. It's like a 1930s actress mixed with a tinge of Israeli flavor combined with the fact you always seem like you've had a cold for the last three days, and it's not getting better."

"That's insulting. Do you ever think about what you say after you say it and realize it was a mistake?"

"What's the girl look like?"

"You're awfully hypocritical."

"I'd never touch another girl. I love Skye. But it's human nature to have curiosities. Even your darling Moreau dreams about other girls. I've seen him gawking at my famed portraits hanging around Campbell Manor."

"You're annoying."

"Come on. What does the girl look like?" he said while continuing to text Skye furiously.

"Sort of like Elle Fanning meets Jenny Humphrey."

"Okay, so younger blonde girl? What's she wearing?"

"Really pretty. Super-expensive clothes. Dolce and Gabbana lily print dress with a Van Cleef clover necklace and Hermès Clic-H bracelet...oh wait. She caught me staring at her."

"Would Skye like her? Maybe I'll take a picture of her. Is she coming over?" He finally lifted his head from the phone.

"She walked away," I said. "More like ran away, actually."

"Her loss."

"Does that happen often?"

"Of course. Comes with the territory."

"Modesty might suit you once in a while."

"There are certain people, people like say: Aeneas, Julius Caesar, Ozymandias, Alexander the Great, George Washington, T.E. Lawrence and maybe..."

"You've seen *Lawrence of Arabia*?"

"Of course."

"Cash has been obsessed with Lawrence. Or really, Peter O'Toole's performance as Lawrence."

"And why wouldn't he be?" Jeff said. "That's a character that is particularly appealing to people from our station. He's an all-time favorite of mine. I can relate to the man."

The match ended, and Jeff instantly changed topics before I could dig deeper.

"Let's go meet some horses. We don't have to be so serious all the time. Moreau always mentions how jocular you are."

Jeff led me on a private tour of the property's stables. We met this magnificent sorrel stud named Serenity, and I was able to brush his mane and feed him a carrot. It was a special experience. That was the point to Jeff. Yes, he said plenty of messed-up things, but his actions repeatedly showed he cared about Cash and me. There's absolutely kindness in that man's heart. And despite all the negatives, some days, I saw what Cash must've seen for many years.

Despite everything, Jeff's frequent generosity made me like him. I mean, there's only one type of person I can't stand—slackers. I can look past and forgive most flaws people have, but not laziness. Regardless of how much money a person has, there are so many activities to experience and people to experience them with. There's nature, arts, sports, history, literature, and just endless opportunities to learn. I've always found the easiest way to have fun in life, regardless of age, is to spend a bit of time outdoors among trees, grass, and animals. But, to my original point, anyone who doesn't strive to seek out their passions and joys is someone I can't get along with. So, I sort of loved this day with Jeff, and our little summer clique, in general. We each had so many passions and never shied away from adventures.

ANOTHER SPECIAL DAY-DATE
WITH CASH — MID-AUGUST 2018

"I HAD ANOTHER CONVERSATION WITH Campbell about his drug intake."

"You did? What'd he say?"

"I've known him for a while, and I think I've been approaching it the right way. I talk about myself and how I've been able to have fun and meet a girl like you without drugs. He has, without question, eased up on his usage—as has Skye. They've been more tolerable lately."

"You mentioned me?"

"Course I did," he said. "You're my hero."

"My little sweetheart." I leaned over and pinched his cheek.

Cash was driving today, so I had free rein on the music selection.

"Play some cheerful stuff, please," he said.

"Doin' It" — LL Cool J
"Ready or Not" — The Fugees
"Have I Told You Lately That I Love You" — Rod Stewart
"Haunted" — Beyoncé
"Tennis Court" — Lorde (Flume Remix)
"Pretender" — Steve Aoki ft. AJR & Lil Yachty
"#Selfie" — The Chainsmokers
"Closer" — The Chainsmokers
"All Gold Everything" — Trinidad James
"Fight Night" — Migos
"Love Me Harder" — Ariana Grande ft. The Weeknd
"Easy" — Sky Ferreira

"Park here," I said.

"I can't fit there."

"Oh, you totally could've."

"Maybe *you* could've, but I'm not risking it in your car."

We arrived in Montauk, parked a few blocks away from the ocean, and walked toward this spot where you could rent kayaks. It wasn't some professional shop with a bunch of guides, just a few yellow kayaks and one local who didn't take credit cards.

"We're lucky the water's calm today," Cash said as we paddled. "Now, we've gotta get into a rhythm. Left. Right. Left. Right."

"You know there's snorkeling equipment in here? Did you pay for that?"

"Yeah, it was a bit extra. We'll dive in once we're farther out."

"You're not scared of the big, bad sharks without Jeff here to fight them off?"

"We'll be safe. Love is a shark repellant. Didn't you know that?"

"What? No, I didn't."

"Oh yeah. The makos can't stand it. Too many pheromones or something. The Moor men in medieval times would take their women out on boat rides in shark-infested waters. They'd go swimming together, and if no sharks came, it meant they had a Biblical, true love. But if the makos or great whites approached, well, either they died, or their love wasn't meant to be."

"Oh. That's certainly untrue."

"I've been meaning to ask you something."

Cash and I were in a tremendous rhythm. Our oars hitting the navy water at precisely the same time.

"Yes?"

"I think I wanna start my own company," he said.

"Wow. Okay. Really? You do?"

"You don't think that's a good idea?"

"No, of course I do. But it's just, you know, kinda outta the blue. What kind of company?"

"Well, I want it to revolve around sports. It could be a sports website where me and some other writers blog, podcast and have a betting and fantasy advice section too. And we'd have a strong social media marketing team that'd film everything and get the word out on all the stuff we did."

"Don't places like that already exist?"

"Yeah, but Coke existed before Pepsi, right? The places that exist right now have flaws I think I can remedy. It's all about how well you do something and how strong your message is. And who the other employees are."

"And you think that's something you'll enjoy doing?"

"Absolutely. Right now, it's the only career path I can think of where I'd like the work."

"Well, you know I trust you. I'll help out however I can, and I know you'll succeed at whatever you do. You're just one of those people."

Cash brought his paddle back into the boat, wrapped his arms around my shoulders, and leaned me back against his lap.

"I love you so much, Kins. Thank you."

"I love you too. But so, are you gonna get Jeff involved?"

"Not at first. He's too much of a wild card to be honest."

"Any other serious topics we need to discuss? I'm ready to see some fish."

"That's it for today, but I'm sure I'll spring more on you shortly."

We stopped at a quiet area, and Cash wrapped a pair of goggles around my head and then his. He was wearing a solid pale-fuchsia bathing suit I'd bought for him at Scotch & Soda. Cash looked as physically intimidating as ever, but inside, he was a tender little cub.

We dove into the water with matching snorkels wrapped around our lips. And even our suits went well together, as I was wearing my mustard-and-violet two-piece from Guépard.

"Kins," he removed his snorkel and shouted in that mumbled, watery tone. "Look. Turtle."

There was a sea turtle about 25 feet away. It was an ethereal little creature gliding along without a care in the world. And then, a few minutes later, we saw a school of rainbow fish.

Dahlia had once taught me you could tell a lot about fashion by looking in nature. Like, if we were in the Caribbean, we could see yellow-and-purple fish or blue-and-orange ones. The colors on their scales could be the inspiration for the base of a dress. I've always adored that idea.

After a few hours of snorkeling and kayaking, we went home, changed, and drove to East Hampton for a super-sweet, romantic dinner at DOPO La Spiaggia. Cash was able to get us a table in their exceptional courtyard area with bushes and trees surrounding us at every angle, vines dripping down the walls, and big, tall lamps creating a subtle and intimate ambience.

He was wearing a washed-out yellow polo I'd bought, although I'm not sure from where. But yellow was always his favorite color. And I had on a simple off-white summer dress from Zara. I felt we looked cute together.

"You look so amazing, Kinsley."

"Thank you, lovely."

"Are you gonna want a drink?" He opened his menu. "I'm happy to drive home."

"Cash?"

"Yes?"

"What was your last girlfriend like?"

"What do you mean? Why do you ask?"

"Well, I know you said you've only had one or two before, and I wanted to know what your last one was like and whether you have a type. I dunno. I've thought about it from time to time."

"You really wanna talk about this? 'Cause I definitely don't want to hear about your ex-boyfriend."

"Okay. And you don't *have* to tell me. I'm just always so fascinated by you. I like to know every last detail, so it feels like I've always been there with you."

"I'll tell you."

The waitress came by, took my drink order, and listened to each of our complex dinner choices.

"What have I told you about her?"

"Just her name, Rania, and that you dated at Penn for a bit."

"Right, well." He was noticeably nervous. Cash *hated* these topics. "Rania was Egyptian. She lived in Shubra El Kheima for 18 years, and coming to Penn was her first time living in another country. She was tall and thin with a thick accent, long curly hair, and these giant eyes with almost-white irises."

"So, she was pretty?"

"Not like you."

"Thanks, but what was she like?"

"Very curious. She wanted to learn absolutely everything about this country and the city of Philadelphia and what to eat and wear and study. She was an excellent student."

"Rania sounds divine. I wish I could date her."

"That's what I thought at first. But after a few months, the spark dissipated. She was a lovely woman, but we had nothing in common. We came from different backgrounds, and she feigned interest in my hobbies for a few weeks, but was more focused on a different path."

"Where's she now?"

"Not sure. But I know she majored in finance. I think I heard she was on Wall Street at one of the big firms, but I never bothered to look her up."

Our food and drinks were brought out, and after a brief bout of silence, I said:

"Whose relationship do you think will last longer? Ours or Jeff and Skye's?"

"Is that a joke?"

Cash's plain tagliatelle with bolognese on the side arrived, and he ate the pasta in its entirety before moving on to the delectable meat sauce that he let me share, as long as I used a clean fork.

"Let me change the question," I said. "How much longer do you think Jeff and Skye will last?"

"No idea. I'm not one to speculate."

"Oh, c'mon. You love betting on sports. Isn't that just speculating on the winners?"

"Fine," he laughed. "That's a good argument."

"You know him better than most. He always says how loyal you are. I bet you'll be pretty accurate."

"I think they'll break up shortly after this summer. So maybe another four to six weeks?"

"That soon? They've been together 11 months."

"They cruised past the first few months, the honeymoon phase, and then Skye was constantly traveling to NYC or Yale. And now they've been living with each other all summer. But what's going to happen when Jeff gets a job, and maybe Skye goes on tour as an opening act at colleges? That's not a duo that can endure a long-distance relationship. They need constant physical touch."

"Who will be more devastated?"

"Given your smile, I guess you're automatically assuming the answer is Skye, and it's an easy question. But I think it's Jeff."

"Oh, I love when we're on different sides. Why do you say that?"

"Well, Jeff has always preached this idea of mutual worship to me. He said the best couples shouldn't just love each other but should worship each other. A god and goddess can conquer anything together."

"That's...odd, to say the least."

"I think Skye definitely worships him to an extent, and it's not easy to get someone to worship you absolutely. It could take months or years before Jeff finds someone that treats him the way she does. He's gonna miss her terribly and won't tell anyone about it. I'm legitimately concerned about him after their inevitable breakup."

"Huh. Mutual worship. I think Jeff loves himself so much he wants her to be exactly like him. He wants to teach her his ways. Make a female Jeff."

"I thought you weren't one to judge people? That sounded pretty judgmental."

"If it did, I didn't mean for it to be. I think they're both intriguing people. I'd love to be either of their psychiatrists. But anyway, I'm ecstatic with the person I'm with."

WOW — AUGUST 31, 2018

"Cash, take a video of me. This is fantastic!"

"Well, slow down. You're going too fast."

"Take...it...vertically," I said while bouncing on my horse. "And we'll use slo-mo."

"Okay, but go maybe five miles an hour slower, please," he shouted from the stable.

"I can't slow down. I'm having too much fun. Just do your best."

Cash and I were on the property of a Mr. Wilkinson. It was one Jeff's, or should I say, one of Jeff's father's many peculiar friends of unknown origins. He was a middle-aged multi, multi-millionaire with a stable on his gigantic property that also had beach access.

"Did you get it? Me and Portia will stop next to you, and you can show me the phone."

I tied my pearl-white horse next to the stable where Cash was stationed with Octavius, the chestnut thoroughbred.

"Show me. Show me." I was so unbelievably elated.

"Here, I took a bunch. Photos and videos."

I scrolled through Cash's high-effort, low-talent videos, and gleamed.

"Mr. Wilkinson," I said. "May you please take a few of Cash and me trotting along your magnificent property?"

"Certainly, madam. But I'm not much of a videographer."

Cash and I shouted gleefully at our horses and off we went.

That Mr. Wilkinson had the most breathtaking house and yard. His home was two stories high and was finished with clean lines of a neutral color that must've let in a ton of light. And the outside was made of that classic Hamptons shaker siding. Then there was a heated gunite pool with a spa and a sprawling terrace overlooking his eight-acre backyard. And finally came the stables.

It was a tall building with the exterior designed in the same manner as the main house, and had about 10 thoroughbreds inside. And each one had plenty of room to run and graze. And the grass was so green, it almost looked painted. The backyard was completely flat. There wasn't a single bump, hole, or even slight curvature. Mr. Wilkinson's place was made up of entirely straight lines and jagged edges.

"I think I'm getting the hang of this, kids."

Our host was a hulking man with a salt-and-pepper mustache that went well with his speckled grey chinos and black polo.

"Cash," I said as we rode side by side. "Thank you so much. This was such a thoughtful gesture. I can't believe you remembered I used to ride horses. I only mentioned that once."

"I never forget anything you say. I'm always hanging on every word, Kins."

"Damn. I think you might know me too well."

Portia and I then broke away from Cash. I picked up my phone from Mr. Wilkinson, scrolled through his shaky videos, and then galloped around the massive property with the wind frizzing my hair and Cash staring from a distance.

"You wanna ride to the beach now?" I said to Cash after pulling alongside Octavius.

"Absolutely."

We trotted onto the snowy-white beach.

"You're always so kind to me, Cash. Thank you for everything."

"You're the most precious person in the world. How could I not be kind?"

After returning to the backyard, I took my shoes out of the stirrups and jumped down.

"How'd you pull this one off, Cash?"

"What?"

"This whole horse thing. I mean, completely out of nowhere. A random house with a random rich guy and his magnificent thoroughbreds." Portia whinnied.

"It took a bit of hard work and some help from our old pal, Campbell."

"Well, however you came up with everything, thank you."

As we were pulling into the stables, I started to get the feeling Cash might propose to me. By the time the horses were back inside, and we were saying goodbye to our host, I felt mildly disappointed. That would've been a phenomenal story to tell all our friends and future children. But then I remembered he was only 23. Well, he was 22, but basically 23. And I was only 24. So maybe we were going to wait a few years. We'd only been dating for 15 months. But then again, everything always seemed so permanent with Cash.

"Kins, we're going out tonight, 9:00 p.m. dinner," Cash said to me when we arrived back at the pool house.

"What should I wear? Where are we going?"

"Wear the nicest outfit you have. And I can't tell you where yet. It'll give away the surprise."

At that point, I was lounging on the sofa, scrolling through images of models on my iPad. Dahlia had given an assignment that required me to find particular types of women that could be the new faces of Guépard, both beauty and fashion. I was mostly looking through Instagram models with between 5K and 30K followers. Dahlia wanted the women to have sharp facial features with high cheekbones, hair that looked luscious whether tied or down, and the women should have objectively infectious smiles on top of poreless skin. I didn't necessarily agree with every one of Dahlia's stipulations, but she had more experience than I did.

"Cash, come here. I need you."

He was wearing no shirt and grey J. Crew joggers I'd bought him. That was when he looked the sexiest. I don't know why.

"What's up?"

"Do you think this girl's cute?" I showed him this influencer's IG page.

"I don't feel comfortable answering that."

"Oh, relax. Be honest."

"I don't...it's...I have no comment."

"Ugh, I don't love when you do this."

"What? Not gush over other girls in front of you?"

"So, you think she's hot?"

"What? No."

"Cash, it's for work. I need to pick models for Dahlia. She gave me specific instructions. I've narrowed my search to 10 women, and I'm only allowed to send Dahlia five."

"Good luck. I know how excellent your taste is."

He walked to the kitchen and grabbed some Muscle Milk out of the fridge.

"You should start getting ready soon," he said. "Do you need to shower?"

"Does it look like I need to shower?"

"N-no, of course not. You look nice."

"Cash, c'mon. I rode a horse for an hour. Of course, I need to shower. Be a little more forthcoming. Don't just try to placate me."

"Okay, okay. You're right. I'm sorry."

"Now, which of these 10 models do you think is the hottest, or would look best in Guépard's new line?"

"Oh, Kins, I don't wanna do that."

"Fine, maybe I'll go inside and ask your old pal, Jeff. I'm sure he'd be happy to help with this task. He may even DM these girls and ask if they're available for some black-and-white nude pics in the frozen tundra of Northern Canada or some bullshit like that."

"Jesus, I'll help."

Cash sat next to me and spat out his choices within seconds.

"Number one, the light-brown hair with the big lips. Number four, the black-haired dimpled one. Number eight, the Arabian-looking girl with the abs. Number nine, that one making the duck face. And then number 10, the girl with the massive tits."

"Cash!"

"What?"

"'The one with the massive tits?' That's somebody's daughter."

"I dunno. You asked for my help and I helped. Just tell me what to do and say so I don't get in trouble."

"Is that how you and Jeff talk? Oh, she's got huge tits. Oh, with lips like that, I bet she gives great head?"

"No. Never. Come on. You know me."

"I'll give you the benefit of the doubt, but clean it up, Cash. What would your mother say?"

"Okay. Let's move on. I love you." He kissed me. "Still mad at me?"

"No. I was never mad. You know it takes a lot more than a stupid comment to make me upset. Just taken aback."

"Sorry. It won't happen again."

"It's just, I like to ask for your help with my work sometimes, and I need you to be supportive. Even if it means doing something that makes you feel uncomfortable, like ranking girls in front of me."

"Okay. I'll try not to be so awkward."

"You've made it very clear how attractive you think I am. I won't be worried or upset if you call a girl 'cute' once in a while."

"Got it. Let's move on. Shower time. You smell."

We both chuckled, and I said:

"That's the kind of honesty I love to hear."

After a 30-minute drive where Cash refused to tell me where we were going, and I blasted Halsey's *Badlands* album the entire trip, we arrived at our favorite spot. The all-time best Hamptons restaurant, the place where it all started: The Crow's Nest.

"Cash," I said while he parked, "it's gonna be so romantic this time of night. Gosh, the lights and moon and fire."

"I brought you a sweater. It's in the backseat. I know you get chilly by the water."

"That's my sweetheart."

Once in the restaurant, Cash pulled my chair out, and we sat and ordered a bottle of rosé.

"I can't believe I'm starting work with my dad on Tuesday," he said.

"Promise me it'll only be temporary?"

"I promise."

"You told me about that sports site. That's your dream right now. That's what you need to be doing."

"I know. I don't have the capital right now."

"Ask your dad for a loan."

"I can't do that. I'm just gonna work for him for a few months while I try to find a few investors. I'll start my own company next year. But can we please keep it a secret for now?"

"Sure, whatever you want. And I trust you completely." I reached across the table and held his hand.

"Don't you wish we could live out here forever?" he said while looking at the sprawling green hills and the calm water in the distance.

"We're too young to live in heaven, Cash."

"I can't believe I'm about to become a boring adult with a day job and a salary. I still feel like a kid sometimes."

"Everyone feels that way. I know I do. Your goal should be to find that mix. You should feel like a child and do childish things sometimes, but also be brave and take on adulthood. I love that you wanna be your own boss."

"Thank you, but can we try to savor our last few nights out here? Let's have some erudite discussion about something other than the daily ennui I'm about to face."

I ordered the scallops with pistachio and lemon orzo, and Cash, of course, got the rib eye with fries. And after the food arrived, he let me have as much as I wanted—my hero.

"You know which day I absolutely adored?" I said.

"The sailing trip?"

"Not exactly...I think when we went to Tetra. Remember that?"

"I'll never forget it."

"And we danced for hours. We were surrounded by fish, and the DJ played Drake and The Chainsmokers and Bailando. And then, even *you* got drunk, and there was that crazy sorbet place. And you had the audacity to put chocolate up my nose."

"That was a ton of fun."

"How 'bout you?"

"When we went to Montauk. Remember the mini-golfing and the catamaran?"

"If we have a mini-golf rematch, I'll one hundred percent beat you—by more than five shots. Guaranteed," I laughed.

"No way. I wouldn't let it happen."

"The other night I loved was that one at Hither Hills Park," I said.

"Oh God, that's right. I couldn't stop thinking about what Jeff must've done in that tent and those raggedy sleeping bags."

"I've never seen someone shower for as long as you did post-camping."

I laughed and grabbed his hand from across the table. The candle in between us illuminated his bright blue eyes and those harsh eyebrows of his—my handsome guy.

"Remember snorkeling and the sea turtles?" I said.

"Or when we watched *The Blair Witch Project*, and you cried out of fear?"

"No, it was the buffalo wings. I already told you that."

"What was your favorite movie we watched in the pool house this summer?"

"*Who's Afraid of Virginia Woolf.* I loved that movie. Oh, and am I getting any of that steak?"

"It might be the best I've ever had."

He picked up a large chunk and leaned his fork toward my mouth.

"Oh wow. Cash? Are you kidding?"

"So succulent, right?"

"Mmm. Are we ever gonna come back here? 'Cause I *need* to get this."

"I'm pretty sure we will."

The bill came, and we just kept chatting. We never ran out of topics.

Cash and I left the table and walked to that funky outdoor bar area by the water. He ordered two glasses of champagne, and we relaxed by the fire.

"It's so pleasant tonight," I said.

"Absolutely."

"You feeling okay? You look a little pale."

"All good. Taking it in."

Then it hit me. Cash was wearing a grey cardigan, and ever since we left the table, his right hand didn't leave his pocket. He was clutching something important. From the pallid cheeks to the hand in his pants to the bead of sweat on his forehead.

"Kins, are you crying again? Should I be worried?"

"Ow, no. I'm getting these embers in my eyes. Like last time. May I please have your sunglasses?"

"Here, switch seats with me."

I got up to move, but then said:

"Wait, I want your sunglasses anyway. They look good on me."

"You're not tipsy, are you?"

"Me? Never," I said.

I finished my champagne and drank Cash's too, while we chatted about last Valentine's Day and that time we took a trip to Duke. I kept waiting for him to drop to one knee. I mean, it must've been 11 at that point. I was worried he might've been too afraid to do it. Too scared of the permanence of the whole thing.

I zoned out and thought about what marriage with Cash would be like. He was so kind and loving. Even though he was younger, Cash knew me so well. He could tell when I needed cheering up or maybe a fiery pep talk. And he was someone who did all the little things to improve my mood. I liked when he came over to my apartment with lilies or Butterfingers in hand. It sounds so simple and corny, but remembering little things is so meaningful. Plus, I felt I could always confide in him. Cash never judged me. Overall, we communicated so well. We rarely fought because there were constant discussions about each other's feelings and never any secrets. I don't know. He was exactly what I wanted in my life. Not too possessive. He wanted us to grow together. Cash Moreau had his quirks, but he was the ideal man for me.

"Are you ready to go?" he finally asked.

I nodded as he lifted me from my stool, and we started walking by the reeds near the water. I'd decided earlier that if he proposed, I was gonna say yes. But by that point, I was thinking he might not be proposing, and maybe all my wild theories were just in my head. But then, instead of walking up the hill toward the parking lot, he made a left and started going along this secluded area of cattails by the lakeshore.

"What are we doing here?"

I was looking out along the water when I said that, and by the time I turned to face him, he was on one knee in front of me. And if he thought I was a crier before, my tear ducts really showed him what they could do.

"Cash? Are you hurt?"

"Kinsley Avital, from the moment you approached my mom and me on that hill 460 days ago, I knew I wanted to do this."

Now obviously, I was bawling and looked super ugly. My makeup was running, and I was barefoot, carrying my shoes. The only positives were my hair and dress.

Cash continued:

"These past 460 days have been unforgettable, and it's all because of you. For my entire life until I met you, I always knew I was missing something crucial, and after meeting you, I realized what it was. Because I love absolutely every part of you. From your uncanny wit to your kind nature to your unmatched fashion sense and your supremely bright mind that seems to teach me something new every hour. And then, obviously, you're so sexy. The closest thing to a perfect person this world has to offer."

"I'm not crying," I said. "It's these damn embers."

"Everything you do is alright with me. Listen, I know I'm only 22 and a half, but I've never been surer about anything in my life. You and I can make absolutely any activity enjoyable."

"I must look so ugly right now."

"Kinsley Avital, I'd be ecstatic if I could watch you cry tears of joy for the rest of our lives. Will you marry me?"

And I now have that mental picture framed in my mind for the rest of my life: Cash Moreau, wearing his navy suede loafers, white linen pants, white polo with navy and scarlet stripes by the collar, grey cardigan with two buttons and two front pockets, and his sunglasses on top of my head, asked me to marry him. And it was no accident each article of clothing he was wearing was something I'd bought for him. He was hands down the most thoughtful human being I'd ever met. And the Harry Winston diamond was enormous. Although that didn't matter to me.

"Cash Moreau, of course I will."

CELEBRATION TIME — OUR LAST TWO DAYS IN THE HAMPTONS 2018

"Cash? Oh, Cash? Your fiancée needs a Red Bull vodka refill."

"Be right there."

I was working on my iPad on the couch while talking to my mom on the phone. And Cash was faintly playing Kanye West's *My Beautiful Dark Twisted Fantasy* album on my Bluetooth speaker. We were both prancing around the house like newborn foals.

"Mom, it was so romantic. Cash is like 10 feet away. He can hear everything I'm saying. He's so smiley. But we went horseback riding, had this amazing dinner at the place we met, and then he proposed in this really scenic, secluded spot right by the water with the moonlight, the stars, and even a frog croaking. Mom, it was the greatest night of my life."

We each spent that morning calling five to 10 people, and then once we'd hung up and I'd had three Red Bulls, two with vodka, I jumped into his arms. We were hugging and kissing and telling each other how in love we were.

"Moreau, notice I'm knocking this time...like you asked." I was actually excited to hear Jeff's voice.

I opened the door to a shirtless Jeff wearing a black bathing suit and his Fendi sunglasses.

"Moreau, your girlfriend's still here?"

"I'm not going anywhere."

"I just assumed my prepubescent friend's proposal would've sent you running for the hills."

"Unfortunately, no. You might have to share him from now on."

"Next summer, you two can have the big house. Congrats, kids. That's all I wanted to say."

Cash walked over and put his arm around me while Jeff continued:

"Also, I'm throwing you guys, I guess you could consider it an engagement party."

"What do you mean, you guess?" I said.

"I had a party planned for tonight. Huge party. Lots of A-list twenty-somethings. Now, my end-of-summer bash will serve a dual purpose."

"So thoughtful," I said, eyes-rolling.

"Thanks, Ms. Avital. I felt that such an...interesting couple deserved an inimitable summer send-off. Love you guys." He hugged us both and jogged off in the other direction.

Cash and I spent the rest of the day packing, calling people, and cuddling in bed together. We went out to grab some lunch in the afternoon, but brought it back to the pool house and ate in bed, much to Cash's chagrin.

The first guests started arriving around 9:00 p.m. Cash had put on the alabaster linen suit I bought for him at J. Crew, and I was wearing my favorite white summer romper from Zimmermann. I also had on ivory-colored Stuart Weitzman sandals and pearl earrings, and then my hair was up.

Cash and I walked hand in hand outside and followed the sound of Skye's super-loud DJing toward the main house.

"Cash, I will say, I'm kinda all for this party's vibe."

"Isn't the music a little loud?"

"Well, yes. But everyone is dressed really well, and it seems like a chaotic, but refined affair."

"Did you look by the pool yet?"

I glanced at where he was pointing and immediately saw what he was talking about.

"Oh dear. Do you think Jeff is aware?"

"That bottomless girls are swimming in his pool? Yeah, I'm gonna go ahead and say he's aware. If anyone were doing anything he didn't want them to, he'd put a stop to it ASAP. Did you see A) How massive the security guards/bouncers are, and B) How many of them there are?"

"True."

"So, what do you wanna do first?" Cash said. "Drink more? Eat something? Tour the house? Dance? The world is our oyster."

"Let's eat first. I'm starving. We barely had any lunch."

Cash and I walked inside toward Jeff's kitchen and found several caterers with about 15 dishes kept hidden and a bunch of signs that said: The Pratincole. The place did an excellent job marketing themselves, and I absolutely adored their logo with the tiny short-legged bird looking off to the left.

"Here, try the shrimp." He handed me a mini skewer. "Or actually, try this pork tenderloin."

"Cash. I mean, oh my God. We need maybe 10 of these this instant. And find me a little champagne. We're celebrating."

We walked outside with plates filled with shrimp, pork, and some bone marrow, and found a spot to sit by the pool where we sipped our champagne and had some solid people-watching seats.

"Here, have some bone marrow." Cash fed me. "This music's not bad once you're farther away. I kinda get the appeal."

"Skye certainly looks like she's having fun. I've never seen her so in her element before. Also, can I finish your champagne? I usually wouldn't, but this is particularly spectacular."

"Go right ahead."

Cash handed me his glass, which I downed pretty swiftly, and then he decided, without me asking, to go find a cater waitress to bring a few more.

"What's with these caterers?" he said.

"What do you mean?" And then I spotted two of them in the crowd and said, "Ah, I know exactly what you mean. They're so, you know, hot and...underdressed."

"Model types, yeah. Wonder how Campbell pulled the whole thing together."

"He made some good calls and some *very* iffy ones...like that." I pointed at a girl's bare bottom that was strolling by us in the pool area. "I thought Jeff was supposed to be classy, and this was supposed to be some sophisticated, all-white party?"

"I mean, I guess he was trying to find the right amalgamation. If it's too stuffy, then people will leave and find a more hedonistic event. But if it's too ratchet, then the more refined people will leave. It's a tricky proposition."

"Wouldn't you call this too ratchet?"

"Absolutely. But it's only five percent of the party. One could spend their whole night dancing by Skye, eating food, and doing stuff in the house or on the beach without ever noticing these girls."

"True...Did you see the Instagram station there? By the beach."

"No, where's that?"

"Look where I'm pointing."

There was a professional photographer with a super-pricey Nikon taking pictures of couples and groups either in front of the beach, on the beach, or in this charming nook of foliage at the edge of Jeff's backyard. There was a big white sign with that purplish, pinkish, blu-ish, orangish Instagram logo everyone recognized.

"Oh, Cash. I'm sure he does a fantastic job. Probably has a lot of cool filter ideas, and maybe he could take a boomerang of us doing something? We gotta go."

"Sure. Now or later?"

"Later." I laid back in my lounge chair. "I need more champagne, more food, and maybe more sleep so I can stay up for the end of this thing."

"No worries," he laughed. "I'll bring you a bunch of stuff. You hang tight. I wanna tour the inside and see what Campbell did with the upstairs and the basement."

"Sounds good. Hurry back."

Cash left, returned to drop off my bubbly, and then went to explore the grounds. Meanwhile, I guess I dozed off for 15 minutes or so.

By the time I woke, Cash still wasn't back, and someone had taken the chair next to mine.

"Oh, excuse me," I said. "My boyfr—I mean, fiancé, is sitting there."

"I'll only be a moment. I wanted to talk to you."

I looked up and matched the faintly familiar voice with her faintly familiar face.

"Oh, it's you," I said. "Having a good night?"

"Could be better. I'm not loving the view. A little too avant-garde for my taste."

"Me too."

"Jeff has so many good ideas. I'm not sure why he'd stoop to this level. I'll have to talk to him about this."

"Well, anyway, you were looking for me?" I said. "And it's Ivee, right?"

"That's right. Good memory. Ivee Petrapoulos. I'm a friend of Jefferson's."

"Is that all you two are?"

"For now."

She may have worn my favorite outfit that night, or at least, the most expensive. Ivee had on a white lace dress from Bottega Veneta with these naked J'Adior slingback pumps and a gorgeous white Dior clutch.

"Why do you like Jeff?" I asked. "I mean, there must be a ton of guys for you. Like, ones your age."

"I've wanted to be with Jefferson ever since I was a seventh-grader. I've seen him at parties like these...well maybe not like these, but I've seen him at a bunch of parties throughout my life and on the streets and at restaurants and clubs. He's this spectacular man who doesn't fear anyone or anything and combines this devilish persona with a sensitive regality. I love that man."

"I don't think you know him very well."

"How do you know him? I never asked. But I saw you two alone together at the polo match and strolling the streets of East. What's up with that? Are you like his mistress?"

"No." I flashed my new diamond ring. "I have a fiancé."

"Can't you have both?"

"That's not my style."

"Speaking of style, is that Harry Winston? That's a gorgeous diamond. Your man is either tremendously wealthy or has screwed you over a bunch of times and wants to make up for it."

"I don't think it's either of those."

"Anyway, how do you suggest I win over Jefferson?"

I'll admit, Ivee was a beautiful young woman with an emphasis on both beautiful and young. She couldn't have been more than 18 or 19, and yet, this girl was incredibly eloquent and well-dressed. She exuded money. Money and innocence. Her defining feature was her long straight blonde hair parted directly in the middle of her forehead. And Ivee kept running her fingers along the hair outlining her face.

"First of all, I don't think you should go after him. My personal view is for all his positive qualities, he's a brooding and disturbed man with a lot of secrets you and I probably don't know about."

"Look, Kinsley, is it? I just wanted advice. I don't need a lecture."

"Why do you want my advice?"

Ivee called over a caterer and had two more glasses of champagne delivered to me.

"Well," she said, "I'm sure you'd prefer to see less of his current squeeze in your life. I think we all would."

"Like Jeff, she has her pros and cons. I don't view anyone as naturally malevolent."

"Then, since you seem like a nice and wise person, may you please help me out? As a fan of love?"

"I can give you a few ideas, I suppose."

At that moment, I'd had quite a few drinks and was missing Cash but decided to dole out a few drunken words of wisdom.

"Your first step to making Jeff like you would be making him dislike Skye. He'll never do anything romantic with you while he and Skye are in a committed relationship. He's not the cheating type."

"Okay. So, remove Skye?"

"Well, that sounds awfully dark. I just mean, you may have to wait until they break up, which I'm sure will happen at some point."

"So once Skye's out of the picture, then what?"

"Be the first pretty woman he sees after the breakup."

"That's it?"

"That's it."

"How can it be that simple?"

"Jeff's a naturally lonely person. And my opinion is he has an addictive personality. If women are a drug to him, he'll need his fix."

"That's a dreary way to look at things. I thought you were the positive, happy-go-lucky woman?"

"Some of what I'm saying is stuff my fiancé, Cash, has told me."

"So, get him to break up with Skye and then be near him after it happens? That's it?"

"Sure, I guess. Oh, and keep complimenting him. Guys like Jeff need the ego boost."

Ivee smacked her crimson lips together, took her phone from her clutch, and started texting someone.

"What do you think would make Jeff and Skye break up?" she asked.

"Cheating."

"Really? One time and that's it?"

"Absolutely. Jeff and Cash are always talking about loyalty. If you want her out of the picture, she just needs to cheat on him somehow. Doesn't even need to be sex. A simple make out session should do the trick."

"You think?"

"I dunno," I said. "I've had too much to drink, to be honest. I need Cash. And maybe a Red Bull."

"Last question, and then I'll find Cash for you and bring him here this instant."

"Shoot."

"So, I'm gathering you're living in this pool house with Cash? And then Jeff and Skye live in the big house?"

"Yeah. How'd you know that?"

"Oh, I don't know. People talk. But my question is, this summer, have you ever noticed Skye being particularly chummy with anyone? Like, if you had to guess who Skye would be most likely to cheat with, even if the odds were infinitesimal, who'd it be?"

"I have no idea. Will you please find Cash for me? I have a headache."

"You must have some idea. You've slept on the same property with her for three months and have eaten meals with her and have had alone time with her. She must've mentioned someone? You talk about your crushes? First loves? The man she lost her V-card to? Anyone that her face seems to light up around?"

"I mean, when you phrase it like that, Bérénice. The French wine girl. The two of them are obsessed with each other. Hands all over one another when I was with them."

"Thank you so much, Kinsley. You're an absolute angel. Love you."

She kissed my cheek and then said:

"I'll go bring back Cash ASAP."

My boyfriend soon returned and sat next to me.

"You okay, Kins? Too much champagne?"

"Maybe a little. What time is it? Did you run into that Ivee girl?"

"I dunno. Around 12:15, maybe. And is that that virtuous-looking blonde?"

"That's the one."

"Huh. Let's head back to the pool house. I'll carry you."

"No, Cash. I want to go to the Instagram booth and the beach. Can we? Please? And we have to dance."

"I wanna do all that too. But you look exhausted. Let's go to the pool house, you can take a quick nap, have a Red Bull, and then we'll attack this party head-on."

I agreed, and moments later, we were back in the pool house, and I was resting my eyes on the couch.

"Kins, wake up," Cash said.

"What? Why? What time is it?"

"After one. I hate waking you, but I wanted us to have an opportunity to do everything."

"Thanks," I said as he helped me put my pumps on.

"Here's a Red Bull."

I knocked that drink back with ease, and about three minutes later, Cash and I were on the dance floor.

"Who's the new DJ?" I shouted as we were approaching a still-packed moshpit.

"DJ Cree Mashun. Jeff and Skye hired her. Eclectic young woman."

This new girl started playing weird gothic, emo, hard rock dubstep, and Cash and I just went with it. We were dancing, grinding, and flailing our arms. We were in one of those mildly tipsy moods that allowed us to go crazy with no regard for who was watching. Cash was a pretty good dancer, actually. He was holding my hips and pressing his body against mine.

"God, you're sexy," I whispered.

He yanked my hair a bit, and then we engaged in a ferocious public make out session. That typically wasn't our style, but the sexy dancing, loud music, and of course, alcohol, made us forget about normalcy and focus on each other.

"Let's go to the Instagram photographer," he eventually whispered in my ear.

"Lead the way."

It was somewhere between one and two-thirty. With most of this writing, I can use my phone's texts and IG messages to pinpoint exactly what day and time events occurred, but that night was all a blur, and my phone had died at some point.

Cash and I listened to the photographer's instructions, and afterward, I posted a few pictures to my IG page and saved some to show my family later. And after we left, Cash and I started to wade in the ocean.

"You should've left your shoes on the beach," he said. "You really wanna hold them this whole time?"

"I'll admit it was a mistake, but I don't want to turn back now."

"What'd you think of the pictures?"

"I had him e-mail me all of them, and after scrolling through, more than half are great, which is, like, an insanely high percentage."

"We might not like them as much in the morning. We probably have that reddish, drunken glow."

"Whatever. Great way to commemorate this very special weekend. Show our kids someday." I smiled at him as we kissed under the moonlight.

It was just our two silhouettes wading in the Atlantic behind Jeff's house. There was that faint, kind of awful, kind of exciting music playing, and the low tide waves kept crashing against our shins.

THE NEXT DAY AND
BEYOND — SEPTEMBER 2018

"KINS, WAKE UP." CASH WAS more aggressive with his wake-up call that morning.

"What? What's wrong? We should be sleeping until three. My head hurts."

"We gotta leave now. Are you packed?"

"10 more minutes. No...60 more minutes."

"Kins, I'm serious. Now."

He lifted me from the mattress that was still lying directly on the floor and handed me some leisurewear.

"What's the rush?"

"Skye and Campbell. It's an emergency."

"What do you mean?" I was fully awake after hearing that word. "Who's hurt? Was it drugs?"

"No. I don't think it was like that."

"Explain to me what's going on. Use words."

"Kinsley, I'm sensing something bad is about to happen. Or already did. I'm worried we could be in danger if we don't leave this second. I'll explain everything in the car. You have to trust me on this."

"Okay. I trust you." We quickly pecked each other on the lips, brought our already-packed suitcases to the door, and just as we were exiting the pool house for the last time, I said:

"Shouldn't we at least say bye to Jeff and Skye?"

"I said bye for you. They'll understand."

So, within 15 minutes of waking, Cash and I were driving toward 27 and on our way back to Manhattan.

"Okay, crazy. Now, what's going on?"

I was driving, and while I typically liked to drive with music on, my throbbing headache made silence seem more pleasing.

"Campbell's gone."

"Gone like where?"

"Gone. Vanished. Location unknown."

"Shouldn't we go look for him? Call him? Call his friends?"

"No. Skye used the words, 'vanished' and 'disappeared.'"

"So, I don't understand, Cash. One of your best friends is missing, and you wanna drive back to Manhattan and wipe our hands of the whole thing? After you stayed in his house for free for three months and he paid for a ton of our meals and stuff?"

Cash and I were both wearing black-and-white Under Armour. We looked quite disheveled.

"Kins, I don't have any concrete evidence. But after talking to Skye this morning, I'm scared."

"Now, why are you scared? I trust you, but I need more info."

"So, I think there's maybe a five percent chance some sort of felony happened or will happen."

"What do you mean? Speak clearly."

"I know I sound nuts, but it was Skye's facial expressions. It was the kind of face you see in movies and TV a lot. Picture somewhere between Kathy Bates in *Misery* or Janet Leigh in *Psycho*."

"Well, those mean two very different things."

"Right. Anyway, I felt she could hurt someone or maybe was afraid of being hurt. I just thought about you and our future together and decided I wanted you nowhere near that house."

"Have you tried calling Jeff?"

"Uh, no."

"Oy. Cash. C'mon. Do it now. That should've been your first move."

He tried Jeff's phone a few times and then texted him. And after not hearing anything for a bit, I told him to message the other Hollandsworth guys Jeff knows in the Hamptons. But no answer from anyone.

"Relax, Cash. Take some deep breaths. We'll stop and grab food. Get you and me a lot of water. If we haven't heard from him in 24 hours, then it'll be time to stress."

"I'm really glad I have you."

We pulled over in Southampton, stopped in The Golden Pear, picked up coconut waters and challah French toast, and then continued toward Manhattan. And by then, I decided we needed some music, so I told Cash to put on this playlist I had:

"Young and Wild and Free" — Wiz Khalifa
"Burn (Remix)" — Meek Mill, Big Sean, Lil Wayne, and Rick Ross
"Often" — The Weeknd
"The Hills" — The Weeknd
"Real Estate" — Wiz Khalifa
"Landslide" — The Dixie Chicks
"Soak Up the Sun" — Sheryl Crow
"Bleeding Love" — Leona Lewis
"Pinocchio Story" — Kanye West
"Power" — Kanye West
"Blank Space" — Taylor Swift

Cash slept for a lot of the way, but by the time we were at the Queensboro Bridge, he woke and said:

"Did my phone ring at all?"

"No, not yet. Can I tell you what I think, Cash?"

"Of course."

"Well, since you fell asleep and left me alone with my thoughts..."

"Sorry."

"I started to think about David."

"Your brother? Why?"

"Well, I mean, he suffered from drug addiction during his college years. I told you that."

"Right, but how's that relate here?"

"I'm only speculating, but I saw a lot of the same signs from Jeff I saw with David. They had the same addictive personalities, they occasionally neglected and mistreated their loved ones, and they both shut off their phones for unhealthy amounts of time."

"I don't think he's an addict, Kins. He's just having fun."

"No, Cash. You and I have fun with alcohol. It doesn't alter our lives or leave us waking alone and afraid in unknown places. He abuses alcohol, drugs, and then, who knows what goes on behind closed doors when he brings girls back with Skye."

"Okay, so what's next?"

"Well, we can't help someone who refuses help and to acknowledge they have a problem. I think he could be depressed also."

"This is a lot of hearsay from someone who doesn't have any experience in the field of psychology."

"I certainly have a lifetime's worth of experience from dealing with my brother. But we eventually gave him a family and friends intervention, and he really took to it. David went to rehab and a ton of therapy, and as far as I know, he's been sober for 18 months."

"Okay. So, what are we gonna do?"

"Nothing for now. We just have to wait until he reaches out and take it from there."

"You don't think he did anything serious?" Cash asked.

"What, you mean like..."

"Suicide."

"No. Jeff's not the type."

"You're so confident about all these things."

"I don't know. I have to rationalize everything. This addiction theory is what makes the most sense to me."

We arrived at our respective apartments, and a few hours later, Cash texted me he heard back from the other Hollandsworth guys, and they didn't know anything. So, after that, we went about our daily lives for the next week or so. Cash started working for his father, and I went back to Guépard. I knew in my gut that nothing was seriously wrong.

I was the first person who "found" Jeff. It's funny. Cash gave me his passwords to all his websites, and about seven or eight days after we returned, I logged into Cash's fantasy baseball league and noticed Jeff had made a transaction. I screenshotted this and sent it to Cash, who then messaged everyone relevant. However, it still took three months before we heard from Jeff.

By December 1ˢᵗ, Cash had moved into my apartment while we looked for a larger place. And the first weekend after he moved in, while we were unpacking boxes, Cash and I heard that unique sound of a Skype call coming through on his laptop.

"Who is it?" I asked.

"It's Jeff."

"Jeff? Really? Are you serious?"

He picked up the call, and I listened in the background.

"Remember me?" Jeff said.

"Jesus, Campbell. What the hell, man? Are you nuts?"

"I know. I know. Slightly abnormal behavior."

"Dude, it's been three and a half months. Not a single text."

"I know, Moreau. I was going through a traumatic experience. I shut off the world and indulged in my numerous vices. Hard to do. Easy to explain."

"Christ, man. You okay? Where are you?"

"Only my father knows. I haven't told anyone else."

"So, what now?"

"I don't want to get into the more plaintive topics. I called because I wanted to offer you a thank-you gift. For your undying loyalty."

"Jeff, I don't need anything. Kins and I are good."

"I think you might want this one."

"What is it?"

"I'm wiring $50,000 to your bank account, which I'd like you to use to start that company you were talking about over the summer."

"$50,000, Jeff?" I shouted and appeared in the frame.

"Hey, Ms. Avital. Or should I say, Ms. Moreau? How the hell are ya?"

"Fine. Fine. But that's too generous, Jeff."

"It's the least I can do. I'm sure I caused you two a tremendous deal of strife. Consider this a small token of my gratitude. And Kins, your gift is coming at the wedding."

"Jeff, I don't want some handout," Cash said.

"It's not a handout. I want to invest in the company. Be the first investor. I want a percentage of the company. Whatever you see fit. Consider me a financier for whatever you wind up calling that place."

"Damnit, man. I don't know what the hell to say anymore."

"Take the money. Start the company. Contact me if you need more, and we'll renegotiate what percentage of the company I own. Always a minority partner, though."

"But why, Jeff? Why ignore me for three and a half months and then send me 50K?"

"I reward loyalty, Moreau. Always have. Always will."

And then Jeff hung up.

Cash and Jeff Skyped about once a month after that first call, and around February 1st, Cash officially leased a small office space in Midtown and hired four part-time, hourly employees and three interns.

Meanwhile, I was promoted to VP of Social Media and Marketing at Guépard as the company's fashion arm blew up pretty quickly.

And so, the final memory I'll bring up occurred last weekend. On June 8th, 2019, Jeff Skyped Cash once again while I pulled up a chair beside my soon-to-be husband.

"The future Mr. and Mrs. Moreau, how's it feel?"

"We're both super excited," I said.

"What is it? 28 days?"

"That's right," Cash said. "And Jeff, I wanted to ask you something about that."

"No need. I already know the question. And yes, of course I'm coming to your wedding. Wouldn't miss it for the world."

"Well, I was gonna ask if you'd be my best man."

"Me?"

"Yeah, you. My old Hollandsworth pal."

"Moreau, wow. I'm flattered. Course I will. Thank you so much. When and where am I going?"

"We're actually having it at Mr. Wilkinson's house in Sagaponack from last summer. I called him about it. Kinsley and I adored his property, and I asked him for a potential quote. The guy said he'd do it completely free. Said he believes in true love. That man's a true class act."

"I may have had a hand in that."

"You always do somehow, don't you? And it'll be on July 6th. I'll message you the details."

"Fantastic. And everything at work's going well? I figure you would've called me if anything pressing came up."

"Yeah, we're off to a fast start. The team I hired has been everything and more."

"Glad to hear it. I always believed in you."

The two of them acted as if they'd never experienced a single problem, and there wasn't a glacier's worth of issues to discuss. I guess in my experience, that's sort of how male friendships could be.

"One more thing Jeff," I chimed in, "what's your romantic situation? Are you living with someone? Do you have a date for the wedding or are you..."

"On the prowl?" he interrupted. "No. I have a clear first choice and a distant second. I have to ask them. Maybe I'll bring both. I'll surprise you. One of them is a blast from my past."

"Can't wait...Also," I said, "you never told me what my wedding gift is."

"Well...I was gonna astonish you in person. I've always been addicted to generosity. But I suppose I can tell you."

"It better not be inappropriate, Campbell."

"I want you two to have Campbell Manor."

Cash and I turned to each other, speechless.

"Frankly, I have bad memories of that place, and aside from a few pieces of memorabilia I need to grab, I'd like to gift it to a couple who deserves it."

"Jesus, Campbell. I, that's, I mean, that's too much. Too generous. We don't need all that."

"Moreau, please. Either I give it to you or sell it and return some money to my family who doesn't need it. Take it. Just make sure to invite me out now and again. I'll stay in the famed pool house that apparently sparks marriage proposals."

"Thank you so much, Jeff," I said.

"Listen, Moreaus, I've gotta get going. I'll check back in later. Peace."

Cash hung up the Skype call, closed his laptop, and stared at me.

"Kins, I'm not sure what to say. About anything. The guy's given me 50K for my dream job and a dream house; well, aside from a few necessary interior design adjustments, of course. I mean, what should we do or say? What do you think of Jefferson Campbell III now?"

"I think he's the one having us write these letters. Him or that Machiavellian Ivee girl."

"Could be Skye too. Let's invite her to the wedding…and you didn't answer my question. What do you really think of Campbell?"

"Honestly, Cash, and I'm not one to be mean, but I think he's an absolute psycho."

THE END

ABOUT THE AUTHOR

WIL GLAVIN WAS BORN IN Philadelphia, raised in Manhattan, and graduated from Tufts University in 2016, where he majored in English with a concentration in fiction writing and journalism. During his time at Tufts, he wrote nine short stories, 40 articles published in the *Tufts Daily*, two feature-length screenplays, and his piece, "Allie," was awarded the runner-up prize in Tufts' most coveted fiction competition: "The Morse Hamilton Fiction Prize." After college, he spent four years working a variety of roles at  Sony Pictures, ICM Partners, and Marvel Entertainment. In August 2020, he released his debut novel, *The Venerable Vincent Beattie*, and on September 15th, *The New York Post* did an exclusive interview on Wil and the book ("The Wild Scandals of NYC's Elite Prep School Scene"). Towards the end of 2020, he appeared on podcasts, guest lectured in college classrooms (over Zoom due to COVID-19), and received inquiries into his novel's film/TV/podcast rights.

Outside of work, he spends his time playing both real and fantasy sports, day trading stocks and cryptocurrency, watching classic Hollywood films, traveling, playing poker, reading, and working on future novels and screenplays. He currently lives in Southampton, NY. You can visit him on LinkedIn, Twitter (@wil_glavin), Instagram (@wilglavin), or his website (wilglavin.com).

CPSIA information can be obtained
at www.ICGtesting.com
Printed in the USA
LVHW030722110721
692392LV00002B/233